Praise for Breathing

Breathing Room is a labor of
course of many years. Steve's  ...w me in
immediately. I found it easy t... ... in my mind the settings &
events as the story progressed. I especially liked how Steve enabled me
to "get behind the eyes" of each person & imagine how it was for them.
This is an inspirational story of grace, redemption & enduring sacrificial
love. There is plenty of real life drama with bits of humor sprinkled in. It
shows the desperation and determination of the human spirit. There is so
much in this book. I would read it again. I think it's an amazing
accomplishment.
~ Jackie Roth

Reading *Breathing Room* drew me right into the story. I felt as though I
were part of the Christopher Family. I felt every struggle and every
victory of the family. Being from South Jersey myself, I enjoyed reading
about the areas that are so familiar to my own childhood. Steven's style
of writing makes you feel as though you are right there experiencing
each adventure & the daily living of the family. Breathing Room is a
story that any American family can identify with, as we each try to find
our own breathing room.
~ Patti Dunfee Pharo

There are certain books that as you read them you can envision the film
version. *Breathing Room* is one of those books, not an action packed
blockbuster, but a slow moving, family drama that draws you in and
leaves you with a sense of loss when it is over. For anyone who has
experienced that longing for a place of shelter from the storms raging
around them, or who has ever hoped for something more than limping
cautiously through every day, this book is for you. *Breathing Room*
reminds us even in our darkest moments, that there *is* a light at the end of
the tunnel and that Hope is *not* dead. Hope is never dead.
~ Rebecca Onkar

Breathing Room
Copyright ©2014-2015
Steven Lange

Edited by: Kimberly Callan

Cover Design by: Jessica Lange

ISBN 978-0-9905882-1-4
Ver. 1-3

www.stevenlangebooks.com

Breathe Easy Publishing
P.O Box 3254
Harvey Cedars, New Jersey

Breathing Room

A Novel by Steven Lange

Breathing Room is that haven of rest that lies between the pains of our past, and fears of an uncertain future. May you dwell in the cleft that is your own breathing room.

Steve Lange

Breathe Easy Publishing
Harvey Cedars, New Jersey

Dedication

Far too many of us are exhausted as we search for that respite from the pains of the past, fears of an uncertain future, and the pressing weight of life's present challenges. May Breathing Room serve as a voice for those too tired to speak, for it is to you that this book is humbly dedicated.

Contents

Forward

Breathing Room is endearing and heartbreaking. The journey of this family echoes what we all know to be true…life can be harrowing, beautiful, and touching. Each family has its' own culture and original fluidity. The Christopher family provides us all with the key to realizing the risk for fragility and that each day is too precious to take for granted.

From innocence to laughter to insightful maturity, this family grows and travels through the intricate details of life that are simultaneously simple and very complex. Family tragedies and illness can cause dramatic shifts in dynamics and relationships. It can break the strongest of individuals and cause everlasting grief. A sense of loss of what could have been and what should have been. We have all experienced this raw emotion. What develops can be devastating and difficult to recover from. Anger, sorrow, shattered hope, dismay, and turmoil.

A chronic illness can have a monumental impact on every part of the family…and can change the dynamics of everyday life. Recognizing and being open to emotional and supportive therapy is imperative to maintaining the family structure as a whole. For some, it is too heartbreaking to bear.

When the winds shift dramatically, it's as if the anchor is lifted and only the strongest of the crew can keep things afloat. The Christopher family keeps us believing. It is a wonderful and healing journey that so many can relate to and gain hope from! It can remind us again to always take a moment and just breathe.

~ Danielle Halbig, MSW, LCSW
Clinical Therapist

Breathing Room

Chapter 1
Brandon and the War on the Hill

November 1967

Unimpeded as they swept across the barren mountaintops, warm, inviting waves of morning light met the unprotected slopes, casting them in a reddish brown hue. Scarcely changing from one day to the next, the new day's sun seemed to have ushered in this customary greeting for countless generations. Today, however, would be different. Today, the blankets of sunlight that painted dawn across the valley floor revealed two massive armies. Grimacing at each other across the open valley floor, the opposing combatants stood motionless while the sun portended favor to neither command.

To the north, an imposing array of knights formed columns at the base of the hill, poised to serve as the first assaulting wave. Their armor and shields glistened as the approaching sun met the dew. A common crest proudly emblazoned on every shield communicated their unmistakable unity. Behind these knights' noble steeds, in what looked like boxes of mobile humanity, were the swordsmen and the pikemen. Entrenched neatly across the rise midway up the hill were the archers, set where the orchestrating commander was confident that the additional elevation would give them a tactical advantage. Projectiles waiting to be set aflame and launched sat beside the trebuchets positioned between each division of knights, bolstering their assurance of victory.

As he surveyed both bands of soon-to-be clashing warriors, the one unarmed witness wondered whether this enclosed valley would be the final resting place for many. After all, the imposing peaks formed a wide arch that extended unbroken from one end of the valley to the other and back again, forming a horseshoe. Ingress and egress from the valley was only possible via the wide opening on the western side.

The witness looked then to the other side, where, every bit as fierce and primed for battle, the adversary stood in final preparation. Positioned in groups of five along the southern flatbeds, 30 idling tanks could be seen, each with a squad of men nearby. Long, dark green gun barrels pointed skyward as a host of artillery awaited the order to commence firing. Riflemen and bazooka men, all in green, stood silently. Were they thinking about home, the witness guessed, before they were thrust into heated battle? Just when reasonable soldiers on both sides might have begun to think that the confrontation would be delayed or perhaps abandoned all together, the green army unleashed a blistering volley of artillery fire. Knight after knight was laid to waste before even advancing.

As the lone young witness watched the armor-clad legions fall, he decided that they had no choice but to call in an airstrike of their own. At that point any adults watching may have become understandably indignant and questioned how such a seemingly ridiculous scenario could be entertained with any degree of seriousness. Such inquiries would have been warranted and understandable, but the answer was as simple as the joy that the young witness had in also being the architect of the battle.

For no one had yet explained to Brandon Christopher the concept of "impossible." His 4-year-old heart and mind were still blissfully free to indulge in unbridled dreaming. Boundless optimism allowed knights to battle army men, for little boys to see themselves as astronauts, and for young Brandon to explore the limitless musings of all that could be. Years from that time, Brandon would—with great fondness—remember these moments lived free from the constraints of conformity. Awash in an ocean of limitless possibilities, he knew nothing of the strains that can be placed on a heart and that deny it the freedom to envision things yet unseen. For a little while longer at least, Brandon Christopher was free to dream. He was free to see a field of battle in what was really a u-shaped mound of earth that had been moved to a parking lot from a nearby construction site.

Rising high above him, the reddish brown hills stretched out to form an almost perfect horseshoe. It was nearly 20 feet wide at the mouth, and the open end was hidden from Brandon's mother, Patricia, as she stood in her front yard frantically calling his name. Although the parking lot was only across the street from his house, the dirt piles also acted as an acoustic barrier, which prevented his mother's fervent cries from reaching their intended target. While Patricia had been waking Brandon's younger brother Richard from a nap upstairs, the triple lures of an unseasonably warm November day, the sheer size of the imposing hills, and a door accidentally left ajar had drawn the young adventurer irresistibly across the street, opposing armies clutched safely in a dirty bucket.

A recent rain, coupled with the decaying conditions in the parking lot made for a 6-inch pool of caramel-colored water that filled the length of the mound's interior. To those who could only see it as it was, the cold muddy mess was unattractive at best. To Brandon, this was a playground with everything a boy could ask for.

As he moved his armies along the outer edge of the open mouth, Brandon's intense focus and concentration were finally broken by the one voice that could reach into his reverie. Looking around the corner, he could see Patricia beckoning from the front yard. Bringing to an end the hostilities unfolding before him, Brandon ran quickly back into the enclosure and began collecting muddied soldiers and returning them to the even muddier bucket.

"Brandon...Brandon!" Not knowing that her son had heard and was even now running his hand back and forth through the coffee-colored water to find the last few of his misplaced figures, Patricia's calls grew more distressed. Unsure of which direction to look, Patricia solicited the help of Rommel, the family's 3-year-old German shepherd.

Unlike Brandon, Rommel was not the imaginative type. Even an open door was not enough of an enticement for him to move from his appointed station next to the staircase. Whether by training or nature,

Rommel was all business and not predisposed to the pointless frivolity that so enthralled other dogs. He sat watchfully next to the steps all day unless commanded to do otherwise, usually by the family patriarch, Jack.

"Rommel", Patricia now yelled while holding the front door open. "Rommel, outside!" Responding to her increased agitation, Rommel sprinted out the door as soon as the words left Patricia's lips. When he reached the base of the front steps, he came to a dead stop and sat, as he had been trained to do. Rommel would go no further than the front steps without specific directives.

"Rommel, where's Brandon? Find Brandon," Patricia commanded with clarity. The strain of concern could be heard in her voice. His mission now clear, Rommel immediately set his nose to the ground in search. To and fro he went, scanning the front yard, his body turning left and right in a graceful sweeping pattern. When Rommel reached the walkway that led to the kitchen door in the back of the house, he shook his head sharply and raised his nose as if acquiring and locking onto a target.

Bolting from the house, Rommel darted across the street to the Thunderstrike Bowling Alley parking lot as Patricia did her best to follow. Reaching the opening of the earthen mounds before Patricia, Rommel reared back on his hind quarters and began barking sharply, sounding his alarm at even 2-second intervals. While he did, he looked alternately between the boy and his mother to ensure that Patricia understood the purpose of his barking. Running into the mouth of the dirt mounds, Patricia found Brandon sloshing through the pool of muddy water, gathering the last of his troops.

"Hi Mommy!" Brandon greeted his mother with obvious delight, despite lips now blue from the chilly waters. "These mountains are cool!" Brandon's feet sloshed with each step as he approached his relieved mother, all the while trying to convey the details of his delightful excursion.

"Oh my goodness, look at you." Surveying her muddy, shivering son, Patricia was for the moment disinterested in Brandon's recap of the past half hour. "Rommel...home!" Patricia knew that the dog would go

16

no further than the front steps until she could get to him. "And you, young man," she said, eying Brandon with feigned disgust. Although the inflection in her voice was purposeful, Brandon knew that he was in no REAL trouble.

Brandon held his precious bucket of men aloft as Patricia picked him up under the armpits from behind. Trying to hold him at arms' length to minimize the mud transfer from her wiggling son to her dress, Patricia turned resolutely toward home. Her son's attempt to turn around during his running explanation of the battle—"the army men were winning," he finished happily—did not aid her minimal success. On reaching the kitchen door in the back of the house, Patricia stripped Brandon of his muddy clothes in what seemed like a single motion. "Go upstairs, get in the tub, and DO NOT touch the knobs till I get there," she instructed him firmly. "And Brandon," she warned, as he paused to feed his watching younger brother a cracker with muddy fingers, "no stopping."

Two years Brandon's junior, Richard had been content in his high chair as Patricia found and retrieved Brandon, especially since it was complete with snacks. Now he happily watched the afternoon drama from the comfort of his perch, pushing pieces of cracker and French toast into his mouth with chubby fingers. Once he finished, Patricia settled Richard into his playpen and prepared to tackle Brandon's bath.

First, Patricia took the armful of Brandon's soggy clothes down to the laundry room in the basement and deposited them in the bottom of a laundry basket. She took several shirts from an adjacent pile and covered the soggy clothes. Coming upstairs again, she followed the telltale path of footprints left behind by the young adventurer.

Starting at the large smear of mud just inside the kitchen door, the trail ran through the dining room and into the sitting room, stopping just inside the front door. Patricia looked at the multiple circles of footprints in and out of the front door, smiling as she imagined their cause. She could picture Brandon, disregarding or more likely forgetting her admonition not to stop anywhere, attempting to summon Rommel into the house. It would not be the first time Brandon had tried to "show

Rommel" how to do something by performing the action himself. In this case, serving as a template, Brandon ran in and out across the threshold hoping that the dog would follow suit.

Since Rommel was much more inclined to adhere to discipline than Brandon, all the little boy got for his trouble was a mess in the sitting room and a perplexed look from a neighbor driving by. If Brandon was disappointed, Patricia noted that Rommel had maintained his position at the base of the steps with relief. If the Christopher house had a "Holy of Holies," it was the sitting room, which was always kept spotless and in which no one ever actually sat. Bad enough she'd have to clean Brandon's footprints; she was glad not to have Rommel's as well.

For his part, Rommel stood patiently while Patricia cleaned his paws and the scruff of his neck with the towel she was carrying, all the while showering him with congratulatory praise.

"Good boy finding Brandon, Rommel. Good boy." Rommel seemed to accept the adoration as his due and waited patiently for his next assignment. Patricia obliged him. "Rommel, stairs," she said, once he had been cleaned. The ever-faithful member of the household resumed his place of duty at the foot of the stairwell.

As she climbed the stairs, Patricia delighted to hear Brandon singing his favorite song. "Davey...Davy Crockett," his little voice piped out. Although those were the only words that he remembered, much to the chagrin of most of the family, Brandon did not let his inability to remember hinder him from singing the song—over and over—all day long, day in and day out. Now Brandon sat contently in the cold dry bathtub, singing happily to himself and the two green army men he had kept in his hand while Patricia undressed him.

Since he appeared oblivious to any of his recent transgressions, Patricia saw no point in bringing them up. Brandon continued his melodic interlude as warm bath water rushed onto his wiggling toes. Watching his foot be slowly submerged, Brandon waited with anticipation for the water to rise high enough to sink his toy boats to the bottom of the tub. Reaching up the lemon yellow tile walls surrounding the tub, Brandon attempted to position one of his toy army men on the black ceramic soap holder. When that didn't work, he put the green figure onto his toy battleship instead. As he plunged the vessel to the bottom of the tub, he broke off singing to vocalize the misfortunes of the doomed ship's crew. "Oh, nooo…I'm sinking…help me…blub, blub, blub," he called out happily.

As Patricia bathed Brandon and he played, she was careful not to interrupt her son's imaginative little world. This was as much for her benefit as his. Like most mothers, Patricia was happy to see her children happy, but she was especially grateful to see Brandon so full of life and exuberance.

His present energetic disposition was a welcome departure from the early difficult days after his birth. Born 6 weeks early and weighing only 4 pounds, 4 ounces, Brandon had many medical complications. His small lungs were underdeveloped, and he needed specialized equipment to breathe. He ate with great difficulty and had a hard time keeping food down. Because dehydration was a constant concern, he had been monitored round the clock.

Perhaps adding to the family's concerns over Brandon's early frailty, his three older brothers had been strong and resilient from day one. Patricia thought perhaps she and Jack had expected this to be a common trait among Christopher children. Jack was particularly nervous about picking up Brandon's frail little body, though by then he was quite accustomed to handling small children. In Jack's thick, powerful arms, Brandon seemed even more fragile, and Patricia understood her husband's fear that he might not know how much pressure he was putting on the gangly infant.

Not that she had ever doubted Jack's love for and pride in his fourth son. Jack had always wanted a house full of boys, and Brandon was a welcome addition to the family, even if his medical difficulties had made both Jack and Patricia understandably nervous.

Now at 4, Brandon was still gangly, tall and exceedingly thin, with thin wispy hair cut in a bowl-shape atop his oblong head. His skinny arms and legs seemed disproportionately long in relation to his torso. In fact, someone less fond than a mother may have seen in Brandon a resemblance to one of those Halloween decorations with the paper accordion arms and legs that hang listlessly that people hang in their window. Even Patricia sometimes observed that the playful little boy frolicking in the bathtub sometimes ran like his torso was trying to catch up to the rest of his body.

She smiled down at his bent head, watching him alternately rescue and drown his little boat and its hapless passengers. Perhaps sensing her attention, he looked up and smiled. His face, sweet and gentle, still held traces of its early distortions, but they were not nearly as distinct as they once were. His large round eyes were soft green in color, but the right eye still often seemed slightly more closed than the left. He also had an overbite and a nose slightly too large for his young face, with a flare of nostrils that seemed to belong to an older child.

Patricia was grateful, though, that none of his early problems seemed to change his sweet optimism. Wanting to believe the best of everything he saw, Brandon had a broad, happy smile that drew attention away from any irregularities and also distracted watchers from the large ear lobes he had inherited from his father.

Chapter 2

Patricia and the Peace at Home

Jack, Patricia thought as she snapped out of her musings. Her husband would be home in a few hours and a mess like the aftermath of Brandon's exploits was not what Jack liked to see when he came home from a long day's work. Continuity. Continuity was everything. Continuity gave a steady predictable rhythm to life. It permitted you to look on the horizon and know, with some degree of assurance, what lay ahead. Continuity infrequently availed itself to Jack; consequently, he enjoyed it wherever it could be found.

However, the finer points of what was required to maintain that continuity were of little interest to him. As far as Jack was concerned, Patricia had all day to clean and maintain the house. Jack would not rant or have violent outbursts to express displeasure. More likely, Patricia would see 2 or 3 days of silence, until she broke the pattern with a favorite dinner or dessert. This simple gesture would almost certainly return relations to normal. Patricia sighed; like any married couple, she and Jack had good days and bad. She realized that there was an edginess to their relationship, but it was this same edginess that had attracted them to each other.

Once Brandon was dried off and sporting a fresh set of clothes, Patricia whisked him down to the living room. Rommel growled intently as they reached the bottom of the stairs, making it understood that he was never caught off guard. Hoping to preoccupy Brandon long enough to get her work done, Patricia sat him in front of the TV with a bowl of dry Quisp cereal.

Brandon was transfixed by the last half of Romper Room, and he looked away from the screen only long enough to throw bits of cereal at Richard.

"No Quisp for Richard, Brandon," Patricia said. Patricia could not help but think that for all her efforts to clean on the other side of the room, Brandon countered her efforts one-for-one.

She redoubled her efforts to get the house in order before Jack came home. Patricia was strikingly beautiful, and most people would not envision her in the role of tireless wife and mother. Her figure would seem more at home seated at a grand piano or gracing the strings of a harp with her long, slender fingers. Delicate and shapely, they were tailor made for musical expression. Her hair was reddish brown, with soft natural highlights and curls that nestled playfully on her shoulders, bouncing as she walked. Seeing her brought to mind the beauties on the war bond posters of a generation ago.

Despite her looks, she was unpretentious and kind, almost to her detriment. Wanting to assume the best in everyone left her unskilled at perceiving guile when it was present.

Patricia loved Jack and loved being a wife and mother. She could not remember ever in her life wanting to be anything other than a wife and mother. Ever since she was a young girl, the security and love of a good husband and the joy of raising children filled her thoughts.

Though Patricia's mother agreed with the idea of her being a wife and mother, Jack had not been Ginny's first choice of husband for her daughter. Ginny had gone to great lengths over the course of Patricia's formative years to ensure that her daughter was surrounded by boys likely to become men of intellect and culture. Academics, musicians, classical artists; these were what Ginny sought. Families of all the eligible young men were familiar to Ginny and her husband Bud after 20 years in their church. Surely, Ginny had thought, she could introduce Patricia to a boy who was going somewhere in life.

Which was not, Ginny's thought, Jack Christopher. Jack Christopher, in Ginny's opinion, which was almost certain to be made known, was the antithesis of everything that she wanted for her daughter.

The man that married Patricia must not only be brilliant, he had to look brilliant. And Jack just didn't.

Despite Ginny's efforts to find a suitable man for her daughter, a man who was stable, consistent, and reliable, Patricia remained uninterested in the boys Ginny introduced her to. Patricia, though not voicing any opposition to her mother, thought of those suitors as "boring." Quietly meeting beau after potential beau, Patricia patiently endured her mother's intrusion.

That is, until Jack Christopher came along. Jack Christopher was a powder keg, and Patricia had been quickly smitten. There was an obvious danger, but she was fascinated when she was with him. Jack showed little predictability or mundane patterns in either speech or action. And yet, beneath the steely exterior, Patricia could see Jack's intelligence and sharp mind. Muted though it was, almost, she thought, intentionally, Patricia could still see a keen intellect wanting to break forth.

Nor was Patricia wrong. Jack may not have looked like he routinely strolled the halls of academia, but he was certainly no dummy. Though he'd never tout it himself, Patricia considered Jack something of a mathematical genius. He could close his eyes and work through mathematical calculations that most of the men in St. Peter's church could not complete using all of the lead in a #2 pencil. Those who knew him well marveled at the uncanny ability that came quite naturally to Jack. Patricia understood from the beginning, though, that he would never be one to don a claustrophobic suit and tie. She didn't care.

And occasionally a word or phrase that revealed vulnerability within the deep recesses of Jack's heart would sneak out. Catching himself in these moments of uncalculated openness, Jack would quickly snatch the words back, biting the utterance off. But Patricia had seen the vulnerability and valued it.

Dating Jack Christopher had been a rare slap in her mother's face from a daughter usually obedient. All too aware that Ginny was much tougher than her 5'2" frame suggested, Patricia did not make the decision to go against her mother's wishes lightly. But, in Patricia's eyes,

Ginny had micromanaged her daughter's life for the better part of 16 years, and the time had come for change. The truth of their assessments can be found somewhere between the protective nature of a mother and the newfound independence of a daughter.

Ultimately, Patricia, though unskilled in the art of confrontation, stood her ground against a mother who felt quite at home going head to head. And she had never looked back. Ginny had introduced Patricia to many fine young men, men who were almost certain to one day be heads of corporations or leading scientists gone on to greatness. None of them had appealed to her then, and none did now. But Jack...Jack was different. Perhaps that was part of her relentless attraction to this rugged man who always wore blue jeans and a fresh white cotton t-shirt. Jack exuded edginess and a confidence that made him seem fearless.

Besides, Patricia never had been concerned with her station in life or what her neighbors may have; Jack and the boys were at the center of everything that was important to her.

Chapter 3

Robert, Shawn, and Russell, and a Continuation of Hostilities

Later That Day

The pleasant aroma of pot roast wafted through the house as Patricia prepared dinner. The smell was as disarming as it was inviting. Filing through her mental "to do" list as she glanced at the kitchen clock, Patricia was relieved. *Four o'clock* she thought. *Brandon is cleaned up, clothes are in the washer, Rommel is washed, sitting room is back in order, dinner is almost ready, and both boy and dog tracks are gone.* She still had an hour to spare before Jack arrived home. While patting herself on the back was not part of her typical daily routine, today Patricia made a well-deserved exception. Treating herself to 60 precious minutes of relaxation on the living room couch was in order. She fixed herself a nice cup of raspberry tea and breathed a relaxed sigh as she reclined on the living room sofa. The previous month's *Woman's World* would prove an enjoyable but temporary haven that the busy mother could claim as her own.

No sooner had Patricia turned the first page when she caught an image in the corner of her eye that promised to raze her rare self-indulgence. Peering out of the living room window, Patricia witnessed her eldest son, Robert, smashing the head of the neighbor boy, Zach, against the backyard fence. Apparently, Patricia had been unreasonable to expect the boys to make the three-block trip home from school without incident. A short distance from Robert, at the end of the yard where the fence met the sidewalk, his brothers Shawn and Russell were piled on top of Zach's twin, Eli.

Patricia sized up the melee as she ran out the kitchen door. Fists were flying, but by all appearances Eli was holding his own against the younger Christopher brothers, who themselves were no strangers to preteen combat. Zach and Eli were tough kids, both sporting involuntary crew cuts. Their pale blue eyes seemed always squinted, as if looking for the next victim to harass or bike to steal. Living in the small two-story brick apartment building directly behind the Christopher's house, the twins prided themselves on being the bane of Patricia's sons' existence. The apartment complex's brick half wall stood parallel to the 7-foot wooden picket fence that Jack had erected. Running the full length of the rear property line, this was the only of the Christophers' fences constructed for the sole purpose of dividing neighbors, since the fence along Mr. Mangold's vegetable garden served more as an anchor for grape vines.

Weighing the intensity of the two fights before her, Patricia decided Robert's altercation took first priority. As the oldest son, Robert had the greatest potential to do physical damage.

"Robert, off of him right now."

Patricia raced down the four short concrete steps off of the kitchen. Out of respect for his mother, Robert disengaged from combat as soon as he heard Patricia's voice. Unfortunately, this momentary distraction allowed Zach to land a solid shot to Robert's right eye before rising to his feet.

"Zach Tollson, get out of here right now!" Patricia pointed toward the apartment complex.

"Zach...out of here," Zach repeated mockingly. Zach then noticed the blood running out of the back of his crew cut scalp. Mocking turned to fear as Zach ran home calling for his mother. As he rounded the corner at the end of the fence, Zach kicked Shawn in the head, and Shawn rolled off Eli, leaving Russell to continue the fight.

The two younger Christopher brothers and Eli had been, to this point, oblivious to Patricia's arrival. Now, following his brother's lead, Eli jumped up and ran for home while simultaneously unleashing a verbal assault at Russell.

"Dumbass," he screamed at the younger boy, who at 6 years old was 5 years Eli's junior. "Wait till you're by yourself!"

Undisturbed by his neighbor's threat, Russell was satisfied with his fighting skills. He was a prolific biter, as Eli had painfully discovered. As they started to recap the highlights of their fight, Shawn and Russell's attention quickly turned to their mother, who was barreling toward them as they spoke. Stopping just short of her sons, Patricia pointed sharply toward the house. Frustration and anger could be seen in her strained neck muscles as she spoke through her clenched teeth.

"You and you, in the house, now! Go to your rooms, and I do not want to hear ONE WORD!" The "one" was elongated for deliberate emphasis. Shawn and Russell offered their mother a fleeting apology as they raced toward the kitchen door. As they reached the foot of the steps, Patricia barked out a final directive. "Do not let me find any dirt tracked through the house. Shoes off!" Patricia, typically selfless, was furious that the one brief hour that she had to herself was now nearly gone.

Robert, still on the ground holding his eye, was determined not to cry. His father frowned on crying. Jack felt it an undesirable habit that undoubtedly became easier and easier to do the more one succumbed to the temptation. *Soft boys do not grow up to be resilient men*, Jack thought. His eyes wide open in a panicked stare, Robert was hyperventilating as he cleared the dirt from his eyes with grimy, rapidly convulsing fingers. Trying to suppress the urge to cry simply compounded the trauma.

Zach's parting shot was the only one that had inflicted any damage, and the fight itself was not the source of Robert's discontent. Patricia was quite certain what caused her son's fear and trembling. What Robert feared above all was his father's reaction to hearing that his boys had gotten into an altercation. Jack had two rules about fist fights. Rule #1: Do not get into a fight. Particularly in a small town, reputations were easily acquired and almost impossible to change. The Christophers had a long family history in Stratford and were well liked. Jack would not tolerate the family name being reduced to a brood of bullies. Rule #2: If you do get into a fight, you had better damn well win it. The only worse

The Christopher home rested on a large open corner lot. Clean, level, uniform sections of sidewalk stretched across the front of the property. Reaching the street corner to the right, the concrete squares then curved to the rear of the house and ended as they met the driveway of the apartment complex behind.

A narrow weathered asphalt driveway occupied the area immediately to the left of the Christopher's home, and a narrow concrete walkway acted as buffer between the driveway and the house. This sidewalk served as the primary entryway into the house via the kitchen door out back. The lawn continued 40 feet to the left of the driveway to where Mr. Mangold's ambitious fruit and vegetable garden could be seen over the wooden picket fence that marked the property line. Large and open, the lawn to the right of the house was interrupted only by a 60-foot oak tree in the center of the yard.

Jack had made numerous and valiant attempts to cultivate a lush green lawn. But five active boys trampling it daily put him at a decided disadvantage. After trying every trick that he could think of over several seasons, Jack finally resigned himself. He stared at the patchwork of barren dirt mixed with random sections of healthy grass that remained, and could see it now with a degree of equanimity. Though not elaborate by any standard, the Christopher home was well loved and well maintained.

Employment as a sheet metal worker meant long, hard hours of work for Jack, but he was proud that he was a good provider, and he had never been a stranger to back breaking work. By the age of 11, Jack had been helping his father as he went about repairing the elevators throughout Center City, Philadelphia. Charles had carried a 70-pound toolbox up and down the stairways of countless high-rises every day; he saw to it that his sons knew the value and necessity of physical labor.

When first compelled to help, Jack did so grudgingly. But many days of difficult labor over the years had rewarded him with incredible strength. Now, as an adult, Jack was a chiseled, impressive figure at 6'2" and always 230 pounds, seemingly without an ounce of fat. The muscles

"It will not be until after you've finished your sticky buns, or whatever the hell you are eating up there, I am sure," Jack retorted. He gave himself a congratulatory laugh for coming up with his zinger.

"This isn't over!" Reena yelled.

"Say goodnight, Gracie," Jack replied as he waved a farewell hand over his head. Jack continued toward the front door surveying the house and yard for irregularities as he walked. One of those "irregularities" must have found its way under Jack's foot. Anger flared up in Jack for several seconds as he seemed to trip over his own feet. The last thing he wanted was for Reena Tollson to see him fall on his ass. Satisfied that she had not seen him, Jack's anger melted away as quickly as it had arisen.

buildings, and empty buildings do not need elevators or elevator repairmen. Dire circumstances and harsh living had carved Jack's views on the foolishness of elaborate expectations. Food for his family, a roof over their heads, and the peace of mind that comes with a measure of predictability were simple pleasures that suited Jack Christopher just fine.

And though Patricia did not share Jack's affinity for structure to quite the same level, she both loved her husband and derived great satisfaction from his contentment and the contentment of others. Order made Jack happy, so that is what Patricia strove for.

The light, playful banter between their parents reassured the boys that Jack was in a good mood. No one expected the topic of Robert's fight with Zach or Shawn and Russell's tussle with Eli to be brought up at the dinner table. These issues were always addressed and decided on *after* the evening meal.

Young Brandon introduced what he had thought was an interesting topic to start the dinner conversation. Dinner, more than any other time of day, provided an opportunity for free speech for the boys. Foul language and disrespectful inferences were still off limits, but the children were otherwise free to broach whatever subjects they might choose.

"On TV today, the people were talking about President Kenny," Brandon began. "They said he got shot, and people were crying." Brandon leaned back in his chair, proud of himself for such a concise recollection of the earlier newscast.

"President Ken-e-dy, Igor; his name was President Kennedy." Brandon's brothers giggled as Jack corrected his son's error.

Brandon felt embarrassed at the mistake until Jack winked at him with a smile.

"Jack, please don't call him, Igor, Patricia whispered to her husband in a barely audible tone. "I don't think that it is healthy for Brandon." Jack did not reply but refrained from using the moniker again during the meal.

"You were born in the year of his assassination, dear," Patricia added to Brandon. "We were supposed to go down to Dallas and visit Uncle Richard, but I was too far along with my pregnancy. Otherwise, we may have been on the parade route." By the time Patricia had finished her story, the boys had completely lost the connection between the former President and their brother's birthday.

As dinner came to its conclusion, each boy grabbed a dish or stack of dirty plates and carried them to the kitchen. Jack did not need to prompt action; they were well aware of what was expected of them. In addition, no one had any expectation of enjoying dessert until the table was cleared. For Russell, this meant he was even less motivated to help than usual, given that he and Shawn would, at the very least, have to forgo enjoying the vanilla custard following the afternoon brawl.

Chapter 6
The Boys and the Trial

The pleasant dinner conversation gave the boys no illusion that they were off the hook, and now nervous anticipation hung over the defendants as Jack led them from the dining room and instructed them to sit on the living room couch. Walking slowly back and forth with a contemplative look on his face, Jack acted as both prosecutor and judge. Patricia took the role of the boys' defender, interjecting support whenever she could. Jack's inflection was stern and left no room for playful banter as he interrogated Robert, Shawn, and Russell.

"You three get one chance: what the hell happened today? If I find out that you're bullshitting me, the punishment will be doubled." Three explanations simultaneously issued forth from the couch as Brandon sat on the sidelines watching, almost as if the family was putting on a play just for him.

Jack parsed each word, shuffling bits and pieces of information into their proper places until a clear timeline of events was established. There would be no punishment for Robert, as Patricia had promised him. Zachary instigated the fight by jumping onto Robert from atop the fence after subjecting him to several minutes of verbal barbs. Patricia and Robert explained the now darkening black eye as well. Jack understood cheap shots. He had received enough of them himself over the years.

Shawn and Russell were not found to be so innocent. In fact, to be completely accurate, Zachary didn't really jump. Shawn and Russell had run around the back of the fence, crept up on Zachary, and pushed him as he mocked their brother. In turn, Eli attacked them as they made their way back into the Christopher's yard. Jack dare not say that he found the altercation amusing, having no sympathy for any of the Tollsons. Shawn and Russell instigated a portion of the conflict, and that fact could not be glossed over.

For this infraction, Shawn and Russell were given the option of two belt smacks on a bare butt, or twice as many strikes with their pants on. Jack thought it fairly magnanimous that he allowed them to choose which method of corporal punishment was preferred. Walking up the staircase, he folded the belt in half and cracked the loop with a loud "SNAP," as he always did when punishing he boys. The approaching sound drawing closer inflicted as much emotional terror as the physical pain that followed.

The belt was a leather regulation police belt that Jack had gotten from his brother, a Lindenwold police officer. Half an inch thick, with a heavy buckle, it was intimidating just to look at. For Jack, there was no emotion involved; he felt no gratification at administering punishment. The belt was simply a means to an end. Correction, from Jack's standpoint, was meant to create an undesirable series of predictable events in response to infractions. This, in turn, should decrease the frequency and number of infractions.

That was the way his father handled correction before him. Charles had frequently found that the insights he wanted to bestow on his own sons were not received with a great degree of enthusiasm. Jack, in particular, flatly rejected his father's attempt to impose what he considered an arbitrary set of rules. The issue was not even the inherent merits of the guidelines themselves. The contention stemmed from a clash of wills, and Jack's boyhood comprised a collective series of standoffs with his father, with both relentlessly obstinate in their ideology and position. Jack refused to submit to his father's will, or give the obedience his father demanded.

Thin white scars across Jack's back served as a reminder of at least one such clash, when Charles had demanded an explanation and apology for some unperformed chore. Jack grit his teeth against the pain but said nothing as his father's belt found its mark across his back. He refused to either cry or offer any sign of repentance. Finally growing weary, Charles stopped the beating as Jack bled from several open slits on his back. Despite his injuries, Jack was satisfied that the closest thing to submission he gave his father was to calmly turn his head as Charles walked out of the room and say, "You'll never hurt me, Pop!"

Countless similar, if sometimes less severe encounters formed the core of Jack Christopher's disposition and worldview. But if he saw any irony in using a method of correction for his own sons that had only minimally altered and perhaps even intensified his own youthful stubbornness and refusal to submit to his father's will, Jack never admitted it, even to himself.

Amidst all the testimony and deliberation, Rommel was the lone innocent casualty. Forgotten in the drama, Jack's beloved dog sat faithfully by the foot of the steps until the morning light ushered in a new day.

Chapter 7
Jack and the Boys, and a Winter Accord

December 1967

"Faster, Faster! Turn-turn-turn-turn!"

Frigid night air mixed with the icy falling snow stung Shawn's cheeks as he flew across the Thunderstrike Bowling parking lot.

"Here we go! Woo Hooo…my face is freezing!" His brothers could not hear his excited screams from the car ahead of him as they leaned out the rear window of the station wagon waiting to see how far he would make it. He could hear their muffled voices as they yelled back, but he could not make out what Robert and Russell were saying. He could see that they were smiling and laughing though, so he surmised that whatever they were yelling was good.

Only Brandon had exhibited any element of concern for the family's current venture, to which his brothers responded by calling him the only sister in the house. As Robert and Russell waited their turn, they reminded him that the evening's entertainment was Jack's idea, if he wanted someone to complain to.

"I'm not saying that it isn't fun," Brandon backpedaled, but only just, "just that Mom wouldn't like it, that's all."

"You're such a momma's boy, Brandon." Russell wasted no time jumping in.

The snow had come down heavier and heavier as the day progressed, and now 6 inches of crunchy powder surrounded the Christophers' car. News reports were calling for 12 to 18 inches by morning. Clogging the streets faster than the road could disperse it, the snow would render the roads impassable until the following evening, at the very least.

Those conditions would leave Patricia stranded at her parents' until then. She certainly had no intention of asking her father, Bud, to drive the 18 miles from their home to hers in such conditions. Ginny and Bud had invited the entire family to stay over for the annual monumental production of decorating their house, during which Ginny, much to Bud's chagrin, spared no expense.

Jack, never too keen on large crowds in small spaces, had suggested an alternative. Since that much decorating would be even more difficult with four boys running around and one in a high chair, Jack made Patricia an offer she could not refuse.

"Why don't you go by yourself, Hon, and I'll stay here with the kids? You could have some time to yourself." Patricia was thrilled with Jack's offer, and he did not have to mention that he had no desire to go to her parent's house. All of the Christopher family would be there on Christmas, and that was enough visiting for him.

Instead, taking full advantage of the wintery invitation outside and Patricia's absence, Jack decided to treat the boys to an evening of fun, the kind of fun that would have given Patricia a heart attack if she had been there to see it. Jack tied 20 feet of rope to the back bumper of the family's Country Squire station wagon and fashioned a wooden T-handle at the end. Robert passed at having first turn, so Shawn sat on an inverted metal trash can lid while holding the makeshift handle. Gunning the engine, Jack headed the car straight toward the earthen mounds Brandon had so enjoyed several weeks earlier. Shawn's head could be seen bouncing up and down behind them as he sped over the bumpy paved surface. Jack executed a wide left turn, having assured Shawn that if he let go of the T-handle at the precise moment, the force would slingshot him up the hill. Jack thought of the adventure as a sort of practical physics lesson.

To the fervent cheers of his brothers, Shawn released the handle right on the mark. The impromptu sled launched up the frozen hill with just enough momentum to clear the crest and gently descended down the other side. Shawn emerged unscathed from the horseshoe with arms raised as though he were a newly crowned Olympic champion.

"That. Was. Awesome! It scared the crap out of me going over the bumps." Shawn delivered this judgment through quivering lips and chattering teeth.

The boys agreed that this was so much cooler than sliding down the hill on your butt and then having to walk back up again. Enjoying two runs each, the boys rotated the coveted position. While Robert admittedly enjoyed the fun, he was also the most hesitant. Though he wouldn't admit it to his younger brothers, he was predisposed, as Brandon was, to wondering what Patricia would think. Robert said nothing but Jack could sense his initial reluctance.

"Come on, Mary," Jack playfully teased. "Don't worry about getting your dress dirty."

Robert's brothers needed no cue to chime in with a chorus of "Yea, Maary."

Jack meant no harm, but his comments, especially in front of the others, had an unintended effect. Several thoughts raced through Robert's mind as he sped along behind the car on his last run. The one absent thought was the one that really mattered: letting go of the handle. With his mind elsewhere, Robert missed letting go at the crucial moment. Instead of flying easily over the snow covered mound, he was hurled end over end through the snow and came to rest at the base of the hill.

He composed himself as quickly as he could and jumped to his feet, limping slightly as he walked toward the car. He was not about to show any signs of weakness to his father. As Jack slammed on the brakes, jumped out of the car, and ran toward Robert, his other sons leaned out the back window with shouts of affirmation.

"That was wild Robert! You looked like a freakin' stuntman!"

"Are you all right?" Jack inquired as he drew closer, relieved to see that his son was standing. "Guess this should be our last run huh?" Jack quipped, hoping to break the tension. Playfully mussing Robert's hair, Jack put his arm over the boy's shoulder as they walked back to the car.

43

Robert took the gesture as an unspoken apology and was glad that they would now be heading home.

To this point, Brandon had been a mere spectator to the action. "What about me, Dad?" he asked now, hopefully. "I can do it. I know how. I was watching the whole time!" Not hearing an immediate "No" gave the young boy some hope.

However, even Jack drew a line when it came to his sons' safety, and Brandon fell short of that line. "You are not doing the hill, Brandon," Jack replied, "but you can ride the rope home. How about that?"

"Yay, thanks, Dad!" Brandon exclaimed as he opened the car door. Jack's concession made Brandon feel like one of the boys. He positioned himself on the sled, and grabbed the T-handle with anticipation. Jack leaned out the driver side window.

"All right there, Igor, hang on!"

"I'm not Igor, Dad, I'm Brandon!" the boy replied.

Jack drove about 10 miles an hour in one long circle around the parking lot as Brandon's spindly arms dangled from the T-handle. Exiting the lot directly across from their house, Jack pulled into his driveway as his tires spun briefly on the fresh snow.

The boys were cold and wet but could not have been happier, and Jack was satisfied that they'd had fun. In his estimation, part of the enjoyment was found in the danger, limited though it was, in his opinion.

The boys were sure to tell their mother of the evening's escapades, but Jack was unconcerned at the prospect of Patricia learning about their jaunt. In fact, her being home and expressing her displeasure at the idea would not have stopped him. But the process was that much easier if Patricia wasn't there to protest.

And though Patricia would have objected, she would most probably have relented and allowed the boys their "fun," trusting Jack to ensure that no one really got hurt. What would have sent her into a fit, however, was knowing that Richard had been in the house by himself the whole time. To Jack's mind, Richard was safely upstairs, asleep in his crib, with Rommel keeping watch from the base of the steps. Besides, Jack thought, since he was just outside, it was really not much different than if he'd been sitting in the living room.

For the most part, Jack did not understand Patricia's fears and would not have sympathized if any of the boys had been afraid to take a turn behind the car. Highlighted in this lack of understanding was a frightening, if sometimes enviable aspect of Jack Christopher's personality. He had no fear, of anything. Whether his fearlessness resulted from genetics or upbringing could be debated, but wherever the trait came from, Jack feared nothing.

"Wet clothes downstairs," Jack reminded the boys as they trudged through the snow toward the kitchen door.

"Yes sir" the quartet collectively replied, still wound up from the evening's events. Once inside, the three older boys raced upstairs half naked, fighting over who got to take a bath first. Jack set Brandon down in the living room, wrapped in a blanket with a promise of hot chocolate to follow. Brandon understood that he would have this in the kitchen. Children and food in the living room did not go together in Jack's vocabulary.

Warm bath water running upstairs, hot chocolate heating on one burner and coffee brewing on another promised a good night for the Christopher household. Homemade toll house cookies that Patricia left put a tasty finish on the evening adventure.

The hot bath and chocolate did not take long to cause heavy eyelids and contagious yawns. Soon Robert, Shawn, and Russell were trudging wearily up the steps as their equally exhausted father carried Brandon up behind them.

Chapter 8
Patricia and a Welcome Respite

Precious memories of past Christmas gatherings came flooding back as Patricia removed a fresh batch of sugar cookies from her mother's oven. Sweet smells from the kitchen could always be counted on to fill the entire house and excite the senses when Ginny entertained at Christmas. Guests anticipated homemade chocolates, hot apple cider, fruit cake, and cookies of every variety, and Ginny never disappointed. Ginny and Bud's brick rancher was always exquisitely decorated for Christmas. Whether it was "over decorated" depended on to whom the question was posed. A new feature, sometimes big, sometimes small, was added to the décor each year. Rushing in to find the heretofore unseen trinket, the grandkids would search high and low for the unfamiliar decoration. The child lucky enough to find the newest addition would get the oversized stocking that was hanging prominently in the kitchen, with the unspoken understanding that the treats and toys would be shared with the other children.

For now though, no laughing children scampered about the house, and the only footsteps were those of Patricia, Ginny and Bud. Bing Crosby played softly in the background as the three of them began to decorate Ginny's pristine 10-foot Christmas tree. As was tradition, Bud had purchased the tree, set it up in the living room, and strung the lights. A band of inner lights was painstakingly strung to wind upward on the tree trunk. Resting gently on the outer branches, more accessible lighting spiraled down in a long, winding band. Ginny and Bud's children and grandchildren would then gather together to hang a multitude of special ornaments. Some had been made by children or grandchildren, and many decorations had been handed down over several generations. Each had its own reserved place on the tree, and each brought to the onlooker's mind a memory that no other ornament could.

This year however, the gathering was unusually small. Patricia's two sisters were snowbound in nearby Philadelphia and were not able to participate in the traditional family gathering. Her two brothers, much like Jack, preferred to be anywhere else and used the storm as a convenient reason to be excused from tree-trimming duty.

Through the large bay window, Patricia could see the Christmas lights that covered the eaves reflecting off the newly fallen snow in the flowerbeds. Patricia thought how strangely barren the flowerbeds looked compared to the splendor to which Ginny coaxed them during the summer season. Ginny filled them with tulips, Russian irises, daylilies, and zinnias, rotating the flowers so that each had its turn to display its colors. The hibiscus had the final say of the summer, as the ice plants crawled their way over the low brick garden wall. Patricia could also see the four blue spruce trees that lined either side of the walk. They were decorated too, and each spruce cast beams of white light into the evening sky.

Delicate holiday figurines were placed throughout the living room in perfect symmetry. Multicolored lights from the Christmas tree in the corner, coupled with the white glow from the front yard had a calming effect on Patricia. When she'd first arrived, Patricia, out of habit, kept looking around, expecting to find one of her children underfoot. Nursing a hot cider while carefully unwrapping ornaments for the tree, she became more and more relaxed, letting her guard down.

As Ginny and Patricia talked, Bud remained quiet but for an occasional "uh-huh" to show that he was following along.

"What are the boys doing tonight?" Ginny asked. Patricia replied with what she thought was an accurate answer.

"Jack said he may take them sledding over at the hill in Lindenwold. It depends on whether it's too cold for Richard to be outside that long." Lindenwold, the next town to the east, had a large, wide hill that was quite popular in the snowy days of winter.

47

"How long do you think Jack will last with all of them?" Ginny gave Patricia a playful smile to assure her that she was just kidding…sort of.

"He's really not THAT bad, Mom," Patricia replied, feeling the need to defend Jack.

Ginny said nothing. Although Jack was not who she had originally planned for Patricia, over the years Ginny had come to agree that Jack was not that bad, for the most part. She could not deny that her son-in-law was a good and faithful provider. He had also given her five grandchildren that she loved dearly.

But Ginny also knew her daughter. She did not believe that the tension and emotional weight she saw etched on Patricia's face when she came in was typical stress, even for a mother of five. Something else was burdening Patricia, and Ginny could tell that whatever it was had been with her for quite some time.

"How are the boys doing, honey?" Her mother's voice was quiet and direct, as if aiming at some specific mark on Patricia's heart.

"Good," Patricia responded with measured intensity. After a pause, she elaborated on her answer. "Robert had five As and two Bs for the marking period. He needs a little help with…" Ginny rested her hand on Patricia's forearm and squeezed gently to get her attention.

"Pat, that's not what I meant. I was more concerned about the boys themselves. Honey, I know that I don't see the kids that often; perhaps that's why I can notice some of the changes in their disposition. Maybe I'm way off base for asking, but Robert seems much more reserved than he used to be. He hardly says anything when he comes to visit. We were wondering if we may have offended him. Has he said anything to you?" Ginny had not raised her voice, and Patricia heard no element of accusation. What came across was simply the voice of love and concern of a mother for her daughter and grandchildren.

Ginny continued, "I love you, Patricia. I just want you to be happy and find joy all through your life."

Patricia tried not to show any indication of the growing stress she could feel returning to her. Even if she had been able to summon enough control over her voice and expression, Patricia's hands would have given

48

her away. Growing tensions deep within her heart had transferred to her fingers, and before she realized how hard she was squeezing it, the glass ornament she was holding shattered.

She looked at the broken glass with alarm.

"I'm sorry, Mom, I'm so sorry." Her voice cracked as she apologized.

"Honey, I don't care about the blasted ornament." Ginny took Patricia by the arm and led her over to the sofa.

"Why don't we finish the tree later? Have a seat on the couch, and Dad will get you a glass of wine. Bud, please do me a favor and pour Pat a glass of the Pinot Noir."

With Bud in the kitchen, Ginny seated her daughter on the Queen Ann sofa. Eggshell white silk with embroidered floral patterns, the sofa had been in the family for years. Ginny hoped that a more comfortable setting would ease Patricia's mind.

"I want you to relax, Pat. When you feel like it; if you feel like it; we can talk later. Otherwise, we will just let it go. For now, have a little wine and take a nap. Ginny grabbed a large afghan from the nearest bedroom and lovingly placed it over Patricia, who had taken a sip of wine and lain on the couch. She found the afghan itself comforting, since it had been made by her grandmother many years ago. Fond memories of spring mornings with her grandmother came to her mind. Bud walked over and kissed her on the forehead.

"Sweet dreams, Patricia," he whispered.

"Thanks Dad," Patricia responded. Though now half asleep, she reached up and gently held her father's fingertips before her hand returned to the powder-blue carpet below her. Once Patricia fell asleep, Bud placed a down pillow under her head. Around 3 am, Patricia woke up and made her way to bed.

Chapter 9
Patricia and a New Day

Cascades of light shimmered across the bed as the bright morning sun reflected off the snow and through the east bedroom window. As the morning progressed the bright band moved from the foot of the bed toward the headboard. Sometime during its travels, Patricia awakened as the bright glow fell squarely across her eyes.

Disoriented at first, she sat up sharply and scanned the room to try to discern exactly where she was and how she got there. Remembering the evening's events, Patricia relaxed and again enjoyed a few final moments to herself. A full night of uninterrupted rest was just what she needed, and her mother, recognizing how desperately she needed it, had been more than willing to forgo normally observed traditions. Ginny's willingness to put off decorating and not push her for an extended explanation meant a lot to Patricia.

Now rested and much more willing to share her burden with Ginny, Patricia hoped that the opportunity would arise again. Her main concern was how to broach the subject without losing her composure. The morning light led Patricia into the kitchen, where fresh coffee made from ground whole beans welcomed her to breakfast. As the smell of eggs and bacon filled her nostrils, she could not help but think this would be the beginning of an enjoyable morning.

Eighteen inches of additional snow had fallen overnight, making the snowstorm everything it was forecast to be. Expecting to arrive home any earlier than late afternoon or early evening was unrealistic. Patricia hoped that Jack's temperament would hold up to the unavoidable extension of his shift with the kids. As for herself, Patricia intended to make the most of her visit with Bud and Ginny, starting with a delicious breakfast that she didn't even have to cook.

"Good morning, Dear," Ginny greeted her as she simultaneously flipped the eggs over easy and turned the bacon. Patricia was suddenly taken back to mornings as a young girl getting ready for school. The feeling of nostalgia suited her. "I hope that you slept well last night. The Queen Anne is nice, but it can get uncomfortable after a while. I was glad to see that you made it into your old bedroom." Patricia had not felt so well rested in quite a while.

She caught Ginny and Bud exchanging a glance.

"What?" she asked playfully, wanting to be let in on whatever joke they were sharing. Bud struggled for an answer.

"Well, Dear, you see…you sort of…"

Ginny finished the thought for him. "You snored like a freight train, Dear. There was no mistaking whether you were asleep or not. I had plaster from the ceiling falling on my head, you were so loud."

Patricia blushed and then laughed along as Ginny handed her a full plate of eggs, bacon, hash browns, and toast. Her mother thought that the light moment may have been a good time to touch on heavier subjects.

"I was hoping that you might talk in your sleep, avoiding the need for probing questions from your mother."

Patricia appreciated the tact with which her mother brought up the subject, and the fact that Patricia did not need to initiate the discussion was also a relief.

"After breakfast mom, I promise. Thanks for not pushing last night. I thought about it and feel much more ready to discuss it today. Let's both get a little breakfast in us, and we'll talk." Patricia leaned back in her chair, free to enjoy their time together in casual conversation for the remainder of the morning meal.

"What time do you have to be home, Pat? It's going to take Bud a while to dig the car out and for the plows to clear the road."

Patricia was in no hurry, and felt some concern for her father.

"I'll give Jack a call later. I'm sure that it's just as bad at home. I don't want Daddy to have a heart attack. I am fairly certain that the mess will still be there when I get home." Patricia finished with a note of sarcasm in her voice.

After finishing breakfast, the ladies cleaned up the kitchen and retired to the living room. Bud stood outside, posed with the formidable task of digging out the car and driveway. He was also mentally preparing himself to watch the plow trucks block his apron in with a fresh wall of slush-compacted snow. A verbal rant—as close to cursing as Bud was likely to get—would almost certainly be required.

Inside, the ladies sat on the couch and placed their bone china teacups on the large, solid marble top of the coffee table. The slab of stone measured three inches thick and was oddly shaped. Smooth on top, it had rough-hewn edges and a light blue color that complemented the carpet. Looking nearly as new as the day Patricia's grandmother bought them, , the handed-down furniture was exquisite.

Patricia was much more composed than she had been the previous evening. She felt it was important that her words were clear and unclouded as she shared what was in her heart. For her part, Ginny wanted to be there for her daughter while resisting an "I-told-you-so" attitude. Ginny wondered if she would be strong enough to tell her hurting daughter that she was wrong if that was where the information led. She didn't know, but hoped that she could, if that's what Patricia needed, no matter how uncomfortable it made her.

Patricia spoke in an even, measured tone. "Mom, you know that I love Jack dearly. Regardless of what you may have thought of him in the beginning, I know you and Dad have come to love him as well. He has so many great qualities. I feel safe with him wherever we go. Jack is about the toughest guy I know, and yet he has this side of him that is so funny; almost like a big kid. You've seen how sociable and engaging he can be. No one could describe him as a sullen, brooding, wandering soul. He's the guy people want to be near at parties and family gatherings, and when he's with his brothers, he's even more so. There is a kind of natural comic rapport between Jack and his brothers. They feed off each other's observations and can have the whole room laughing.

"But then there's this other side to him. I think of all that he has overcome in his life and how hard he's worked all these years to give the kids and me a good home. I just wish that somewhere along the way he could catch a break from the pressure that is on him, even a little break."

Patricia stopped to let her mother respond, but Ginny remained silently attentive, signaling her to continue.

"But Mom, I walk through every day on eggshells, not knowing whether all hell is going to break loose." Patricia's voice grew shaky as she clasped her hands together tightly in front of her.

"I, I don't really know if Jack is even aware of what he is doing. We could be having a wonderful day; Jack is cracking jokes and we are having fun with the kids. Out of nowhere, like a flash of lightning, comes this frightening rage. It could be as stupid as the door taking too long to unlock or water tracks on the kitchen floor. Jack sends his hand through a wall, or window, and then five minutes later you would never know anything had happened. There have been times when we've talked about it, but I think that even Jack doesn't know where it comes from, and it certainly isn't deliberate."

Ginny offered a non-partisan solution. "What about seeking professional help? We all need a hand now and then."

Patricia shook her head, knowing that counseling was not an option. "Jack said that patients are an easy retirement plan for people like that. They fix you just enough to keep coming back."

Ginny posed the question heaviest on her mind, "Patricia, does he ever hit you or the kids?"

"No, no, Mom, I promise you. Nothing like that at all," Patricia assured her mother.

"Well, how do the kids feel about it, Honey?" Ginny came to the heart of Patricia's distress. Tears welled up in Patricia's eyes as she ran her shaking hand back and forth across her forehead. Ginny wanted so much to embrace Patricia and let her cry in her arms, but refrained it, knowing that Patricia would not be able to continue getting the frustration out if she did.

"It's so hard to explain to them, Mom, when he sits in his chair with a wide glazed look, and everything else is blocked out. This is not to suggest that Jack is taking anything, Mom. Jack despises any pills or medicines; you know that. To him, relying on them is a sign of weakness, and he has never been drunk a day in his life. The idea of not being in control is repulsive to him."

Patricia paused for a moment, fearing that she may have begun rambling, and sipped her now lukewarm tea. Ginny also sipped her tea, giving Patricia a chance to regain her composure. When Patricia continued, her tone was calm and even again.

"What scares me most, Mom, is that I can see the toll that this is taking on the kids. They can seldom relax in their own house. Each day brings varying degrees of tension. I'm most worried for Robert. He already puts so much weight on himself as the oldest son. The anxiety from day to day is slowly wearing him down. A little today, a little tomorrow; eventually there will be nothing left to inspire him or bring him joy. I can see it in his eyes. He tries to hide it, but the frustration is there. I'm sorry if you and Dad thought Robert was upset with you. He loves you both dearly. Bringing him with me had crossed my mind, but the other boys would have had a fit. In hindsight, perhaps it was best that he stayed home. I am sure that you and I wouldn't have been able to talk if he were here." With her last words, Patricia became aware that her mother had scarcely said a word.

"So, what do you think? Am I driving myself crazy?"

Ginny strained to be as impartial as possible.

"Honey, your father and I knew that something was wrong. Naturally, we couldn't put a finger on what it was. Sometimes it's hard for your father and I to know where the line is between helping, and sticking our noses in where they don't belong. Have you talked to Robert about this?"

Patricia nodded. "Robert feels as though Jack has always been the hardest on him, that he can never measure up to Jack's expectations. With the best of intentions, Jack is tough on Robert. He picks apart much of what Robert does. Is it excessive? How am I supposed to know what

54

'excessive' is. I can tell you that I hate that belt of his," she said, gritting her teeth. "I can see why the boys are afraid of it. It's scary to even look at."

Patricia sighed. She felt that Robert had experienced more than his share of episodes with the belt. Since he was the firstborn, what was and was not an infraction was developed on a case-by-case basis for Robert.

"Mom, Robert is afraid of dreaming he could become somebody. He's afraid of failing and Jack teasing him, so he finds it easier to not do anything at all rather than risk the humiliation. All of the beautiful things that I see in him are dying, and it breaks my heart. You know he's very athletic, but he doesn't think enough of himself to pursue any sports. Several months ago, Jack punished him while his friends were over at the house. He hasn't had anyone over since then."

Hearing her voice catch, Patricia paused and swallowed hard before continuing. "His grades are okay but far short of what he achieved last year. And I've gotten several notes from his teachers concerned about the change they see in him. Jack calls it 'bullshit' and won't meet with them. It seems like Robert just tries to get through the day he has ahead of him, and that's all. Jack thinks I'm making too much of it all; maybe I am, who knows?"

Patricia felt relief wash over her as she poured out the last of her worries to her mother. Regardless of her mother's answer, she had finally been able to say all that was on her mind.

"Let me put some water on for tea before we continue, dear," Ginny said, using the few brief moments to think through all that Patricia had told her. Returning from the kitchen, Ginny took Patricia's face tenderly in her hands.

"Honey, listen to your own words. I saw something. You saw something, and the teachers expressed concern. I seriously doubt that all of us are making this up. Too many people have noticed that there is a problem." Patricia started to feel as though perhaps she had represented her husband too harshly.

"Mom, I know that Jack loves the kids, and that is why he wants them to grow tough enough to make it in life. How do we get somewhere between where Jack is and me?"

Ginny noticed that most of Patricia's concerns had pertained to Robert. "How about the other boys, dear?" she asked. "Do they feel the same way Robert does?"

"Robert seems to have been affected the most," Patricia replied, taking a more reflective tone. "I wonder about Shawn, to be honest with you. Shawn probably sees himself as sort of 'skipped over'. He is quite happy not to be in Robert's shoes, but I think he wishes he were a little more like Russell. Shawn tends to keep to himself and is very sensitive to criticism. I'm sure that it must bother Shawn that Jack favors Russell. Russell is very much like his father in that he fears nothing. Russell is a fighter and has even told Jack during spankings that 'you can't hurt me'. So Russell has Jack's respect. He still gets spanked, but he has his father's respect."

Stopping to look out the wide bay window, they gauged the extent of Bud's progress. Patricia figured he still had an hour's work before they could leave, but she'd need to leave shortly thereafter. She was emotionally drained but thankful for the time with her mother. Still, she also missed being with the boys, and despite the concerns expressed to Ginny, missed Jack.

"How about Brandon dear? How is he?" Ginny asked, breaking the momentary silence.

"Brandon?" It took Patricia a few seconds to switch from watching her father and thinking about her family back home. "Oh, Mom, he is nonstop as usual." Patricia's face lit up. She felt good to be able to switch to a more pleasant topic. "The little bugger is always into something. Of course now everything is Santa this and Santa that. Has he been good? Do reindeer get sick? The questions never end. He is such a happy boy, especially when he gets to play with his brothers. He drives them nuts singing that infernal 'Davey Crockett' song. I have to admit, sometimes I give him snacks just so he'll stop singing."

Patricia's face changed quickly as her mind landed on a more serious contemplation. "I hope that my little one grows into his arms and legs. Things would be so much easier for him with the other children, Mom. You know that kids can be so cruel about the slightest differences. Jack is still awkward around him sometimes. It's as if he's not sure what to make of his son's physical shortcomings. Richard is a sweetheart, but I can see his father's tenacity in him. He does not give in to anyone. Maybe after New Year's we can spend a weekend together, and I'll bring Richard."

Patricia leaned over and kissed her mother on the cheek. "Mom, thanks for listening. I feel much better not having all of this bottled up inside me. Maybe I worry a little too much, but I'll sit down with Jack during the week and tell him how I've been feeling."

Ginny smiled and refrained from expressing her doubts that Patricia would bring her concerns to Jack.

"I'll be praying for you dear...always am." Ginny's support brought great comfort to Patricia. "Let us know if there is anything we can do," Ginny continued.. "By the way, Bud's boss is letting us use his cabin in the Poconos next month. We would love to take the three older boys skiing, if it works out for you and Jack. We will take care of the cost." She paused before adding "And it might be the break you both need, with the boys away, to work things out."

The sleigh bells hanging on the kitchen door jingled as Bud came in, stamping the snow off of his boots. Nose running and cheeks red, he gave them the latest update on his battle with the township workers.

"I know darn well those plow guys are laughing every time they push a fresh wall of snow across our driveway. Three times! Three times, I had to clear it back out. Well, anyway, it's done, assuming that the plow guys have had their fill of tormenting me."

"Thank you, Daddy," Patricia said warmly as she kissed his receding hairline. Tiny balls of ice hung from his thin strands of hair.

"Let me get a shower and warm up, and then we can head out," Bud said, before forewarning Patricia, "Driving on roads like this at night makes me nervous: too many knuckleheads out there. We're cutting it a little close, but I should be able to get you home and be back before dark." Cold and tired, Bud slowly made his way toward the bathroom. He'd been thinking about a nice hot shower for the better part of the last hour. But before he could get to the bathroom door, Ginny called out one more item of business.

"By the way Bud, Robert, Shawn, and Russell are going to the Poconos with us next month. You'll need to buy some sleeping bags and extra lift tickets."

Not willing to enter into a protracted exchange, Bud simply raised his hand without turning around. This silent reply brought amusement and a feeling of sympathy from Ginny and Patricia. They knew that the still icy and slick roads promised a long, slow ride home. Patricia felt sorry that her father had to drive in such conditions, but for her, the trip was well worth the effort, and she went home feeling much better than she had only a day before.

Chapter 10
Jack and the Boys, and the Long Road Home

While Patricia was sharing concerns with her mother, Jack and the boys used the day to walk the mile or so up the hill to visit Jack's father. Two years had passed since Charles' beloved wife, Agnes, had died, and the holiday seasons were especially difficult for him. The back roads that led to Charles' house could be hard to navigate. The snow would make them impassible for Charles, potentially adding to his isolation.

The kids loved "Grandpop Charles" and his big house. The many rooms of the large old multilevel manor always left them full of wonder as to what might be behind any given door. They had freedom to run around inside and out, with one exception: they could not enter the locked back room at the end of the upstairs hallway. That room, where Agnes had died, had been locked ever since, and was unmistakably off limits.

Charles was surprised but pleased that his son and the boys had trudged all the way over from their house. Charles Christopher was as tough as his son, but he was not above playing "got your nose" with his younger grandkids.

The visit was enjoyable for all, until Brandon attempted to "fix" the colored light shining on Charles' Christmas tree. The tree was 6 foot, and made of silver aluminum. It stood in front of the unused fireplace, as it usually did and was adorned as usual with several dozen red Christmas balls and nothing else. In fact, having become somewhat used to seeing it there, Charles now left the tree in the same spot all year round.

The living room remained completely dark, with all of the shades drawn. The only light came from an illuminated color wheel at the base of the tree. Hues of blue, green, and yellow shone on the tee, cycling through in a continual pattern every 10 seconds.

Earlier in the day, Charles had stopped the wheel, leaving the Christmas tree bathed in blue light. Since Brandon had never seen the wheel stopped before, he naturally assumed it to be broken. Attempting to turn it by hand, Brandon snapped the wheel off its mount. Jack heard the snap and tinkle of glass and walked in on the frightened would-be mechanic. Grabbing him by the upper arm, Jack lifted his son into the air and plopped him down in a nearby chair, directing him not to get up. The jolt to his arm frightened Brandon more than his father's yelling.

Finally, after the mostly enjoyable visit with Charles, Jack and the boys made their way down the icy streets of Linden Avenue. Grouped together, Jack and the older boys walked as Jack carried a whiney and restless Richard and pulled Brandon on a Flexible Flyer sled. Brandon nursed his aching arm as he rode over the snow-covered streets. Compounding Jack's discomfort was that after a full day on his own with the boys, he had little energy or patience left. Overnight accumulations were too deep for Brandon to have kept pace on the walk, and since Charles' house sat four blocks off of the White Horse Pike, only now had the plows begun to make some headway along the secondary roads. Once they reached the White Horse Pike, the Christopher's house was a little more than a mile west, at the bottom of the hill.

As they walked out onto the Pike, Jack thought again what a beautiful town Stratford was and remembered the thousands of times he had raced up and down this same hill as a boy. Jack was proud to have grown up in this town, and he could never imagine living anywhere else. Slightly more than two miles square, Stratford was tucked in between the larger towns of Lindenwold and Somerdale, Hi Nella, Laurel Springs, and Gloucester Township. Part of Stratford's charm was that it seemed to have arrived at the 1950s and decided that it was quite content there. Consequently, it retained an attractive small-town charm evidenced by mom and pop storefronts that lined the White Horse Pike, Stratford's answer to Main Street.

Surrounding municipalities had opted for large expansion projects, courting several retail chains. While that strategy might have some fiscal merit, to Jack's mind, that meant that much of the character and irreplaceable uniqueness of small town life was lost. That uniqueness could still be found, alive and well, in Stratford.

There was another aspect of small town living that appealed to Jack. With six boys each as wild as the next and two beautiful girls, Jack's family had been well known. It was commonly understood that you did not mess with the brothers or disrespect the sisters; or if you did, it was at your own peril. Moreover, aside from a reputation for toughness, the Christophers were also known to be a fun bunch. After the hard times of the Depression were over and they settled in Stratford, their reputation, rightly earned, gave them the freedom to enjoy being kids, and as a result they were well liked throughout town.

By design of the township planners, all commercial buildings were situated on the White Horse Pike. This foresight meant that side roads like Linden Avenue could display the beauty of stately Victorian homes unencumbered by retail signs and shops. Large majestic oak trees, generations old, now provided a grand canopy over the quiet side streets. Rarely did anything but local traffic have reason to traverse these back roads.

As Jack and the boys turned left onto the Pike, the view down the hill was strangely beautiful. They saw no signs of moving vehicles; the only cars were several stranded sedans dotting the roadway. Abandoned cars, most on the side of the road but some stuck in the middle of the roadway, left the boys wondering as to the disposition of their occupants.

Later in the evening, neon roadside signs would cast a luminous glow on the hill. This was particularly true when the signs themselves were blanketed with fresh snow. The vibrant colors cast on the street in the dark of night would bring life to the silent hillside.

There was something about the ability to point at any building on the hill and know the owner and his or her stories that gave Jack a wonderful feeling of belonging. Across from Linden Avenue stood St. Anne's Catholic Church, where Jack received his first holy communion and his confirmation and which was still the family's church. St. Anne's had hosted his two married brothers' weddings, and it was here that Jack said goodbye to his dear mother. Jack's boys joked that if you attended early mass, you got to hear the sermon of "Father Fast." Parishioners who slept in and went to the later service would end up sitting through "Father Slow's" drawn out sermon.

Two doors down was the Hilltop Diner. Local teens still used it as a hangout and to argue with older patrons. Five years before, it had burned down, but, against all odds, its owner, Donna Delaprutti, had it rebuilt. Jack thought she showed the same boundless grit and determination that her father had. Next to the diner was The Smoke Shop tobacco store, run by Chuck Lester, who had gone to school with Jack. Chuck and Jack had hated each other as kids but laughed about it now. Chuck insisted that he overcharged his friend for smokes.

Next to the Smoke Shop was the Full Bloom Florist, and any of the men frequenting the shop would certainly describe the owner as being "in full bloom." Tina Darling was a divorced Jane Russell look alike. Jack was not one of those men, however, once Patricia found out that Tina hit on Jack when he went into the shop. Soon after Patricia found the note with her phone number that Tina had a habit of slipping into any of the bouquets that Jack bought, Patricia found the family another florist.

On the corner of Stratford Avenue across from Jack's house was Thunderstrike Bowling Lanes. Packed several days a week, and always lively with Mike O'Brian behind the counter, Thunderstrike Lanes was the social center of Stratford. Jack remembered the exciting nights of his youth bowling with his father as all the men started coming home from the war. Men hugged without apprehension as they found that dear childhood friends had survived the war.

"I need the sled, Brandon," Robert said as he gently nudged his younger brother off. "Dad, can I?" Robert asked, motioning toward the icy hill.

"Let him have the sled, Brandon. I'll carry you the rest of the way home." Jack took Brandon up in his left arm, with Richard continuing to squirm in his right.

"I'm sorry that I broke the light Dad," Brandon said as soon as he was in Jack's arm. He was unsure to what extent his earlier mistake still hung over him. "I was just trying to help Pop-Pop."

Jack regretted the intensity of his initial response to Brandon's offense and wanted him to know it.

"I know, Buddy; Dad was just really tired. I got a little too upset. How is your arm? Is it feeling any better?" Brandon's eyes lit up as the cloud dispersed from over his heart.

"My arm is fine now. Look." Brandon rotated his arm in a wide circle to prove his point.

As Jack walked with Richard and Brandon at a controlled pace, the oldest three boys navigated the hill in a much quicker and more exciting fashion. After a running start, Robert and Shawn flopped on the sled and went careening down the hill. The sled moved down the hill so fast that even Shawn, on top of his brother and so further off the ground, was blinded by the snow flying into his eyes. Just before they the sled hit the back of a stranded car, the brothers bailed to either side, rolling end over end. They lay in the road, snow covered and laughing over their wild ride. Russell followed behind them, sliding down the hill on foot.

Jack and the 2 youngest boys continued their more leisurely pace. They passed Integrity Jewelers on the left. Sye Cohen, the owner, had never gotten over losing his only son in the Korean War. Each Valentine's Day Sye raffled off a beautiful 2 karat wedding ring in honor of his son.

Further down the slope on the left was Capolla Shoes. Everyone loved Tony Capolla. His favorite line was, "You're not Italian, but I like you anyway." Tony was the type of man who really would give another the shirt off of his back. At the bottom of the hill, across from Stratford Avenue, was the Dark Arts Tattoo Shop. Although many in town initially thought that the shop was a blight, most changed their minds on learning that owner Jake Watson was a highly decorated veteran. After this came to light, both other vets and bikers went out of their way to support the business. Jack looked around at the other stores on the hill: pawn shop, garden center, bank, and auto store. Jack knew all their stories.

Now, though, Jack was relieved to be so close to home. Strong though he may have been, his arms were tired. Jack was even happier to see Bud's car come into view. This meant that Patricia was home. Tracks scattered over the front yard in no discernible pattern were a telltale sign that Rommel had been outside recently.

As soon as they caught sight of their grandfather's car, the three oldest ran ahead. As Jack turned into the driveway, he saw Bud standing with his closed fists held in front of him, playing "guess which hand is the dollar in". Bud derived as much joy as the boys did from this. Every time Bud played, each grandson seemed to win two dollars without fail.

"Hi, Jack," Bud greeted him warmly. "Did you survive the odyssey?" Both men laughed, knowing he was only half kidding.

"Barely, Bud, barely. I'm not wired to be a homemaker. I'd make a terrible housewife."

As the two men entered the kitchen behind the boys, Patricia had just returned downstairs from doing an initial survey of the house.

"Not bad at all, Jack; I'm impressed," she said, hugging him tightly, and pressing her fingers against his back. She was pleased to feel him reciprocate with equal zeal.

"I'm going to start back home, Patricia," Bud said, making his way toward the kitchen door. "You know how I am about driving in the dark. I can still make it before dusk if I leave now. Jack, it's been good to see you. I imagine we'll be seeing you over the holidays." Bud adjusted his scarf and fedora as he readied himself to leave.

"Have a safe trip back, Bud, and thanks again for everything. We'll see you in a couple of weeks," Jack replied.

"Bye, kids!" Bud yelled as he ventured out the back door. As the boys yelled goodbye from the living room, Patricia caught her father at the door and kissed him on the cheek.

"Thank you, Dad,…for everything." Bud knew that his daughter meant the night's sleep and talk with Ginny as well as the ride home.

"Take care, Schpunky," he said in a lowered voice." This was the name he had given her as a little girl, and that no one else knew, not even Ginny. It was a secret they shared and a name she adored.

Turning her attention to her family, Patricia's first instinct was to start her mental "to do" list of house chores. Looking at her husband, she decided that the cleaning could wait.

"Would you like coffee, Jack?" she asked.

"Thanks, Hon, but I won't be awake when it's done." Jack kissed her before heading upstairs for a hot shower and then bed.

"Thanks again, Jack," she answered. "I really appreciate the break." Patricia knew that Jack was too tired to hear any of the details, especially any concerns she had regarding the kids. She was probably too tired as well.

Patricia had only to look at the huge pile of wet clothes in the basement to know how she would most likely spend the rest of the day. Despite that, and the problems that still weighed on her, it was good to have everyone safely back home.

Chapter 11
Jack and the Unkindest Cut

June 28, 1968

Biting winds and bitter cold temperatures were but a distant memory as Jack continually wiped accumulating sweat from his brow. To him, fanciful depictions of beaches and amusement parks usually associated with the mid-year months were a waste of time.

"You can always put more clothes on in the winter," he argued. "But you can run around bare ass in the summer and still sweat to death." The searing July sun had done little to dissuade Jack of his opinion.

1968 marked Jack's 10th year at Kutter Sheet Metal, and every summer was just as miserable as the one that had preceded it. As June drew closer and closer, the temperature on the floor of the machine shop grew more oppressive by the day. And though the 300 machine operators felt like the dial on an oven was being turned up by degrees, their floor bosses and the company owner showed little sympathy from the air-conditioned glass-fronted offices that overlooked the production floor.

Watching us sweat is some kind of sick amusement for those SOBs upstairs, more than one worker had thought.

Measuring 100 feet wide and 300 feet deep, the production floor held 75 machines spaced five across and 15 deep over the entire floor. Shaved and heated metal cast a decidedly industrial smell over the entire floor. The building also had no windows, which made it virtually devoid of meaningful ventilation from the outside. A large vent fan just below the roofline at either end of the building provided little relief. The deafening sound of running machines was so intense that the vibrations seemed to penetrate the body, and heavy ear protection often did little but delay permanent damage. Driving home with a piercing migraine was, by now, all too common for Jack.

Heavy industrial machines of every conceivable type —lathes, presses, milling machines, and large sheet metal cutters, all painted forest green—were constantly in use. Jack's work station for most of the past 10 years was a sheet metal cutter. Each machine was enclosed within a perimeter of 3-inch red tape that extended 4 feet from the machine on all sides, forming a box that forbid entry by anyone other than the operator. Established under a pretense of safety, the operators thought that the intent was more likely to keep them boxed in. Within this cube, the operators stood for 12 hours a day under the watchful eye and disgruntled calls of the foremen.

Establishing a production pace that would bode well for their own performance reviews, the foremen were relentless. "All machines should be running all the time, no excuses," was the standard set for the machine operators. Neither mechanical nor personnel problems were of any interest to the men upstairs in their crisp, buttoned down shirts. Missed quotas would bring the heated wrath of the foreman on anyone who did not measure up to standard.

Powered by 3000 pounds of hydraulic pressure, an imposing 10-foot cutter blade ran the full length of Jack's table. Sheets of metal, 8 feet long and 4 feet wide would be rolled out to Jack's station, where he used two pedals to bring down the razor sharp blade and cut them into 8'x2' or 8'x3' pieces.

After positioning the ¼" thick sheet of metal on the table, Jack pressed the first pedal with his left foot. This #1 pedal acted as a safety interlock and had to be depressed first. With the #1 pedal down, Jack triggered pedal #2 with his right foot. When the two pedals were depressed, the 100- pound cutting blade sliced through the thick metal in less than two seconds. The blade then automatically retracted itself to the "ready" position, three inches above the table.

Pete Wells was Jack's foreman and had a penchant for, if not a preoccupation with, pissing Jack off. Although Pete feared Jack and knew when he had better back off, as Jack held his temper over the years, Pete ran the risk of moving the line in the sand, daring Jack to cross it. By the summer of 1968, he had been making life miserable for Jack the better part of four months. Jack's #1 pedal was not working. Half the time it would not allow the blade to come down even after the #2 pedal was triggered. Bitter arguments ensued between Jack and his superior. The bosses upstairs refused to pay for repairs, not that Pete had even dared to suggest shutting the machine down.

"I'm not going to shut it down Jack, so that you can stand around drinking coffee while you wait for it to get fixed," was Pete's answer. He rode Jack constantly for missing quotas and had even threatened to fire him.

This conflict and stress from work also found its way home, and days with Patricia and the kids that used to be amiable had become somewhat more contentious. Finally, Jack was so frustrated with the situation that he bypassed the #1 pedal by rewiring the machine, without authorization. While this circumvented the safety circuit, it also got Pete off of his back. Pete could not have cared less about the switch as long as quota was met.

The production floor was particularly humid, and vapors from penetrating and lubricating oils mixed with the heavy air and beaded on the skin. Irritability was a natural and noticeable byproduct of the surrounding elements.

"Christopher, get your ass moving! How much longer are you going to draw this out? Look at your station; you've gotten nothing done!" Pete was particularly acrimonious this day. Forced to stay on the floor for most of his shift, Pete resented not being able to stay in the air-conditioned offices. He was determined to take his anger out on anyone and everyone.

Although not able to decipher his words amidst the background noise, Jack could tell that Pete was livid. Jack fought to compose himself against the urge to grab Pete by the throat that was welling up within him.

"I'm resetting the fence; back off!" Jack retorted while flipping gestures that left his own opinion unmistakable.

Jack's sign of disrespect was the final straw for his boss. Crossing over the safety tape, Pete moved quickly toward the operator's side of the machine. Once and for all he was going to make clear who the subordinate employee was.

Pete grabbed the table and flung himself around the corner of the machine, landing next to Jack. Momentarily losing his balance, Pete stepped on the #2 pedal. Immediately pulling his foot back, the foreman watched as his worst fears unfolded, and his anger turned to horror as he watched the massive cutting blade come down on Jack's fingers.

"My fingers, my fingers!" Jack screamed as blood poured from his hands and pooled on the cutting table. Searing pain rushed through Jack's hands as he saw six of his fingertips lying in the blood on the cutting table. The index, middle, and ring fingers of both hands had been cut even with top of his pinky.

Jack pulled his shaking hands to his chest, blood running down his arms and falling in steady drops from his elbows. Half hunched with his hands to his chest, Jack frantically paced back and forth for several seconds until Chuck Mitchell ran to him. Pete, frozen with panic, sat on the floor nearby, crying hysterically, his face buried in his hands.

"Oh God, oh God, oh God..." was all that he could mutter.

A trail of blood led from the machine to Jack and continued to splatter onto the floor as Jack paced several feet away, hoping to somehow alleviate the pain. Finally reaching his agonized coworker, Chuck grasped Jack firmly by the shoulders and yelled directly at his face, hoping to secure his attention.

"Jack, listen to me! I need you to help me by laying down on your back. Lay flat on your back, Jack!" Chuck screamed through the din.

Though Jack was disoriented, Chuck managed to get him to lie on the floor. Men from nearby machines rushed over to assist. They placed an inverted parts bin under each arm and applied pressure at the elbows in an attempt to stop the bleeding.

"My fingers, get my fingers!" Jack yelled as he strained to motion up to the cutting table.

"Stay still, Jack; ya gotta stay still." Chuck reiterated several times. One of the men pulled the emergency handle, cutting power to all of the machines. The 30,000 square foot room fell strangely silent. Three large red lights continually flashed overhead, relaying the existence of an emergency to the bosses upstairs.

While lying down, Jack's attention turned to his foreman, still seated on the floor nearby. "You, you son-of-a-bitch! I'll kill you!" Jack pointed toward Pete with his bloodied hand. Chuck and two others held him down as he fought to get up and make his way over to Pete.

"Get him out of here" Chuck yelled while pointing at Pete. Seeing Pete ushered out of the area settled Jack down, and he recognized how weak the loss of blood made him feel.

Bursting through an exterior door, the Emergency Response Team Seemed to include an inordinate number of firefighters and rescue personnel carrying all forms of specialized equipment. As the EMTs worked to stabilize Jack and get him on a gurney, the lead rescue worker leaned over to him. "You're doing fine, Jack," he said. "I just need you to stay awake for me till we get you to the hospital, ok?"

With Jack on the way to the hospital, the task was now on the men in the glass booths to inform Patricia.

Chapter 12
Patricia and Collateral Damage

Tears streamed down Patricia's face as she was directed through the emergency room doors and escorted to the small curtained-off enclosure where Jack was being treated. The day's events would have been horrible enough, but coupled with the unremitting stress on the family in the past months, they were almost more than she could bear. Stress from conditions at work had made Jack very dark, almost unapproachable. Patricia had always understood Jack's dual nature, but now the strength and force of personality that had made her feel safe and secure left her uneasy.

It seemed to her that the demands of work had taken everything out of Jack. Interaction with the kids was minimal other than to discipline them. Punishments for the kids had been frequent and more severe, and infractions that had previously only warranted verbal reprimands were now met with corporal punishment.

The boys also felt the pressure. In recent months, Brandon had stopped singing the "Davey Crockett" song and began displaying some worrisome compulsive behaviors like frequently washing his hands. Already self-conscious about his physical irregularities, Brandon had been crushed to learn that "Igor" was not just an amusing moniker that Jack had invented. One Saturday morning as he was watching TV, the movie "Frankenstein" came on. Brandon was only 5, but still old enough to piece together what Jack's nickname for him implied. He had come out to the kitchen in tears and escorted Patricia back to the living room.

"Is that me, Mom?" he cried, pointing at the TV. "Does Daddy think I'm like Igor? I don't want to be like Igor!"

It did not matter that Jack had not meant to hurt Brandon; Brandon was crushed.

Patricia had always prided herself on being a devoted, submissive wife. She never flared up at Jack, especially around the kids. But seeing pain in the kids' faces every day and Jack's seeming indifference to it angered Patricia deeply.

But if Jack's actions were on trial, where was *his* legal counsel? Patricia had laid out the case clearly and concisely in her mind, and only one logical conclusion could be reached. And yet, she had reached her conclusion with only the prosecution in the room. Would no one inquire as to the daily trials and strains besetting him? Had no one asked about his rebukes from Pete each day? What of the migraines that were down played, or concerns that went unvoiced, even to Patricia? These circumstances may not exonerate her husband, but might they not mitigate the sentence?

Against this backdrop of conflicted emotions, Patricia received the call from the offices of Kutter Sheet Metal.

"Mrs. Christopher, this is Winslow Billson at Kutter Sheet Metals," the carefully controlled voice began. "I'm afraid that there has been an accident. Mr. Christopher is at Kennedy Memorial Hospital, in the emergency room. Please do not be alarmed; your husband's injuries are not life-threatening. Unfortunately, I do not have any more information than that at the moment. Let us know if there is anything that we can do." Before Patricia had even drawn a breath to respond, she heard a "click" and the other end of the line fell silent.

Patricia's immediate worry for Jack was laced with anger at the message. The owner of Kutter had delivered his terrifying message in a voice devoid of human emotion, as though he had repeated the same words a thousand times before, with equal detachment. The call was minimally informative at best, and as glaringly dispassionate. Patricia had no time for Mr. Billson; she had to compose herself enough to figure out how to get a ride to the hospital.

72

Chapter 13

Jack and Patricia, and the Beginning of a New Normal

Avery Mangold strode through the emergency room doors just behind Patricia, with long, even strides and a neighborly smile. He had been more than happy to give Patricia a ride to the hospital. There was not much that he would not do for Patricia, or any neighbor in need of assistance. Such things, in his mind, were a natural expectation of those living in a community.

Patricia's searching eyes found Jack as soon as she passed the nurse's station. Huge balls of white bandaging covered both of his hands.

"Jack!" Patricia exclaimed, burying her tear streaked face in his neck. All of the conflict and disagreement melted away as she hugged her husband, careful to avoid bumping his heavily bandaged hands. Tears fell from her face to Jack's as she kissed his forehead.

"Honey, I'm so sorry that this happened to you. You're gonna be fine. We'll do whatever you need us to do." Patricia stroked Jack's hair with her fingers, and stood back to give him a little space. Groggy from the loss of blood and pain medications, Jack caught only about half her words.

Moving his arms even slightly sent throbbing pain through his hands so he tried to keep them at his sides.

"It's all right; I'm fine," he nevertheless tried to assure his worried wife, with marginal success.

"Howdy, Jack," Avery greeted his neighbor in his usual kindly manner. Jack was glad it was Avery who'd given Patricia the ride to the hospital.

"What did they say, Jack?" Jack liked that about Avery when he talked, he was to the point.

"That I won't be stealing any of your strawberries, Avery," Jack joked, trying to lighten the mood. Avery smiled his broad smile.

"I'll pick you some," he promised. "Patricia, you ok getting back home?" he asked. "I can stay if you need me." Avery blushed as Patricia walked over and hugged him.

"No, thank you, Avery." Patricia answered with real gratitude. "You've done so much already. Thank you for all of your help, and keeping me focused. I can get a cab to pick up the car from Jack's shop." Avery's offer to stay was genuine, but he did need to get back home and check on his wife. He was not accustomed to leaving her alone in the house for any period of time.

"Alright then folks; let me know if I can be of any help, now or when you get back home. Take care, Jack." Avery gave Jack a friendly tap on the foot as he departed.

As Avery left, Patricia realized that the ambulance she'd seen racing past their house a few hours earlier was carrying Jack, since the route from Kutter to the hospital ran right past their house. Patricia got the chills as she made the eerie connection.

Jack started to give Patricia as much information as he knew, or thought he knew, given his medicated state, although at that point he knew little more than she did. To Jack's relief, this responsibility shifted to Dr. Bonner, the emergency room physician, as he entered Jack's enclosure.

"Mrs. Christopher?" Dr. Bonner extended his hand. His gesture was both cordial and a means to verify her relationship to Jack before providing details of his condition.

At her nod, he turned to Jack.

"Hi Jack, how are you feeling? Is the pain medication working?"

"I feel a hell of a lot better than I did a couple of hours ago, Doc. I still feel a little dizzy." Jack's answer was no surprise to Dr. Bonner.

"We gave you an injection and I have a prescription for Darvon to help mitigate the discomfort at home. Part of the dizziness may be from the medication. But remember, you've lost a lot of blood as well. I'd like to keep you overnight for observation. We've also put you on an IV antibiotic to prevent infection. If nothing changes, you can go home tomorrow."

Jack interjected, slightly raising his bandaged hands. "How bad are they?" he asked. Dr. Bonner understood his patient's concern and that his answer could change an entire family's future.

"I have to say that you are very fortunate, Jack," He answered and saw some of the tension leave Patricia's and Jack's faces as both breathed a sigh of relief. "Two inches lower and you would have no fingers. The blade cut just above the top of your pinky." Dr. Bonner drew a line across the top of his own hand with his finger to illustrate. "I do not foresee you losing any functional capability. Your hands were perfectly even with each other. What were you doing?"

Jack thought of Pete, and his anger started to come out again. "I was setting the fence for the next cut, when my jackass supervisor hit the blade pedal," he said.

Dr. Bonner had not intended to take Jack's thoughts in that direction, and he quickly moved the conversation back to the prognosis.

"The good news is that you should regain full function and movement. Now, you may experience 'phantom limb'. This is when you feel pain or other sensation that the lost portions of your fingers are still there. We've cleaned up and closed the wounds, but unfortunately we were not able to reattach the severed digits. As contaminated with dirt and oil as they were, the risk of infection outweighed the benefit of reattachment. I'm sorry, Jack."

"Thanks for everything, Doc. You did what you had to do," Jack replied, genuinely grateful for the doctor's care of his injury.

"You will need to change the dressings every day," Dr. Bonner continued. "We will give you instructions, and we will change them just before your release tomorrow." He turned to Patricia. "I would like to see Jack again in one week, assuming that no problems arise between now and then. Should you see any signs of infection, or he develops a fever, call me right away."

He turned back to Jack as he said, "Minimizing movement of your arms as much as possible will help with the pain. I would stay seated for a few days after returning home. There is the chance that you may feel weak or experience dizzy spells until your blood levels build back up. Here is the script for the Darvon. If you have any questions feel free to call." Dr. Bonner excused himself and continued methodically down the row of enclosures.

Patricia resumed playing with Jack's hair, running her fingers in his thick locks to reassure him. "I know it is really painful, Hon, but it sounds like the accident could have been much worse." Patricia gave in to her motherly desire to put the best face on things. "I'll stay with you until they move you to your room. Try and get some rest. Robert is watching the boys until Mom and Dad get to the house, so once you are in a room, I'll take a cab over and get the car."

She slowly leaned over and pressed her forehead against his as she closed her eyes. "I love you, Jack. I'm sorry that circumstances have gotten the best of us lately."

"I love you too," Jack replied with a tired voice. Instinctively, he started to raise his hand up to touch Patricia's face, only to be reminded by the white bandages why he was in the bed. Patricia kissed Jack softly and departed; leaving him to get the rest that he desperately needed. In spite of their recent difficulties, she was not looking forward to seeing his side of the bed empty tonight.

Chapter 14
Brandon and Dreams of Jet Pilots and Belonging

"Mosquito truck! Mosquito truck coming!"

The announcement of the mosquito truck's impending arrival was akin to a prepubescent call to worship. Neighborhood kids poured out of every house as the glorious word spread from street to street. Every boy or girl who had a bike was on it. The strongest riders vied for the coveted spot right behind the fogger as the township vehicle made its way down the street. Children without bikes, or whose bike had just been highjacked by a neighbor, ran to position themselves as best they could.

Mosquito trucks made their rounds twice a month. Their stated purpose was to help control the swarms of insects that invaded towns across the state during the long, hot, summer months. Routine dispatch of these vehicles presented an unforeseen and unintended side effect. The same vehicles that roved the streets as the nemesis of the insect world were a source of rare and profound entertainment for the younger residents. As the trucks moved through the neighborhood, they dispersed enormous bluish white clouds with plumes that rose up 20 feet in the air.

Riding through this haze, the faithful followers imagined themselves to be jet pilots cruising through the clouds at 30,000 feet. The distinctly sweet smell accompanying the fog only added to the appeal. The sweet fragrance belied the true nature of the clouds, but probably not a single participant in the ritual would have been deterred, even if they understood the clouds' true nature. The fog was meant to kill, and DDT, an insecticide agent, provided the aroma that the children so enjoyed. To the enthusiasts, both pedaling and on foot, the trucks were a form of entertainment generously provided by the state.

Patricia made attempts to discourage the boys from following the truck but never went so far as to forbid the activity, and the fact that she was not home at the moment removed any lingering inhibitions. Bud and Ginny had come over to watch the kids while Patricia was at the hospital getting Jack, and much to the boy's satisfaction, had expressed no opinion regarding the mosquito trucks.

Robert, with his long, powerful legs successfully secured the #1 or #2 spot behind the fogger. Shawn was not far behind, and Russell blended into the larger group of bikes further behind. Although Brandon was left to run through the widely dispersed cloud on foot, the bi-monthly event probably meant more to him than to any of his brothers. Within this exuberant mass of humanity, Brandon felt like part of something bigger than himself. Such an opportunity was not incidental in Brandon's mind. Neighbors relishing the awaited revelry laughed *with* him not *at* him. Some kids, even a few of the older ones, high-fived Brandon as the cloud dissipated. Chasing the truck as fast as possible, no one had the time or inclination to make the usual insulting comments regarding Brandon's appearance, or the way he looked when he ran.

With few other 5-year olds around to play with, Brandon often tried to hang out with his older brothers. His siblings were accommodating, to a point. Beyond this point, they became aloof and tired of waiting for their younger brother to catch up with them; and tired brothers are not always kind.

Several weeks prior to the latest arrival of the mosquito truck, the three older boys had been playing "trike in a drum" in the bowling alley parking lot. Taking full credit for the game's inception, Shawn admitted to his mother that he'd thought of it because he was bored. Patricia did not need this admission to recognize that this was the type of game that could only be conceived by a group of bored preadolescent boys.

An empty, 55-gallon steel drum lay on its side in the parking lot, which led Shawn to issue a challenge. Accepting the challenge, one brother would sit cross-legged in the drum, with his back against the inner bottom. The "defender" faced the open end, holding a block of two-inch-thick foam padding off of an old dining room chair as his sole measure of protection. Pushing a small tricycle toward the barrel from 25 feet away, the "bike master" released the trike at a premarked point 10 feet away.

The "defender" was to prove his bravery by allowing the bike to run into the barrel without first peeking past the protective cushion. The boys were sure that points should be deducted for peeking, although they never bothered to establish a measurable point standard to begin with. The "bike master" received skill points for guiding the tricycle into the barrel. Since proving endurance was the main purpose of the game, the defender scored points for not looking and for the number of consecutive turns he was willing to take. Quitting after the first turn meant forfeiting prospects for another.

Beaming with excitement, Brandon accepted the invitation from his brothers to play. But sitting inside the drum holding his meager protection, Brandon had no real concept of the game's negative possibilities. At the worst possible moment, he succumbed to the temptation to peek, and the trike's handle bars crashed squarely into his forehead.

The resulting purple lump and need for stitches on their brother's forehead brought an infrequent display of rage from Patricia and a long night of Jack's belt. No intercessions for mercy came from Patricia that night. Ironically, though, Brandon was more thrilled that he had been included as part of his brother's endeavors than upset at his own injury.

Since that temperate November day less than a year earlier when the dirt mounds cultivated all that he could imagine, a portion of Brandon's unbridled exuberance had been lost. Or perhaps "stolen" would prove a more accurate term for optimism's diminishing influence in him. Months of relentless teasing from kids in the neighborhood and issues at home had caused Brandon to start doubting his self-worth.

Still lingering in Brandon's thoughts was the "Igor" incident. Even at 5, Brandon understood with part of his mind that his father did not mean to hurt his feelings; he also understood that the issue was not worth revisiting. What continued to bother Brandon was why his father thought of him that way. Although he was very aware that he looked and moved differently from the other kids, that he was potentially less of a person because of this had never occurred to him…until now.

Chapter 15
Jack and the First Homecoming

June 29, 1968

Since Jack had showed no signs of complications overnight and had enjoyed the benefit of a medically induced good night's rest, he was authorized to be released. His hands still throbbed, a condition he was told would not go away any time shortly. His hands were encased in a fresh sphere of bandages as the nurse wheeled his chair out of the hospital's main entrance. At the car door, the nurse gave him discharge instructions and asked if he had any questions. Raising both bandaged hands up in front of him, Jack posed the question that had worried him since the doctor had removed the catheter.

"What if I have to go to the bathroom?"

Maintaining her professional bearing, the nurse smiled and looked at Patricia. Taking the nurse's obvious cue, Patricia raised her own hands and wiggled her fingers.

"If you behave I'll even warm them up first, Jack," she said.

Patricia and the nurse burst into laughter, and Jack soon followed suit. Patricia's risqué comment was uncharacteristic and appealing. As the nurse walked away, Patricia could not help but tease Jack further as she got him settled in the car.

"You had better behave or I'll put my hands in the freezer, Jack," she laughed. They had not laughed together in a while. Breaking the impasse felt good.

"Dad said that he would like to take the kids tonight and then fishing down in Long Beach Island tomorrow, Jack," she continued. "Your first day home promises to be a quiet one if he takes the kids for the day.

What do you think?" Patricia preferred that she and Jack make any decisions together, though she didn't expect him to dislike the proposal. Given the chaotic nature of the preceding two days, the last thing Jack needed was for one more circumstance to arise that was out of his control.

"He doesn't know what he is getting into, but God bless him for trying. Tell Bud we'll owe him and your mother a night out for this."

Though he was still quieter than usual, Patricia was happy to notice that Jack's voice was not as weak as it had sounded the day before. Unwilling though he was to admit it. Jack would grow tired if he tried to talk for any length of time. Shock, emotional trauma, the maze of medical minutiae, and her own lack of sleep had left Patricia in little better condition than Jack, and by the time they pulled up to the house, both were exhausted.

Lingering discomfort in both of Jack's hands was scarcely alleviated by the pain killers. Increasingly troubling, the broader implications of his injuries now gripped him on his arrival back home. Looming over the coming eight weeks was the uncertainty of his job, as well as question as to what degree he would regain the normal use of both hands, despite the doctor's assurances.

"They're home! Mom and Dad are home!" Running en masse out the kitchen door, the boys raced up to and around the car as it pulled up the driveway. Ginny followed just behind, carrying Richard.

"I'm sorry you two, I was hoping to have them out of here before you arrived home. Bud insisted on running out and buying hooks and sinkers for tomorrow. For the life of me, I don't know why he couldn't have picked them up when he got to the shore tomorrow. But you know how your father is when he gets something in his head." Ginny could hardly be heard above the excited shrieks of the kids as they peppered their parents with questions.

"Off the car, Russell. I said off of the car!" Jack snapped.

Russell climbed back off the hood, where he'd jumped with excitement, and hugged his mother. Jack and the boys succumbed to a momentary awkwardness. Presented with the sight of large bandages obscuring both of their father's hands, the boys' natural tendency was to inquire, since Patricia had decided it best not to elaborate on the extent of Jack's injuries the previous evening. But which, if any questions were appropriate was far from obvious to Jack's sons.

The younger brothers were all relieved to hear Robert take the leap, and ask their father how he was. "Tired, Robert, really tired, but thanks for asking. They said it will take about 8 weeks to heal. Too damn long if you ask me."

Russell stood next to Jack, tightly grasping his leg. He was almost overcome with the temptation to poke Jack's ball of bandages with his finger, but the reaction he'd expect from Jack was enough to restrain him. Jack understood their curiosity, but hoped that his simple answer would suffice for now.

"Boys, why don't you stay outside for a few minutes and wait for Grandpop?" Ginny broke in. "He should be back very soon. Your mom and dad are really tired and want to get settled into the house. We'll stop in and get your things for the shore before we leave, and you can say goodbye then."

One thing Ginny was good at was crowd control, Jack thought. He was glad that she saved him from playing "20 questions." The boys' questions were understandable, but when your mind and body only promise to function for the next 30 seconds, the cognitive challenges of answering them were a bit overwhelming.

Ginny's tactful deterrent benefitted Patricia as much as Jack. As the boys ran to the other side of the house to play jailbreak, Patricia and Jack took advantage of the distraction and made their way toward the kitchen. Patricia watched in horror as Jack stumbled, falling to his knees and landing hard on both elbows. He screamed as he impacted the hard ground and pain shot into his hands. At Jack's cry, the boys came running from the opposite side of the house as Jack rolled onto his back.

"Your dad is ok, boys; please just go to the other side of the house." Ginny shouted. She was less concerned this time that they believe her. Ensuring that they followed the directive was her utmost priority.

Jack pressed his back against the wheel of the car and shimmied to a standing position. He politely shrugged off Patricia's attempt to help, and they both understood that his response would have been much worse if the kids had seen him fall.

"I got it," he insisted. "My damn foot fell asleep. I just want to get inside and sit the hell down."

Reena Tollson, watching from her apartment window, saw the incident but stayed silent. She still didn't like Jack, but she couldn't help but have sympathy for his present condition.

As Patricia held the door open, Jack went straight to the living room recliner. He had never been so happy to sit in his own chair. He could feel the traces of warm blood running down his fingers under the bandages as he waited for the intense throbbing to stop, but he was not about to say anything to Patricia.

"I have all of the boys' overnight bags packed with a change of clothes and toiletries, Patricia. I think it best now if I get them over to our house." Ginny handed Richard to her daughter and gathered the boys' supplies as she called out to them. Somehow, her grandsons always seemed to respond faster and were more accommodating when Ginny made the request.

"Boys I want you all to take your things and get ready to leave. Grab your clothes and whatever else you are bringing and put it in the driveway so Grandpop can load the car." Ginny stood in the doorway and handed overnight bags out as the boys came to the kitchen. Soon a pile had formed at the head of the driveway, and all was ready for Bud.

Ginny left no room for misunderstanding as she ushered the boys in to say goodbye to Patricia and Jack. As only a grandmother can do, she spoke with a sweet and cordial tone and the underlying expectation that things would be done exactly as she instructed.

"One at a time I want you each to come in and say goodbye. We have a great day planned for tomorrow, and you will see your mom and dad around dinnertime. Robert, you can go first."

Sheepishly making his way through the kitchen door, Robert crept silently across the kitchen and into the living room. Approaching Jack,

Robert stood stiffly off to the left side of the recliner. Too timid to stand directly in front of him, Robert spoke to his father while standing behind his left ear. Jack was still waiting for the throbbing in his hands to subside after the fall and sat with his head back and eyes closed.

"Bye, Dad," was all that Robert squeaked out. Trying to maintain a neutral composure, he was trapped between wanting to show compassion and wanting to appear strong. Which would his father prefer? Was showing compassion the same as showing weakness?

Jack's voice was quiet. His words conveyed trust, but also placed a measure of accountability on his son. "When Grandpop is not there, you are in charge, Robert. I don't want him to have to do everything. Have fun, and I'll see you tomorrow."

Neither offered a hug or kiss goodbye. Robert turned and quietly headed back into the kitchen. He wanted to cry both for himself and for Jack, but restrained himself. He held back, that is, until he approached his mother. There was no inhibition as he threw his arms around her and cried softly. He didn't want Jack to hear his sobbing, but he could not contain himself as he embraced Patricia.

"Dad will be OK, Robbie" Patricia answered, her voice weak but reassuring. "Go with Grandpop and have some fun. Catch me a big fish, Honey." Patricia cupped her hand under Robert's chin, and lifted his face gently as she kissed his forehead.

"I will, Mom, I promise." Robert vowed.

Shawn did not enter the living room at all to say goodbye. Seeing Jack's head slightly visible over the back of the chair, Shawn gave one deliberate salute from the kitchen doorway. "See ya, Dad."

"Bye, Shawn." Jack offered one response. That was it. Shawn walked over to his mother, who was standing by the kitchen table.

"Bye, Mom. Hope you feel better." Patricia and her son shared one hug that started and disengaged almost as if on cue. Patricia knew that her son's sentiment was genuine. And yet, holding back was not unusual for Shawn as of late. She wondered if it was growing worry about the future, if Shawn felt that holding back protected him from unforeseen hurts.

Russell burst through the kitchen door within seconds of hearing his name, announcing both his arrival and pending departure as he came. "I'm going now, Dad; where are ya?" Seeing Jack, Russell ran with a full head of steam toward his father's chair. Hearing the thumping footsteps approaching, Jack cringed, anticipating that the energetic boy would slam into him at full speed. Much to Jack's relief, Russell came to a screeching halt right next to the arm of the recliner.

"See ya, Dad! Can I give you a hug? Grandmom is waving for me to hurry up."

Jack welcomed Russell's exuberant request. "Sure, Buddy." Leaning his neck to the left so that Russell could grab it, Jack simultaneously swung both arms over to his right, clear of Russell's excited display of affection.

"Bye, Dad, love ya. OK, Grandmom. I'm coming!" To his father's amusement, Russell had grown irritated with Ginny's gestures to finish the goodbyes. Though tired, Jack enjoyed his son's animated display of affection for him.

In stark contrast to his brother, Brandon hesitated to come in the room.

"Maybe he's too tired, Grandmom; we can just go," he said nervously.

Ginny turned him toward the living room and gave him a gentle push toward Jack. "You haven't seen your dad in 2 days, and you won't be home till late tomorrow; now go in and say goodbye."

Slinking through the kitchen door, Brandon called ahead for permission to enter. "Can I come in, Dad? If you're too tired, I can come back later." Jack was growing increasingly tired, but made his voice welcoming. "Sure son , come on in ," he said.

Jack could see Brandon's nervousness as he approached the chair, But surprisingly Brandon stood directly in front of his father rather than off to the side.

"I hope you feel better, Dad," Brandon said with a slight quiver in his voice. As he spoke, Brandon's eyes darted right and left. He stood with shoulders slumped forward and his head bowed slightly as he periodically glanced up to gauge his father's reaction.

"Thanks, Igo..., I mean, thanks, Brandon; that means a lot." When he heard from Patricia how upset Brandon had been, Jack swore that he would never again call Brandon by the unwanted nickname. His father's deliberate effort to refrain from calling him by that disliked name was not lost on Brandon, and tears welled in his eyes.

"Can I hug you, Dad?" he asked. Jack leaned forward while moving his hands clear, as he had done with Russell. Brandon threw his arms around Jack's neck and pressed his smooth face against his father's five o'clock shadow. Neither could remember the last time they'd hugged.

"Catch a big one, son," Jack said. That was all that Brandon needed to hear to make his day. He ran into the kitchen with an uplifted spirit. After saying goodbye to Patricia, Brandon burst out of the kitchen door, his heart joyful and racing, to rejoin his brothers.

Now that the goodbyes were complete, Ginny turned to Patricia. "Here, Dear, let me take Richard," she said. "He can stay with me while the boys go fishing." Patricia hesitated, not wanting to impose, but Ginny was insistent. "Nonsense," her mother answered Patricia's protests. "It will give me a chance to spoil him. Besides you promised me last Christmas that I could steal him for a day. Both of you should make the most of a quiet house tomorrow. Lord knows that it does not come that often."

Ginny was right, and Patricia knew it. Though she did not say it, Patricia was happy that Ginny had insisted on watching Richard. Even with the other boys gone, rest would not a reasonable expectation with a 3-year old running around the house.

"Jack, Mom is leaving," Patricia called to the living room. Ginny saw that Jack was getting up and said quickly, "Don't get up dear. We'll see you tomorrow. Both of you try and get some rest."

"Thanks, Ginny. We'll see you tomorrow. Tell Bud I said thanks," Jack called as he carefully raised the footrest on his recliner with his elbow. With a little help from the pain killers, he would soon be asleep.

After a quick head count, Ginny and Bud backed the station wagon out of the driveway as the boys engaged in several loud competing conversations in anticipation of the next day's fishing trip. They had no idea what to expect. Watching them turn onto the Pike as she stood at the end of the driveway, Patricia felt much the same way. She had no idea how the coming difficult weeks would pan out.

She sincerely hoped that Jack had a strong physical recovery, but also that the two of them could repair some of the damage the previous months had done to their marriage. Patricia prayed that as she and Jack faced the challenges to come, their relationship would strengthen.

Chapter 16
Bud and the Boys, and a Separate Peace

The Next Morning

Although odds were good that Jack's Country Squire station wagon would come home smelling like a combination of clams, squid, fish, and possibly vomit (depending on Russell's proclivity toward car sickness), Jack felt the risk was well worth letting Bud use his car. Oddly enough, Bud really enjoyed trips like this with his grandsons. Outings with his own grandfather when he was a boy had left an indelible mark and many fond memories. Being remembered in a similar manner by his own grandsons would be more than Bud could ask for.

Bud's friendly, unflappable nature and steady temperament also permitted him to enjoy outings that would have left the average person hanging on their last nerve. All of the Christopher siblings adored "Grandpa Bud." The grandkids could count on one hand the number of times they had ever heard Bud yell, but even the youngest understood that he was no pushover.

In his late fifties, Bud was still broad shouldered and did not fit the stereotypical image of a stock fund manager. He stood 6 feet tall and had a slight paunch, but the physique of Bud's football days was unmistakable. One of the boys' favorite greetings to him was to pat the top of his balding head. Their grandfather was always accommodating except after those hot summer days when he had forgotten to wear his fishing hat. Ginny had ensured that Bud took one on this trip, leaving it on the dashboard so that he would remember to wear it.

Following a good night's sleep, Ginny woke everyone before sunrise for breakfast. Whenever they stayed at their grandmother's, the boys could count on a sumptuous breakfast. Ginny delighted in watching the boys eat. She let them "order" anything they wished and she would cook it, but they knew they had to eat what they asked for. Wasting anything, especially food, was a pet peeve Ginny developed during the Great Depression. Ginny had originally intended to make the ride to the shore with Bud and the gang, but after considering the daily needs of 3-year-old Richard, decided to stay home.

Prepared to a fault, Bud had methodically removed all six fishing poles from the shed, checked the reels, and replaced last year's line. In perfect working order thanks to Bud's meticulous care, the reels were older and held memories of fishing with his father.

Bud had also prepared crab traps to help keep the boys busy. While waiting impatiently for fish to bite, each boy had a crab trap that he could check as often as desired. The traps were made of four triangle-shaped steel mesh sides connected to a square bottom, with string at the top of each side. When the string was pulled, the sides would rise up and snap shut, trapping anything that had wandered inside. The amusement factor of these traps was just as important as any bounty they may ensnare.

The final element of a successful fishing trip was contributed by Ginny in the form of a large wicker picnic basket, and the boys had a ravenous Pavlovian response whenever she brought it out. Since they were forbidden to open the basket, they went to work like a pack of bloodhounds as soon as it came to rest on the floor just inside the tailgate. They relied heavily on the aromas filling the station wagon to determine the contents. Though "forbidden" may be an overstatement; Ginny layered the top of the basket with juicy purple grapes, fully expecting little fingers to find their way into the basket before lunch. Chicken salad sandwiches, bologna and cheese, chips, brownies, apples, and two cold sodas for each boy and Bud rounded out the staples for the day. With a final check and a kiss on the cheek from Ginny, Bud tooted the horn and they were on the 2-hour trip to Long Beach Island.

Fa-fump, fa-fump, fa-fump, fa-fump. The tires repeated the sound all the way from Moorestown through Mount Holly, Hammonton, and on to

Pemberton where they turned on to the connecting road that would take them to the shore. The steady rhythm sounded out every two seconds as the car's tires passed over the evenly spaced ridges of Route 38. Almost like the car's heartbeat, the noise went unnoticed after the first five miles. As annoying as the sound might be during the day, Bud could count on it to lull the exhausted boys to sleep on the way home later that evening.

The journey started in a heavily suburban community, by the time they had driven from Pennsauken to Pemberton, the landscape had changed considerably. Family farms, handed down from generation to generation, surrounded the day trippers as they drove the five mile connecting road from Route 38 to Route 72. A patchwork of blueberry farms, stables, and roadside produce stands dotted the roadway until it ended onto the long, final stretch to the beach.

Long and straight, Route 72 ran through the New Jersey Pine Barrens for 40 miles until it crossed the bridge onto Long Beach Island. Perhaps most arduous part of the journey for the eager young fishermen, this section of the drive included very few reference points to indicate just how far they had traveled. No encouraging signs read "10 miles to LBI," no local landmarks with which they were familiar. Tall scrubby pines, sandy soil, and low-lying brush on either side of the single lane road added to the feeling of isolation, though an occasional deer could be seen lying dead on the roadside or grazing in groups of three or four on the grasses.

Adult motorists can find the topography relaxing and enjoyable. However, a quite different response may be expected from young boys.

"Are we there yet Grandpop? I think we're lost. Are we running out of gas?" Each grandson seemed compelled by some unknown rationale to ask the same questions, even though he had just heard the answer given to a brother. Bud tried as calmly as possible to repeat his responses as though the question were fresh and unique. Mercifully, Robert unwittingly relieved Bud of his repetitive duties.

"Oh, cool, parachutes!" Robert's observation turned everyone's attention skyward.

Not far off of the roadway, six large troop transport trucks slowly descended to earth with the assistance of four enormous green parachutes per truck. Floating 50 feet above the vehicles, 50 smaller chutes with personnel floated earthward, as if trying to catch up with the heavy machinery.

"War games, kids," Bud explained. "The Army is practicing combat maneuvers. If you look closely, you can see that the backs of the transport planes are open."

Droning overhead, huge transport planes seemed to skim just above the treetops. The boys could see the last plane shutting its rear loading door after releasing its cargo. In perfect unison, the three aircraft banked left sharply to make their landing approach at nearby Fort Dix.

"Someday I'm going to be an army guy," Brandon said, proud of himself for being the first to make the assertion.

"You'd be too scared, Brandon," Shawn answered. "Besides, you don't even know what they are called. They're not 'army guys,' they're soldiers." Shawn extracted a strange sense of satisfaction from cutting his brother's aspirations short.

"Yeah, well you're too stupid, Shawn," Brandon shot back with a degree of fire in his voice. "Grandpop, can I be an army guy if I want to?"

"Brandon, you can be an army guy, but don't call your brother stupid."

Sweet and salty, the smell of the bay mixed with sea spray, greeted the fishermen as the car approached the foot of the bridge onto Long Beach Island. Arching over Barnegat Bay, the bridge connected to the island at the midpoint of the island's 18-mile length. Rectangular lights were inset into the rails every few feet for the entire long expanse, and at night they cast a white luminous glow on either side of the roadway.

This morning the boys could see seagulls wheeling effortlessly overhead and hear their laughing call at several men already fishing from the bridge's sides.. Morning crabbers dotted the marshes and sand bars, taking advantage of the low tide. The roaring engines of powerful boats could be heard from the waters below. The apex of the bridge's arch offered a beautiful panoramic view of the island. On either side of the bay, the shore line was dotted with boat rentals, dockside eateries, and vacation homes.

A jewel protected on all sides by water, LBI was for many a haven from all that was transpiring in their lives on the mainland. At half a mile wide along its full length, it allowed vacationers to make only a short walk from the ocean to the bay.

As Bud turned left onto Long Beach Boulevard, the boys saw Barnegat Lighthouse come into view in the distance.

"There it is boys," Bud announced at the sight of the lighthouse. "That's where the fish are."

The boys met this announcement with a renewed sense of purpose. All were determined that they were going to catch fish.

"Is there a bathroom there, Pop Pop?" Russell correctly established the first priority

"I think so Russell. If not, we have a bucket," Bud replied as seriously as he could without cracking a smile. Robert laughed at Bud's suggestion as his grandfather glanced over to him as if to share an inside joke.

The bulkhead stretched hundreds of feet along the inlet, offering ample parking as Bud pulled up to the water's edge. At 5 feet above ground level, it was ideal for fishermen to sit on with legs dangling while waiting for a bite. Just to the right of Bud's parking spot, a family diner and gift shop rested next to the water's edge. Owned by a long-established local family, the unassuming eatery consisted of 10 tables and several booths and served as a welcome start to, or break from, fishing. Wooden planked walkways surrounding the diner gave it a welcoming, unpretentious appeal that was matched by the proprietors' welcoming attitude.

A fishing pier built by the diner's owners jutted out into the inlet immediately outside the entrance door and had long been a popular attraction for tourists and anglers. It was constructed of seasoned wood planks stretched across pilings sunk deep into the inlet's floor; the pier stretched out for 100 feet and doglegged to the right an additional 50.

93

White wooden handrails ran around the perimeter of the pier, giving weary or lazy fishermen something to lean on. Andy, the owner, charged $3.00 per day for use of his fishing facilities.

The bulkhead extended toward the mouth of the inlet, eventually running even with ground level until it met the lighthouse. Falling from this section meant a precarious 15 foot drop onto the large boulders lining the water's edge of the lighthouse.

Called "Barney" or "Old Barney" and beloved by most locals, Barnegat Lighthouse is a majestic structure, with an enormous base and a lens perched 170 feet above dangerous waters. The structure's cylindrical shape was painted white on the lower half and brick red on the upper segment. Mounds of boulders, many larger than the Country Squire, were placed on the water's edge to protect Barney from the strong currents and buffeting waves known to be dangerous to novice and experienced mariner alike.

As the boys began unloading the car, the wailing of the local firehouse siren signaled the arrival of the noon hour. Since eating a sandwich with bait-covered hands was not an attractive proposition, the boys decided to delve into Ginny's culinary treasure trove before venturing out onto the pier. Topics of conversation as their appetites were satiated ranged from the prospects of catching fish to the cute girl collecting the fee for the fishing pier. Shawn was particularly smitten by the lively red headed girl in appealing denim shorts.

Rarely had the Christopher boys felt such a freedom to relax and be themselves. Seated in a circle with the basket of provisions in the center, Bud's grandsons were in no particular hurry to disband the lunchtime gathering.

For his part, while Bud was anxious to know how Robert and his brothers were doing, he did not probe. Instead, favorite movies, jokes they had heard, and stories of Bud's childhood were the preferred topics of the day. Bud's lack of prying into the details of his grandson's lives was the very quality that made them comfortable talking to him about more sensitive areas when they needed to. Today, however, laughing, busting on each other, and an occasional game of "pull my finger" were as serious as any of them wanted to get.

Stomachs now full and inspired by watching several nearby fishermen catch flounder, the boys helped Bud unload the poles and gear from the car.

Rationalizing that all of the big fish were at the end of the pier, the boys convinced their grandfather to set up stations on the far end of the dogleg. Robert and Shawn marked out territories at the very end, with Brandon and Russell off to either side. Bud had no illusions of sitting in one spot for very long. His would be a day of constant roving from one boy to the next as he addressed their questions and equipment issues. Bud's principle concern was for the safety of his grandsons. The waters beneath the pier were twenty feet deep, and ran swiftly with the incoming and outgoing tides. He would not tolerate horseplay on the pier.

With poles ready, Bud gave them a few last minute instructions. "Ok men, here we go. I know that the fish are down there. Remember, put your thumb on the spool like this," he said, providing a visual demonstration like a veteran flight attendant. "Let it drop down until it hits the bottom. Oh, and our rule is no casting! The fish are not all hiding waaay over there, I promise," he joked with an animated gesture. "We then have to wait for the tug. Boy, I hope that there is room in the car for all of our fish!"

This last was met with choruses of, "Grandpop!" from several quarters. Though the boys were well aware of their grandfather's exaggeration, they appreciated it just the same. Dropping all of their lines in the water, the grandsons watched as Bud set up a crab trap next to each of them. Then each began the process of waiting for a bite, in his own way.

Recalling his promise to Patricia, Robert's expression was one of determined concentration. He was going to catch a big fish for her, even if it killed him. After only 10 minutes, Shawn began to question where he had gone wrong. *Bwoop.* Shawn dropped the line in the water and reeled it right back up, dropped it in the water and reeled it back up.

"Shawn, ya gotta let the line get wet before you reel it back up, Buddy." Bud laughed to himself as he coached. Shawn thought that perhaps his bait wasn't right, or that he was holding the pole incorrectly. He also second guessed his choice of fishing spot.

"Grandpop, I think that I should move next to that guy over there," Shawn said, pointing to a rotund old salt sitting mid pier. "He just caught a fish." Bud peered at the man, and decided he did not look like someone who enjoyed the company of small children fishing next to him. Bud exercised his gift for diplomacy.

"Patience, Shawn, you'll catch a fish. Check your crab traps while you are waiting."

Chapter 17
Brandon and a New Détente

Facing the inlet, Brandon watched as boat after boat passed by, wistfully gazing on the occupants. Who were they? Where were they going? What wondrous tales do they have of life beyond the mouth of the inlet, where the vast ocean offered unlimited travel? Where do the boaters get gas in the middle of the Atlantic?

Brandon was startled out of his daydreams by an unfamiliar but friendly voice. "Hey, kid, did you catch anything?"

"Not yet, I just started to…" Brandon responded while turning, but his reply trailed off as he saw that the inquisitor was a black boy about 7, sitting in a wheelchair.

"Helloooo, did you have any luck yet?" The boy asked again, with bright eyes and a broad smile that diffused any suggestion of impatience at Brandon's unfinished answer.

Brandon was taken aback. He had never spoken to a black boy before. He could not remember seeing any black boys in Stratford, and he most certainly had never conversed with *anyone* in a wheelchair. Trying not to appear too obviously unsettled, Brandon said the first thing that he could think of to say and immediately regretted it. "What happened to your legs?"

Unfazed by the question, as though he had answered it a hundred times before, the boy in the chair adeptly turned the question back. "Is that your fishing pole?" he asked. Brandon had no idea how this related to the present conversation but gladly answered "yes."

"And do you know how to fish?" the boy continued.

"Not really," Brandon answered. He had to be honest; he did not know the first thing about angling.

"You have a pole that works, but don't know how to fish. I have legs that don't work, but I know how to walk if they did. I guess that makes us even." The boy finished with a big smile, his bright disposition dispelling any awkwardness. The two shook hands and laughed at Brandon's fumbling introduction.

"I'm Lucius," Brandon's new friend informed him as he popped a wheelie in place. "That's my mom near the diner. I told her that I wanted to come on here by myself. She let me, but she worries a lot." Brandon waved to Lucius's mother as she kept a watchful eye from a table outside of the diner. Lucius expounded on his reason for being in the area. "I live here, and my father works on the big fishing boats. He goes out for a week or so, and then comes back. We are waiting to see his boat come back in sometime this afternoon. "

Brandon returned Lucius's greeting. "I'm Brandon; sorry about the stupid question. I just…," Lucius cut short the apology.

"Don't worry about it; just catch some fish, Brandon. Don't just let the bait sit on the bottom. You have to bob your bait up and down every once in a while to attract any fish." Brandon appreciated the tutorial, and planned to pass the information on to his brothers.

"Does your dad have cool stories when he comes home?" Brandon asked with anticipation. Stories of the open sea fascinated him, and he would gladly listen to any stories that Lucius's dad had shared with his son.

"Lots of times," his friend replied. "Once when we were out we stayed up till midnight fishing." Lucius' firsthand account caught Brandon off guard.

"We? You mean that you went out to sea with your dad? How…?" Brandon caught himself before he could say anything to offend Lucius. "What did you see? How far out did you go?" Just the thought of going so far out to sea stirred something magical in Brandon's heart. He could hardly contain his feeling of wonder.

Lucius continued to paint a picture of the open sea for Brandon. "One morning, we were fifty miles off shore, just as the sun was rising. Dad called me out of the cabin onto the aft deck. There on both sides of the boat were hundreds of dolphins. They were jumping out of the water as if they were playing. It was the most beautiful thing I had ever seen." Part of Brandon wanted to believe that the young boy in the chair was predisposed to embellishment, but in his heart was sure that Lucius was telling the truth.

"Do you think someday your dad could take me?" Brandon asked excitedly.

"Sure, that would be cool, Brandon," Lucius said. Though neither boy had any idea how to make it happen, but sentiments on both sides were genuine, and they high-fived to cement their plan.

Before they could work out details, Lucius' father's fishing boat came into view as it passed the lighthouse.

"Dad, Daaad, Dad, over here!" Lucius called with increasing urgency. After the third call, a heavily muscled man on the boat's deck flashed a great smile and a zealous wave. Pointing toward the pier around the bend that facilitated his boat's mooring, Lucius' father gave his son a hearty thumbs up. Lucius returned his father's signal with great fervor.

"I gotta go, Brandon," he said, turning his chair effortlessly. "The next time that you come down, you can meet my dad. Good luck fishing, and remember to bob your line." He patted Brandon on the shoulder, and headed off of the pier.

"Bye Lucius," Brandon called. Halfway up the length of the pier Lucius again called to Brandon. Turning, Brandon saw Lucius pop a wheelie in place and spin his chair 360 degrees.

"It's all in here, my brother," Lucius yelled, pointing to his own head. "It's all in here."

Although his mother did not seem pleased with this display, Lucius flashed a mischievous smile to Brandon as he departed onto shore. Impressed with Lucius' ability to look past his own physical impediments and just be a kid touched something in Brandon's heart. Whether he caught any fish or not was now inconsequential. For him, this was a wonderful day. Comments on Brandon's awkward appearance had never passed his new friend's lips.

Chapter 18
Shawn and Reconnoitering New Territory

"Grandpop, I have to go to the bathroom."

Drinking both of his sodas, and stealing one of Robert's, had caught up with Russell. Bud was currently untangling Shawn's fishing line from that of a nearby fisherman but could not let Russell go running off by himself.

"Robert, would you mind taking Russell up to the diner? He can use the bathroom in there."

Robert had no interest in his brother's need to perform bodily functions, and had not lost an ounce of his intensity. He did not want to miss his big fish to tote Russell to the diner. He beseeched his grandfather to find an alternate guide.

"I just changed my bait, Grandpop. Can't Shawn do it?" Robert was desperate enough to implore his brother directly. "Shawn, could you *please* take him. I'll give you my last brownie."

Never convinced that he would catch anything and now bored with pulling up the crab trap, Shawn agreed. At least he would get a brownie for his efforts.

Bells jingled as Shawn opened the thin wooden door leading into the diner. The lunch crowd had gone, leaving a few of the locals nursing coffee at the counter. Immediately behind the counter stood a middle aged woman, her appearance hardened by the sun and coastal winds. She wore a white smock over a pink T-shirt and blue jeans and sported a white pen behind her sun-toned ear. Standing a few feet away, at the hostess stand, was the red-haired girl in the denim shorts.

"Can I help you?" she asked, with an accent that took Shawn a moment to recognize as Irish. "Would you like a table, or would you prefer sitting at the counter?" Her diction was perfect, and she spoke with a both practiced air and enough energy to make them feel welcome. She looked a little older than Shawn, with bright blue eyes, and fair skin.

Shawn found himself fumbling for words. "No...I'm sorry...Er, Um...my brother...just needs to use the bathroom," Shawn finished in a rush. But if the little girl was upset that Shawn and Russell had no intention of purchasing anything, she did not show it.

"Oh, that's fine," she smiled. "The bathroom is just past the counter to your right."

Russell darted back toward the rest room without any further prompting, leaving Shawn alone with the girl to languish in the post-lunch silence of the almost empty diner. As if she sensed his unease, the young hostess began filling the silence with casual small talk. Shawn rarely ever talked to girls, and speaking to one for any period of time, especially while surrounded by silence, was his worst nightmare. On the other hand, he thought that she was cute, *really* cute.

"My name is Kati. I help my parents out here during the summer." Kati paused and looked at Shawn expectantly.

"My name is Shawn," he replied quietly.

"This is my parent's place," Kati continued to Shawn's relief. "I meet a lot of..." Kati paused as she looked Shawn in the eyes, and then turned as if catching herself thinking out loud. "...nice people here." She quickly changed the subject. "Have you caught any fish, Shawn?" He liked hearing her say his name.

"No, not yet," he replied. "If I do, that's great, but I just like being down here." Shawn was starting to feel surprisingly at ease talking to Kati.

"I saw you sitting around eating lunch with your group earlier," She answered. He was surprised to have warranted her attention.

"Oh, those were my brothers and my grandpop." He liked Kati's sweet Irish accent, and the way she accented her Ss and Ts.

"Have you been to the top of the lighthouse yet?" Kati asked.

"No, but I bet it's cool to look out from up there," Shawn answered, wondering why she asked. She looked at him expectantly for a moment, then smiled a little shyly.

"Look Shawn, we're slow in here right now. I just need to set a few tables, and I'll be done for the day. Would you want to go to the top of the lighthouse with me? Looking out from the top is really awesome, but I don't like walking up to the top by myself." Without waiting for an answer, Kati directed her attention to the woman behind the counter. "Mom, is it okay if Shawn and I go to the top of the lighthouse?" She asked, not realizing that her mother had been quietly listening to the exchange as she tinkered behind the counter and had already drawn conclusions regarding the visitor.

"That's fine, Kati, but I want you either here or at the lighthouse. Do not go out onto the jetty at all. And be sure to finish up your tables before you go."

Shawn realized that he too would need approval to go to the lighthouse, and hoped that Grandpop would not feel slighted by his absence. "I have to go check with my grandpop, but I think it will be fine with him." Shawn's heart was pounding, but he went to great lengths to control his excitement when Kati turned to smile at him again.

"I will see you back here in about 20 minutes if you are permitted to go, Shawn," she said. Shawn thought her voice sounded like singing.

"I had to flush twice!" Russell declared as he bounded around the far end of the counter. If there had been any kind of tender moment between Shawn and Kati, it was most certainly gone now.

"Russell, not so loud!" Shawn cautioned as several older customers laughed at his exuberance. Shawn felt terrible until he noticed that Kati was still smiling at him.

"See you soon, Kati. Nice meeting you, Mrs.…Kati's mom." Shawn was sure that he had botched his exit, but Kati's mom only smiled and waved at his attempt at etiquette.

As they made their way back onto the pier, they saw Brandon waiting for them.

"Look in the cooler; I caught two fish! I did just what Lucius told me to do," he informed them. "The little one is a snapper blue, and the big flat one is a flounder." Brandon proudly educated his older brothers once the cooler was opened, having learned the information himself only a few moments earlier.

Both fish were small, and Bud had told Brandon that they would soon need to be returned to the water. Brandon did not mind this; his main concern was that everyone beheld his prize catch. Brandon then launched a dissertation on the techniques he had employed in catching the fish. Robert feigned excitement for his little brother but was really just frustrated by his own lack of success. Brandon's ramblings did nothing to educate him, but much to agitate him even further. For his part, Shawn was not distracted by Brandon's news and attempts to educate him.

"Grandpop, I met this nice girl in the diner. She invited me to go to the top of the lighthouse. Would you mind? Fishing is really fun, and I promise to come right back." Shawn looked for the disappointment in his grandfather's face to register, but it never appeared.

"She's a smart girl for inviting a good-looking fellow like you, Shawn. Go and have fun, but do not go out onto the jetty." Bud put his arm around Shawn and pulled him off to the side, facing away from his brothers. Speaking softly as he reached into his pocket, Bud withdrew a five dollar bill and slipped it to his grandson.

"Here, Shawn; the gentleman always pays. Treat your friend to the lighthouse and a soda. That's how I landed your grandmother." Shawn's face lit up at Bud's generosity but blushed at his last comment.

"You're awesome, Grandpop," Shawn whispered as he hugged Bud.

"I know," Bud responded with a wink. "Now go and have fun. Meet me back here in 2 hours." Shawn ran off to help Kati finish with the tables before their outing.

Turning back to the other boys, Bud noticed that Russell had the strange contorted look on his face, and he was jerking his head back and forth as if looking for something or to get away from something.

"Russell, what's the matter? Did something happen?" He asked with alarm.

"Well, I was in the bathroom and…" Bud jumped into action as his grandson shifted back and forth with both hands in his pockets.

"Did you poop yourself? We can't leave you like that all day!"

"Ewww, no!" Russell answered, humiliated. "Why would you think that?"

"Russell, I'm sorry." Bud felt horrible for jumping to conclusions too quickly. "But why are you so nervous?"

Russell looked around to make sure no one else could see, and pulled a 20 dollar bill halfway out of his pocket.

"I found it next to the toilet in the bathroom. Is that stealing, or can I keep it?"

"Let him keep it, Grandpop!" Robert chimed in immediately. Apparently Russell was not successful from shielding his newfound wealth from his brothers.

"I'll tell you what I'll do," Bud set about answering the burning question. "We will tell the diner of the lost money. If no one claims it before we go, it's yours, but keep the money in your pocket until then." Russell was thrilled and relieved that he had a fighting chance of keeping the money.

The revelation of Russell's sudden windfall turned Robert and Brandon into his best friends. Suddenly, the two could not do enough to accommodate their newly-swimming-in-cash brother. "Hey, Russell, I'll bait your hook for you. Hey, Russell, do you want my last soda? Hey, Russell, do you want my spot? This is where I caught the fish." As Robert and Brandon jockeyed to get onto Russell's good side, Bud decided to diffuse the situation.

"I have an idea, boys. Why don't we all catch some fish in our own spots for now? Let's not count on spending that money just yet." Out of respect for their grandfather's wishes if for no other reason, they all returned to their respective fishing poles.

Chapter 19
Robert and the Mission

Efforts over the next 2 hours showed mixed success. Brandon had a few promising bites but caught nothing. More often than they cared to hear it, he reminded the others that he had already caught several fish using his new technique. Russell, content to have use of Shawn's trap as well as his own, had caught six nice-sized crabs. Robert became more sullen and anxious as time passed, and was now hardly speaking. He had not felt even a bite on his line, and watching other kids on the dock bring in fish just added to his distress.

After 2 hours, Bud could see Shawn on the bulkhead, moving back to the diner from the lighthouse, as promised. He and Kati were walking with their index fingers interlocked as their arms swayed slightly, something that thankfully for Shawn, his brothers did not notice. The tender connection was disengaged as the two approached the diner. Shawn glanced over to Bud and gave him half a wave to acknowledge that he knew his time was almost up.

Shawn's brothers had inquired as to his absence several times. Bud told them that Shawn wanted to go to the lighthouse, leaving out the part about his female friend. Brandon was frightened by the idea of walking to the top of Barney, and Robert had no intention of leaving the fishing pier without something to show for it.

"We will be leaving in 15 minutes guys," Bud announced. The finality of his grandfather's words pierced Robert's heart. He was sure that he had failed in his mandate and that the promise to Patricia would go unfulfilled.

Shawn bounded onto the pier smiling from ear to ear, his normally somber expression nowhere to be found. He and Kati had a wonderful time together, and she seemed genuinely interested in getting to know Shawn for who he was. Kati made Shawn feel as though he was inherently worth something. As they walked along the bulkhead and talked, neither felt the need to force conversation. Kati had even kissed Shawn on the cheek as they stood looking over the island standing atop the lighthouse. For Shawn, that alone was worth more than catching 100 fish. Replaying the previous two hours over in his mind, Shawn was more than happy to help load up the car. As he made repeated trips from the pier to the car, Shawn smiled at Kati as she watched him from a table just inside the diner window.

Bud had the crab traps on the deck and began removing the bait. Seagulls hovered overhead, well aware that an easy meal was soon forthcoming. Walking off of the pier with fishing poles in hand, Shawn, Russell, and Brandon arrived at the car, leaving the rods against the back window as Bud had instructed. Only the crab traps and Robert's pole remained on the pier as they headed back to grab the last few remaining items.

Robert, still on the pier, felt thoroughly dejected. While he enjoyed the ride down, the fishing endeavor turned out to be one protracted disappointment. He saw no benefit to even holding the fishing rod, preferring by now to leave it on the deck. His grandfather would soon be telling him to reel it up anyway. But not wanting to appear ungrateful for all of Bud's time and effort to show the boys a great day, Robert helped his grandfather prepare the crab traps for the ride home.

Suddenly the normally soft-spoken Bud let out a sharp yell, "Robert, your pole!" Dragging across the deck for 2 or 3 feet, the rod was just about to fall into the water when Robert dove and grabbed it by the reel. The rod was moving with such velocity that Robert might have found himself in the water had Bud not grabbed both his shoulders. As Robert stood, still holding the rod, the line continued to pay off of the reel.

Ziing! "Robert, tighten the drag! Lean back! Keep reeling!" Bud's directives confused an already flustered Robert. Reaching around Robert, Bud tightened the drag, which immediately bent the rod into a full arch. The tension and strain on his young arms were like nothing that Robert

106

had ever felt before. His biceps screamed from exertion while his hands fought to turn the handle. Settling down after the initial tumult, Robert determined that whatever was on the other end of the line would not get away. Curious onlookers started to gather both on the pier and along the bulkhead.

"Go, Robert! Keep reeling!" Calls of support from his brothers steeled his determination. Under Bud's direction Robert walked to one side of the dock and then the other. The danger of the fish wrapping the line around a piling was ever present.

A combination of anticipation and fear gripped Robert's heart. Beads of sweat formed on his forehead from the constant strain imposed on his body. He could see the line's entry point into the water drawing closer and closer, raising his hopes. Following 15 minutes of grueling effort, Robert finally saw it. A thunderous splash above the surface of the water briefly revealed Robert's prize.

"Look at it, my boy; it's a beauty!" Bud said. He could see that the fish was tiring and knew that his grandson's victory was at hand. The fish darted back and forth like quicksilver just under the surface of the water.

"Shawn, grab the net and give it to me," Bud said; taking no chances, he would net the prize himself. "Keep reeling, Robert; he's almost done." Bud's years of experience paid off as he hoisted the fish onto the deck, making sure that it did not flip out of the net.

"I did it, I did it, I really did it!" Robert cried as congratulatory pats on the back fell on him from every direction and cheers rose from the excited spectators.

"That's a weakfish, boys, and a big one at that!" Bud noted. "He's probably over 10 pounds, Robert! Let's get it on shore." Robert beamed as Bud removed the hook and slipped his fingers into the fish's gills, lifting it parallel to his leg.

Robert felt 10 feet tall as they walked off the pier. People he did not even know were extending their hands to him. But most precious to him was picturing Patricia's expression when she saw his catch. He had kept his promise to her after all.

With the fish on ice, the boys finished loading the wagon, and everyone took a last bathroom break. Shawn was glad for the excuse to see Kati one more time. He had hopes of talking to her again, because although her mother did not think it prudent for Kati to give her number to him, she allowed Shawn to leave his with her daughter. Finally, the boys and their grandfather began the long drive home.

Peering out the back window as they watched the diner grow smaller and smaller, the boys shared an unspoken consensus that the day had handed a little something to each of them. For Bud, this had been a rare opportunity to spoil the boys. Robert would later enter the house with his grand catch, bringing Patricia to tears of joy and eliciting a hearty hug from Jack. Jack would make him feel as though he were one of his fishing buddies, and that meant the world to him.

Shawn found the approval of a sweet girl and got his first real kiss, even if it was on the cheek. He began to wonder if perhaps, just perhaps, he was not as messed up as he thought he was.

Lucius reminded Brandon of all that was possible, even with physical limitation. Perhaps Brandon would one day find himself past the mouth of the inlet, where the hope of the open sea offered limitless possibilities. And Russell was now 20 dollars richer and enjoying new leverage with his brothers. They were all his best friends…for now.

Like clockwork, just as Bud had anticipated, the boys began to curl up and drift off to sleep as they turned onto Route 38 and heard the familiar refrain. *Fa-fump, Fa-fump, Fa-fump, Fa-fump.*

Chapter 20
Jack and a Brother in Arms

The Day Before

Rommel was not interested in the hour-long episode of Red Skelton playing out on the Motorola in front of him as he sat attentively next to Jack's recliner in the living room. As Jack's favorite show progressed in the quiet after the boys had left, Rommel's master found himself in an increasingly accommodating mood, evidenced by a command he gave Rommel that the dog rarely heard when he was next to Jack's chair.

"Lay down," Jack quietly commanded. Rommel was so surprised at the utterance that he hesitated to follow through until Jack repeated the instruction. Stretched out on the brownish gold pile carpet, Rommel was content to poke his nose under the olive green skirt at the base of the crushed velour chair, but he stayed on guard for any signs that the footrest was coming down.

An unusual quiet fell over the house. An afternoon nap had taken some of the edge off of Jack's pain, although his hands still throbbed from the earlier fall. Shortly after he woke up, Patricia brought in a steaming plate of precut steak, mashed potatoes, and green beans. Avoiding the indignity of watching her cut a new portion after each bite made the meal more enjoyable, but they were still both feeling awkward as Patricia raised the fork to Jack's mouth.

Patricia fed him forkfuls of food from a TV tray placed between the recliner and the kitchen chair she'd placed near it. He knew she was trying her best to time each forkful so as not to be too intrusive or pushy. Having to sip milk through a straw as Patricia held the cup brought to light just how unsettling the next 10 weeks would be. He reminded himself that it was only for 10 weeks, and wondered if Patricia was doing the same.

Jack intentionally allowed milk to dribble out of his mouth, hoping to relieve the obvious tension.

"Jack, that is so gross," Patricia said, but could not help but laugh. Unchastened, Jack thought that a little levity was just what they needed. Patricia kissed the side of his face as she removed the empty dinner plate.

As Patricia went to the kitchen, the chilling realization came over Jack that, joking aside, this would be the norm for the next few months. Feeling helpless, vulnerable, and needy bothered Jack much more than any of the physical discomfort. He realized that even the most incidental attempt to function would now require assistance. Scratching an itch, tying a shoe, opening a door, even going to the bathroom; he could accomplish nothing on his own. This affront to individual sovereignty threatened to make Jack feel like a burden, and useless.

Patricia came back into the room and arranged dessert plates on the coffee table. She and Jack eagerly anticipated their guest's arrival, and the desserts adorning the coffee table were all their visitor's favorites. Jack's brother Joe was sure to love the lemon bars, chocolate-covered almonds, pretzel nuggets, and biscotti all neatly displayed in clear glass serving dishes shaped like oak leaves. The sticky buns with wet walnuts on top were still baking and filling the living room with a delicious aroma.

Traveling as a sales representative led Jack's brother away from the Stratford area for long periods of time, but when he heard of the accident at Kutter Metals, he immediately left the conference in Ohio and started the drive home.

Joe would do anything for Jack, but his actions also personified the idea their parents drilled into them as young men: "Family *always* comes first." Besides, ever since they were little kids, Joe considered himself Jack's guardian. All of the Christopher brothers were close, and though this closeness did not preclude them from beating the hell out of each other, the bond of brothers and the responsibility that each felt to another

110

was unbreakable. Joe and Jack especially shared an intense closeness and mutual respect, the type that did not need to be constantly verbalized or reaffirmed. Neither ever doubted that the cohesion was there. That they were polar opposites had as much to do as anything else with their relationship.

Joe was nothing like Jack in his approach to life. In the same way that Jack could (and possibly would) fight his way out of anything, Joe could talk himself out of a bind. This is not to say that Joe could not fight if it was necessary, though perhaps not on Jack's level. But Joe's real gift was as a smooth talker. He was not a disingenuous man, and his version of smooth talk was not slick or meant to be deceptive.

Instead, he had an honest, down-to-earth humor, and a natural, if usually hidden, intellect that combined to make it nearly impossible not to like him. He also had the capacity to listen, which made people comfortable around him. Moreover, Joe loved to laugh, and he enjoyed life, and in the process he helped other people enjoy it, too. Consequently, people naturally gravitated toward Joe. In fact, though Joe never saw himself as the "Cary Grant type," that's how Jack thought of him. Since he had never fit the suave mold himself, Jack admired this quality in Joe.

Joe never attained the dominating strength of Jack's personality, but it was Jack's complete disregard for self-preservation that Joe truly admired. He remembered his brother taking on four loudmouthed boys when they were kids. Although two had bats, when all was done, all four lay unconscious. Joe wondered what that feeling of complete self-assurance must be like. This playful dynamic between the two brothers brought them great joy when they were together, though Joe's traveling schedule and Jack's long hours at work made getting together a considerable challenge.

The little brother in Jack sprang to life as the headlights from Joe's car made their way up the driveway. Rommel was somewhat less enthusiastic about having visitors, and a low growl rumbled within him as he resumed his watchful sitting position next to the recliner.

"Stairs, Rommel," Jack commanded. Reclaiming his position next to the stairs, the shepherd understood that this would be his domain for the remainder of the evening.

Patricia could see Jack coming to life now that his brother had arrived. Like a comedian getting ready to perform, Jack was "on." He was now at his social best.

As Joe jumped out of his Mustang and trotted briskly to the kitchen door, Jack went into the kitchen and instinctively reached for the doorknob only to remember his bandaged hands. Slightly embarrassed, he looked at Patricia.

"Hon, maybe you could…." he gestured toward the doorknob with his head. By this time Joe had his face pressed against one of the small glass panes of the door, his eyes darting back and forth.

"Joe, it is so wonderful to see you!" Patricia called out enthusiastically as she opened the kitchen door.

"Patricia, you are looking as beautiful as ever," Joe replied. Taking her face gently between his hands, he kissed Patricia on both cheeks as a brother who had not seen his sister in years. Patricia recognized the familiar smell of Blue Aqua Velva as he embraced her. Joe had used it for years, and Patricia came to expect the clean fresh scent when her brother-in-law was around.

"That is more than I can say for the ugly bandaged bastard behind you," he ribbed his brother in a smooth, matter-of-fact tone. "How are you doing, Jack?" The brothers embraced and kissed each other on the cheek.

Joe patted Jack on the back with an open hand, and then pulled back to look him in the eyes for a moment. He wanted Jack to understand just how much Joe had really missed him.

"You look good, Jack. Well, except for those two damned Q-tips at the end of your arms. What the hell is that all about?" Joe mussed Jack's hair, knowing that his brother could do nothing in return.

Joe was sharply dressed, as usual, in a pair of beige cotton slacks, reddish brown Italian dress shoes and an earth-toned button-down short-sleeved shirt. His leather belt perfectly matched the color of his shoes.

His jet black hair was combed straight back, neatly trimmed above the ears with a crisp neckline in the back. Joe's baby smooth face never had razor stubble or five o'clock shadow; he seemed to be perpetually clean shaven, and he somehow always managed to appear slightly tanned. His darkened skin accented his infectious smile.

Contrasted to Jack's heavily muscular build, Joe's physique was more like an acrobat or trapeze artist. Standing 5'11", he was lean and toned, with little fat, just like his brother.

He started taunting Jack, taking advantage of his brother's encumbered state.

"You know, Jack, I can't remember when I could hit you without worry about you tagging me back." Taking up a boxing stance, Joe taunted Jack with light taps to the head as his brother stood defenseless. Left,-right, right, and then a quick left grazed Jack's head.

"This was worth the drive here, I have to admit."

"Just remember, I will find your ass as soon as these bandages come off." Jack pulled back from the jabs laughing.

Before he could say more, Joe noticed the smell in the kitchen.

"I'm done with you, Jack," he laughed. "I want sticky buns." He turned to the kitchen table like a little kid, but Patricia chased them both off.

"Why don't you relax in the living room? I'll put some coffee on and leave you guys alone. The kids will be home tomorrow, and I have a lot of housework to catch up on."

Jack understood that Patricia was excusing herself tactfully to give them some privacy, and he appreciated the gesture.

Patricia started the coffee, took the sticky buns from the oven, and drizzled white icing over them before cutting them into squares and placing them beside the other snacks on the coffee table. Joe promised that he would tend to the coffee when it was done, so she retrieved cleaning supplies from the kitchen and went upstairs to give it a good going over before her sons returned.

"I'll be back in a little while. You boys enjoy yourselves. I'm so glad that you're here

Joe."

Joe turned the TV down so that it was little more than background noise. Neither minded; recalling childhood days was much preferred to the "idiot box" as Jack sometimes called it.

Having not seen each other for almost a year, Jack and Joe had a lot of ground to catch up on.

"It is nice to see you, Jack, although different circumstances would have made it even better," Joe started. "What do you say I set up a golfing day together? You were always a lousy golfer, but with those mittens on you it would be a hell of a lot of fun to watch." Uncertain whether his brother wanted to open up, Joe thought it best to interject some levity, letting Jack take things where he wished. His brother's deadpan delivery was just what Jack needed.

"Keep eating your sticky buns, you bastard," Jack replied.

Pulling a cigarette from the ever-present pack of Kents in his shirt pocket, Joe lit up, knowing he needed no permission from Jack. He took a second smoke out and extended it toward Jack.

"Do you want me to light one up for you?" he asked. Jack feigned indignation.

"What, one of those girlie smokes of yours? Hell no. There's a pack of Pall Mall in the kitchen drawer. Someday when you grow up, I'll give you one of those."

Joe mussed his brother's hair as he walked past him, and Jack thought just how happy he was to have his brother there. For that moment, Jack found himself as close to tearing up as he had been in quite some time. Jack rarely allowed himself to be vulnerable, but he could be with Joe. They, along with their brothers and sisters, had been through so much together.

Jack was sure that his aversion to crowds and crowded places was rooted in how they had been crammed into the house on Maple Avenue. When they finally had a real house of their own, all 6 brothers—Richard, Charlie, Jim, Bill, Jack, and Joe—had spent most of their life sleeping in one room. As younger boys, they thought it was the coolest thing in the world, but by the time the eldest turned 15, the allure of communal living

114

had long since worn off. Sisters Annie and Janet taunted the boys with all of the extra space that the girls had in their room.

Jack felt the memories of events long since locked away, even from Patricia, stir in his heart. Joe knew how to reach the painful areas that were off limits to others, and he understood his responsibility for tonight. Jack needed to vent his emotions every once in a while. Allowing pent up anger and frustration to build up inside was like shaking a soda bottle. Sooner or later, some poor soul was sure to come along and pop the cap. In those instances, Jack could not control his response. Most often, after going into a blind rage, Jack would not even remember the details of the altercation. Tonight Joe wanted to open the cap slowly, allowing the pressure built up in his brother to slowly dissipate.

Joe returned from the kitchen with the pack of Pall Malls and two mugs of coffee, one with a long straw.

"Here you go, Jack. I even gave you a sippy straw." Joe set the mug down on the dinner tray that Patricia had been using earlier. "Let me know when you want a smoke." His tone was now more tempered, and gone was the playful banter of earlier.

"Thanks, Joe, for everything," Jack said. "I appreciate you coming in all the way from Ohio to check on me. I'm doing OK all things considered."

Joe leaned in toward his brother, placing one hand on Jack's knee. His words cut to the heart of why he was compelled to come see Jack.

"Jack, you know I will be damned if I will ever leave you hanging out there by yourself. You were never one to sit there pissing and moaning your way through life. Brother, I can tell how frustrating this is for you before you opened your mouth. You're not used to sitting on your ass while someone else dresses you, bathes you, and spoon feeds you; none of us ever were. Listen, before you know it you will bounce right back. Until then, you can count on family…always. What did the doctors say was the prognosis for your hand? How long is the recovery?"

Jack looked at his bandages. "According to the doctor, I should regain full use of both hands. I'll just have the nubs on each set of fingers. Losing my thumbs would have made it much worse, and I would

115

have had no chance of returning to work. Hearing myself say it sounds funny, but I am anxious to get back to work. Ten weeks, and it's barely started."

"How are you for money, Jack?" Joe asked. "I could front you some until you go back to work if that would make things easier." Though Joe did not expect his younger brother to say yes, he'd meant every word of the offer and stopped at the bank on the way over.

"I appreciate that, Joe, I really do, but we're fine. Things will be a little tight, but I have some savings, and I'm on workman's comp until I go back." Jack paused for a moment. He pondered whether to say what he was thinking, even to Joe. There was a question that burned in Jack all through his years growing up. He hoped it wouldn't be necessary to talk about as an adult, but he still felt it. Joe and the others had been there for him time and time again, and he thought Joe would know where he was coming from. Besides, Jack wanted to hear what his brother would say. Joe could always be counted on for a clear, honest opinion. He did not think that Patricia, even with her best effort, would really understand. Jack decided to drop his guard.

"Joe, do you ever wonder why it all happened the way it did?"

Joe looked at Jack quizzically. He felt like Jack had let him in midway through another conversation.

"Why what happened, Jack?" Joe asked.

"Why did we go through all that shit that constantly fell on us growing up? I wondered so many times as a kid if God got pissed, and we were just the dog in front of him that got kicked. He keeps kicking and kicking, never moving on to another dog. So what happens? You never sleep, 'cause you're getting kicked. You never relax, 'cause you're getting kicked. You can never enjoy life because you're either getting kicked or waiting for the next kick to come."

That's me Joe. I'm always waiting for the next foot from heaven to kick me in the ass. Hell, Joe, you know me. I've never asked for or expected a free ride. But this:" Jack raised his bandaged hands. "God tells us we're supposed to provide for our families. You do what you think He wants you to do, and you're still screwed.

116

I envy you sometimes, Joe. I don't know how you are able to be as easy going as you are. You always take things in stride. Just once I would like to be able to roll with the punches like you do. Even when I really want to relax, it eludes me."

Joe wanted to assure Jack that he too had problems and setbacks, but he allowed Jack to continue without interruption.

"Here's an example, Joe," Jack continued. "You're taking a day trip to Seaside Boardwalk; you think that it would be a fun day. But, no, not for me. I'm waiting for the next fight with some punk; sizing them all up. Does that sound crazy? Maybe, but think about it, Joe. All those years, every time we thought there might be some breathing room and we let our guard down, the other shoe dropped.

How many times did Mom and Dad have to wake us in the middle of the night when we rented? We were packing up at one o'clock in the morning because we didn't have the rent. The next morning you are in a strange town and don't know a soul. Remember walking into class? Hell, how many times were we the new kids, Joe? And then there was always some son-of-a-bitch that had to start with us, just to prove something."

Jack caught himself. "I'm sorry, Joe; dumping on you was not the way that you planned to spend the evening. Like I said, Patricia tries to be understanding, but she really has no frame of reference to go by."

The men lapsed into a comfortable silence as Joe thought through his answer. Jack respected Joe's hesitation; it told him that his brother's answer would not be off the cuff. When he finally spoke, Joe did not give a long oration. As he saw it, the answer could be delivered with a few words.

"Forgetting what took place was never an option for us, Jack. Trying to forget would only get us more frustrated. Thinking of what I have now keeps me looking forward to something better." He looked seriously at Jack. "You have good things, too. You have a beautiful wife and five great boys. I know you love them and would do anything for them. And that's a long way from where we started as kids."

Jack nodded, but elaborated on his previous concerns. "That's what worries me, Joe. All that I ever wanted was to not have to worry anymore about where our next meal is coming from. Remember the lard sandwiches and how mom looked at us when we asked about food? What the hell was she supposed to do with an empty cabinet? After all those years, is it too much to ask that my wife not be put through the same hardship? Who tells God when to stop? He has more than gotten his pound of flesh out of us."

Joe held his hands out over the coffee table. "Look at the food on this table, Jack. You are grinding yourself down with 'what ifs', and things that have not happened yet. Your trouble is that you won't cut yourself any slack at all. There will always be *something* that you can kick yourself in the ass for. Losing the fingers and being laid up for two months is bad enough. I get that. Beating yourself up on top of it is not going to do you any good."

Joe looked at his brother's face and saw that he was treading on very sensitive ground. He understood the importance of choosing his words carefully. He also understood that Jack's blaming himself was rooted not with Patricia and the kids or even the financial struggles of his youth, but with the death of Gary Mayer when Jack was eight. The tall oak tree on Linden Avenue still reminded Jack of his pain and guilt every time he went to visit his father.

Gary Mayer was Jack's best friend. The two eight-year olds were alike in every way. Both tough and fearless, they were always trying to outdo each other. One of these friendly challenges took them to the base of the 60-foot oak tree on Linden Ave. Protruding from the tree 8 feet above the ground, the first branch that climbers could get to was not reached easily. One had to ascend a series of notches in the trunk to reach the limb. Each boy tried to make it by using the notches as a foothold and grasping whatever rough surface they could. Jack had made it to within a foot of the branch but lost his footing and could not grasp it.

The exhausted boys had nearly given up when Jack dared Gary to give it one more try. Begrudgingly, Gary made his way up the trunk and was finally able to grasp the lowest limb. Holding onto the branch with one hand with his feet propped against the trunk, Gary let out a victorious Tarzan yell.

Suddenly, Gary's voice fell silent and his eyes rolled in the back of his head as a spray of red covered the tree beside him and he fell limp to the ground. Blood covered Jack's chest and tears streamed down his face as he held Gary, trying to revive his friend.

Gary had been shot in the head. Police assumed he'd been struck by an errant rifle round from the nearby fields. No shooter was ever identified or turned himself in. Perhaps the rifle's owner never knew of the consequences of that fateful shot.

Whoever fired the bullet, Jack blamed himself for daring Gary to try climbing again. To a lesser extent, Jack faulted God for allowing such a senseless loss of life.

And something in Jack changed that day. Part of the change was obvious almost immediately though still other parts were like seeds planted in a vulnerable mind; unnoticeable at first but coming to debilitating fruition years later. In Jack's mind, every waking moment, no matter how relaxed it may appear, was a hair's breadth from a crisis that needed to be addressed. Life had become a continuous leapfrog from one emergency to the next.

Joe also knew that one aspect of Jack's burden was heavier than any other. It was the fact that Patricia did not know about any of this. No one had ever mentioned Jack's friend Gary to Patricia. She had never understood the scars from this tragedy in her husband's heart.

What Patricia believed were random outbursts were actually anything but inexplicable. Patricia never knew about Gary or about when Jack fell off the wing of a B-29 plane while in the Air Force. The fall had split his head open and the then young airman needed a steel plate to close the gaping wound. This Neanderthal form of surgery left Jack with almost unbearable cluster migraines. Patricia remained in the dark about this as well. Jack believed that to tell her would be fishing for sympathy. Besides, there was nothing she could do to help him.

And where was God? Jack wondered how he was expected to see God as good while misery after misery was piled on his life. The loss of

Gary challenged all of the tenants and convictions that his religious family had long embraced. If God was good, why did he let Gary die? The dichotomy arose in Jack's mind that every mealtime grace was directed to the One who let his friend die. Each Christmas and Easter would ring with the same pang of contradiction. How could a God who called himself good be that uncaring?

Could any priest explain that to him? Two years had passed since Jack had last been to St. Anne's Church. Patricia took the kids most weeks, but for Jack, the pain of his last visit there just added to his questioning of God's mercy. The last time Jack was in St. Anne's Church was the day of his mother's funeral. Jack was her youngest son…her baby. Even after 2 years, his heart still ached to hear her gentle voice and touch her sweet face. He still felt the anger of how she died. She'd raised eight children faithfully; she'd poured out her life for them. She did not deserve to die of cancer.

Joe was aware that Gary was never too far from his brother's thoughts. For Jack, the inability to take action, the lack of an obvious foe, ironically, brought more stress. Although certainly glad that Jack was able to vent some of his frustrations, Joe felt that he needed to lighten his brother's mood.

"Hey, Jack, do you still have those 8-mm films of our fishing trip with Pop at the cabin?" he asked when he thought Jack was ready for a change of pace. "You know, the flounder trip?" Several years prior, Jack and all of his brothers had gone with Charles to Brigantine Island for an entire week. It was the last trip together when their father was in good health. The older boys had come up from Texas to surprise their father.

Jack thought for a moment, then directed his brother to the basement to retrieve the films, projector, and screen. Coming up to the living room, Joe set the projector on a tall plant stand with a phone book added to get the projector high enough to cast images onto the screen.

Setting the screen up was a clumsy process. Joe extended the tripod legs and rotated the 6-foot steel cylinder that held the screen itself. He unlocked the height rod and extended it. He unfurled the screen, like a giant window shade, and struggled a little to hook it onto the bottom.

"Jump in and help any time, Jack," Joe teased his brother.

"I provided the snacks," Jack returned in kind. "This is the least you can do." Jack appreciated Joe's sense of when to lighten the atmosphere. They spent the rest of the evening happily recalling fond memories of their past. Patricia came down as they ran the last few films. She sat next to Jack, her hand resting gently on his forearm.

When Joe was ready to leave, Patricia kissed him on the cheek, and thanked him for the visit. Heading back upstairs, she allowed the brothers a private goodbye.

"Promise me something, Jack." Joe's request was slow and deliberate, and he placed one hand on his brother's shoulder as they stood by the back door.

"Promise me that you will look for the good, Jack. It's often buried under all of the crap that piles up, but it's there. You know I love you, brother, so never hesitate to call. I'll be up in Pittsburg for a few weeks, and then I'll stop back. Maybe we'll shoot some pool...or something." Joe waited to get a laugh out of his brother and was not disappointed.

Chapter 21

The Christopher Family and the Long Summer Battle

July 1968

Adjusting to the new paradigms of life over the ensuing weeks proved a steep learning curve for the Christopher household. In some respects the new challenges galvanized the family. Everyone, including Jack, understood that the petty squabbles that tended to occupy each day had to be set aside. They had no time for bickering, because they needed all their energy, and each would have to carry his share of the load.

This is certainly not to say there were no arguments or an occasional fist fight. Such a suggestion would be disingenuous. It could be said, however, that everyone made a concerted effort to minimize disagreements. If not for altruistic reasons, then because no one wanted the additional stress and aggravation that conflict invariably brings.

For Jack, the physical limitations and pains were less disconcerting than the hindrances imposed on his freedom of self-determination. The litany of orders the doctors gave him did not sit well with a man who had rarely set foot in a physician's office over the past 10 years. Onerous restrictions that could not be appealed left Jack in a submissive role that he was not accustomed to.

He did not doubt that the doctors had his best interest at heart and had that they had not given him these orders to be condescending. This did little to suppress his frustration. Any vestige of control had been rescinded for the duration of his recovery.

Take this antibiotic.

Take your pain pill.

It's time to change the bandages.

Don't try to pick that up.

It's time for your bath.

The list of directives never seemed to end. By necessity, Jack had to plan on when to go to the bathroom. He had no alternative but to time this function to ensure that Patricia would be home. Even in the later stages of healing, Jack's fingers were bandaged and useless. Whether he used the handheld urinal or needed a bowel movement, Jack needed help in these sensitive realities. Taking a bath was an hour long process.

While Jack felt emasculated, Patricia felt physically drained. Recognizing her husband's unease also weighed heavy on her heart. She tried as much as possible to remember, and remind him, that each day brought them closer to the end of the 10-week ordeal. Compounding Jack's frustration, it had been weeks since he and Patricia had been together romantically.

One saving grace for Patricia was the accident's timing. Since the injury had taken place during the summer, the boys were home to help out with the myriad of chores. They were not happy about spending the summer cleaning, but the jobs got done.

Otherwise minimizing the day to day impact of the accident on the children was a Herculean task for Patricia. When not needed for chores, the boys could always find something to do. There was always a pickup game of baseball or a walk to swim at Crystal Lake, as long as Robert was willing to go and watch out for the younger boys. Bud and Ginny could also be counted on for a day trip every other week.

On several of these outings, Patricia was able to relax, particularly when Jack insisted that he needed some down time of his own. Even better, Joe was back from Pittsburg and had taken Jack to the Garden State Race track once or twice. Betting results aside, Jack was happy to hang out with Joe and get the hell out of the house.

But not all frustrations for the family could be eliminated. Not being able to have friends over for the better part of the summer proved frustrating for the boys, but Jack simply could not deal with the difficulties of the injury itself while simultaneously listening to the shrill voices of excited preteens. The chore rotation also aggravated the boys by summer's end. The imposing schedule mounted inside the kitchen door was managed by their father with no room for excuses. As the long, tiresome summer dragged on, the Christopher boys almost looked forward to the start of school. Unfortunately for Brandon, he did not have the luxury of thinking about school. Too young for school but old enough for simple chores, Brandon envied Richard, who was still exempt from both.

Moreover, payments from workman's compensation were not nearly what Jack usually brought home. As much as he complained about it, the overtime had made a big difference in the number at the bottom of his weekly check. His payments now were less about 20 hours of overtime per week, and that, coupled with the loss of concrete-pouring side jobs that Jack could count on each summer, meant that the Christophers were living on less than half of what they were used to.

The financial strain added to the far-reaching impact of the accident on the Christopher house. Gone was the pleasantly predictable meal schedule: Monday, steak; Tuesday, breaded baked chicken; Friday, pot roast. Culinary patterns that had existed for as long as most of the family could remember were now spotty at best. Casseroles were the new staple, particularly those that required little or no meat. Three-cheese macaroni with small bits of ham found its way to the table quite often.

Jack recognized the challenge that the budget posed to Patricia's food shopping and did not complain if he found an experimental dish less than appealing. *Telling* his children not to complain either was not necessary. When Jack locked eyes with each of his sons at the table, they all understood that the wisest course of action would be to shut up and eat everything on the plate.

"Thank God it's almost over," Jack thought to himself by close to the end of August. He would be back to work in two weeks.

This year the boys would have to recycle last year's school clothes until he was back at Kutter and caught up on some bills. Torn clothes or jeans were a pet peeve of Jack's—having been the youngest, as a boy Jack had to wear hand-me-downs that had been previously worn by all of his brothers—but they had little choice at the moment. Patches on existing jeans would have to suffice for now.

By the end of the summer one thing was painfully clear: the Christophers were ready for the whole ordeal to be over. Despite best efforts, tempers had flared, frustrations had led to periods of acrimonious silence, and money woes had produced their domino effect of self-doubt, agitation, and depression. But now, each family member saw a break in the dark cloud that hung stubbornly over their lives. The coming weeks would mercifully restore life back to normal and they could all move on. Like soldiers back from the front lines of battle, they would recall the conflict, nurse their wounds, and claim victory for having survived.

Thus, mid-September found the Christopher boys strangely happy to be back in school, with only Brandon and Richard at home. After the emotionally and physically grueling summer, the older three Christopher boys found following the normal predictable patterns of daily education a welcome change.

But they still faced some challenges. For the first week, students were allowed to display trinkets on their desks, testimonials to summer travels around the country or even abroad. Seeing that several desks other than their own were also devoid of such novelties did not bring the Christopher boys much consolation.

The boys also dreaded the customary "What I Did on Summer Vacation" essay. This year, writing such a report held a particularly potent sting. Where would they begin such an assignment? "I emptied a urinal" is usually not a compelling opening for a school report. Therefore, Robert, Shawn, and Russell devised a plan: they would lie about the summer. They agreed that the best course of action was to keep the story simple and make certain that their accounts were similar in case teachers cross checked with each other.

Robert laid out the details: "our grandmother lives in Florida. We went to Grandmom's for 2 weeks. We went to Disney World. We saw gators. That was it." Robert implored the others to stick with the story. Do not embellish or add activities. Keep it simple. Since they had spent so much time working in their house over the summer, no one would

125

question 2 weeks absence from the neighborhood. Most important was that no one got creative and somehow transported the family to the Grand Canyon. Much to Robert's relief, all the brothers adhered to the game plan, and all of the essays were accepted as plausible.

The boys got one source of relief in not having to return to school in last year's clothes. As Jack's optimism increased, prompted by anticipating his return to work, he allowed Patricia to shop for school clothes. Although less than $500 in savings did not amount to much with little income and five boys to feed, Jack felt that one new set of clothes each, along with school supplies, was not unreasonable.

A new outfit could not ease all their discomfort, however. While most children return to school feeling refreshed, the Christopher boys were more exhausted than they had been when the final bell had ushered the summer in. Living so far out of the norm also left them feeling disjointed during conversations with their friends. The giddy lighthearted banter of their classmates rang foreign in the boys' ears. Innocent, whimsical notions that they had held the previous spring would not return immediately or easily. But knowing that their father would soon be back to work and life was returning to normal helped to move the healing process along.

Chapter 22
Jack and the New War

September 1968

What could only be described as euphoria swept through the Christopher house on a bright morning in mid-September. Jack was himself again after months of being fed, bathed, driven about town like a schoolboy, dressed, and coddled. Having endured humiliating circumstances that he never wanted to revisit, Jack retook command of his life. Reliable, predictable patterns would once again prevail, bringing with them the satisfaction that Stratford itself had long given the Christopher family.

"My return to work order should be coming any day now," he had told himself time and time again for the past two weeks. He hoped that after *this* morning, the mantra would no longer be needed. Acute anticipation over the long days slowly ticking by brought a disgruntled feeling that he believed was now near an end.

When the last of his bandages were removed during the previous week, Jack was relieved to find that he had lost no dexterity. Gone were the phantom pains in his severed fingertips. Clenching his fists as hard as ever, Jack decided that the real test of his hands would be whether they could absorb sudden impact. Initially playing it safe by striking the back of his recliner, he was soon punching everything around him, gauging his recovery. First he hit the walls, then the refrigerator, the countertops, culminating with the cinderblock wall in the basement. Jack was ready to return to work in full capacity.

The only slightly disconcerting note in the last days of his recovery was the absence of any visits from the guys at work. Granted, several coworkers had sent cards and Chuck Mitchell even had a large gift basket delivered. But being able to keep in touch with his coworkers would have made these past few months a little more bearable. In his coworkers' defense, Jack was aware that if the workload over the summer was anything like it had been previously, little time would have been available to the guys for social visits.

Rommel's single bark and deep growl alerted his master to the postal delivery as it had a thousand times before. Profound jubilation came over Jack as he rifled through the mail that had just arrived through the slot at the base of the front door and saw the certified letter from Kutter Metals.

"Making my shop buddies feel guilty and dragging it out for a couple of days should be good for a few free lunches," Jack laughed to himself as he poured himself a cup of coffee, minus the straw. Performing even such a mundane task was now gratifying.

"Here's your sandwich, Hon," Patricia said as she set a fully loaded BLT on wheat bread, one of his favorites, on the table. A big bag of chips and a tall glass of cold milk created the perfect setting for this grand occasion.

"Thanks, Pat. Thank God this day is here." Jack could hardly contain himself as he showed her the newly arrived envelope.

"We may need a week or two to catch up on bills; after that you should be OK to finish the kids' school shopping.

Brandon could not have been happier listening to his parents as he played in the living room. The conversation in the room next door was every bit as amusing as the Colorforms that he was playing with. Such carefree moments had been scarce as of late. Brandon's brothers would be thrilled when they arrived home, he was sure of it. Life had returned to normal. Richard was blissfully oblivious as he slept in the boys' room upstairs.

Jack's hands shook with excitement as he opened the letter. But the color drained from his face as he read the note. In a moment, his demeanor went from playful schoolboy to someone in mourning. Patricia watched as her husband's face then went from shock to welling anger and his hands began to shake uncontrollably. She saw the frightening, wide-eyed gaze that she so feared on his face. Eyes bulging, staring straight ahead, Jack sat without blinking, as if he looked through, rather than at the room in front of him.

"Jack, Jack, what is it? What does it say? Please talk to me!" Patricia burst into tears.

"What's the matter, Mom? Is Daddy OK?" Standing in the doorway, Brandon could only see his father from behind. But the look on Patricia's face told him that something was very wrong. Fear now gripped Brandon's young heart. The rapid transition of his parents' mood left him shaking and in tears.

"Brandon, Daddy will be OK. Why don't you go up and check on your brother. I'll come up soon." Her voice was shaky, but Patricia had to dispatch her son as quickly as possible. Brandon was visibly still upset as he ran upstairs, but there was little she could do. Whatever had just happened, Jack could not be left alone like this.

Carefully taking the letter from him, Patricia read it as he held his forehead between shaking hands, moving them up and down. "No, no, no, no," was all Jack could say as Patricia took the paper from his hand and read.

Dear Mr. Christopher,

On August 30th, 1968 the Advisory Board of Kutter Metals met in conference to render a decision as to the disposition of your accident and future employment at Kutter Metals. After reviewing all of the pertinent facts associated with the incident that transpired on June 28th, 1968 we, the Advisory Board have made a determination.

It was found that the primary cause of the accident was an unauthorized alteration of the wiring in the #1 pedal of the cutting press. Subsequent inquiry has found that you, Mr. Christopher, had made the alteration and were thereby responsible for the unfortunate resulting mishap. Such a safety

129

violation is contrary to the practices and policies of Kutter Metals.

Accordingly, we at Kutter Metals are left with no alternative but to terminate your employment with us, effective immediately. We regret having to come to this inescapable conclusion. The final workman's compensation check will be issued on September 30th, 1968. This will conclude your association with the company. We wish you the best in your future endeavors.

Sincerely,

Winslow Billson
President, Kutter Metals

Tears filled Patricia's eyes as she finished reading the letter. The mortgage, food, and mounting bills, weighed heavy on her mind, and she felt profound grief. How could they keep the house? Even heavier on her heart was watching the man she dearly loved as his hopes were ripped out from under him. Jack was crushed and so filled with rage that she feared what her husband might do if he left the house.

Jack bolted up from the table and began frantically pacing the kitchen floor. His mind reeled at the cold, heartless contents of the letter. Since when did Kutter Metals care about safety? They were the ones who refused to fix the machine. Jack pictured Pete laughing when he heard that his troublesome subordinate was fired.

"Sons of bitches; those sons of bitches," Jack said as he walked erratically around the kitchen. "They take these," he said, raising his hands to Patricia, "and then tell me it was my fault? *My* fault? That arrogant bastard sits up in his office riding my ass about not getting enough done and then tells me that it's *my* fault that I lost my fingers?"

He slammed his fist on the kitchen table and then was suddenly calm. Gone were the jolting movements and rapid pacing. But what replaced them filled Patricia with even greater terror. Jack's voice rang with pure hatred and calmly declared intent.

"You know what, Hon? I'm going down there. Hell, if he thinks I'll just quietly disappear, he's mistaken. I got all the time in the world now! Let's see how Billson likes sitting around recovering for 3 months!"

Jack moved from counter to counter, hurriedly looking for his car keys. The sight of his face, now bright red with veins bulging in his forehead, moved Patricia to try to block the kitchen door.

"Jack, please, *please,* don't go down there!" Patricia cried out in sheer exasperation, crying uncontrollably. She fell on her knees in front of the kitchen door, her tear streaked face imploring her husband.

"Jack, no please. I'm begging you! We'll figure something out, but don't go down there!"

Jack was recalcitrant. Pulling open the kitchen door, he bumped his wife over enough to get past her, slamming the door behind him.

The tires of the station wagon screeched as Jack backed out of the driveway. The car made black tire marks across the street toward the bowling alley as Jack slammed the brakes on pulling out. He gunned the engine, and didn't even attempt to pause at the intersection of the White Horse Pike. Fishtailing as he made a wild left, he narrowly missed an oncoming car.

Patricia collapsed on the living room couch and looked out the window, watching helplessly as the car disappeared over the hill. Her chest tightened, as her heart pounded. She could only wonder what Jack was capable of at the shop.

Brandon could not possibly grasp the complexities that had so radically changed his family's mood this morning. However, Brandon clearly understood one thing: his mother was hurting. Crying softly as he went to the couch, Brandon said nothing, but slowly positioned himself between Patricia and the edge of the cushions. He lay down on the couch and draped one small arm over Patricia's neck, both giving and seeking reassurance.

Silently praying for Jack to forgo retribution, Patricia lay still with her eyes closed. She gently stroked her son's light brown hair with one hand. Patricia was despondent wondering how she was going to tell the boys what happened when they arrived home from school. They had left this morning with optimism and a jovial air. Why must they return to grief and the certain prospect of hardship? Worse yet, this time the days could not be so easily marked off.

As she contemplated the new wave of difficulties threatening to crash over her family, Patricia questioned God. She thought she at least deserved an answer to why He had taken a beautiful, long-anticipated day and turned it into a cauldron of lamentation. What transgression had the Christopher family committed that another plight should befall them so soon? What malice on their part had so quickly incurred God's wrath? Was it not enough that her husband had lost his fingers?

All of the stories that she had heard in church as a child, all the messages of God's goodness on a given Sunday, were like dust in Patricia's hand, and she could only ask silently, "Why God? Why?"

Patricia held Brandon close to her, trying to comfort him. She had no control over what Jack would do, and for now, chose to cease praying to the One who allowed this to happen. Richard's cries from upstairs reminded Patricia that she needed to compose herself and carry on.

"Thank you, Brandon. Mommy feels much better" she said, smoothing his hair with a gentle hand. "Why don't you sit here on the couch, and I'll get you some milk and cookies." Placing the Colorforms in front of Brandon and turning on the TV, Patricia hoped her son could find a partial distraction from the day's turmoil. She wanted so much to tell him that everything would be back to normal shortly and that Jack would be fine. She could not bring herself to lie, and she could not be reasonably certain that it was true. As she went upstairs to get Richard, Patricia stopped to pet Rommel. He had not abandoned his station but was clearly agitated by the commotion.

Passing zone marks in the center of the road flew by like one solid line as Jack barreled down the Pike. Reaching the top of the hill near St. Anne's, the car went airborne for a short distance and then sprayed sparks from the rear as it struck the road when landing. Afternoon traffic was mercifully light as Jack navigated the bend to the left at the bottom of the hill. Two more miles of straight road would take him to the Berlin Circle, with Kutter just around the corner. Jack slowed, remembering the long-standing speed trap just ahead. Much as it killed him to drive slowly, getting pulled over would delay him even longer.

He had no grand plan of what he would do when he arrived at Kutter, but one thing Jack was certain of was that Billson had wanted him gone a long time ago. Winslow Billson resented that Jack was impervious to intimidation. Billson was used to and expected people to jump when he said jump, and Jack gave flak back to management as good as they gave it out.

Most guys in Jack's section of the floor just let things roll off of them, no matter how onerous management demands were. Not Jack. He would walk right up to Pete's office unannounced to voice his displeasure with company policy, which really ticked his boss off. Jack pegged Pete as a "company weasel." The more bad reports about the crew that he could drop on Winslow's desk, the happier Pete would be.

Further aggravating management was Jack's ability to meet his production quota. He was used to working incessantly. Jack found a certain gratification in frustrating the "white shirts" each week. He had felt for some time that they were gunning for him, but as long as he met the daily quota, they could say little.

Week after week, month after month, Jack had made his deadlines. Typically, one size plate would be cut one day, another size the next. Around the time of the accident his orders had him cutting two, sometimes three, different plate sizes per day. Each different size required him to stop, set the machine for the new plates, and complete a new set of paperwork. Jack was sure that management was trying to make his numbers look bad. They would then have the excuse they were looking for, and their "troublemaker" would be gone.

Jack believed that management feared his production floor bravado would spread. Jack saw no danger of that in his section. Not one of them had a backbone. Nice guys...but no back bone.

Not fixing the # 1 pedal was management's last act of sabotage as far as he was concerned. They were confident that this would be his undoing. When the repair crew was instructed not to fix the pedal, setting Jack up for failure, he fixed it himself, and again management was outwitted. He didn't believe they'd intended to harm him, but when the accident happened, they saw an opening to rid themselves of Jack Christopher. It was this deliberate calculation of his demise from the company by the "white shirts" that made Jack livid. They had won and were sure that he could do nothing about it. He had not only lost his fingers but had also handed Winslow Billson the final victory, and there was nothing that Jack could do about it…, or so they *thought*.

Safely navigating past the speed trap, Jack continued driving within the speed limit to avoid attracting unwanted attention making his final approach to the shop. Selecting the target of his retribution as he pulled into Kutter's was easy. Pete was not worth Jack's trouble. He was an idiot and little more than a glorified coffee boy for the white shirts. Pete lacked the brains or stones to plan how to railroad an employee. The white shirts said do it, and Pete followed along, but he was no mastermind. That distinction was reserved for Winslow Billson. Billson was the one with whom Jack had the axe to grind.

Exiting the car, Jack was pleased that the lot, though full of cars, was devoid of people. How many times, he thought, had his car pulled into one of these spaces each day over the years? How many birthdays and family events had been missed because he was told he had to work late? What did it profit to have spent countless summers in the sweltering heat until he thought that he was going to pass out? Bosses expected you to bend over and kiss their asses in gratitude after informing you of a 10 cent raise. All the while Billson sought a way to fire him.

Jack's heart was racing, and his anger had not subsided at all since he'd left the house. Instead, rehearsing the litany of grievances riled him up even more as he walked through the employee entrance like he had done thousands of times before. There was a calculated advantage to using the employee entrance. Coming through the main lobby would attract immediate attention from the always present receptionist or the countless office workers milling about.

The employee entrance opened onto the production floor, and Jack burst through with heavy, deliberate steps. Anger radiating from every movement, Jack turned right to the open staircase that would take him up to the production offices.

For a moment, Jack looked out onto the production floor at his old machine. This would have been his shift. He should be out there operating the machine instead of the new guy. Jack harbored no ill will to this new employee. He's just another poor slob trying to feed his family. It was just a question of time before Kutter started shitting all over him as well.

Jack slowly looked down at his fingers and then at his old machine, and the magnitude of the affront flashed into a boiling point in his mind. He turned sharply and stormed up the straight open, metal staircase. At the top, long open walkways extended to the right and left for 50 feet. Offices to the left handled production matters; vendors, contractors, and personnel were to the right.

Billson's office was right in front of him at the top of the stairs. A large brass, engraved plate on the door read "Winslow Billson, President/CEO". Jack opened the door and walked in as if it was his name on the door. The closed door to Billson's inner office was behind a receptionist's desk staffed by sharply dressed but quite startled receptionist. Seeing what she considered a shabbily dressed man enter unannounced, she immediately became defensive.

"You cannot come in here, sir; you will need to make an appointment! Mr. Billson will *not* see you!"

Jack dismissed her before she even began to speak; he walked right past her protests to Billson's door.

"Sure he will," Jack said as he landed the heel of his foot just to the left of the doorknob. Sharp cracking followed as splintered wood littered the floor. The doorknob sheared off of the door, leaving a gaping hole. This explosion of noise and shattered wood seemed to feed Jack's hunger for perceived justice.

Jack's barbaric entrance gripped Winslow Billson with sudden terror. The mug of custom blend Columbian coffee that he had been drinking was now spilled prominently across his tailored white cotton shirt. Since he was accustomed to projecting power, Billson did his best not to show his panic. At 5'9" with grayish hair on a balding head and a distinct paunch, Winslow Billson was by no means physically intimidating. However, the fiftyish executive had always coveted position and power and the ability to control other people. Even when he was terrified, power was Billson's default position.

"Mr. Christopher, you do realize that security will be here any minute," he said, holding his voice steady with some effort. Jack knew that "security" meant a skinny, pasty-complexioned kid with a white shirt and an arm patch who walked circles around the production floor. No older than 20, the boy was lucky if he could don his ill-fitting uniform by himself.

"My fault, you miserable son-of-a-bitch?" Jack shoved his termination notice across the desktop, and it came to rest in front of Billson. Resting his closed fists on the desk across from his former boss, Jack leaned over until his face was as close to Billson's as the wide desk would allow.

"I want you to look me in the eye and tell me that getting my fingers cut off and losing my job was my fault! C'mon, Winslow, let's hear it!" Jack's nostrils flared and his speech launched spittle into Billson's face.

"I'm sssure that all of the details have been spelled out, Mr. Christopher," Billson said, but his attempt to remain composed enraged Jack even further. What Jack saw has Winslow's dismissive attitude seemed to flip a switch in his brain. Taking the back of Billson's balding head, Jack slammed his forehead into the top of the coffee stained mahogany desk.

"It's"…*bam*…"not"…*bam*…"in there"…*bam*…"Winslow," Jack shouted as he slammed his former bosses head into the desk. Billson fell limp, as blood poured from a large cut on the front of his head. Jack heaved the heavy, cumbersome desk back towards its semi-conscious occupant, bringing it to rest atop his disoriented former employer.

"Still think that you've won, Billson?" Jack snapped. "Well, I hope you're enjoying it!"

136

Jack turned calmly and passed through the receptionist's area as she frantically called for help. Disregarding her, Jack walked onto the open staircase. Men and women came out of their offices on either side. The men seemed in no hurry to confront Jack as the women yelled for "somebody to do something," at which Jack smiled.

As Jack made his way down the staircase, Chuck Mitchell peered up at him from the base of the steps. "Aw hell Jack; what did you do that for Buddy?"

"He had it coming, Chuck." Jack was unremorseful. "You know he had it coming."

"I'll check in on the family for ya on my way home," Chuck did not agree or disagree with the statement, but offered an act of kindness.

"Thanks, Chuck; I have a feeling I won't be there tonight," Jack laughed, patting Chuck on the shoulder as he passed by.

Leaving the employee entrance, Jack was surprised not to see police. Jack got into his car, but rather than go home and further upset Patricia, he made the familiar left onto Linden Avenue. Entering his father's house through the screen door to the kitchen, Jack found his father as he often was, drinking coffee at his small, yellow formica dinette table.

"Hey Pop, mind if I grab a coffee?" Jack hoped to keep the conversation fairly routine. He saw no sense in getting his father riled up. He was sure that it would not be too long before the police arrived. "Yeah, grab some coffee, Jack; you can help me with this damned crossword puzzle," Charles responded. He adjusted his thick wire-rimmed glasses as he searched for his next clue. "Six letter word for Hornpipe dancer, Jack. Hornpipe dancer…Hornpipe dancer…" Charles was slightly irritated with his son's lack of input. "You're not much help, Jack."

Jack was distracted, but not nervous or upset. He had no intention of hiding from the police; his was far too familiar a face to attempt anything so futile. No, he would just wait. He knew the police would not take long to find him here, and being arrested at home in front of Patricia and the boys would have been entirely too chaotic. Being arrested at his father's house was much less dramatic.

In the long run, as far as Jack was concerned, it was all worth it. Billson would think twice before setting anyone else up to get fired. Of course, nothing was going to change for Jack, not for the better anyway. Nonetheless, he felt some satisfaction that the score was a little more even now.

Light tapping sounded from the screen door off of the kitchen, but Jack and Charles saw no one in the doorway. After a second round of taps, a voice followed the knocking.

"Jack…Jack, are you in there? This is the Lindenwold police. We want to come in Jack. We see that your car is out there." Jack had no plans to make this harder for the police than it had to be. They were only doing their job.

"I'm in here, guys, and I have my hands on the kitchen table." Cautiously, two police officers opened the screen door.

"We're coming in, Jack; I don't want this to be difficult." As the two officers entered the house, the senior policeman, in the lead, had his hand on his gun. The patrolman behind him carried a nightstick. Jack saw that the first cop was Mike Arnold. Mike and Jack had been friends since grade school. They had hung out a lot together and always gotten along well.

"If you could slowly stand up and put both hands on the countertop, I'm going to have to cuff you, Jack. I'd feel a little safer that way," Mike said, a little regretfully.

"No problem, Mike; I have no beef with you," Jack replied.

Mike cuffed Jack and read him his rights, then turned to greet Charles. "Good afternoon, Mr. Christopher." For his part, Charles was unperturbed. He had seen plenty of police as his boys were growing up. He would eventually find out what happened.

"Afternoon, Mike; how is your father doing?" Charles knew Sergeant Arnold very well. Mike had spent many days of his childhood running through Charles' house with the Christopher brothers.

"Still getting his golf in, so he's happy. I'll tell him you were asking about him," Mike replied.

"There's some coffee in the pot boys, just leave me a little," Charles offered.

"Thanks, Mr. Christopher, but we should probably be getting Jack down to the station."

Charles went back to trying to solve his crossword puzzle.

"C'mon, Jack, a six letter word for Hornpipe dancer. Aw hell, I guess you better go with them son; I'll call Charlie, 'though he's probably heard by now. Stop by when you get out son."

If Jack and Charles did not appear too concerned with the impending incarceration, it was with good reason. Jack's brother Charlie was also a Lindenwold police officer. Though no one expected him to fix Jack's mess, Charlie was well respected around town. Jack and Charles expected he would eventually stop over and talk to Winslow Billson, asking him if the charges could be lessened or dropped. Perhaps there was some other way his brother could make amends. Jack put a lot of stock in his brother's good name in the community.

"You scared Mr. Billson to death Jack," Mike told him as he led him out of the house. "He's banged up, and was out cold when they took him over to Kennedy. You can call your wife once the paperwork is done, and bail is set." As they walked Jack out the kitchen door, Sgt Arnold stuck his head back in the screen door and called to Charles. "By the way, Mr. Christopher, the word you are looking for is "sailor"…you know, Hornpipe dancer."

As they made their way to the patrol car, Jack's right leg gave out from under him. Fortunately the two officers had him on either side and were able to support his weight, so that he did not fall.

"Did you hurt yourself over at Kutter's, Jack? Do you need medical attention?" Mike asked.

Jack paid little attention to the embarrassing slip.

"No Mike, it just decided to give out on me. I'll be fine, thanks," he answered.

Upon arrival at the Lindenwold Police Station, they began the mundane tasks of booking. Questions were followed by commands such as, "look straight, turn right, turn left, roll your fingers, sit there, follow the yellow line." The officers were professional and direct, and Jack was smart enough to keep his mouth shut unless asked a question. Everyone in the station knew that Jack was Charlie's brother, but they did not offer him special treatment. Charlie was out on patrol and could not attempt to see Billson until the following week at the earliest. Jack also knew his brother would have a few choice words for him. Charlie did not like expending his hard-earned reputation mending his brother's fences.

Shortly after 6 pm, Patricia was cleared to bail her husband out of jail. However, by then all the banks were closed, leaving no means by which to obtain the needed bail money before morning. Jack would remain a guest of the Lindenwold Police for the remainder of the evening.

Chapter 23
Patricia and the Spread of Hostilities

The Next Day

Bud offered to come down the following morning from Pennsauken to shuttle Patricia from the bank to the police station, as he did not think that she should be driving in such a jumbled emotional state. As the darkness gave way to morning, Patricia was not tearful, upset, or even despairing. She was furious. Patricia was consumed with a deep, quiet, dark anger. Gone were her usual graceful flowing movements. Instead, she moved with short, angry gestures that needed no verbal reinforcement.

The tears and sadness so overwhelming earlier had been supplanted by sheer disdain for what Jack had done. His bitterness and disappointment in Winslow Billson was understandable, but compounding the burden on the family for the sake of his own satisfaction had Patricia livid. Dwelling on the price that her children now had to pay for Jack's impulsive indiscretion incensed her all the more.

Patricia was careful enough not to let the discontent to spill over and be vented onto the children, but they could see clearly that something was wrong. Their mother's disposition came as much of a shock to them as anyone. Patricia had made it quite clear that dissention within the ranks would not be tolerated this morning.

Approaching the house, Bud could see Patricia coming out of the kitchen door holding Richard. Like baby ducks with no clue where they were being led, the children filed out onto the yard behind her.

"Hi, Daddy. Thanks again for coming on such short notice. I've had to keep the kids home from school; not sure as to whether we would be back from all of this running around before school let out. And I'm sorry to say it Dad, but the station wagon is at his father's house. Would you mind leaving your car there and bringing the station wagon back here? I told Jack's father that you would be parking there." Patricia began to look a little flustered as she tried to ensure that she had all of her bases covered.

"I am so mad that I can hardly see straight, Dad," she told her father through gritted teeth. Bud watched his daughter with concern. Brooding anger was a side of her that he could not remember seeing as far back as his memory served him. He invoked his usual unflappable air of stability to calm her down.

"Relax Honey; just wait here and I'll be right back with the station wagon. Don't worry, we'll sort this out."

Bud then directed a few unsolicited instructions toward the grandkids.

"Listen, Boys," he said, "your mom is having a hard day and really needs your help. I want you all to behave on your best today. You boys like *nice* Grandpop right?" His grandsons all responded in the affirmative. "You would never want to see *grumpy* Grandpop." Bud gave them a playful wink, but the serious message tucked into his banter was understood.

"OK, Grandpop," they responded in unison, slightly impressing themselves.

Bud was back with the station wagon in 15 minutes. The boys had heeded his admonition and stood in silent patience until he returned. They needed little encouragement to refrain from misbehavior after witnessing Patricia's disjointed attitude earlier in the morning.

At the bank, Bud and the boys amused themselves with stories in the parking lot while Patricia and Richard went inside and waited in line. His mother found that Richard was not nearly as cooperative as the rest of his brothers. His fidgeting and steady whine proved uncharacteristically bothersome at the worst possible time. Patricia's anger was acerbated by

142

the stares and murmured comments from other patrons. The callous disregard of those inside had Patricia returning to the car in no mood to even be around people.

"You take out $400.00 of your own money, and they act like they are doing you a favor," she said as she reached Bud and the boys. Bail had been set at $300.00, but Patricia was taking no chances. She had withdrawn all but twenty of the funds they had in the account. She hoped that lollipops taken from the bowl on the teller counter would appease the boys for the next 15 minutes. They began to argue over who got what color lollipop, but a short-tempered threat to take them all back cut the discord short.

"I'm sorry Dad. We can go now," she said a little sheepishly.

Patricia was growing more and more uncomfortable with her own volatile behavior. Midway to the police station, Patricia decided that she had enough of feeling miserable for something that Jack had done. The kids deserved better.

"Are you hungry, Dad?" Patricia asked out of the blue. Bud thought it a strange question, but felt he ought to humor his daughter.

"Am I...hungry? Well I ate a bagel before I left the house, but that was about it. Why, Honey?" he asked.

"Let's go to breakfast, Dad!" Patricia proposed. "The Hilltop Diner is up here on your left. We're gonna treat the kids to breakfast."

Erupting at the promise of an unexpected detour, the boys cheered while Patricia's father tried to figure out where all of this was going.

"Honey, we don't have time for breakfast," he reasoned. "Jack will be..." Patricia cut in before he could finish his thought. She was tired of worrying about Jack.

"You know what, Dad? We *do* have time for breakfast! I have just spent the last 10 weeks waiting on Jack hand and foot. I spent yesterday morning crying on the kitchen floor after he ran out even though I begged him not to go. My crying and pleading meant nothing, because Jack wanted to get even. My father is now giving up his day to drive down here early in the morning and sit in a bank parking lot, while I am standing in line listening to complete strangers complain about my son who is cranky because he had to get up at 6 am to pick up his father from *jail*. Dammit, Dad, we *do* have time for breakfast. Jack can wait!"

At the end of this speech, cheers erupted from the backseat. 'Yay, breakfast! I'm getting pancakes!" "I'm playing the music box!" The boys all began exchanging diner aspirations.

Patricia was suddenly not overly concerned with unexpected costs that may come along with posting bail. She had taken out plenty of extra, and she was hungry. She was well aware of how dire finances would become very shortly. With what little extra she had in her pockets, she could think of no reason why her children should not be the beneficiaries of her fleeting ability to treat them. Jack could wait.

The boys were slightly awkward at the onset but soon settled in and enjoyed a lively breakfast. There was no talk of bail or any of the other issues sure to be soon pressing down upon them. They all got to pick a song on the tabletop jukebox, flipping through the rolodex of songs.

Bud had witnessed a previously unseen side of his daughter. She was finding her voice, and Bud could tell she liked it. Patricia had found the line that pushed her too far when crossed. Imposing unwanted burdens needlessly on her boys crossed her threshold of tolerance. Patricia had no desire to take on this persona permanently. Her role as wife and mother was gratifying, and she excelled at both. What had changed was the protective mother's recognition that there were times when a raised voice was required, and occasions on which it would be necessary not to be the soft-spoken wife.

After finishing a leisurely breakfast, Jack's liberators made the last leg of their trip to the police station. After dinner mints and toothpicks scattered in the car were a dead giveaway of the unscheduled pit stop. Relaxing at the diner took some of the edge off for Patricia, but she was still irritated.

Bud and the boys once again waited in the car while Patricia went inside the station to post bail. Jack was brought out from the holding area as the clock on the wall ticked past 11:30. His hair was disheveled and clothes wrinkled, and he looked as though sleep had not been a principle aspect of the previous evening's agenda. Assuming that his wife would inquire as to his wellbeing and how he had endured the uncomfortable incarceration, Jack was taken aback when Patricia said nothing as she signed the release forms. After several minutes of silence, Jack broke the verbal impasse with a less than ingratiating question.

"What took you guys so long, Hon? The bank should have opened at nine. Were you at the bank at nine?"

Patricia did not even turn herself to face him. Looking up briefly from the paperwork she had been filling out, she rested her chin slightly on her left shoulder and spoke to him through gritted teeth.

"I was at the bank at 9:00, Jack. At 9:30 I was at the Hilltop, and now I'm here." Patricia's acerbic remark was delivered with deliberate annunciation. Jack was thrown so completely off guard by the comment and Patricia's terse tone, and he was momentarily unable to respond.

Recollecting his thoughts, Jack began again after a pause, now irritated by his wife's lack of compassion.

"What's the matter with you? I sat on the damn cell floor all night."

"Sat on the floor last night?" Patricia's head snapped up with her response. "Really Jack? Was it like I did yesterday while you pushed your way out the door? Maybe if you had shown an ounce of concern for me then, you would not be in here now! Let's just end this and go home." For the first time in their marriage, Patricia decided when the conversation was over. She had no intention of hashing things out in the police station.

Outside at the car, the children were more welcoming to their father, much to Jack's delight. He hugged them all and thanked Bud for coming. Once she was with the children, Patricia shrouded any overt contentions with her husband for their sake.

After dropping off Bud at Jack's father's to get his car, the Christopher family finally arrived home. Jack had weighed the possibility of staying with Charles for a few nights. Surely his father's reception would not have been as frigid as the one he had received thus far. But for the sake of maintaining minimal peace, Jack decided to bite the bullet and go home.

Arriving at the house, everyone scattered in different directions. Most of the boys began playing freeze tag around the tall oak in the yard, happy not to be in school. The creamed chipped beef on toast that Russell had for breakfast was not sitting well with his gastrointestinal tract. He was the only one to find the humor in his flatulent condition. Jack went inside the house just long enough to put Rommel on his leash and then spent the next few hours walking the streets of Stratford. He felt that a little distance would serve both Patricia and him well at this juncture.

Patricia went inside, settled Richard in the living room, and started on the pile of dirty dishes next to the sink. Richard lasted only a few minutes playing with Brandon's Colorforms before falling fast asleep on the living room couch, compensating for the early wake up earlier.

Busying her hands provided Patricia a form of therapy. Temporary as it was, the sink acted like a sudsy disconnect from all that had transpired this morning and the legal problems to come. Despite the task's soothing nature, Patricia's hands shook as she retrieved another cup from the basin. For Patricia, the morning's combative posture was an anomaly. She found going toe to toe with her husband unpleasant, and it had left her feeling hurt, guilty, and alone. Crying, however, was out of the question. She had shed enough tears.

For his part, Jack did not doubt that, after a mutual cooling-off period, he and Patricia would get past this divot in their marriage. Of greater concern was Winslow Billson's inclination, or lack thereof, to show any mercy toward his former employee. Jack had placed himself in a position in which he had no control over the outcome. That he had brought this latest tribulation on himself and the family by his own hand made the sting that much sharper. His brother Charlie's longstanding reputation and rapport with local leaders was the only thing standing between Jack and Billson's potential revenge on him. And they would have more weeks of uncertainty before the court hearing would mitigate or confirm Jack's fears for the worst.

Chapter 24
Jack and the Sentencing

Early October 1968

Following the assault on him at the office, Winslow Billson had been ready to crush Jack once and for all. Leniency was the furthest thing from his mind. Once and for all, despite Jack Christopher's bravado, it would be Billson who had the last laugh.

Charlie Christopher understood that Billson would need to both physically heal and get past the embarrassment of being beaten unconscious in front of his employees. Allowing time for the dust to settle, Charlie made no attempt to intercede until 3 days before the hearing.

Charlie, Billson believed, was the antithesis of his brother. With 18 years on the police force and an exemplary record, Charlie had cultivated a myriad of solid relationships with community associations, businesses, and organizations through honesty and integrity. Most of the kids loved Charlie, and even those who disliked him knew not to take him lightly. He had coached many of those now entering high school in little league and was familiar with all of their parents. When Charlie offered an opinion, people listened.

It was only out of this longstanding respect that Winslow Billson agreed to meet with Charlie. Billson was fully aware of and unexcited about, the agenda which his friend most likely had for the visit. Still nursing a pronounced gash across his nose, Billson made it clear at the onset of their discussion that he was in no mood to, nor saw any reason to, extend mercy to Jack Christopher.

147

The battered executive was surprised that Charlie wasted no time or energy trying to defend or exonerate his brother, though perhaps he should not have been. Certainly it was pointless to do so. Jack's anger may have been understandable, but the manifestation of it was indefensible. Secondly, Charlie's own integrity would not allow him to explain away Jack's actions. Instead, out of heartfelt concern for Patricia and the boys and believing that a different approach may be better received by Winslow, Charlie tried an appeal to Winslow from the other innocent victims. They too, Charlie contended, were innocent bystanders who would ultimately suffer far greater than the one who perpetrated the act of senseless violence.

Winslow remembered Patricia from several corporate picnics as a sweet, soft-spoken woman, not the abrasive type that Billson thought her husband to be. He had felt compassion for her on the day of Jack's accident at the shop, even though he hadn't been able to convey it in his call to her. A host of legal, administrative, regulatory, and investigational entities, all clamoring for attention, had hovered around his desk while he made the call to Patricia. In retrospect, Billson wished he had handled the call much differently. Perhaps Charlie's visit would allow him to rectify that regret.

"One thing that I have always liked about you Charlie: you have always been straightforward," he now turned to his friend. "You've come here and made a reasonable argument. Had you gone down the road that I had anticipated you to take, this would have been a very brief meeting. Outright pardon is out of the question. Every man on the production floor is wondering what price if any Jack Christopher will pay for his actions. Wholesale dismissal of charges would be an open door for the next disgruntled employee." He paused and looked Charlie straight in the eye. "And to be honest Charlie, I want some satisfaction; something that causes Jack Christopher to regret walking into the building that day.

That said, your concern for the plight of Mr. Christopher's wife and children is well taken. I cannot sit here and spell out exactly what I have decided or intend to do. Right now I have no definitive answer to give

148

you. What I can do is tell you that I will discuss these factors with my legal team and weigh them against the punitive measures that need to be taken against your brother. You know that I have great respect for you Charlie, and nothing that has happened will change that."

Charlie assured him that he'd expected no more than a fair consideration. He confirmed their mutual respect. Finally, thanking Winslow for his willingness to meet, Charlie excused himself so that he could get a few hours' sleep before starting his shift.

Prospects for spending 6 months to a year in prison hung precariously over Jack's head as he spent the day of his hearing on his best behavior. Defense counsel had warned Jack that one ill-placed comment, gesture, or reaction during the proceedings could offend the judge and seal his incarceration for a year. Jack was cautioned not to speak, respond, motion, or react unless specifically instructed to do so.

Striking the wooden block upon which it normally rested quietly, the judge's gavel fell, and the preliminary hearing was called to order. Now the Christophers would learn if Charlie's plea to Winslow Billson had produced any fruit. As the legal teams prepared their statements, Winslow Billson entered the chambers and sat down next to his team of lawyers.

This morning was the first time Jack saw his former boss since slamming his head onto the desktop. Jack could not let the slightest hint of disdain or loathing toward Billson cripple any hope of leniency, so he looked straight ahead toward the judge and kept his mouth shut.

After the judge read the charges, lawyers for Winslow Billson were granted permission to address the court.

"Your honor, my client has instructed counsel to craft a plea bargain agreement that we hope would, along with sparing the court and parties involved a painful trial, also accomplish two stated objectives. The first goal is to compel Mr. Christopher not to pursue such actions in the future as a remedy to disagreements. Secondly we wish to minimize the negative impact of Mr. Christopher's actions upon his family. We hope that they need not suffer for his foolish actions. Should Mr. Christopher confess his guilt and accept this plea, and should the court authorize its implementation, Mr. Christopher's jail time would be reduced. Our proposal is as follows:

1.   Mr. Christopher plead guilty to all charges;

2.   Mr. Christopher serve 3 months incarceration with no early release, to begin immediately;

3.   Mr. Christopher repay Mr. Billson and Kutter Metals for all medical bills, court costs, and repair bills directly resulting from his actions;

4.   Mr. Christopher will be barred from coming within 1000 feet of Kutter Metals and the Billson residence; and

5.   Mr. Christopher will provide a handwritten letter of apology of 500 words or more. The letter must be to Winslow Billson's satisfaction, and will be posted on the Kutter Metals bulletin board for not less than 90 days.

Only the full and unconditional acceptance of these aforementioned conditions will be accepted. Thank you, Your Honor."

The judge looked at the defense table to measure their response. Lengthy discussion was not needed. Jack's guilt was never in question, and picking the offer apart in search of some small symbolic concession might provoke Billson to withdraw it completely. At a nod from Jack and anxious to accept the plea while it was there, the public defender rose to his feet.

"Your Honor, we accept the plea bargain as it has been stated, with no requests for modified conditions."

The judge conveyed that he considered the terms to be reasonable, and was prepared to dispose the case immediately. He motioned toward Jack, calling him to his feet. Repeating the conditions from Billson's offer, the judge addressed Jack directly.

"Mr. Christopher, how do you plead with regard to the charges against you?"

"Guilty, Your Honor," Jack answered quietly.

"Do you do this of your own volition, free from any pressure or outside coercion?"

"Yes, Your Honor," Jack answered.

"And do you accept and understand the terms of the plea deal offered, foregoing a criminal trial?"

"Yes, Your Honor."

"Very well," the judge answered. "I hereby order that Mr. Christopher be remanded to the custody of Gloucester County Department of Corrections for 90 days, with no early release, to begin immediately. All other terms and conditions of this agreement shall be met to the satisfaction of the court. This hearing is adjourned."

Patricia sobbed softly as Jack was placed into handcuffs. Though saddened that the whole incident had taken place, Patricia was thankful for Winslow Billson's extension of grace. She understood that things could have gone much worse for Jack.

Kissing Patricia before being led away, Jack told her how sorry he was. If not for the act itself, Patricia was convinced of his remorse for the impact of his actions on his family. Jack's repentance, which had gone virtually unstated for weeks, was of some comfort to her pained heart.

"December 30th will be here before you know it, Hon. I love you," Jack tried to paint as bright a picture as he could.

"I love you, Jack. Please keep quiet for the next 90 days will you?" She finished with a tentative smile. Jack offered one parting bit of guidance for his wife.

"Call Joe or Charlie if you need anything. You'll be safe with Rommel there."

"Let's go, Mr. Christopher," the sheriff's deputy intervened. He'd tried to be as accommodating as possible, but had a job to do. The deputy then led Jack through the courtroom side door for processing.

Drying her eyes, Patricia went into the marble hallway. She saw Winslow Billson and stepped toward him. When it was apparent that Jack's wife was approaching him, Billson became uncomfortable. Sensing his unease, Patricia stopped at a respectable distance.

"Mr. Billson, I just wanted to tell you how sorry I am for all you have been through, and to thank you for your grace to my husband," she said, looking him in the eyes so he could see that she meant her words. Winslow was glad that his gesture had not gone unappreciated.

"Mrs. Christopher, you have done me no harm and owe no apology. I hope that this agreement eases the burden placed on you. You do understand that there had to be some degree of recompense on the part of your husband. Any grace in my gesture was directed toward you and your children. I hope that it was successful. I sincerely wish the best for you and your family. Good day, Mrs. Christopher."

As Winslow turned and walked away and the last echoes reverberated down the marble hall, Patricia found herself alone. She was still alone as she lay in bed that night. Seeing Jack's side of the bed still neatly arranged, Patricia's heart sank within her. Jack's unrumpled pillow reminded her that she would be on her own for the next 3 months.

Chapter 25
Patricia and the Boys, and the Long Autumn Siege

October 1968

Three steaming bowls of oatmeal sat on the kitchen table, two of which had a side plate of sliced bananas ready and waiting. The third bowl was adorned with blueberries and sugar. Patricia was working feverishly to get the boys off to school on time.

"Robert, Shawn, Russell, BREAKFAST!" she shouted through the dining room archway hoping to motivate them. Shortly thereafter, the rumbling of six feet running down the staircase startled Rommel out of an unusually sound sleep; an intrusion about which he was not the least bit happy.

Patricia watched the boys giggle and whisper as they began eating their breakfast. Barely noticing their behavior at first, she became certain that she was the subject of some inside joke. After several rounds of hushed conversation and finger pointing, Patricia could ignore them no longer.

"What is it you boys find so funny?" The thought of a spider on the back of her lavender housecoat might be humorous to her young ones but would be far less amusing to their mother.

"Ummm," Robert began, "are you cooking Dad's breakfast?" The other two boys laughed while pointing at the two sizzling pans on the stove. She glanced at the stove in dismay. The boys were right; Patricia was cooking two eggs over easy, bacon, sausage, and hash browns in the pan before her, as she had done countless mornings before. So established was this daily ritual that Jack's pronounced absence from the morning meal did not stop her from cooking the familiar culinary combination.

But if a blunder on her part brought the boys a little levity to start the day, as far as she was concerned it was worth it. Besides, by now it was quite clear that talking her way out of the obvious lapse was impossible. Therefore, Patricia chose to laugh along.

"I guess Rommel will eat good this morning, then, won't he?" she laughed to the boys.

She could enjoy the light ribbing from her sons, but the reminder that she was on her own proved far less entertaining. Before she had the chance to dwell on her new situation too much, the boys startled her with a strange request.

"Mom, can we tell our friends that Dad is in jail?," Shawn asked, with Russell nodding hopefully. "If they ask why, we can show them." Shawn pretended to slam Russell's head onto the kitchen table, giving a play-by-play as he mock-assaulted his brother. "Take *that*, stupid boss!" His mother was not amused by the re-enactment.

"Enough," she snapped. "I understand it is useless for me to tell you guys not to say anything, but could you please try not to make it sound like going to jail is such a great thing?" As she expected, the request fell on deaf ears.

"But Tyler will think that this is so cool, Mom." Russell said, looking forward to his role of being the day's best storyteller.

"All right you three, off to school," Patricia said, choosing not to comment on their friends' idea of "cool." As they headed toward the kitchen door, Patricia double-checked backpacks, books, and lunches. Today of all days, she did not want a call from the school. She kissed each of them on their way out, and could hear Shawn and Russell busy putting the details of their story together. Patricia could tell that Robert was less inclined to say anything, walking slightly behind the others to avoid getting involved.

As she walked back into the house, the sudden pall of overwhelming silence caught Patricia off guard. Rommel was asleep, as were Brandon and Richard. Normally, this would be a rare, sought after oasis that any mother coveted. But now her thoughts once again turned to how much she missed Jack. This was often their time together before Jack went to work. Some mornings the conversation was lively and risqué, other mornings hardly a word was spoken, but it was a comfortable silence.

Since the early days of their marriage, Patricia and Jack had agreed that nothing pressing or utilitarian would be discussed during their morning time. Jack knew how important this time was for Patricia and tried to violate that understanding as little as possible. All of the recent fighting and contention aside, it was in their early morning talks that formed many of the ties that held their marriage together.

Patricia was still angry about Jack's retribution against Billson and its aftermath on the family, but she also wondered if she had underestimated the daily stress her husband had been subjected to. The more she pondered the whole mess, the more she decided that she was equally upset with both Billson and Jack. Billson got the last laugh after making life miserable for Jack, and Jack enjoyed a pseudo-vacation in jail for 3 months, but Patricia was left to clean up the emotional, legal, and financial mess. Jack would get three square meals a day and would surely know many of the men in jail with him. He will have to follow rules, of course, but it was not as if he were out every day on a chain gang.

She scraped the leftovers and Jack's freshly cooked breakfast into Rommel's bowl, and the dog's head popped up as he waited for the call to come out into the kitchen. As Rommel bolted for the bowl of food, Patricia thought of how life had certainly never been dull with Jack. The recklessness and spontaneity that had attracted her to him years ago was still there. Expecting her husband to have settled down and become docile would have been like trying to have it both ways.

Patricia vowed to do her best to hold down the fort for the next 3 months. The challenge would be formidable, as heretofore she had had no involvement in the family's financial records, bills, banking, or repairs. All of these were Jack's responsibility, and Patricia had no interest in handling such things. She did not even really know how much Jack made. He gave her money each week to cover shopping and other household expenses. Patricia had no idea of the fire that she would now be thrown into.

Chapter 26
Patricia and the Next Battle

October 1968

Hardly a week had passed since Jack had gone to jail, and already the Christopher's phone was ringing off the hook. Calls came in all hours of the day and night, sometimes waking Richard shortly after Patricia put him down for a nap. The next hour would be spent trying to convince her son to go back to sleep. Explaining her circumstances garnered no sympathy from overbearing bill collectors. She had been barely able to get a handle on the scope of their finances before she was subjected to unyielding demands from people who would remain relentless until payment was made. Each day was the same. The sun had barely broken through the kitchen window and it started all over again.

Never had Patricia been so repeatedly spoken to as if she was worth nothing. Several calls left her physically shaken. One collector for the mortgage company called her a "dumb bitch." Her home was threatened with foreclosure; she was told her utilities would all be shut off and liens placed against her. Several collectors went so far as to come to the house demanding payment. Thankfully, Rommel saw to it that these attempts were short-lived, and the visits were not repeated.

Patricia could not fathom the mindset that permitted callers who had never met her—did not know her or anything about her—to speak with such venom.

"I just need time to figure out what we owe," Patricia pleaded during one call.

"I told you what you owe, Mrs. Christopher," came the unsympathetic response. "You just seem to be unwilling to fulfill your obligations."

This cold, heartless world had been foreign to Patricia for years. Now languishing in it for 10 days, along with the weight of her children's daily needs, Patricia began to feel as though the demands on her might be greater she could meet.

This particular morning, Patricia was surrounded by 10 to 15 bundles of bills, both previously paid and outstanding, covering the living room floor. The bundles were arranged by category, but the contents of each group were not in any chronological order. The imposing thickness of the stacks intimidated Patricia before she had even taken the rubber bands off. This conglomeration of paper represented Jack's filing system, such as it was.

While she sorted through this daunting assemblage of records, Patricia answered another call. The misguided collector was overzealous to retrieve an outstanding debt.

"Mrs. Christopher," he railed, sounding as if well versed in child welfare law, "if you cannot manage your financial affairs, do you think that the state will continue to trust you with the welfare of five children? We could start actions to have them become wards of the state. I want you to think of that when you look at your youngest..." There was a pause as if the collector was referring to written material regarding the Christopher household. "Richard. Now when can I expect to come to your home and pick up a check in the amount of $157.29?"

Anger surged through Patricia's body as she had never felt before. She had tried to be polite for days, to the point of sleeplessness, emotional breakdown, and physical exhaustion. Such oppression, Patricia could grit her teeth and bear. Threatening her children, however—using Patricia's own flesh and blood as a tool against her—sent her into a protective rage. Raw maternal anger and instinct filled Patricia with a power and control she could not remember experiencing.

"My children?" she raged. "My *children*? You *dare* to use my children against me? Listen to me, you bastard! I'll tell you when you can come down and get your money! Any time you that you want. By the time you knock, my dog will have your throat in his jaws. So I'll leave it up to you, but don't you *ever* threaten my children again!" She slammed the phone down, her arms shaking with rage. The release of frustration felt really good, and Patricia felt only slightly guilty for having cursed. Jack, no doubt, would have been proud of her.

That was the first taste Patricia had that surviving on her own while Jack was incarcerated would demand that her skin become a little thicker and her nails a little sharper. For the children's sake, remaining a doormat was not a luxury Patricia had the option of exercising.

The family bank account was tapped out, creditors were still calling, and now Billson was demanding the $500.00 restitution owed for his office repairs. Patricia had an idea but wondered if she could go through with it, and had no one she could talk to about it. She did not have the heart to tell Ginny what she was about to do, knowing that her beloved mother would pull out her checkbook to try to fix the problem. And yes, money would rectify this particular dilemma; that point was not in question. Bud and Ginny were always willing to help out in a pinch, and that was part of the problem. Patricia was so tempted to just pick up the phone and call them, certain that money would soon be on the way. But she settled in her heart that the time had come for that to stop. This was *her* family, *her* problem, and *her* responsibility.

Still, sitting in the car outside the pawn shop, she debated within herself whether to go in. Twirling the two-carat diamond ring in her fingers, she thought about how much knowing it would be sold would have broken her grandmother's heart. Patricia dreamed of one day giving it to her own daughter or granddaughter if she were to have one. Patricia tried to console herself by thinking that Grandmom would have done the same thing Patricia now contemplated doing, if it meant feeding her children. Patricia was confident that she could get $1500.00 for the ring. This would provide a small measure of breathing room even after settling up with Jack's former boss.

She remembered how beams of light had danced off of Grandmom's fingers as she wore the ring. Patricia could not remember a day in her childhood when Grandmom wasn't wearing her ring.

Present circumstances dictated that Patricia suppress her feelings of self-loathing for what she was about to do. Jack had given precious little thought to one other important implication of his violent departure from Kutter Metals: his outburst and subsequent assault on Winslow Billson had rendered him ineligible for unemployment compensation. Patricia could be certain that no financial help would be coming from the state offices. She was completely on her own as she tried to garner some means of providing for the family. Grandmother's disappointment from beyond the grave would have to be superseded by the needs of the five confused faces currently watching her. This ring could buy them a little time, time Patricia needed to formulate a longer range plan. She turned to hide her pained face from the boys as they wondered why they were sitting in a parking lot.

"Wait here and behave yourselves, boys. Listen to Robert. He is in charge. I'll be right back out." Robert relished his declared authority and scanned the faces of his siblings to ensure his mother's words were understood. Stepping out into the steady rain, Patricia left her coat in the car, too distraught to be bothered putting it on in the confines of their vehicle. Running the short distance to the front door, she entered the shop, finding the store filled with a potpourri of miscellaneous oddities. Ill lit and smelling of mold and cigarettes, the inside of the shop did not feel much different than the cold chilly weather outside. It looked like the home of a hoarder who had made a feeble attempt to organize. Patricia walked across what were presumed to have once been white linoleum tiles toward the long glass case that stretched across the back wall.

A tall, gaunt man in his thirties, though he looked much older and weathered, stood behind the waist-high glass case. His long greasy hair hung down over the counter as he leaned on the glass with his elbows. He had large droopy eyes with distinct bags underneath, the cumulative result of hard living. Eyeing Patricia from head to toe, the owner stood up as he addressed her.

"Hi, Sweetheart, I'm Neil. What can I do for you?"

"I want to sell this ring," Patricia said. Disconcerted by the man's greeting and smoker's voice, Patricia still stated her business as clearly as possible. Knowing her propensity for being perceived as naïve, Patricia also wanted to show him that she knew the ring's value. "I know that it has been appraised for $1500.00." She wanted to start off strong in the bargaining process to come.

"May I see it?" he asked, reaching for the ring. Flirtatiously placing his fingers across the back of Patricia's right hand, he removed the ring from her grasp with the other. Pulling her hand away but saying nothing, Patricia endured his nauseating gesture, just hoping to finish the transaction and leave.

"It's worth $1500.00, I agree," the owner mumbled as he looked at the ring through a jeweler's lens. "Of course, if I bought it for $1500.00 and sold it for $1500.00, my shop would be soon closed." He looked up and gave her a leering smile. "I'll give you $1100.00"

As repulsed as Patricia was by the owner's personal traits, she was surprised that the offer was reasonable and quickly agreed. That $1100.00 would be helpful, and Patricia wanted very much to get out of the store.

She was happy that the man wrote up the paperwork quickly. Patricia signed the agreement of sale, and Neil counted the money out on the glass countertop. Handing the stack of bills to Patricia, he startled her by grasping her hands in his.

"You know," he said, winking, "if you wanted to show me a little something, I could come up with another $100.00 pretty quick." He smiled at her again with his stained teeth.

"How dare you!" Tears streamed down Patricia's face as she ran out into the rain, clutching her money. Raindrops masked her crying as she jumped into the car and rested her head on the steering wheel, not wanting to upset her sons. Feeling violated and degraded was bad enough, but tearing at her soul was the knowledge that none of this would have happened if Jack were there with her. That walking piece of filth inside would not have opened his mouth. Perhaps she had taken for granted the security that was found whenever she was with Jack. Right now her protector was gone, and Patricia felt frighteningly vulnerable.

Noticing that her boys were beginning to get upset, Patricia pulled herself together. Thankfully none of them saw what had transpired, for surely they would have told their father.

"I'm sorry, kids; nothing is wrong. I'm just upset without your father here." This explanation seemed plausible and sufficed for all but Robert. He was sure that something in that pawn shop had upset his mother, but he had no idea what it was. Lacking any details, he had nothing to tell Jack at whatever future point he would see his father.

Arriving home, Patricia started a large pot of water for spaghetti. Simpler meals now constituted the new paradigm: pasta for the older boys, peanut butter and jelly for Richard. Notwithstanding the creep at the pawn shop, Patricia began to feel a little better. Settling up with Billson would have him out of their lives permanently. Filling the fridge and some of the cabinets with food was certain to be a morale boost not only for Patricia but the kids as well.

Patricia was also finding that the monumental task of juggling bills and creditors was not as daunting as it had been just a few weeks ago. Though Jack had the bills bundled into their respective groups (gas, electric, mortgage) the fact that they were not in chronological order made the stack useless. After sorting for more hours than she cared to remember, Patricia filed according to date, with all stacks in order and arranged in her new accordion file.

She'd also decided on another change that had drastically reduced the number of calls coming in from collection agencies. Each month, Jack would pay several bills off in full, leaving the remaining debts until the following month. When a steady cash flow was coming in each and every month, her husband's system worked fine, but current circumstances required a little more creative accounting. Patricia paid 25% of four bills instead of 100% of a single debt. The creditors were less inclined to call as long as they were getting something, taking this as a good faith attempt to meet the obligation.

Proud of her performance in light of the overwhelming administrative mess she was left with, Patricia liked to think that Jack would also be pleased. She had not seen her husband since the hearing, because demands on her time over the past few weeks made such a visit impossible. When she'd spoken with him over the phone, Patricia had clarified that her absence was not out of anger or resentment, and Jack took it in stride, telling his wife to come see him when circumstances permitted.

Chapter 27
Patricia and New Strategies

November 1968

By mid-November, six Sundays had passed since that day in court, and Patricia was thankful that they were at the halfway point in Jack's sentence. The past three Sundays had found Patricia and her family in church. Father O'Donnel's face lit up the first week that she returned to church with the boys. Though she did not try to explain this to him, Patricia had begun to feel that as many times as she had been brought to her knees begging for strength and intercession, coming to church on Sunday was the least she could do to say "thank you."

Patricia assumed a kind of quid pro quo relationship with God. She petitioned, God came through, she owed God a Sunday visit, and so the cycle continued. Breaking this arrangement, she thought, would be like throwing salt on an already gaping wound in her life. Even if pressed, Patricia could not explain the rationale for presuming that this was how God operated. The closest she could come to an explanation was that her mother had told her and her grandmother had told her mother and so on. No one ever thought to challenge the underlying premise.

However, whatever benefit and blessing Patricia found in Sunday mass was lost on her sons. Getting up early each week, putting on ill-fitting clothes, and sitting in hard pews for more than an hour was, to them, a useless, redundant exercise. And why on earth were they putting money into a basket when they were broke? It made no sense. Shouldn't members of the congregation have the option of withdrawing from the collection basket if they needed money? As far as the boys were concerned, this made perfect sense, though they never exercised the option.

As they sat in church on Sundays, Patricia's sons would dwell on the irony of singing while mired in the collective misery of their present circumstances. As to the boys' opinion of God, they felt He was at best indifferent and at worst vindictive. The boys' minds could not reconcile how a faithful, loving mother like Patricia deserved to be subjected to such oppression and heartache. For the benefit of their mother, the boys made it a point not to complain aloud too much on Sundays, but disapproval of all that accompanied the "day of rest" was still palpable.

Richard was the only male member of the family who felt a benefit of this recently revived ritual visit to St. Anne's. Being given milk and cookies in a room full of other toddlers to play with suited him just fine.

Too much had changed for the other boys to feel much inspiration. Sumptuous meals lovingly prepared had given way to hot dogs, lunch meat ends, and more pasta and rice than they cared to remember. Scant amounts of hamburger or tuna were thrown in to make you think it was a full meal. Who had ever heard of putting tuna in the oven?

A previous highlight of weekly trips to the supermarket was the chance for each boy to pick a favorite name-brand cereal, each with a prize inside. Generic boxes of cereal now filled the shopping cart. Most of the boxes did not even have a picture on the front, and there were certainly no prizes inside. Potato pancakes and oatmeal were now the only other breakfast items available. Mr. Mangold brought over whatever vegetables he could to help the family out.

The boys also suffered socially. The last thing they wanted to do was to tell their friends that they could not go bowling or to the movies because they couldn't afford it. Finally, after a long series of lame excuses, some of their friends began to catch on and stopped inviting them. Patricia tried to minimize the effects and thought that she had the perfect solution: roll pennies from the jar upstairs. Her sons were much less enthusiastic. The thought of placing nine rolls of pennies on the counter at the bowling alley, evoking stares from all around, was too much.

Some evidence was impossible to hide. Bud could only cover so much ground making repairs while Jack was gone, and the deteriorating condition of the house advertised a family in decline. One morning Patricia and the boys awoke to find that the water had been turned off, and the anxiety of leaving for school with ratty hair, no bath, and no water when they got home pitted the siblings against each other. They knew that neighborhood kids had begun talking about them, and the knowledge ate at them even if they had not heard the comments directly.

The cumulative stress of their circumstances began to show in contentious behavior. For the first two weeks of Jack's incarceration, the mention of his name was sufficient to keep the boys in line. As time wore on though, all of the brothers, especially Robert, began to explore the new boundaries of a home devoid of the usual repercussions for disobedience.

One Saturday, as she walked out to hang clothes on the line, Patricia smelled the familiar scent of cigarettes in the morning air. She found it almost pleasant at first, since it reminded her of Jack, but she quickly wondered how the smell could be so strong if Jack wasn't there to smoke. Turning the corner near the sidewalk, Patricia found Robert and Shawn crouched down on the other side of the fence, puffing away on their father's cigarettes. After a verbal tirade, Patricia instituted her own form of corrective punishment. She forced each boy to eat three Pall Malls as she stood and watched before sending them to their rooms. The resulting vomiting convinced the brothers not to test any more boundaries for the remainder of the day.

The boys were not the only members of the household to feel the strain. For Patricia, maintaining a positive outlook and trying to foster a sense of optimism for the kids grew increasingly difficult as the weeks wore on. She and the boys counted down the days until Jack's release, but financial realities threatened to dampen any exuberance as that date got closer. No consistent money was coming in, and though it would be good to have him home, Jack's impending release promised no solution to their troubles.

Selling the ring had brought some relief, but that money was now gone. Bud and Ginny offered help, but Patricia did not feel that was a viable solution. Besides, Jack would not want to give Ginny the satisfaction of holding a penny over his head. Payment for the mortgage was now a month behind, and satisfying this debt threatened to leave little for food or heat. With the winter months approaching, Patricia decided the mortgage would have to wait, but the very real prospect of losing their home loomed over her.

Jack may have believed that Ginny was not the most congenial person on the planet, but one thing could be said for certain: she took the bull by the horns when confronting adversity. In true fashion, once she understood that Patricia would not accept her financial help, she approached her about the money troubles in a different way.

"Patricia, do you remember the Raggedy Ann and Andy flip dolls that I taught you to make? I am sure they would sell very well at the flea mart."

Ginny loved the Columbus Indoor Mart and sold items there most weekends, or at the Englishtown market in fall. They were limited to the indoor market this time of year, but the venue was still packed each weekend with people checking out the multitude of rented booths. Ginny sold homemade apple dolls that looked like old people. She also sold flower arrangements, needlepoint, various craft items, candles, and homemade jams.

The Raggedy Ann and Andy dolls were one of the pricier items at between $50 and $75. The finely crafted dolls stood 48" or more. Raggedy Ann could be inverted to reveal Raggedy Andy in a different outfit.

Patricia considered her mother's suggestion. The dolls were extremely labor intensive to produce, but might bring in some much needed resources. Best of all, Patricia did not need go to the flea mart herself, as Ginny could sell the dolls for her.

Willing to bank on the chances of a good return on her investment, Patricia spent $75 of her remaining funds on material, batting, and other items needed to begin production. A feeling of dread came over Patricia as she envisioned the arduous task of crafting the doll's curly red hair hour after lonely hour. The pastime formerly pursued as a quiet pleasure now held more foreboding stakes. However, with no other cash flow for at least the next four weeks. Patricia had no other options.

Over the next month, Patricia's soft, gentle features began to reflect the harsh realities that had now beset her. Tired eyes met the boys each morning. The beautiful hair that normally hung in soft locks soon bore the lines of fingers frequently run through it in either concentration or exasperation. Her usually graceful steps soon resembled those of a marathon runner straining to complete the last mile. Few callings to persevere match a mother's sense of duty to her children. Accordingly, Patricia plodded forward day by day.

Chapter 28
The Christophers and a Fragile Christmas Peace

Christmas Day 1968

"Oh my God, Mom, a bike! It's a freakin' three speed!"

"Language, Shawn," Patricia calmly cautioned. "I'm glad that you like it. How do you like the color?" Patricia already knew the answer to her questions, but she wanted to hear the excitement in her son's voice. The cobalt blue bike shimmered with metallic flecks. Shawn was rarely this verbal about his enthusiasm, but this was not the Christmas that any of the boys had anticipated.

Only the night before, Robert had given the boys a late night admonition to like or pretend to like "whatever Santa leaves for you."

"No complaining," he'd added sternly. He didn't have to tell them that his motive was to mitigate disappointment for everyone during what promised to be a bleak Yuletide celebration.

Their surprise was intense then, when they descended the stairs Christmas morning to find piles of wrapped presents in the living room. Each mound was affixed with a placard bearing the child's name. Initially hovering anxiously over their respective piles, the boys started out with a well-orchestrated present opening, but waiting to open presents in turn predictably devolved into a gift-opening frenzy, with shouts of unrestrained joy blessing Patricia's ears.

Gleaming and twinkling lights from the finely contoured tree in the corner reflected off of Shawn's blue bike. A jumble of rechargeable race cars, trains, and a wagon bore evidence of the elation of five boys who had not been this happy in quite some time. As she watched them,

169

Patricia silently thanked her parents for giving her children their glad hearts back.

"I am not offering you a loan or trying to give you money," Bud had insisted 3 weeks prior, when he had instructed her to compile a list of toys for each boy. "This is our present to you."

Nothing was to be mentioned of their grandparents' involvement. Ginny, Bud, and Patricia waited until the boys begrudgingly went to bed at 9 pm Christmas Eve, dreading the lackluster morning to come, before shuttling in the wrapped presents. Christmas gifts were brought in all ready to go, as Bud and Ginny intended. Bud graciously made two trips from Pennsauken. While waiting for him to return, Ginny and Patricia decorated the tree and living room, and with hushed voices, the dining room. Ginny could not help herself but to bring all of the food needed for breakfast as well.

No complaints were heard from the boys as they left for church Christmas morning. Robert and Russell were even inspired enough to sing one of the hymns. Standing in church with her parents and frighteningly well-behaved brood let Patricia free herself, relax, and enjoy the day. Should trouble come tomorrow, she would deal with it. Today, she would rejoice. The Christopher house was once again filled with laughter as had not been heard since their troubles began the day of Jack's accident.

Jack's reaction to hearing of his in-law's shopping spree was, much to Patricia's delight, just as happy as hers had been. There was no objection to Bud and Ginny's gesture and he raised no concerns about owing them repayment. Her husband had even seemed to get choked up as Patricia visited him. Patricia was careful not to make too much of his emotional display, especially when other prisoners were only feet away.

Focusing on details of the boys' reactions, Jack's excitement touched Patricia's heart. She could hear how much her husband missed being home and how much he wanted to see the boys. "What did Shawn say when he saw the bike? Tell Robert I'll help him set the train village up. Maybe we could run over to the hobby shop and pick out some buildings for the platform. I can imagine Richard loading every toy he has into that wagon."

"It will be good to have you home Jack. Oh, by the way, Dad even bought an enormous chew bone for Rommel," Patricia grinned. She knew how much Jack loved and missed his dog.

For his part, Jack was now more anxious than ever to return to the family. He wished that he could reach through the glass window and hold his wife. There was consolation in counting down the last few days of his sentence.

"Pat, I'm sorry…for all of this. I know that so much has fallen on you and that you deserved none of it. I can't say I've changed completely, or for good, but I love you and don't want you to go through anything like this again."

As he spoke, Patricia watched Jack repeatedly close his fist tightly and then open his hand back up with fingers outstretched. She had not seen this habit before.

"Are you ok, Hon?" she asked with concern in her voice.

"It's this damn numbness," he replied. "I must be sleeping on it or something; who knows. This place is not renowned for its accommodations."

"Maybe you should get it looked at while it's free," she said. Her suggestion was met with a polite but unenthusiastic answer that told her that the chances of Jack making an appointment were nil.

"Time's up, Mrs. Christopher." The officer's announcement ended any further goading for Jack to see the doctor. Patricia put her hand to the glass and Jack matched it with his.

"Merry Christmas, Jack. I'll see you in a few days, and this will be all over," she said with a smile." Jack smiled back.

"Do I get my present when I get home?" His wife knew where that mind of his was taking him.

"Let's see if you can be a good boy first, and we'll see." Patricia shot Jack a sultry glance that she rarely used outside of their home. As Patricia turned from view, Jack was reminded of all that waited for him at home.

Recalling one of his other extended stays in police custody, Jack remembered how then, as now, Patricia had faithfully stood by him. There had been some differences, though. For one thing, the brig at McGuire Air Force Base had been considerably less friendly than his hometown jail. He'd spent 6 months there rather than 3, but maybe the reasons were not too dissimilar. Jack thought of his vitriolic hatred at the very sight of Lt. Burns, the supply officer Jack had served under in the Air Force; not that he was likely to see him again soon. The last time he had laid eyes on the Lieutenant, Jack had knocked him out cold and left him with a broken jaw.

Jack did not feel any guilt, since he'd decided long ago that Lt. Burns deserved the punch, probably as much as Billson did. From the very beginning, Jack and Lt. Burns had disliked each other. Lt. Burns had had it in his mind that Airman Christopher was going to spend his entire enlistment as a mess cook and mockingly told Jack as much. Jack would have none of it and went AWOL until his father convinced him that he had little option but to turn himself in.

Three days back from having been AWOL for several months, the Air Force returned Jack to Lt. Burns, the very same officer that had driven the young airman to jump the fence and go on the run. Lt. Burns, elated at his subordinate's return, saddled Jack with every greasy, slimy, unpleasant task that he could think of. When his superior intentionally knocked over a drum of fryer grease so that Jack had to clean it up, Jack had had enough.

Patricia's faithfulness stood as resilient now as it had in his days at McGuire though they'd only been dating at the time. Patricia took the long bus ride from Stratford to Lakehurst every weekend, a full day's commitment.

Thinking of Patricia reminded Jack of another difference: this time around, his actions had more far-reaching implications. Truth be told, the first week in jail for Jack had been somewhat relaxing. He and his cellmates got along fairly well. There was a lot of card playing, smoke breaks, and workouts. Ironically, each inmate was now insulated from the outside problems that had landed them in jail. But hardly had his first few nights in jail passed, before Jack began to consider the breadth of the imposition on his family. Further, within the first month, the recreational novelty had worn off and Jack's thoughts turned to leaving this mundane, orchestrated existence.

Now only a few short days away from freedom, Jack was determined to make amends to Patricia. Finding a job would be his first priority. While visiting Jack , Patricia had been very careful not to expound on how dire the family's financial circumstances were, since she saw no benefit to it. Jack understood, and repairing the family's financial insolvency and any scars in his relationship with Patricia would be the first steps needed in returning the Christophers to normalcy.

Chapter 29
Jack and the Second Homecoming

Dec. 29, 1968

Rommel's tail wagged feverishly back and forth while he trotted in place at the foot of the stairs. He maintained his assigned position, but his front paws danced up and down, as a slight whimper highlighted his growing restlessness. Abandoning his regimented bearing, he let out a single, crisp bark as he heard the car door close from the road outside.

Jack was home! The frost on the living room window obscured Patricia's view of the approaching figure now coming down the walkway, but she did not need visual confirmation. Rommel's reaction signaled the fruition of Patricia's long awaited hope! Scarcely had her husband walked through the door when Patricia latched her arms tightly around his neck as she buried her face in his chest. Hugging his wife with equal fervor, Jack celebrated how much nicer this moment felt than the last time he and Patricia were in the kitchen together.

"I missed you so much!" Patricia cried as she pressed her wet cheek against his. Jack pulled away enough to take her face in his hands while looking with unbridled love into her eyes. Just outside the still-open back door, the morning sun glistened off of the untouched snow in the back yard, casting a golden glow onto the wooden fence.

"Pat, I can't tell you how much I've missed you and how proud I am of you for holding everything together," he said, looking in her eyes. "I promise you, this will never happen again."

Caressing his wife's cheek softly with the back of his index finger, Jack sought an answer in Patricia's eyes. She could tell that this was not a cold, pre-staged formality that Jack was walking through. Jack's mannerisms did not demand an immediate response. After three months, he sought to understand where Patricia's heart was. "Are we...OK?" he asked.

Patricia could not remember the last time Jack had sought any type of affirmation regarding their relationship. Though he did not implicitly say so, she heard the "I'm sorry" in his voice, and that was all she really needed. Now she just wanted to move on.

"We're OK, Jack; now please go say hello to your dog before he has a heart attack."

Rommel was by now talking to his master in low guttural growls. Though ever obedient, he had not left his station near the stairs. As Jack turned the corner into the dining room, Rommel pulled his ears back and lowered his head to the ground. Playfully pressing the left side of his face to the floor, Rommel gazed up at Jack from his right eye. As Jack was halfway to the steps, he gave the command that his loyal friend had waited months to hear: "Rommel, come."

Rommel bolted towards him. When they met, Jack buried his face in the beloved dog's neck and tussled the scruff with both hands. Only now did Jack appreciate how much he missed his dog. "Good boy, good boy," Jack repeated as he held out his powerful arm for the dog to mouth playfully.

The boys had heard Rommel fidgeting and growling, but at first did not care enough to investigate further. Only after hearing their father's voice were the boys aware of the impetus for the dog's excitement. Soon shouts of "Dad's home! Oh, my God, Dad's home!" came from upstairs, and frantic footsteps could be heard as the boys spread the word from bedroom to bedroom.

A thunderous procession approached the top of the stairs. Jack looked up to see three of the four eldest boys racing down the steps like firemen responding to an alarm call. With each son jostling for position, Shawn gained the lead, but only by a few steps.

"You're back," Shawn cried as he embraced Jack, the two of them falling over. Russell and Brandon gang-tackled Jack, crying with joy.

"You don't have to go back, do you?" Russell asked after a spirited bout of wrestling.

Jack sat on the dining room floor, his hands propping him up from behind as he listened to the boys recount the previous 90 days.

"I got a new bike," Shawn said.

"My friends said you are the coolest dad ever. None of their fathers ever went to jail." Russell wore Jack's stature with his friends as a badge of honor.

"Well, I don't plan on getting any cooler, Russell,'" his father joked as he playfully wrestled with the boys.

"Mom makes us go to church now, Dad," Russell said. "Do we still have to do that?" Jack was not about to deal with such matters his first day home.

"If your mother says go to church, then you go to church," he answered.

Noticeably absent from the reunion was Robert. Using the need to go to the bathroom as a pretext, he had let the other boys run downstairs. Certainly, he was happy that Jack was home and out of jail, he thought to himself as he sat on the edge of the bathtub. He was though, not keen on running downstairs and wrestling on the floor. He could hear the others yelling and thumping around the dining room. He didn't know why he didn't want to join them. Maybe he had been banged around enough already.

Pangs of guilt overcame him as he slid down the side of the tub onto the tile floor, trying to resist the urge to cry. *How horrible I must be*, he thought. His father was finally home and here he was trying to decide whether to be happy. He loved his father. He did believe he was pleased by Jack's return, but he was worried, too. Would Patricia tell his father of his disobedience while Jack was away? Was today's rejoicing a brief pause before certain retribution?

Not wanting his absence to appear overly conspicuous, Robert washed and dried his face. Running down to the dining room, he too exclaimed, "Dad, you're home!" and threw himself around his father's

176

neck. After exchanging greetings with his father, Robert slowly retired to the background, content to let his brothers have the limelight.

Patricia watched through the doorway as she sat on the living room couch, content to hear laughter in the house again. She was more than happy to allow the boys their roughhousing moment.

Patricia and Jack allowed the kids to set the agenda for the rest of the day. The boys showed Jack all their Christmas gifts and they ventured out onto the untouched powder for an afternoon snowball fight. Both parents wanted the children to feel that life was getting, as much as possible, back to normal though they themselves were admittedly not quite sure what the new "normal" would look like.

As the day wound down and the newness of Jack's homecoming wore off, the boys drifted off to other rooms, and Patricia and Jack were left alone to catch up on time lost. To Patricia's surprise, Jack did not shift the conversation to the nuts and bolts of more utilitarian matters. She understood that he was, by nature, a get-it-done, no-nonsense head of their house and that avoiding such discussions took concerted effort. Patricia found Jack's self-imposed restraint endearing. Letting her do most of the talking about how she felt and what her hopes were signaled a change in Jack. She did not know how long it would last, but Patricia drank in his undivided attention while she had it.

Patricia expected that Jack would want to have sex that first night, but she did not expect him to take such care in their love-making. Blissfully for Patricia, Jack made the night—as the day had been—about her needs. The small talk late night moments just lying together with the house still were more than she expected. They even got up around midnight to share a late night snack in the kitchen. When Jack finally drifted off to sleep, Patricia looked over at him and felt safe and secure again.

She did not forget her own accomplishments of the last months. How much of the bolder, more resilient Patricia should remain out of the bottle was a question that she was not yet ready to answer. For tonight, she was glad that for the first time in months, the sheets on the other side of the bed were once again rumpled.

Today had been a better day than Patricia had hoped for. Not only was Jack home, but he had shown a rare conciliatory side. They had even shared an optimism that the family will prevail over its present tribulations. She prayed that her children's lives could return to some semblance of normalcy. Patricia had not heard them laugh like today in quite some time. *Children deserve the freedom to be insulated from the burdensome weight of their parent's' struggles*, she thought to herself.

As she wondered how long this newfound synergy between them would last, Patricia felt the realist in her surface. *Oh, if it were possible for Jack to remain so approachable and optimistic every day! How much easier things would be for all of them!* Deep down Patricia knew that it was only a matter of time. Even the kids understood that their father could not stay this way for too long. Even if he wished a lasting peace, the ramparts of Jack's heart and mind had suffered too many cannon shot to declare it.

Patricia feared that not knowing when the optimism would end, and the wounded, brooding Jack return would deny any permanent calm from presiding over the Christopher's home. She wondered if they were destined to return to those days when she and the boys felt like someone walking across a wooden suspension bridge. Hanging onto the shaky ropes, you hope for the best, not knowing when a plank may give way under the pressure imposed on it. Looking across the wide expanse you just hope to make it to the other side without crashing onto the jagged rocks below. At best, you arrive, shaken, on the other side of the bridge knowing full well that the next day is sure to bring another expanse before you.

Patricia stopped her train of thought with a conscious will. She decided that she would not allow her fears to ruin the day. Pulling herself closer to Jack, Patricia enjoyed a sound, peaceful sleep for the rest of the evening.

Chapter 30
Robert and Shawn, and Comrades in Arms

Dec. 30, 1968

Sitting on the front steps enjoying an early morning cigarette, Jack watched as Rommel rolled on the front lawn in the freshly fallen snow. Rejuvenated, Jack felt wonderful after sleeping in his own bed. What a change from lying for three months on a mattress that had probably been there for 20 years. While Jack began shoveling the car and driveway out from the weekend snow, Rommel made the most of his rare vacation from guard duty, jumping through deep drifts and chasing an occasional bird until it took refuge in the branches of a barren tree.

Anxious to get back to work and aware of the need for cash coming into the house, Jack was not about to waste any time. Tomorrow would be New Year's Eve, and any attempts to secure a job then would be pointless. Today was the last day businesses might be even remotely interested in work-related matters for several days.

Jack remained optimistic, but this morning he had begun to notice the changes inside and outside the house that mirrored the increasing seriousness of the family's financial plight, and that the reunion with his family had initially obscured. Although the inside was still generally neat and tidy, the exacting attention to detail Patricia usually maintained was no longer there, though he recognized that it could hardly have been expected to be, given the pressures already placed on Patricia. Outside, the chipped paint and hanging gutters were a far cry from the showcase building that he had maintained less than a year ago.

Nonetheless, Jack was hopeful. Stratford was, after all, *his* town. Considering the number of business owners that Jack knew and had grown up with, not to mention the contacts he had in town with any number of contractors, he was confident he would find work. One of the advantages of having lived in this small town for so many years, Jack thought, was that he had no lack of friends, and friends were always willing to help you out in a pinch.

His snow clearing completed, Jack got Rommel inside and saw to getting him dried off and back on station. "Pat, I'm leaving," he called into the kitchen where Patricia was cycling the boys through bowls of Maypo and slices of peanut butter toast.

"I'm sure your job hunt will go well, Jack," Patricia said, wiping her hands on a dishtowel as she came out to wish him luck. "Just remember, it may not be the first place or even the second place that you apply to. Stay positive." Patricia paused and placed her hand on Jack's shoulder as she smiled at him. "Oh, and Jack, no applications at the Full Bloom Florist," she quipped while playfully snapping the towel at her husband. Jack smiled at the joke, but he also understood the underlying message. Patricia wanted him to head out on a lighter note, hoping a more jovial mood might make for a better first impression with potential employers.

"I'm going to stop over Dad's when I finish up. I'll call you from his house and see you tonight," he said in answer. Patricia said a quick prayer as he kissed her and headed out the door.

Robert and Shawn went upstairs and started putting on their snowsuits. Today in particular, they did not dare risk putting them on in the kitchen. The noise they generated as the arms and legs rubbed together would be a dead giveaway and would almost certainly trigger an inquisition from Russell and Brandon.

As the oldest, Robert was used to the pattern: "Where are you guys going? When are you coming back? Why can't we go too?" The litany of questions was almost always followed by a petition to their mother, which would initiate the following request from Patricia: "Why can't you take Russell and Brandon with you? It won't kill you to invite them."

As far as Robert and Shawn were concerned however, it would kill them. With four other boys and two girls, they had formed the "Double Digit Club" over the past summer, as they and their friends took turns

180

lamenting the task of dragging younger siblings around with them. Thus, the club rules were simple and strictly enforced: 1. No one under age 10 is allowed to join or visit. 2. Blab about the club and you're out. 3. Betray the secrecy of what is said in the club, and you're out. 4. When it is your turn to bring snacks to the meeting, bring them. Since the most important tenant was that they did not want to hang around with anyone under 10 years old, Russell and Brandon did not make the cut.

Actually, most of the group wouldn't have minded Russell. After all, he was tough and, by all measure, pretty cool.

The group had unanimously decided that no exceptions could be made. Brandon, on the other hand, never stood a chance of gaining membership. The consensus among the group was that he was too young and dorky.

Finishing their preparations, Robert and Shawn carefully moved from the bedroom to the top of the staircase. They peered past the angled staircase ceiling, but saw no sign of their younger brothers. Neither Robert nor Shawn could do anything to mitigate the squeaking of their rubber boots as they slowly descended.

"Listen," Robert put up his hand like a platoon commander signaling a halt. The tinkling of dishes could be heard as Brandon helped his mother clean up from breakfast. This activity only solidified their belief that Brandon was a shameless kiss-up. They saw no signs of Russell, but assumed that he was also in the kitchen, *not* helping.

The creak of the wooden steps, the squeak of the rubber boots, the creak of the wooden steps, the creak of the rubber boot—the pattern was agonizing. For what seemed like forever, the boys inched down the steps, finally reaching the front door. Rommel gave them a routine sniff, but seemed generally uninterested in them after his morning romp. Finally reaching the front door, the pair gently closed both the wooden and storm doors behind them.

"Yeah, baby," Robert congratulated Shawn as they patted each other on the back. They turned left out of the front door and made their way to the corner of the property. Once at the next corner, they could look across the street at the object of their planning efforts: the Bat House.

The Bat House was an old abandoned two-story stone block house that sat in the center of the large, overgrown lot across the next street. Worn and weary looking, its windows long since removed or damaged, the house's side profile faced the Christopher house. None of the town's residents, except perhaps Avery Mangold, could remember the last time it had been occupied. In most months, weeds and tall grasses covered the entire yard and obscured any signs of a walkway. At night, bats could be seen flying in and out of the top floor windows, which is how the abandoned house with the crumbling gray mortar façade got its name.

Robert and Shawn did not remember who first realized that the first floor of the Bat House was the perfect location to congregate. The Bat House met all of their needs. It was secretive, secluded, local, and accessible. Long-abandoned furniture in what was presumed to have been the living room made it all the more inviting, and since the end of the summer, the Double Digits had been meeting surreptitiously once a week whenever possible.

With its proximity to their house, Robert and Shawn understood that walking onto the lot and straight up to the house was ill advised. Fresh tracks in the snow and flattened strands of the tall grass that poked through it would surely leave a path for the ever pursuing Russell to follow. Instead, they crossed the street and continue down Stratford Avenue to the far side of the dilapidated property. There, they ducked into the woods adjacent to the old house and doubled back through the field and into the house without leaving a telltale path.

By the time the brothers arrived, most of the group was already there. Denise Davis had started a small fire in the fireplace, mindful that anything too much larger would give them away.

No particular agenda was initiated on the arrival of the group's members. No minutes were taken, and no important measures were voted on. Even if someone had thought to propose an itinerary, it would have been summarily dismissed. Instead, several decks of cards, a Twister game, and a Monopoly game comprised the standard means by which the group entertained themselves.

Robert, like most of the others—though no one ever articulated the thought—felt a sense of ease here that eluded him at home. With his friends, he didn't need to parse every word he spoke. In fact, Robert was the dominant voice in the collective. Shawn, insecure as ever, noticed this shortly after the friends began gathering. In this small world of the members' own creation, Jack Christopher held no sway. No "yes, sir" or "no, sir" weighed down their every move. In the Bat House, each inductee could be him or herself. Though no one knew it, perhaps not even Robert himself, the Double Digits had been what carried Robert through the long difficult months since his father's accident.

Being the oldest son posed a burden on Robert for as long as he could remember. Jack permitted his son little or no room for error. While this was true for all of his sons, Robert felt the greatest retribution for an infraction. After all, Robert was the first son to represent the family name in a town where everyone knew the Christophers. Any lack in ability, aptitude, or execution on Robert's part was construed as a negative reflection of his parents and the family name. Jack took this very personally, and was quick to respond.

One particular means of correction had plagued Robert for years. Though not a formally trained academic, Jack was incredibly adept at math. Trigonometry, calculus, and physics all came easily to him. Jack seemed to believe that if he was proficient, it stood to reason that his sons would also excel. Jack would oversee and quiz Robert in his grade school math homework. Standing behind him, Jack rested his hand against the back of Robert's head and asked homework questions.

When Robert answered incorrectly, Jack let him know with a sharp smack on the back of his head. Though to Jack's mind, such methods of instruction were perfectly logical—negative repercussions for mistakes will inevitably reduce the number of mistakes—Robert's head, body, and heart had carried the scars of this flawed philosophy of instruction.

The designation of "man of the house" during Jack's incarceration compounded the stress upon him. The formidable weight of this responsibility put a continuous added burden on Robert's heart. The specifics of what such a title meant, or the expectations it carried, were at best ambiguous. Robert was never sure what the criteria were; as a result, he battled against the constant fear that he was somehow not measuring up to the task.

Thus Robert, perhaps more than anyone, saw the beauty of the Bat House. Robert loved that the Bat House expectations were few, clear, and reasonable. Here, Robert could be "Robert Christopher" and not "Jack Christopher's son," though even he was uncertain of what such liberation would be like for him.

Shawn, meanwhile, set his expectations considerably lower. He was just glad to be allowed in the Bat House at all. Though Shawn could not have articulated it, there existed a kind of fellowship among the Christopher brothers and their friends. All were looking to get away from something, and at the same time for something to run to. Constant discussions belaboring the point were unneeded. The desire for acceptance and grace prevailing at the Bat House was so common among its fellows as to be as understood as it was unspoken.

This meeting began as each did, with a sense of anticipation as the members discovered what each had brought from home.

"Alright, everybody, pony up and show what you've got," Billy Holland suggested as he pulled a bag of Hershey Kisses from his Harley jacket. One by one, the others followed suit. Heather Proscow, ever the hair–flipping gum chewer, true to form, laid two big packs of bubble gum on the table. David George had convinced his mother to make brownies by telling her they were for the wrestling team. The sheer audacity of this plan garnered much praise though any surprise regarding his contribution was lost with the aroma emanating from his paper bag.

"Oh shit, I forgot," Denise Davis said as she rolled up her flannel sleeves to the elbows.

An awkward silence fell over the group as they looked back and forth at one another, wondering how to address this transgression. Robert's face became serious as he approached her, but before he could chastise her, Denise cut him off.

184

"Ahh, burned, dumbass; I'm just messing with you," she laughed. She reached into her solid green Army jacket and pulled out a box of salt water taffy. "Compliments of Granny; she just doesn't know it yet."

After a few minutes of teasing Robert for behaving so seriously, the group got back to contributions. Max Schuler's contribution was somewhat obvious. Several bottles of Coke protruding from his down ski jacket left no doubt that he had met his obligation. Meanwhile, Benny Larosa shifted in his chair slightly outside the main group, seeming uncomfortable. Benny was Shawn's friend, but he was well liked among the group. Living above the laundromat that his mother managed, Benny experienced a lot in life every bit as tough as the Christophers'. Knowing his circumstances, the group would be less harsh if he was unable to add to the group's kitty. Benny would avoid the tongue lashing Robert had almost given Denise.

"It's ok if you're a little short this time, Benny," he said to the younger boy. "We'll make you the banker in Monopoly."

Benny sought to correct their error. "I could not stop to get food," he said, "but I did bring something."

Benny's answer sounded anti-climatic to the group, but they humored him.

"What have you got?" Robert asked. Benny stood and started to unload handfuls of quarters from his bulging pants pockets. The metallic disks had been the reason for his constant shifting.

"Oh my gosh, Benny, where did you get all of this?" Denise asked.

"My mother left the coinbox key out, so I took the change out of a dryer downstairs while she was getting a shower. I hope that this can cover me for awhile."

Like the Christopher brothers, Benny saw the Bat house as something of a lifeline, even if the rest did not realize how important being accepted into this exclusive enclave was to him. If keeping in good standing meant stealing from the Laundromat, Benny felt it was worth it.

"Benny, I think it's safe to say that you are covered forever!" Billy assured him. "We'll keep the money in the vase on the mantle above the fireplace so that everyone knows where it is until we need it. That just leaves Frick and Frack to chip in," Billy mocked, jokingly referring to Robert and Shawn. Only one item was needed per household, as the group had agreed early on that requiring both Shawn and Robert to snatch something could jeopardize the whole group.

"Wow, matches,"…someone muttered with feigned enthusiasm as Robert pulled a pack of matches from his pocket.

"In case you haven't noticed, there's a fire in the fireplace, but thanks, Robert," David commented, throwing in an extra dig.

"Well, if you have matches, you might as well have these…" Robert paused for dramatic effect before pulling two packs of Pall Mall cigarettes from his coat pocket. To most present, Robert might as well have produced the Holy Grail. Only David George, who lived for football and wrestling, was completely uninterested in the packs. For the others, only lack of opportunity had prevented them from trying the habit, and only Robert and Shawn had ever actually smoked.

"Robert, are you crazy? Dad is going to *kill* us," Shawn said with a rising panic. Preferring not to bicker in front of friends, Robert glared at Shawn to tell his brother he was killing the moment.

"Relax, Shawn," Robert warned. "Dad is never going to remember how many packs he had. He bought the carton before he was arrested. Just change your clothes as soon as you get home, and tell Mom and Dad we went to the bowling alley—everybody there smells like cigarettes. Everybody save a piece of gum for the walk home."

Even Shawn was surprised how well Robert had thought through covering his tracks. His brother's remedy for getting caught eased Shawn's fears.

The rest of the day was spent doing what most typical kids on the early threshold of their teens do. Games, gossip, stupid jokes, and idle banter filled the passing hours. Finally, the fading sunlight struggling to pierce through the remaining dirty windows on the west face of the house signaled the end of the Double Digit's meeting. The group heaped snow from just outside the door into the fireplace, and puffs of steam and ash plumed into the air. The members left the Bat House at 5-minute intervals to limit the possibility of drawing unwanted attention. The

186

games and the vase of quarters could safely remain behind. No one felt like carrying them, and the group liked the idea of marking the house as their own territory.

Robert and Shawn were left to close up.

"That was fun, Robert," Shawn commented. "Do you think I did ok?"

"You did fine Bro, don't over think it," Robert assured him, thinking that Shawn worried too much, always concerned that he had said or done something stupid or offensive.

Shawn was the first to realize that something was not right as they crossed the street toward their house.

"Robert, why is your baseball glove in the snow?" he asked.

The two stopped and looked at the snow directly beneath their bedroom window. Robert's brand new glove was joined in the frozen drift by his baseball trophy, pillow, several of his comic books, and an old GI Joe action figure.

"Russell!" the brothers shouted in unison. Gathering the items, they ran into the house and up to their room. Once inside the bedroom door, they found more comic books scattered on the floor, Robert's bed disheveled, and his tooth brush floating in the fish tank. Russell was lying on his stomach on the bed, reading a comic book.

"Russell, what the hell are you doing, you jerk!?" Robert shouted as loud as he dare while reminding himself not to draw Patricia's attention.

"Maybe you guys won't ditch me next time," Russell answered without looking up. "Where did you go anyway?" He started sniffing the air with his nose and finally sat up and stared at his brothers. "You guys stink. How would you like me to tell Mom that you were smoking?"

Startled by their brother's threat, Robert and Shawn sought to diffuse what was becoming a potentially explosive situation. Shawn spoke to Russell in a much softer tone.

"Look, Russell, we always have fun doing stuff together. I'm sorry, but where we went is just for big kids." He reached into his pocket and pulled out the half-full bag of Hershey Kisses he had brought home from the Bat House.

"If you don't say anything to Mom, you can have this bag of kisses," Shawn said temptingly.

"AND we will play with you outside until it gets dark," Robert added. Neither inducement alone would have secured Russell's silence, but adding a bag of chocolates all to himself to the chance to play with his older brother in the snow sealed the deal.

As the three spent the next hour playing outside, Russell was oblivious to his older brothers' ulterior motive. Were they to discard dry, smelly clothes in the basement, Patricia was sure to smell the smoke. The bowling alley cover was not a bad story, but not guaranteed. A more-secure solution was to ensure that Patricia saw them playing with Russell in the snow. Sure, they would get yelled at for not wearing snowsuits, and they might also freeze half to death, but the larger issue of the stinky clothes was resolved without a problem.

Chapter 31
Jack and the Difficult Repatriation

The Same Day

Finally feeling wind at his back, Jack set out with a spring in his step, hopeful that the beginnings of a new career were right around the corner. He felt that, relatively speaking, things were looking up. The crunch of the previous evening's snow beneath his feet was much preferable to the cold, painted concrete floors of the county jail. Even the inconvenience of the traffic in front of him paled in comparison to the iron bars through which he'd recently viewed the world. Infused with a feeling of renewal by the approaching New Year's holiday, Jack was ready to meet the day's challenges head on.

Patricia had suggested that Jack consider applying for a position with the post office. Jack was a veteran, and had a keen memory. Perhaps, she thought, a postal route would suit him. After some thought, he agreed that walking a delivery route instead of being stuck behind a machine all day, might not be a bad idea.

Surprised that anyone was applying for a position this close to the New Year's holiday, the branch supervisor at the local office was initially polite but noncommittal. Jack was surprised however, when the official's disposition changed from accommodating to snarky after viewing Jack's credentials. His dishonorable discharge from the service removed any helpful feeling that the veteran in the postal uniform may have initially felt towards Jack.

For his part, Jack tried to explain that though he had struck an officer, he believed the real reason for the less than impressive discharge was actually a medical issue. Jack tried to explain that he was forced out after an accident to avoid medical liability on the part of the Air Force. Jack grew more frustrated by the feeling that the more he tried to clarify the Air Force situation, the less that the postal official wanted to hear.

"Conjecture does not overrule documentation, Mr. Christopher. We do not hire dishonorably discharged service members. I'm sorry," the man finally said. Jack felt this dismissal was only slightly better than, "Don't let the door hit you in the ass on your way out."

Moving on to other prospects, Jack found much the same outcome at every interview. A local cannery, several construction sites, a rival sheet metal shop, and even the hardware store expressed little interest in giving Jack a job. Instead, Jack found himself spending hour after hour feeling helpless in front of people he did not even know, parsing every word he spoke so as not to offend them. Years had gone by since Jack Christopher knew the subservient feeling of needing to beg for employment.

Most prospective employers had been polite, but even under the best of conditions, the humiliation grew intolerable. Jack was peppered with endless questions, tests, forms, and at times, intrusions into areas of his life that had nothing to do with the issue at hand. Nine stops, nine applications filled out, nine explanations of where he saw himself in 5 years. What Jack really wanted to tell them was that he was too damn busy trying to find food for this month to develop a 5-year plan. Jack just kept smiling because he knew that he needed them much more than they needed him.

Some interviewers seemed to enjoy delving into these personal areas more than others. The pasty little bookworm in front of him at one stop, for example, had the power to decide whether his family would eat, or if the utilities would be paid before being shut off. Worse yet, after all the interrogation and paperwork, Jack was told they were not hiring right now, but his name would be on "the list". Jack was sure that the interviewer would then go to lunch and brag about how he had held a carrot in front of some "chump" and then pulled it away, and everybody at the table would have a good laugh while Jack moved on to do it all over again.

By day's end, any positive inkling in him had dried up. Slowly, with each interview, the emotional drought spread through Jack's body. The inescapable position of feeling helpless and subjugated to another human being ate away at Jack. He felt that he had been treated no better than someone who had wandered into town from out of state. An aloofness had hung over each interview, and his standing as a lifelong member of this community accounted for nothing. Jack had given everything to his town and now felt dismissed as a total stranger.

At the end of the day, Jack stopped at Sharp's Liquors for a 6-pack and continued on to his father's house. The day had drained everything out of him, and a few beers with his father in a quiet house seemed appropriate. How many days or weeks would Jack have to repeat this day? He tried reminding himself that all of the prospects in Stratford had not yet been exhausted and to convince himself that a better attitude was assured the next day.

"Happy New Year, Pop," Jack called out as he walked into his father's kitchen. Charles was where Charles *always* was, at the kitchen table doing a crossword puzzle.

"Don't say that too soon, Jack. God is liable to flip the switch on me at 11:59 out of spite," his father answered. Charles was in a jovial mood, which is just what Jack needed. Jack popped the top on a beer and handed it to Charles.

"Well you better drink this fast, then, before it's too late, Pop."

"Charlie said that he took you home the other day when you were released. What are you going to do for work now that you are out?" Charles swirled his beer in the can as he spoke.

"Nine stops today, Pop, and not a single "we'll call you back.'" Jack said, finishing his account of the concerted effort made that day, and the disappointing results. Leaning against the countertop across from his father, Jack could see that Charles had something on his mind.

"I've worked day in and day out since I was a kid, son; never did I have a problem finding work. Hell, I could go out there right now and come back in 20 minutes with a job. Why are you even looking in

Stratford? You'll never find a job in Stratford, even Charlie knows that. Maybe you got used to sitting on your ass in that jail."

Jack could tell that his father was joking about the jail, but today was not a good day for sarcasm. This is not how he'd wanted this conversation to go.

"Pop, I know plenty of guys around here," Jack began. He wanted his father to know that he was giving the search every effort. "It's just a matter of time. By the end of next week, I…"

Charles slammed his still-pronounced forearm on the table, interrupting his son for what he believed was a needed dose of reality.

"Are you that damned stupid, Jack," he said, clenching his fist as his irritation peaked. Jack had witnessed the same reaction many times as a young boy, but he found it strange to see the look coming from his father's tanned, wrinkled, normally cordial face.

"I just told you that Charlie said that you will never find a job in this area." Charles pressed his point home before Jack could respond. "He's not ripping on you, but telling you like it is! If there was a brain in that head of yours, you would have spent the day looking somewhere else."

His own irritation primed by the long day, Jack was in no mood for a lecture, even from his father.

"Is that how it is, Pop? Charlie makes a proclamation, and all of a sudden he's the friggin' Pope? What does Charlie know? Does he have a crystal ball now?"

"It's not a guess, Jack, those are the facts! You screwed yourself up real good around here. Nobody is going to hire you. Your brother has been asking around for you while you were locked up. Everyone knows what happened at Kutter. Who's to say you won't do it again? Even the owners that like you said they can't take that risk. You've been blackballed around here, son. Oh, they'll smile when you're standing there, because they are afraid that you might snap again." Charles stopped to look at his son and saw his well-intentioned words were not reaching him.

"Nobody can tell you anything, Jack! You're so damned smart, aren't you, son? Go ahead and keep filling out applications around here.

192

All that I can say is that I'm glad that your wife is still making those dolls!"

Charles' last comment cut Jack to the core. Frustrated to his boiling point, Jack decided that distance would be the best arbitrator. He forcefully slid the four remaining beers across the table in front of his father and headed towards the kitchen door.

"Happy New Year's, Pop; thanks for nothing," Jack grimaced to Charles as he left. Jack could hear his father's response as he got to the car.

"I'm only trying to help you, son!"

Jack banged his fist on the steering wheel as he made his way home. He knew deep down that his father and Charlie were right. The financial burden this realization portended paled in comparison to his feelings of betrayal. Unable to trust even the town with which he had for so long identified himself, Jack felt pangs of hurt and anger run through him. All of his life, Jack Christopher had lived in crisis mode, and this confirmed his need to insulate himself and stay on guard. Who was to say that Patricia and his children would not also inflict such pain on him?

Though she hardly expected Jack's optimism to last forever, Patricia was still surprised and frightened to see how agitated and despondent he was when he arrived home. Hoping to comfort her husband after a long and frustrating day, Patricia passed on the encouragement that she had heard at the previous Sunday's service.

"God knows what we need, Jack," she said, resting her hand on his shoulder.

Her husband's response was visceral.

"Does he, Pat? Well he's got a piss poor way of showing it," he said, shrugging off her hand. "Don't even get me started on that crap. He can't get me a job, but I'm supposed to thank Him?" Jack's voice took on a mocking tone. "I'll tell ya what, Pat, let's pray for a miracle. Give me one miracle, and I'll sing my ass off on Sunday!"

He held up the back of his hands toward her and then raised them over his head in mock prayer.

"Here we go, God, give it your best shot…1…2…3!"

He lowered his stubby fingers, showing them to Patricia.

"Well, I guess He's all out, isn't He, Pat?"

Patricia knew that to answer Jack with what she was feeling would only exacerbate the situation. She stayed silent and let her husband's outburst run its course.

"They throw that damned basket in front of you and bitch if you don't reach into your pocket! Well I'll tell ya what, Pat; when you can tell me what the hell I'm supposed to thank Him for, maybe I'll go to church. Till then, you and the kids do what you want, but leave me out of it!"

For a moment, Patricia wondered whether she could explain the comfort that she sometimes felt in church and thought about encouraging him one last time to join them. After a quick glance at her husband, she quickly withdrew instead. His glazed stare had returned, and the shock of seeing it again made her almost unable to speak.

Chapter 32

Jack, Rommel, and Brandon, and the Start of the Cold War

December 30, 1968

Finding the car in the driveway, Brandon and Russell ran inside the house hoping to rekindle their wrestling match with Jack, oblivious to his changed disposition. "I got ya now!" Brandon laughed as he clung to his father's leg from behind. Russell approached quickly, hoping to repeat Brandon's attack.

"Not now, dammit!" Jack barked as he flipped his leg to shake Brandon off, unwittingly hurling the boy against the coffee table, and banging his head on the table top. Brandon put his hand to his head and felt the warm trickle of blood from a cut which, though small, was sufficient to send him into a panic.

"Get a rag and stop crying Brandon! What the hell are you grabbing my leg for anyway?"

Russell backed off before making contact with his father, thus avoiding a fate similar to Brandon's. "I just wanted to play, Dad," Brandon explained through hyperventilating tears. Across the room, Rommel made no attempt to greet his master, preferring to keep a safe distance unless called.

Throughout the Christopher home that evening, everyone tread lightly. Patricia had advised the boys to remain upstairs as much as possible. Her sons needed no further coaching, and had every intention of removing themselves from the lower half of the house unless called. Patricia shuddered to imagine what a long, drawn out job search would mean for her family. How much heavier would her heart weigh as the days and weeks wore on? How often would this rending and convulsion of her spirit repeat itself? She wondered how many unforeseen ways grief could be administered to one family. She could not have known then that, in its own way, this day was but a sampling of things to come.

December 31, 1968

On New Year's Eve, the contrails of several bottle rockets could be seen streaking into the night sky from the bowling alley parking lot through the lower pane of the storm door. Such a vantage point was truly rare, as the front door was almost always closed. Flashes of light from the bottle rockets and roman candles, accented by a disjointed collection of loud explosions, agitated Rommel. Unfortunately, Brandon's earlier fear of missing any of the excitement had overridden his obligation to ensure the front door was secure as he ran out, leaving the wooden door ajar. It was this lack of diligence that provided the family pet with an unwanted ability to see the controlled mayhem unfolding across the street. Low heavy growls emanated from Rommel as unfamiliar faces ran to and fro, up and down the street.

As darkness settled in, neighborhood kids ignited all manner of pyrotechnics under the less than watchful eyes of their parents. Thunderous booms of M-80s and the endless crackle of full packs of firecrackers exploding particularly unnerved Rommel.

The Christopher boys had no fireworks of their own but for the uninspiring boxes of sparklers that Patricia had stored from last year. While these were sufficient to amuse Brandon and, to a lesser degree, Russell, the sparklers were considered "lame" by the two eldest boys. Pretending to be waiting until later to set off their explosives, Robert and Shawn did everything they could to hide that they had none. That Jack and Patricia had not bought fireworks this year promised a very bleak New Year's celebration, but the boys were not about to discuss anything to do with money with their parents. Instead, moving among their friends throughout the parking lot, the brothers pilfered a few items from the other kids' bags of goodies.

The barrage of light and sound flashing through the storm door pushed Rommel into sensory overload, leaving him ever more agitated. Seeing something through the glass, Rommel suddenly stopped pacing back and forth in front of the staircase and pressed his wet nose against the lower pane of the storm door. Illuminated by a sparkler carried in front of him, Rommel could see Brandon racing down the sidewalk on the other side of the street with something or someone chasing closely behind him with showers of sparks.

Convinced that Brandon was in imminent danger, Rommel scratched feverishly at the door glass as the hair on the back of his neck stood erect. His growls and repeated barks went unnoticed among the hordes of exploding firecrackers and projectiles. Seeing the light that had been chasing Brandon converge with him, Rommel could stand idly by no longer. He took several steps back and settled onto his haunches, then thrust himself through the lower pane of the storm door. Shards of glass showered the porch as the canine landed halfway down the steps, rolling once on the front lawn and then continuing, hell bent on taking down Brandon's aggressor. Fierce repeated barks rang out as Rommel ran towards the street.

"Jack, your dog!" one of his neighbors shouted.

Brandon and his playmate froze in horror as Rommel stepped into the street.

"Rommel, noooo!" Jack shouted, but he could only watch helplessly as a black sedan barreled around the corner of Coolidge Avenue and struck Rommel, tossing him into the air and 10 or 15 feet down the street. He landed in the center of the street and lay motionless, whimpering. Frightened by the mass of people coming towards him, the driver of the sedan threw the car into reverse, backed onto Coolidge, and disappeared down the icy road as several neighbors ran behind him.

"Somebody call the police!" someone shouted from the crowd.

Patricia responded by running back to the kitchen to notify the authorities. Jack knelt with his face buried in his beloved dog's bloody neck. Rommel tried to lift his head to respond, but could barely get it off the ground. Several neighbors reached in to help Jack move the dog as gently as they could to the relative safety of the side of the road. A pink and red trail followed Rommel to the new, frozen spot. Jack said nothing as his heavy tears mixed with the blood in Rommel's fur. Through all the years, Rommel had never abandoned Jack, never disappointed, never contested a command. Rommel still exuded unconditional loyalty, love, and faithfulness as he struggled to breathe.

After a few moments, Ben Turner arrived in his squad car and made the heartbreaking assessment that Rommel was dying.

"I'm sorry Jack, I've got to put him down" he said, regretfully. "I know that you don't want him to suffer needlessly."

Jack knew, as painful as the decision was, that Ben was right.

"Let me do it, Ben," Jack pleaded as he used his shirt to wipe Rommel's blood from his face.

"All right, Jack. Let me clear everyone out first." He turned to the crowd. "All right, folks, you all need to clear out. There's nothing more to do here." Motioning with both hands, the officer moved the neighbors on their way.

Jack returned to Rommel's side while the officer dispatched the crowd. He knelt back down as his boys could be heard crying on the front porch. Finally, Ben compelled the rest of the Christopher family inside before returning to Jack.

"I'm going to empty it except for one round, Jack," he said. After prepping the .38-caliber revolver, the officer handed it to Jack and then helped him move Rommel onto the lawn, so that the expended round would not ricochet off of the pavement.

"Goodbye, boy," Jack said and softly kissed the top of Rommel's head. Rommel's eyes met Jack's for one last time as his master began to stand back up.

"Anytime you're ready, Jack." Ben said. "Make it clean." Jack did not answer, but took careful aim for Rommel's temple as the squad car lights bathed the macabre scene in garish light.

In the living room with her sons as they wailed over Rommel's fate, Patricia pulled the drapes closed so no one would be tempted to watch the gruesome drama unfolding outside. She flinched slightly as the single gunshot resounded in the now-still night. Rommel was gone. Almost instinctively, all of the Christopher brothers looked over to the base of the stairway when they heard the shot.

"Do you want me to take him in, Jack? I mean…dispose…" Ben faltered with the difficulty of asking the question.

"I'll take care of him, Ben; he'll stay here." Jack saved him from going on. "Thanks for everything."

The officer excused himself but assured the grieving owner that the police department would do everything it could to find the driver of the black sedan. Moments later, Jack stood alone in the cold night holding Rommel. Streaks of blood ran down his t-shirt, collecting in a band of crimson around his torso. Slowly, Jack proceeded to the corner of the yard, where the back fence met Avery Mangold's property line. Laying the dog down, Jack went into the house without uttering a word. He went into the basement and retrieved a pick axe and a shovel before returning outside to Rommel.

Meanwhile, Patricia settled Richard in bed and gave Robert the task of making sure that the others followed right behind him. Little prodding was needed, since each brother wanted time to himself to sort through the evening's events. They could hear tinkling glass downstairs as Patricia cleaned up the glass in the hallway and discarded the dangerous shards still stuck in the storm door. Patricia missed Rommel's growls and groans, so prone as he'd been to express his disapproval of a disturbance in his domain. Patricia already missed the comfort of that secure feeling the Christophers had felt when Rommel stood watch at the base of the steps.

Jack toiled against the frozen ground well into the night. After a while, Patricia walked out to him. She did not speak, but, without fanfare, hung a heavy flannel shirt on the fence near him. Jack had cleared a wide, deep swath of snow to expose the dirt beneath it, and began cutting into the frozen earth with the pick axe until large frozen chunks could be removed.

After watching from inside for another hour, Patricia came back out and quietly convinced Jack to put on the fresh flannel shirt in her hand, since the one she'd offered previously was now wet from snow where it still hung on the fence. Jack thanked his wife as he rolled down the heavy flannel sleeves over his bright red arms. Soon after, as she walked back to the house, she heard the "thud" of the pickaxe cutting into the deep earth again. Several long hours passed before Jack made his way toward the house, dirty and bloodied, with tools in hand. Rommel's collar hung from the horizontal bar of a makeshift cross marking the beloved canine's final resting place. Patricia cautiously approached Jack as he walked into the kitchen. She slowly embraced her husband's freezing torso and was relieved to feel his arms returning her show of affection.

Exhausted both emotionally and physically, Jack sat at the kitchen table, and Patricia put a mug of hot tea in front of him and began gently rubbing his shoulders. As her weary husband nursed the cup of tea, Patricia hoped it provided him some comfort and did her best to be there for him. "I know it hurts, hon. If there is anything I can do…" she trailed off, hopefully.

In a voice that was tired but uninterested in compromise, Jack commanded, "Go get the kids. I want to talk to them."

Patricia assumed that Jack was not aware of the late hour and started to tell him that everyone was asleep. "It's after midnight, dear…"

"I didn't ask what time it was, did I? I said that I want to see Robert, Shawn, Russell, and Brandon in the living room now!" Though his voice was controlled, Patricia knew that Jack was leaving no alternative open. Still, she attempted to spare the boys having to be awakened before morning.

"Jack, please; they've been through a lot. For their sake, could we address this in the morning?" Patricia's suggestion that "they" had been through a lot did not sit well with Jack. Weary and mentally drained, Jack thought Patricia's statement minimized his own tribulations, though her willingness to stay up with him all night as he buried Rommel helped Jack not take this perceived offense too far.

"Pat…just…" he faltered. "Just go get the boys, and have them come to the living room…*please*."

Realizing that any further intercession would serve no purpose, Patricia made her way upstairs and Jack remained in the kitchen with his mug of tea, still trying to shake off the bitter cold. Through the kitchen window, he stared out at the collar hanging from Rommel's grave marker as the moonlight reflected off of the information tag.

A pall of bewilderment hung over the four boys as they adjusted their eyes to the foyer light and stumbled toward the living room couch. They said not a word as they lined up and seated themselves, waiting to hear the reason that they had been rousted out of their sound slumber. Reaction to Jack's call to muster ranged from frustration from Robert to outright fear in Brandon. Though the emotions were obvious in their young faces, none of boys expressed these feelings verbally. Looking haggard, wet, and cold, with his bloody t-shirt visible beneath the flannel shirt, Jack walked into the living room with mug in hand.

Normally the boys would have been relieved to notice that there was no belt in their father's hand. Tonight, however, the strange hour that they were summoned coupled with the events of the previous evening, made their uncertainty regarding their father's disposition much more troubling than the sight of Jack's usual implement of correction.

Jack paced silently to and fro in front of the coffee table without a glance toward the boys. After making several passes, he began to speak with cold, clear annunciation, his eyes still avoiding contact with his sons. As if reciting from a speech, Jack recounted the night's events.

"My dog was killed tonight," he began. "I had to watch a car hit him and send him flying until he landed, crippled, in the street. I listened to him whimper in pain as I carried him off the street, while his blood ran down my shirt." Jack's voice grew shakier as he continued. "And then…I had to put a bullet in his head as he looked up at me. I spent the last hours digging his grave as I looked at him every time the shovel went into the ground. Rommel *never* disobeyed me, *never* bit me in anger, and learned everything that I taught him. He jumped through the front door tonight, probably thinking that one of us needed help."

Tears welled up in the boys' eyes as they relived how Rommel died.

"Now what I want to know is, why is my dog dead?" Jack stopped, turned around, and faced them as if he had no intention of moving again until he received a suitable response.

Upset as they were over Rommel's death, Robert and Shawn had no reason to exhibit any signs that they bore responsibility.

"We loved Rommel, too," Robert reminded his father. "We don't know what happened. Shawn and I were in the parking lot with you. We never went back to the house once we had walked over to the parking lot after dinner, not even into our yard. We were collecting fireworks; I can prove it."

The two brothers were relieved when Jack's attention shifted away from them. Jack was sure Shawn and Robert were telling the truth. He had warned both of them to stop mooching fireworks from the other kids several times.

"Mom made me stay with her cause Robert and Shawn wouldn't let me go with them," Russell added, also certain he bore no guilt. I hate you guys; you suck!" Russell was not thrilled with getting ditched again by his brothers, and couldn't resist complaining, even through his grief.

"That's enough, Russell!" Jack was in no mood for peripheral arguments.

Not wanting to incriminate any of her sons, Patricia did not speak, but silently observed from the doorway to the kitchen. She offered heartfelt, albeit silent, moral support to her sons.

Brandon sat on the couch with his knees pulled up to his chest, his arms tightly clasped around his trembling legs. Invisible puffs of air escaped from quivering lips as he began hyperventilating. Patricia cried within herself, wanting so much to run over and comfort him, but she refrained, because she knew Jack would not allow it. In Jack's mind, this was a formal hearing, every bit as real as the one that he had been through. No emotional outbursts from the gallery were tolerated.

Brandon could no longer function, as the weight of Jack's eyes pressed down on him. Bewildered as to why their brother was in such a state of panic, his brothers looked around, searched for a concrete resolution to their father's interrogation.

202

"I'm…ss…sorry…D…d…dad" His lips quivering so violently that he could hardly get the words out, Brandon looked pale and terrified as he tried to speak.

Jack signaled to the other three boys that their participation in this gathering was no longer required.

"You…you…and you, back to bed," he said as he pointed sharply to each, making it clear that no delay would be tolerated. All three looked briefly to Patricia as she nodded her head for them to make haste. They bolted off of the couch without another word and ran up the steps back to their bedrooms. Patricia dared not go up after them but offered a brief "G'night" as they scampered out of the living room. Leaving Brandon with Jack, not knowing what her son would say or what husband might do

Leaning over and resting his hands on the coffee table, Jack stared into Brandon's eyes. The answer to why his treasured companion was dead sat on the other side of the coffee table, and Jack wanted to hear it, *now*. Ghost white with fear, Brandon fought not to pee himself as he gave an account to Jack.

"Chris and me were having fun running with the sparklers. Mom was with Russell, so I didn't want to bother her. When I needed to light my sparkler, I ran home and lit it on the stove."

Frightened, Brandon hoped to soften the blow of his recollection by reminding his parents that he had repeated this the previous evening without incident. "Lots of sparks flew off when it lit, so I ran really fast to get out of the house. I was trying to be safe, Dad, I promise!" The young boy's arms shook with fear as he awaited his father's response. He did not wait long for Jack's reply. With the coffee table still acting as a barrier between them, Jack leaned over once again to address his son. His voice, to Brandon's surprise, was calm, almost placid.

"I'm *not* going to hit you Brandon. Is that what you were afraid of?"

Brandon nodded rapidly. He allowed himself to relax a little, relieved by Jack's assurance.

"Do you know why I don't have my belt, and I'm not going to hit you tonight?" Jack continued. Brandon felt more and more relieved as his father spoke.

"'Cause it was just an accident?" Brandon surmised. His tone did not change, but Jack's face morphed into a cold, hard, frightening mask.

"No, son, not because it was an accident. I'm not going to beat you because if I start to spank your dumb ass, I may not stop, and I might wind up back in jail. That's why I don't beat you." Jack stood. His face was unchanged but his voice hardened.

"I want you to stay away from me, Brandon. When you see me in a room, go to another room. I don't care where. You are not to touch me, talk to me, write me a note, nothing. As far as you are concerned, I am not even here. Right now, I wish I could just drop you off at an orphanage and drive away, so thank your mother that you are even in this house. Until Mom tells you different, just stay away from me!" Jack turned away sharply, leaving Brandon alone on the couch as he went upstairs to shower.

Brandon was crushed. He felt as if Jack had torn him open and watched as everything in Brandon spilled out onto the floor. He considered himself disowned, and began to cry uncontrollably as Jack disappeared from view. Guilt gripped his heart for killing his father's loyal friend and the family's beloved pet. His wrenching feelings of worthlessness could not be driven away by Patricia's embrace and words of comfort.

Worst of all, Jack had set forth no timetable for forgiveness; Brandon had nothing to count down toward, no set end to being ostracized. His father's boiling resentment was left to linger. Healing? Healing was left unpromised. If it came at all, would healing come too late to repair damage done to Brandon's heart?

Chapter 33
The Christopher Family and the New Siege

May 1969

Patricia's discomfort resounded in her own ears as she buried her head deep within the toilet bowl. Quickly grabbing a nearby hand towel, she wiped her mouth as she brought herself back to her feet with some difficulty. Leaning her head back, with hands resting on hips that felt somewhat wider than a few months before, Patricia drew in a long, slow, deep breath. That she would soon need to resume her previous position over the toilet was certain, but it felt good just to stand and breathe again, however briefly. Looking out the second floor window, the crocus and daffodils straining to poke their colorful blooms above the dark soil provided her with some measure of peace before she once again had to fall to her knees.

Late nights toiling to finish as many dolls as she could was burdensome enough; getting sick all morning was no help at all. Ginny still took the dolls to the flea markets, which were soon to start their spring season, as eager buyers and sellers converge at Columbus and Englishtown. Patricia had pushed herself, sewing and cutting and weaving in doll hair, almost to the point of exhaustion, but she had recently broken the news to Jack that after completing the projects on hand, she did not have the physical strength left to keep the manufacturing process going. Careful to make her point clear, Patricia told her husband that this was not an issue of motivation, but the physical capacity to see the job through.

Patricia had given him other news as well. She was pregnant. Lately the retching and nausea competed with sleepless nights for her attention.

While she was thrilled to be carrying another beautiful baby, Patricia had to admit that her life currently was not the most conducive to nurturing her baby the way she had so enjoyed with the other boys. For the previous several months, Patricia also struggled with when and how to tell Jack, as well as concern about what his reaction would be. She decided to forgo telling her husband until a month ago, which meant that the first 3 months of the New Year were a daily cycle of frustration, guilt, and exhaustion. Fear of sending her husband over the edge with yet another mouth to provide for, gnawed at Patricia each time she thought to tell Jack of her pregnancy.

Circumstances of the Christopher's financial straits had grown considerably worse than during the time of Jack's incarceration. Necessity forced a whole host of new unpleasant practices upon the family. Unable to afford repairs to the washing machine, laundry was done either at the laundromat or on an "as needed" basis by hand in the tub. This resulted in large piles of unlaundered garments piled in the basement and scattered around the house. Waiting to be cleaned, the collective components of blood, dirt, grease, food stains, and body odor sent a noxious odor wafting not only down in the basement, but also throughout the house.

It also meant that the boys sometimes had to wear the same clothes for two or three days until Patricia could get over to the laundromat. Taunts and whispers directed at Shawn and Robert at school had resulted in several fights and suspensions. Incidents like this only compounded Jack's frustration. The house was falling into disrepair in multiple ways, and the challenges of trying to keep it up were never ending. Beyond the washing machine, sections of basement pipe had frozen over the winter, flooding the basement floor with the first thaw. Cobwebs and dust now settled in places that had never seen them before. Once neatly arranged knick knacks were askew, having no one to position them. Outside, melting snows revealed the home's external shortcomings for all to see. Parting into several pieces, the dryer belt had rendered the unit unusable for the past two weeks. An embarrassing clothes line was strung up between the back fence and the tall oak tree on the north side of the house.

Constant fear of finding the heat shut off greeted the family each day. The utilities company could not deny service during the cold winter months but was now free to shut service off. It was now only a matter of time before they did so. When this happened, all cooking would have to be done on the grill, and Jack would also be denied use of the oven as a means to dry some of his clothes if he needed them on short notice.

Patricia had gathered every candle she could find and placed them strategically throughout the house, along with booklets of matches in case the electricity was turned off. She had also taught all the boys to recognize the Water Department truck. The boys understood that once it pulled up, they had about 10 minutes to fill up as many sinks and basins as they could before the technicians shut the supply valve off.

Losing electrical power was the most disconcerting to the boys. The utilities company was barred from cutting off the gas for heat during the winter, but never the electrical power. On nights the power was turned off, Shawn would be denied the simple pleasure of listening to "Radio Mystery Theatre" as he drifted off to sleep. Many winter days were spent with icicles forming off of his scalp as he walked to school, eliciting taunts and curious awkward inquiries on his arrival. Clothes donned while still damp would freeze into a stiffened suit as the boys walked the three blocks to school.

"Stop bitching and walk faster," was about all of the guidance that Jack would offer on the matter.

Strains and external pressures on both Jack and Patricia kindled heated arguments that never would have seen the light of day had their nerves not been stretched thin, and their tempers short.

"How hard is it to dust the damn table once in a while, Pat? The living room looks like a pig sty," Jack said more than once. Patricia was no longer the wilting flower of 2 years ago, and after her many sleepless nights was in no mood to hear Jack's ranting,.

"You're home every day, Jack," she retorted. "If it really bothers you that much, I could use some help around here!"

207

The boys spent many nights hunkered down in their rooms listening to heated exchanges from the living room below. Slowly, such nights began to erase memories of the carefree days a few years before. Patricia was grieved that the financial crisis coupled with the latest round of emotional vacillation, which had its roots in the events of New Year's Day, was taking such a noticeable toll on the children. Patricia could see that the almost continual challenges imposed on the Christopher household over the past few years created a new and troubling trend. Robert was incrementally becoming less fearful and more angry. She saw a sullen, quiet foreboding overtaking her son. Robert maintained a healthy respect for his father's ability to dispense justice and correction when he saw fit, if for no other reason than self-preservation.

Even Patricia did not know that Robert's futile attempts to recall midwinter walks to Grandpop's,or sledding behind the car in the Thunderstrike parking lot rendered them faded and distant. The sporadic, brief memories of normal life—roast dinners on Thursdays, Jack full of laughter—were nothing but logs that burned on the fires of Robert's suppressed anger. Patricia also did not realize that Robert disliked this change in himself every bit as much as she did. Was it wrong for Robert to withdraw from contact with his own father? Did the relative calm found in continual solitude come at the price of Robert's sense of respect and decency? Guilt over disassociating from Jack plagued Robert at every turn. He felt himself beginning to hate Jack, and he hated himself for his own anger.

Even if Patricia could not see his guilt, she could see the boldness to dream or to envision any kind of bright future for himself leeching from Robert's heart. She tried to infuse some hope in him in church on Sundays, but Robert saw the church as just more rules and another authority playing to it's own agenda.

"You go there every week, Mom. *You* go to *them*. Have you ever once seen any of *them* come to *you* when you need it? When does the church get dressed up and come to *us*, Mom? "

In Robert's mind, this hypocrisy told him everything that he needed to know. Church could not give him hope, and he continued to attend on Sundays only out of respect for his mother.

Shawn carried none of the simmering resentment of Robert. He was not angry, but instead felt immersed in a pool of self-deprecating doubt and inferiority. He harbored no ill will toward Jack or anyone else in particular, because he was on a constant quest to identify and fix the innumerable deficiencies of character he was sure *he* possessed. Shawn felt no need to resent Jack's recently absented displays of affection because he was convinced that he didn't deserve affection.

Meanwhile, both Robert and Shawn envied and admired Russell's sturdily entrenched disposition, though they would never admit it to him. While respecting his father's obvious physical advantage, Russell would not cede an inch of emotional ground.

"Hit me, and I won't cry; you can't hurt me," Russell told Jack on a number of occasions. So sure was young Russell of who he was and what he would and would not do that he went about living his life in a kind of self-styled vacuum. Shawn especially, wished for even a small slice of Russell's tenacity.

Brandon was vulnerable and sensitive, very much his mother's son. Being drawn to music and art, he did not, at times, exhibit the rugged bravado that his father would have preferred. Even at his young age, Brandon was a people pleaser and he found great joy in watching the response of those he aspired to make happy.

Jack did not fully realize how devastatingly painful his shunning of Brandon's attempts to show affection, which had lasted for about a month, had been to his son. Even now, Brandon kept a safe distance while he strained to find the words or actions to make everything right again.

Jack was well aware that it had been an accident, but while trying to make a point of some kind, even for Brandon's good, Jack did not understand how the cancer of rejection threatened to leave Brandon hollow. Small and little noticed for now, left untreated, the cancer was sure to resurface with a vengeance.

Though each responded to it differently, an atmosphere of constant crisis began to settle among the Christopher boys. Whether a perceived emergency was real or imagined was now immaterial. The resulting impact on the psyche remained the same.

Patricia worried for all her children, but she worried for Jack as well. She felt he needed to know that he had an advocate in her. Finding the delicate balance between the extremes of a protective mother and a supportive wife siphoned off a great deal of Patricia's much-needed strength.

As she freshened up after her bout with morning sickness, Patricia celebrated one small victory, one less worry to vex her mind. Thankfully, and surprisingly, Jack has been excited to hear of her pregnancy when she'd told him last month. His enthusiasm was an enormous relief to Patricia. While she feared that their current circumstances would cause Jack to feel even greater stress upon learning she was expecting, her husband saw it quite differently. For as long as he could remember, the Christophers were always keen on having large families. Any additions were always welcome and were considered a feather of honor in the cap of the respective patriarch. Charles would be pleased to hear that his daughter-in-law was expecting. This was certain to curry Jack some good favor with his father until their financial circumstances improved. Having his next child born in a new residence might also promise a bright new start.

Two years ago, Jack would never have believed that he would be unceremoniously starved out of his own town. By spring of 1969 however, he had reluctantly concluded that selling the house was the only way out of this spiraling descent into abject poverty. Jack had become convinced that Charlie's prognostication was right. For months, Jack had repeated the same daily, mundane process of job hunting, both in Stratford and in the neighboring boroughs. Believing that the town that he had so loved now shunned him, Jack became slowly convinced that his family could not continue living in Stratford. Jack now showed an unfamiliar air of disdain and mistrust as he went about his once beloved town. Ironically Jack's countenance confirmed the apprehensions of those who had put it there in the first place.

Nearly as emasculating and unsettling were the care packages. Jack recognized that the intentions of the deliverers were good and the packages did take some of the pressure of feeding the family off Patricia, but he found having the name "Christopher" in some book of needy families humiliating. How many cars passed by his house each day with passengers who pointed to his house and said, "We delivered food to that house. Poor souls, they have five kids, and the father can't find a job." Each sunrise made the prospect of staying in Stratford more infeasible.

Chapter 34
Jack and New Advances

May 1969

Walking out the kitchen door, Jack could see that the last of winter's snow had melted from Rommel's burial site. The sting of losing Rommel had still not yet completely subsided, and he had not, as yet, gone too far to rekindle the broken relationship with Brandon. He was not quite ready to let bygones be bygones just yet.

Surveying the hanging gutters, worn paint, and missing shingles firmed Jack's resolve to sell the house and move. Somewhat nervous, and with a bit of melancholy, Jack decided he would call his brother Bill tomorrow to see if his offer to put a word in for him at Crown Steel Press in Pennsauken still stood.

Bill had made the offer while Jack was incarcerated, and though appreciative of his brother's efforts, Jack saw little need at that time to consider leaving Stratford. The entry position would be temporary, but Crown was a union shop, so even a temporary position could be an open door to join the union. Bill could not promise it would happen, but there was a distinct possibility given Jack's experience. He had encouraged Jack to apply. A long time foreman for the heavy equipment operators, Bill was always willing to make a few calls to help someone out. In many ways, Bill and Jack were alike. Bill was also tough and had no tolerance for bullshit. He was direct in his dealings, with little or no mincing of words. Bill was however, different from his brother in some significant ways. Sporting a full head of prematurely silver hair, Bill had a distinguished manner about him and was always polite and gracious. People liked that Bill was always "others minded"—how others felt, what others thought, what others needed. Unlike his brother, Bill was not prone to explosive episodes; his anger curve was much more gradual. This combination of traits meant that he was always getting invited to a football game, or concert or formal dinner. Everyone felt at ease around him, a quality that had won his bosses many a contract and had won him their appreciation.

Entrance into the ranks of the Sheet Metal Workers Union would bring a number of benefits, but when Bill initially made the offer, Jack wasn't sure a temporary position was worth the daily 45-minute drive to and from Pennsauken. In addition, though Jack greatly admired Bill, he was never anxious to be beholden to anyone, even his own brother. Since leaving Stratford was the furthest thing from Jack's mind at the time, he'd thanked Bill but passed on the offer. The past months had certainly changed a lot.

Standing over the stove, Patricia felt morning sickness rise again. The smell of frying eggs did her little good. As he made his way in through the kitchen door, Jack could see that most of the color had drained from her face. .

"Don't worry about breakfast, Pat; I'll find something," he offered. "You look terrible. Why don't you go lay down on the couch."

Though she wasn't sure if being told she looked terrible warranted a "thank you," Patricia appreciated the sincerity of Jack's awkwardly worded gesture.

"Thanks, Jack, I think I will. I'm not sure how much longer I could have taken the smell of fried food."

"I'm going to call Bill tomorrow," Jack announced after a brief pause. Patricia waited for the rest of Jack's sentence, given that she had no idea what her husband was talking about. She did not remind him that he had not shared whatever internal conversation had brought him to this conclusion. Since he had never told her of his previous conversation with Bill regarding the job, though she was happy to see that he was in somewhat better mood, Patricia had no notion as to why. As Jack finally recounted his conversation with Bill, Patricia, still queasy, fought to maintain her attention. She was unsure as to whether what Jack was

213

explaining would pan out, but she had no doubt about one thing. She was certain that her current position on the couch was more conducive to recovery than standing over that greasy pan of sizzling eggs. Patricia celebrated what little victories she could claim.

The Next Day

Numerous awards mounted on carved wooden plaques adorned the wall of the Sheet Metal Worker's Union Hall in Haddonfield. As Jack waited for his meeting...or interview...or whatever this actually was, he was sure that had anyone but Bill given him this lead, the drive up the White Horse Pike would have been a waste of time. As it was, he could not help but feel just a little optimistic. If he had no chance at all of getting this job, Bill would not have sent him.

Jack saw a deliberate, planned atmosphere of unity and cohesion as he gazed over the wall plaques and looked through the brochures spread out on the table of the waiting room. This stood in sharp contrast to anything seen at Kutter Metals. None of those guys had the slightest notion to address work conditions. While he was looking at photos from various job sites, Jack heard the distinct clack of heavy footsteps echo throughout the open foyer. He turned to see a man, larger than anyone he could remember ever meeting, ducking his head to clear the steel-framed glass doorway. Jack estimated that he would have been about 6'7" in bare feet, and the burly man's black cowboy boots added another 2 inches to his imposing stature.

Heavily muscled and walking with quick, purposeful steps, the stranger wore blue jeans with a crisp white cotton button-down shirt, opened at the collar. A silver stick pin stood out above his shirt pocket, presumably an indication of official status. Seeing no one else in the foyer, the big man walked up to Jack and extended his hand. "Jack Christopher?" he asked in a friendly baritone.

"Yes," Jack replied as he returned the handshake. Jack was not intimidated by his host, nor did he feel the need to project his own strength.

214

"Pleased to meet you, Jack. My name is Wes Morgan. I am one of the members of the Executive Board here. My office is on the third floor." Wes directed Jack toward the elevators and invited him to walk ahead. "Bill told me a lot about you while we were golfing the other day. Do you golf, Jack?" Jack laughed as he held up his hands.

"I'm one of those guys playing ahead of you that pisses real golfers off, Wes."

Wes laughed at Jack's self-deprecating joke. He was accustomed to people shrinking or taking a defensive posture when they met him, and he appreciated that Jack responded naturally to the question. Morgan quickly switched to a more serious demeanor while looking at his guest's fingers.

"Bill told me about your accident. I'm sorry to have heard that it happened. That kind of shit gets me fired up. I'm all too familiar with Billson; he's a low life as far as I'm concerned. How are your hands doing now?"

"Pretty much back to normal now, thankfully," Jack replied. He began to feel more and more at ease. So far, the meeting didn't even feel like an interview.

These guys get it! he thought to himself. Everything that he had been saying for years at Kutter until he was blue in the face was what the union was about.

"Word got around when you busted up Billson, Jack. A lot of my brothers in the union were ready to buy you a beer. Listen, I know that you can run a press. I'm not worried about that. One of the reasons that I had told Bill that I would meet with you was because I know that you're not a shill for the company. You've got balls Jack, and that's why I respected you enough to give you a fair shake."

As they arrived at the heavy mahogany door to Wes's office, Wes ushered Jack in and offered him a drink.

"No thanks Wes, I have to drive home."

Wes sat behind his desk, and Jack sat opposite, appreciating that the "guest chair" seemed equally comfortable. Wes looked over some notes, then reached into his large desk drawer and pulled out several official-looking pamphlets.

"Here, Jack, I'd like you to read these so that you have a better idea of who we are, and where we've come from. I am sure that you will appreciate who we are after spending all of those years at Kutter. I see no reason why we can't find you a spot in our Pennsauken shop. We would bring you in as a journeyman and see where it goes to from there."

Jack closed his eyes briefly. He could not believe that relief had finally come in sight after so long. His expression was not lost on Wes.

"I'm glad we could help, Jack, but if I didn't think that you were a good fit for our shop, I wouldn't have offered."

Jack stood, extending his hand once again to Wes.

"You don't know the weight that you just took off of my shoulders."

"I'll have to make a few calls and get the paperwork started," Wes said, motioning Jack to sit. "I'll set a day up for you to get your physical, and meet with the shop steward so that he can get all of your information. We can probably have you back on the press at the end of the month."

Nothing could have sounded better in Jack's ears. He already felt a difference between this and the wasted years at Kutter.

Wes paused and seemed to consider carefully before he turned again to Jack.

"Are you doing anything this afternoon, Jack? A group of us are going down to support a strike that's going on in Deptford. You could follow us; that way you won't have to ride back here to get your car."

Rather than be offended, Jack was glad that Wes thought enough to invite him.

"Sounds good to me, if it's OK by you," he responded. "I wasn't sure if there was a problem with me not being a member." Wes waved a large hand to dismiss Jack's concern.

"Are you kidding me, Jack? They'll be happy to meet the guy that decked Billson! Besides, they'll see that you're with our group." Wes paused again, then offered, "One more question if you don't mind my prying, Jack..." Jack was taken a little off guard, not sure what was left

216

to discuss. "…how are you getting along until you start work? I know that Bill had said that you have five kids."

"It's going to be six soon, actually, Wes." Jack was proud to update his family status. "You can tell my brother that you found out about number six coming before he did." Wes chuckled at the idea that he could now use this tidbit to chide his golf buddy.

"Congratulations, Jack. I guess what I'm getting at is, how are you fixed for money? Will you be able to make it until you start work?"

Jack's pride would not let him ask for money, and he clumsily searched for a polite answer. Wes spoke again before he could put one together.

"I understand that you wouldn't ask Jack, but hell, you've got six kids. If it makes you feel any better, it's not charity. We can take a little out of each check once you start until it's paid back." Wes took something out of an imposing cabinet flush mounted in the wall behind his chair. He rotated back around, sliding 10 crisp $100 bills across the desk. "Hopefully this will make the transition easier for you."

Picking up the cash with his left hand while extending his right in gratitude, Jack assured Wes he intended prompt repayment.

"I've decided to sell my house and move to Pennsauken; as soon as I do I'll…"

Wes interrupted. "We'll work it out. Don't lose any sleep worrying about it, Jack." He looked at his watch. "Damn, 1 o'clock already; we've got to get going. We can grab something quick to eat on the way down."

Jack was tempted to ask Wes to use the phone, but he changed his mind after learning that they were running late. Jack was incredibly anxious to tell Patricia all that had happened. Finally, some good news! Jack worried for a moment about what Patricia might think, especially remembering the aftermath of his job hunt in January. Patricia was sure to assume the worst this time around as well. Today's results had been so blissfully different, he decided that his news would be well worth the wait until evening.

Following Wes and a couple other men down to the picket lines, Jack wondered why it had taken him so long to become affiliated with

217

guys like Wes. Jack had made all of those attempts over the years to change things at Kutter for a bunch of guys that had no interest in improving anything. Now it was all worth it; all of the frustration and pain were well worth it, if everything was as it appeared. The salary advance from Wes went a long way to convince Jack that these guys were on the up and up.

As he was turning into the parking lot behind Wes' car, Jack saw a sea of picket signs part in a single motion for the car in front. The access quickly sealed again before Jack could gain entry. Jack looked at the multitude of faces peering into his windshield, and he could tell that the onlookers were at best circumspect as to his intentions. While he wondered what to do next, Jack saw the looks of disdain and mistrust melt from the faces around him. Those in the immediate area began to applaud and pat the sides of his car in an apparent expression of appreciation. Again the picket signs parted, and he drove through.

Celebrity status followed Jack over the next 2 hours as Wes introduced him to a number of union members. Being seen with a man of Morgan's stature within the organization, along with the revelation to the rank and file of Jack's exploits at Kutter, afforded him a hearty welcome. Around 4 o'clock, Wes bid farewell to Jack and said that he would begin the employment process for him first thing in the morning.

"Don't feel obligated to stay," he said, "but you are welcome to hang around if you like. They're a great group of guys." Jack appreciated what Wes' parting comment said of his affinity and commitment to his union brothers. Feeling quite at home, Jack decided to stay.

Jack spent the next half hour in lively conversation, some casual and some related to the status of the negotiations and grievances, and he noticed one of the men start to excuse himself. Jack had noticed Justin Decker, glance at his watch several times over the last half hour and become increasingly excited. The man was short and thin, and had a weathered brown face that made him look much older than his voice and mannerisms. He spoke in short, rapid sentences, and Jack wondered if he seemed to be always on edge like this, as if he were waiting for the next shoe to drop. Justin looked like the kind of guy who enjoyed the perception that he was "in the loop.".

"So, Jack. You know Wes, huh? Big man around here; big man, ya know."

"My brother knows Wes pretty well," Jack began to explain, "but..."

Justin interrupted before he could finish. "They're gonna be pissed around here tomorrow, I tell ya; pissed!" Justin shuffled his feet while he talked, and Jack noticed his hands darting in and out of his pockets. "All the big mahoffs up there are gonna be plenty pissed," he finished, and looked around for confirmation. Varying degrees of agreement were expressed from the other five men standing with Decker and Jack. The other men seemed to have no concern that Jack would betray their trust, and one explained the upcoming plan that led Justin to his excited conclusion. Jack sensed that his demonstrated "in" with Wes Morgan was all the assurance anyone needed.

"They're going to bring in scabs tonight to finish the production run so that they can load up the trailers," the man explained, referring to non-union workers, "hoping to get them all out of here around midnight when only a few of the striking workers are around. That's why we blocked your car; we thought that you may have been one of those bastards."

"Hey Jack, why don't you come with us?" Justin suddenly asked. "We could use an extra hand; what do you say?" Jack hesitated. In the first place, he had no idea what he was getting into, and in the second, Justin was impetuous and Jack was unsure if the others approved of letting a relative stranger in on such matters.

"We'd love to have you with us, Jack," one of the others noted, seeing the hesitation on his face. "That's the first good idea you've had, Decker," he joked.

"In that case, hell, yeah," agreed Jack. Although not explicitly stated and probably not planned, Jack felt this brief exchange was a test. His acceptance of their offer to help further the union's cause could get him the real inclusion that is elusive to outsiders.

As several men gathered together to finalize their plans, Jack felt a great pain shoot through is head as the sirens of a nearby fire station signaled deployment of their trucks. Jack had nursed one of his frequent migraines all day but had done well hiding the pain till now. The deafening screams of the firehouse alarm pierced like an ice pick, and Jack closed his eyes in agony, waiting for the pain to subside. When the sirens stopped, Jack pushed the pain aside. In truth, he was excited about the upcoming maneuvers.

Just after 5 o'clock, ten men formed a small cluster, and the mood became much more focused. Justin was silent as the obvious leader of the group began to speak.

"All right, listen up," he called in a deep baritone. "There is no way in hell those trucks are leaving tonight. Our brothers are counting on us to come through. They can make all of the 'scab' parts that they want to in there, but I'll be damned if one part is leaving here." He spoke like a coach before a big game, and the men around him responded to his urgency. "We're going to walk outside of the perimeter fence and make our way through the woods, along the fence, until we reach the loading bays. We'll stay outside of the fence until 8 o'clock. Then, two at a time we'll jump the fence and make our way behind the scrap metal dumpster just on the other side. One man will disable each trailer; there are eight bays in all. It's about 100 feet of open ground between the dumpster and the trailer rigs, so you'll have to move fast. Sye and Harry will keep lookout from the scrap metal bin. Spike all of the tires as fast as you can, and get the hell out of there and back over the fence.

"Wait for Sye's signal before spiking any tires. If one of you gets jumpy and starts too soon, the roving watch will hear the air coming from the wheels. If that happens, the rest of you are screwed. Wait for the signal!" Ice picks were handed out to each of the men as he spoke.

"You all know that the yard dogs get let out at 9, which gives us an hour as long as they don't think anything funny is going on. If they do, the roving watches will set the dogs on us early. As soon as you finish your tires get out of there and over the fence. Beers are on me when

220

we're done," he finished. A great cheer rose up after this last announcement.

As the group milled around, several men, including Jack, moved their cars to a large parking lot three blocks away, where they would raise no undue suspicion. No one wanted to walk back to the shop parking lot once the rigs had been disabled.

Just after six , the group made their way into the cover of the dense woods and underbrush outside of the perimeter fence. Leaving in groups of two spread several minutes apart, each team navigated through the untouched wooded terrain to the rear property line. Finally arriving just outside of the scrap bin, the men stopped and waited for all of the teams to assemble.

Although not voicing any particular objection, the group leader had seemed less certain than his compatriots about Jack and had stayed with him. By the time they had reached the rendezvous point, it was apparent that Jack was neither nervous nor tentative and he had not talked a blue streak, which also seemed to assure his team leader. He couldn't know that Jack's still pounding headache had as much as anything else to do with his silence. He was correct that Jack felt no fear about the endeavor. Jack's heart was surely racing, but out of exhilaration. This would be another long sought after shot at guys like Winslow Billson, and this time he did not have to go it alone.

Just as the teams were about to hop the fence at a little past eight, a large black school bus pulled up to the bay entrance door preceded by the flashing lights of a police cruiser providing escort. A surge of noise from the bus's airbrakes echoed through the empty parking lot, which was now empty, but for the eight tractor trailers, each backed up to loading bay doors. The team was relieved to see that all eight of the loading bay doors were closed.

As the bus door opened under the watchful eye of a police officer standing just outside, 20 or 30 men filed quickly and silently off of the bus and into the building.

"Scab sons of bitches!" Justin Decker barked.

"Shut up, Decker!" the leader growled while trying to minimize the sound of his own voice. "You want to get us all caught?"

Several minutes later the police escort and empty bus made their way out the same way that they had come in. The solid steel entrance door closed with a "thud," and the lot once again fell silent.

"Eight fifteen, you guys. We have 45 minutes before the dogs are out," the leader warned. Two by two the teams of saboteurs began to deploy themselves over the fence. Sye and Harry looked out for the roving watch while waiting to see the faint image of a man under each of the eight trailers so they could give the signal. Jack crouched between the set of tires closest to the bay doors as he awaited the call to action. He would work his way down the underside of the trailer towards the cab end and drive a single heavy puncture into the wall of every tire. Then he would dash across the darkened lot and escape the same way they came in, before anyone could spot them.

Around 8:40, Sye confirmed that all trailers had a man crouched down between the tires looking back at the scrap bin. Lying on his stomach behind the dumpster, he waved his hand low to the ground to get the men's attention, and pointed up to the light and to the sportsman's sling shot in his left hand. Various forms of acknowledgment were returned from under all of the trailers, and each man readied himself to start.

Placing the brace on his left forearm, Sye grasped the upright posts of the slingshot in his heavily veined hand and grabbed a single ball bearing, about the size a marble. He got to his knees and leaned out from behind the metal bin to get a better shot. He placed the bearing into the sling, said a quick prayer as he slowly exhaled, and released the ball bearing, sending it towards the lantern. The bearing hit the globe dead on, and the men heard a loud "pop" followed by the sound of tinkling glass as it rained down onto the asphalt below. The parking lot was plunged into total darkness.

Almost as soon as the glass hit the ground, a "hissss" of escaping air vented from a symphony of tires. Mild at first, the sound quickly grew to a thunderous crescendo as tire after tire was punctured. Justin finished first and tore across the parking lot as the vandalized trailer settled onto its newfound posture. Six others soon raced after him, hurriedly throwing themselves over the fence. Jack struggled to run as fast as he could, but he found himself hobbling across the pavement dragging a useless leg behind him. The barking of the now released guard dogs could be heard drawing closer with each step.

"Son of a bitch! I can't feel my leg!" Jack told Sye as he collapsed behind the scrap bin just as Harry threw himself over the fence. Jack and Sye, the only two left to clear the perimeter, could see the glint of the guard dogs' eyes as they rounded the far corner of the building.

"Oh shit, Jack! Pull yourself up on the fence and I'll push you over!" Sye yelled. Jack used the one leg he could move to jump. He grabbed the top of the fence, and pulled himself up using his upper body strength. Sye gave him the final push that sent him rolling over the top of the fence, and scaling the fence like a monkey, quickly followed him over.

They could hear the four angry dogs behind the dumpster barking wildly and see headlights come screaming toward the trailers, the cars stopping with a loud screech in front of the now-disabled vehicles. One by one the bay doors flew open as foremen and spectators gathered on the docks and in the parking lot, not quite sure which way to run in pursuit of the vandals. Cursing and curt orders could be heard from several directions around the loading docks as security officials converged.

"I think we're clear, but keep moving," Sye called to Jack as they made their way deeper into the woods. Jack moved with some difficulty, struggling to regain the use of his right leg.

The commotion behind them faded as Jack and Sye made their way further and further into the woods, and the sounds eventually died out completely. The two men emerged on the other side of the woods, a mile down the road from where the cars had been parked at the water treatment plant. They waited in the tall grass 30 feet off of the roadside as the flashing lights of police cruisers raced by.

Jack turned and offered Sye a hand in thanks. "I would have never made it if you had not been around, Sye. My leg must have fallen asleep while I was crouched under the truck."

"Don't mention it," the other man responded with a humble shrug. "We're glad that you came with us, Jack. How's the leg now?"

Jack picked up a nearby stick and whacked the offending appendage.

"Tingles a little, but I've got the feeling back," he said. "So, where are we meeting the others?" he asked, absently rubbing his weakened leg.

"Why don't you go ahead and I can meet you there," Jack noted when Sye mentioned a familiar bar. "It might not be a good idea to go walking out of these woods at the same time. Thanks again, Sye."

"I'd say I'll buy you a beer, but that's already covered," Sye acknowledged the thanks as he readied to move on alone. "It's been a hell of a night, Jack. Welcome aboard."

Sye tapped Jack on the shoulder before disappearing into the tall grass. Minutes later, Jack stepped onto the roadway and pulled a broken cigarette from his shirt pocket. Casually smoking as he made his way to the car, Jack wondered what Patricia must be thinking. It was now almost 10:30. He decided he would go the bar but stay only long enough to recap with the others. Blaring music and loud conversation was the last thing Jack needed with his pounding headache.

He made it to his car unchallenged and drove down the desolate winding back roads to the Eagleside Bar. Jack could hear the raucous celebration from the outside, and incessant pounding filled his head as he opened the door.

"Hey, here comes Limpy!" He heard someone call as he entered. "We've been waiting for you, Jack!"

Rather than be offended, Jack took it as a badge of honor that the men had bestowed him with a nickname. The bar was packed with union members, and the night's events had it lively. Many of the men inside wore the logo-emblazoned jackets, and one by one the union brothers came to expressing appreciation to Jack. He understood that by putting

224

himself on the line with them, he had passed the test of true brotherhood for them.

He felt a pat on the back and heard a familiar voice from behind him say, "Hell of a job tonight, Jack; let me buy you that beer."

He turned to see the leader of the group hand him a heavy frosted mug of beer. "By the way, I'm Hank Cerra," the man added then frowned. "Too damned loud out here," he said and pointed to a door with a large man standing in front of it. "Some of the guys are playing cards in the back." Jack wasn't sure what was on the other side, but he was pleased with the option of escaping all of the noise. He spent the next hour or so playing cards with 15 guys and nursing two beers.

He was not sure what set this group apart from those out in the noisy room, but he could see by the gourmet spread and the privately stocked bar that these men were not just the rank and file. Only his arrival with Wes explained why they had invited him in from the larger crowd. Jack liked the crowd in the back room. He would have enjoyed himself even more if he didn't have this migraine.

As midnight rolled an hour into the new day, Jack said his goodbyes, and looked forward to seeing them all again at the end of the month. All that Jack could think about on the long drive home was how nice it would be to fall into bed. The unlit roads repeatedly teased him into thinking that he was almost home, only to throw another bend in front of him.

Dirty, exhausted, and disconcerted that he had nearly gotten caught, Jack could not have been happier to pull into his driveway. He was barely able to keep his eyes open as he moved through the kitchen into the dining room. Patricia bolted down the staircase, ran to him, and threw her arms around him.

"Oh my God, Jack, are you all right? Look at you. I was so worried about you. It's 2 am; where have you been?"

Patricia's flurry of questions was not helping Jack's headache at all. Fighting to keep his eyes open, Jack just wanted to satisfy her curiosity as quickly as possible and go to bed.

"I know, hon; I'm sorry. There was no place to call from," he answered wearily.

Patricia would not be so easily appeased.

"Let me make you some tea. How did you get so dirty? Where were you anyway?" Patricia's voice trailed off as she walked into the kitchen. Jack had hoped to continue the conversation while walking upstairs, and had gotten to the foot of the steps before begrudgingly turning back towards the kitchen.

"Hon, I just want to go to bed. I really don't need any…" Jack trudged awkwardly to the kitchen when he heard a gut-wrenching cry from Patricia.

"No, Jack, no! What did you do? You'll go back to jail! I can't go through this again!" Patricia began to hit Jack in the chest with the stack of bills that he had, with little thought, thrown onto the kitchen table as he'd walked through.

Patricia was now crying hysterically, almost on the verge of collapse. However she had expected Jack to respond, it was not with the hearty, rolling laugh he let out as he supported his exhausted body by bracing both hands on his knees.

"Hon, listen to me! I'm not going back to jail," he said as he helped her to stand and giving her a hand towel to dry her tears. With no energy for long, drawn out explanations, he gave her a few quick bullet points to calm her down.

"I'm not going to jail. I didn't rob anything. It was a great day, but it's late and I can hardly stay on my feet. I have to go to sleep, but I will tell you all about it tomorrow; I promise."

Patricia looked into his eyes and was certain he was telling the truth. Now embarrassed at her outburst, Patricia playfully hit Jack with the hand towel. "You scared me to death, Jack. Do you know how frightening that was?" As much as she wanted to know where all that money came from, she could see how exhausted Jack was and decided to spare him any further delay in his quest for slumber. She kissed him and picked up the thin stack of bills to take upstairs. Once the shock of the event itself had worn off, Patricia was heartened to think of how many of

226

the Christopher's immediate problems this could help resolve. Jack planned to tell Patricia everything the next morning in exacting detail and thought she was sure to sit in rapt attention as he recalled the entire day. Jack would relay to his wife almost the entire day. She didn't need to hear about Jack's legs going numb. Patricia, Jack rationalized, did not need the added worry, and he would rather not be nagged about it. But that was all for tomorrow; for tonight, sleep…sweet sleep.

Chapter 35

Jack and the Boys and Continuing Hostilities

July 4, 1969

"Robert, we don't want to inflate the rafts until we get to the beach; they'll take up too much room." Patricia's voice was every bit as light as her heart as she delegated loading responsibilities to the boys. Not loading the car herself was not only enjoyable, but necessary considering that her due date was only 12 weeks away. Robert released the air from the blue and red canvas rafts, pressing the last of it out as he folded them into compact squares.

Looking better than it had in a long time, the house was nearly back to normal. The money Wes Morgan had loaned Jack, along with countless hours of hard work by Jack and the boys, had made quite a difference. Commuting to work in Pennsauken the last few months, Jack had worked on the house when he got home each night, almost as soon as he walked through the door. He worked on the house any spare mornings, nights, and weekends; the smell of sawdust, mineral spirits, or fertilizer giving Patricia an idea of what current project was under way.

Fixing the house up helped Jack feel more in control, but he also had another reason for the feverish pace. Jack's new job was going well. The strike in Deptford, much to his delight, had ended several days after their evening assault on the trailers. The commute to Pennsauken was working out fine as a temporary measure, and Jack and Patricia had begun house shopping in Pennsauken. They had their eye on a sturdy-looking two-story on Remington Avenue on the border with Camden, but they also knew that any hope of buying the home would include selling the house in Stratford.

Jack had even drafted the boys to rake, weed, scrape, and paint for the past three months. Robert, Shawn, and Russell were all but certain that they were destined to once again lie about their summer vacation this year. Jack and Patricia were shocked when the house had a buyer almost as soon as they had put the "For Sale" in the ground. They found out that the apartment complex that they had battled with for so many years was now their means of salvation, as the owners wanted to buy the Christopher's property to expand the complex. For a few weeks, a construction variance for the property was all that stood in the way of a guaranteed sale. Now they had word that the variance had just been approved, and Jack, feeling magnanimous, was taking the family to Atlantic City for the day.

In light of the string of fortuitous events lately, even the normally guarded Robert was cautiously optimistic. It seemed to him that everyone had been in a good mood lately. The Christophers had all gone to the Two Guys department store to buy new bathing suits and a couple of rafts. Patricia spent the previous day preparing meals and snacks. She was excited that this would be Richard's first look at the Atlantic Ocean, and an atmosphere of rarely felt anticipation was spreading throughout the house. Unfortunately, a natural by-product of all this exuberance was talking, lots of talking, about nothing in particular. Fast talking. Loud talking. Patricia did not try to inhibit the boys from expressing themselves as the family prepared to depart. She prayed that they would be talked out before the long drive to the beach had begun.

With car fully loaded with boys and supplies, Patricia adjusted the pillow behind her back to get as comfortable as possible for the long drive. The smell of chicken salad and fruit filled the car, but the older boys would not take the same liberties with these baskets as they had on the fishing trip with Bud. They knew that if they transgressed, even crouching in their seats could not provide escape from Jack's heavy hand from the driver's seat.

Cold jets of air conditioning were a welcome contrast to the sweltering, oppressive heat outside. As the Phillies game squawked on the car's AM radio, shrill excited exchanges that only young ones can produce prompted several cautionary warnings from their mother to "keep it down". The traffic became progressively heavier as the car drove down Route 30, until the cars in front of them came to a complete stop. Although this might have been expected for a shore outing on the Fourth of July, it was not what Jack had envisioned for the family's outing.

"Awww, what the hell is this? We're going to spend half the damn day stuck in traffic," he complained. He tapped the heel of his right hand repeatedly on the top of the steering wheel, until his agitation prompted Patricia to try to diffuse his frustration.

"It's the Fourth, hon; there's always going to be traffic on the Fourth. We'll get there soon." But looking ahead, they could see steam rising from the hoods of several cars ahead.

"Now we've got these piece-of-shit cars blocking the road."

"Why don't I get you a soda, Jack? Robert, reach back and get Dad a ginger ale, will you?," Patricia tactfully suggested.

As Patricia motioned to Robert with her eyes, he could see that Jack was growing more and more restless. But this trip was all Jack's idea, Robert thought. One day to relax for the family after working nonstop for 3 months. What Robert didn't know is that Jack had days before pictured in his mind how today would go: an idyllic day with the family. Unfortunately, the further the day deviated from his idyllic picture, the more frustrated Jack became.

As the car inched slowly through traffic, a distinct and continuous "ping" began in the engine compartment. The family was left little doubt as to the cause of the rattling when warm air started coming out of the air conditioning vents.

"That's just great! Are you freakin' kidding me?" Striking one of the vent panels with his hand, Jack cracked the housing.

"Put the windows down, kids." Patricia hurriedly prompted the boys.

Once the windows were open, Robert folded his arms in resignation, leaned against the right passenger door, and stared out the window. He had really hoped that this trip would be different. He had let himself discount past disappointments. Now he felt as though he had only set himself up to be let down again.

Shawn, Russell, and Brandon were semi-oblivious to their father's growing frustration as they played "Bug Bite" out the rear window of the station wagon, hitting each other on the arm each time one of them spotted a VW Beetle. Richard was not so oblivious. As the fumes from the surrounding cars and the heat overwhelmed the broken air conditioner, he became more and more irritable. He began complaining that the smell was choking him and that the rising temperature was unbearable. Patricia tried to soothe him, but she really couldn't disagree with her young son. She herself shifted back and forth, alternating positions as she tried to rest her chin on either palm. Jack was livid that the car had not traveled more than 2 miles in the last 30 minutes.

Glancing into the passenger side mirror, Jack saw a car approaching quickly on the shoulder of the road. Whizzing past car after car, the vehicle was doing about 35mph.

"He's got another thing comin' if he thinks I'm going to let them past me," Jack shouted to no one in particular. "Who does this bastard think he is?"

Turning his wheel to the right, Jack waited until the offending vehicle was just four car lengths back before he hit the gas and lurched the Country Squire onto the shoulder, forcing the other driver to come to a screeching halt. Jack opened up his driver door and yelled over the roof of his car. "Go ahead you bastard, get out! I would just love it!"

Patricia looked at the petrified expression of the teenaged boy driver and knew there was no chance he was going to confront Jack. Instead, the he backed the blue Nova he was driving about a block and turned down the nearest side street. Jack's victory was short lived; however, as they watched the Nova re-emerge further ahead, make a right, and continue driving on the shoulder. Patricia could see Jack's gaze become wilder at the thought that the teen driver had gotten the best of him. She tried again to calm and distract him.

"Hon, why don't we just go to the lake? It's closer," she suggested in the most festive voice she could muster, hoping to salvage the rest of the family outing.

"Because I wanted to go the damn shore!" Jack rifled back. "Is that too much to ask? You've got all these assholes who don't know how to drive!" Directing his hand toward the windshield, Jack pointed out the innumerable cars in front of them to Patricia. His father's voice jolted a previously inattentive Brandon.

"We're not going to the shore?" he whined. "I thought we were going to the shore. I don't want to go to the lake!" Hot, sweaty, and uncomfortable, Brandon began to cry despite Robert's subtle signals to stop. Jack turned back toward Brandon to accentuate his point.

"Are you ignorant or just stupid, Brandon? One more word out of any of you, and I'll turn right around and go the hell home! Push me, just go ahead and push me!" Jack spun back around in his seat still seething to see all of the traffic around him.

Brandon's siblings tried to calm him down, both for his sake and theirs. True to form, Russell, in his characteristically blunt manner, seemed unaware of how close to the edge Jack was. Without raising his voice, Russell stated in a matter-of-fact tone what he thought to be true, "I hate this trip. This sucks."

Before the last word had left Russell's mouth, the family was thrown to the right side of the car. Writhing in a convulsive pile, each boy tried to reestablish some distance between himself and his brothers. Patricia fought to pull herself off of the front passenger floor as the contents of her lovingly prepared picnic basket scattered through the rear of the car. Jack had yanked the wheel in a hard left turn, screeching the tires as the station wagon was now propelled headlong in the opposite direction.

"Where are we going, Dad?" came several cries from the back. Already sensing with dread what their father's response would be, they attempted to rectify the infraction, still not quite sure exactly what the offense was.

"We'll be good, we promise!" they all pleaded.

"You want to know where we are going? Home! That's where we're going! I'm tired of all your bullshit!"

Patricia looked at her husband's set countenance and was certain that pleading was futile at this point. Instead, she turned a tearful face to the boys and raised her hand to let them know that the trip was over and that any further discourse would only make things worse. The remainder of the ride home was a mix of the engine scream as Jack floored the gas pedal, sudden violent stops at red lights, and frightful restarts when the signal turned green again. Looking out the passenger window, Patricia kept her eyes fixed as the barbeques and patriotic banners sped past. No one uttered another syllable until Jack pulled the station wagon into the driveway.

"Unload the car," Jack ordered. "Your mother will tell you where to put everything." With that, Jack stepped out into the yard, lit a cigarette, and started to walk around the block to settle down. Upset by the day's turn of events, Brandon and Richard began to cry as they carried the untouched sandwiches and snacks into the house. The three older boys were no less disappointed, but they refused to shed a tear. Previous excursions that ended in a similar way had taken the shock, if not the sting, out of the occasion.

Working with Jack on weekends had precluded Robert and Shawn from making the Double Digit meetings for the past few months. This morning, they had allowed themselves to think that a fun-filled trip to Atlantic City was worthwhile compensation for missing these cherished get-togethers with their friends. Both boys vowed that they would not repeat this lapse of judgment any time soon. They already dreaded the end of participation in the club when the family moved to Pennsauken. Tomorrow would come, and the weekend was bound to be spent like many others, working on the house.

After they had unloaded the car and stored the gear, Patricia placed an egg salad sandwich, some chips, and a pear on each of five plates on the kitchen counter, along with a can of soda. Sounding almost apologetic, Patricia called the boys to lunch. "Come get your lunch, kids. You can take your plates outside if you like." This small, unusual gesture of letting them eat outdoors was offered as a feeble compensation for the morning upheaval.

Leaning against the front of the car with their sodas resting on the hood, Robert felt the need to vent.

"Here I am, stuck in our stupid driveway, smelling like suntan lotion, standing here like an idiot! Happy Independence Day!" The sarcasm in Robert's declaration was unmistakable.

"This summer stinks just like the last two summers," Shawn chimed in to show solidarity with Robert. "Thanks a lot, Dad!"

Brandon took exception to his older siblings' affront to their father, knocking Robert's soda out of his hand. "You're a jerk, Robert. You shouldn't say stuff like that. What if God hears you?" he finished.

"I don't think that you have to worry about that, Brandon," Robert laughed sarcastically. "The way things have gone, God hasn't heard too much of anything that we've said for the past few years; but you can keep dialing, and let us know if God picks up."

The smell of hickory chips and grilling hamburgers from the neighbors' houses hung over the Christopher's house as a taunting reminder of what they might have enjoyed, had their trip gone as planned.

"Don't worry, Brandon," Shawn added. "When days like this happen to you about 10 more times, you'll be as mad as us," he predicted.

"I don't like this. I don't like it at all!" Richard chimed in. The other three were surprised that a little boy could be so perceptive, and were going to curtail their complaints, when they realized that the 4-year-old's real discontent was that the juice from his pear was making his hands sticky.

"C'mon, Richard, I'll take you in to Mom." Taking the child by the hand, Brandon did not care to hear any more of the present conversation. Robert and Shawn exchanged glances, sure that it would only be a matter of time before Brandon's naiveté wore off. Looking past Mr. Mangold's, Robert could see Jack coming up the street from the White Horse Pike.

234

Fearing that their father would put them to work if he saw them, the boys disbanded before Jack arrived back home.

Chapter 36
The Christopher Family and Moving Camp

July 1969

"Kids, I want you to take one more walk through the house and find anything that is yours," Jack called into the almost-empty house. "This is your last chance. If you don't get it now, just assume that you donated your belongings to the next family. Everyone should be in the car in the next 10 minutes so that we have time to stop and visit Grandpop before we go. We have to meet the moving van and the workers at the new house in 3 hours."

Careful to acknowledge Jack's warning to make a final round, his sons were fascinated by the echo of their own footsteps as they reverberated throughout the empty house. Running up and down the hollow staircase was never so much fun. Still, Jack's caution had merit; they hated the idea of a cherished possession being lost forever to people they did not even know or worse, thrown away in the rubble when the house was eventually knocked down so the apartments behind could expand.

Patricia could not have been more excited that this day had come. She found it hard to believe that she was moving into her new home with a fresh start and new décor. Still, in the middle of her anticipation, she felt a strange melancholy as she made her own sweep through the house, which was now devoid of any significant style or character. Running her hand over several sets of ascending lines, Patricia saddened at the thought that these notched testaments to her children's growth would soon be demolished without a second thought. No one else would care that each set of lines on the inside of the bedroom doors chronicled the progression of her own flesh and blood. These markings, some with personal notations next to them, would only be graffiti to the incoming owners.

Each room she entered brought another memory that warmed Patricia's heart. From the first crib for Robert, to the mobile hanging from the ceiling for Richard that she never had the heart to take down; all of those special moments came back. She remembered the house full of people for Robert's First Holy Communion and the time Russell spent half the day sliding down the stairs in a cardboard box. Looking up the stairs, she remembered the look on Jack's face when his brothers Joe and Charlie had snuck upstairs to pull a prank on him during one visit. As they heard him get out of the shower, they opened the bathroom door and threw a whole bag of flour on him just as he stepped out. Patricia could still see the look on his face. She felt those moments of time, though not captured on film were never the less preserved is if under glass in her memory.

"Mom," Brandon approached hesitantly. "Ummm. We...I mean, all of us were wondering...if we could..."

"Oh my goodness, Brandon, just ask!" his mother found Brandon's fumbling amusing.

"Can we, just this once, slide down the banister?" Brandon's trepidation in asking was understandable. Never in all the years that they had lived in this house had anyone been allowed to ride the banister. It was out of the question. Jack always feared that one of the boys was sure to land on Rommel; not that the idea would ever even be suggested while Jack was home. Certain that Jack no longer cared at this point, Patricia nodded her head in approval.

"She said yes!'" Brandon yelled out to the others waiting on the stairs. Patricia watched the boys and could hear the "squeak" of their hands on the polished wood as they took turns sliding down. After each had enjoyed a few runs, Patricia told them to head out to the car.

Patricia watched the time carefully. The Christophers had to be out of the house by 11 am to allow the buyers a full afternoon to make their transition. Patricia just couldn't resist pausing for a moment with her memories. How many times had she looked out the living room window to watch her sons play in the yard, Patricia wondered as she ran her fingers across the windowsill. Even now, the boys were recklessly chasing each other around just outside. Walking into the kitchen, Patricia could almost hear the laughter of the dearly loved, some now departed, as they prepared holiday meals of years now long since passed.

For Patricia, these refreshing memories offset the wearisome thoughts of recent years. She needed to remind herself that there were indeed happier days before the mire of more recent difficulties. Only in pulling the pleasant memories to the surface could Patricia breathe life back into the belief that something more awaited them beyond the wave of misfortune that had washed over her family.

As she walked outside, Patricia called to Jack and the boys, and the entire Christopher family walked toward the front door of the Mangold home. As they strolled past Avery's impressive garden, Patricia could see the thick vines of bright red beefsteak tomatoes, heavily bent as if the weight of the huge fruit was more than the branches could bear. A light wind blew across the garden, bringing the smell of strawberries, basil, thyme, and oregano from the herb garden. The combination was intoxicating.

Approaching the front door of Avery's humble single-level cottage, all the Christophers but the very youngest felt the permanence of the move, and understood that the Christophers would no longer see their beloved neighbors. Jack surveyed the quaint home with its blueish gray tile siding and mini walkway fence, and wondered suddenly why the neighbors had not visited each other more often. Jack was not sure, and never wanted to intrude to ask why the Mangolds seldom hosted guests. He knew of no one who had met them who felt anything but affinity for them.

At Jack's knock, Avery Mangold answered the door with his usual gentle smile. He wore an olive green T-shirt and dungaree blue jeans.

"Jack, Patricia, Robert, Shawn, Russell, Brandon, Richard, and…" Avery matter-of-factly pointed to Patricia's belly and smiled. "I don't know the name of this one yet, but…"Hello."

Jack did not want to impose by making Avery feel obligated to invite the family in. "We won't keep you, Avery, but we could not leave without saying 'goodbye'." Jack was really going to miss his friend. As he shook Avery's hand, Jack could sense the strength of a man many years Mangold's junior returning the grip.

"You've been a wonderful friend and neighbor, Avery." Patricia kissed Avery on the cheek almost as if he were her father. They had never met Mrs. Mangold, but hoped he understood that their sweet sentiments extended to them both.

"Just doin' what neighbors try to do is all," Avery humbly replied.

"We brought you a little something to let you know how much we care for you. Here are a couple of bags of the peppered beef jerky that you love so much, and a nice bottle of wine," Patricia said. She was gratified to see the old man's eyes light up as she gave him the bag. She knew that the jerky was a culinary indulgence that Mr. Mangold rarely permitted himself. She was certain the same was true as it pertained to the wine. "The guy at Sharp's thought that you might like the wine. He said that it has a real fruity taste."

Avery seemed touched to the point of being overwhelmed. He ran his hand along the sides of his face, seeming to struggle for the right words to say. Jack saved him from the uncomfortable silence.

"Here is our address. You are always welcome to visit. I'm sure that I could stop in when I come back to visit my Pop."

Patricia sniffled as she hugged Avery and stepped back. As Jack extended his hand, Avery grasped it in both of his. Looking to Jack as a father would his son, the normally silent neighbor was compelled to speak.

"I'm an old man, Jack; happy, but old. I see so much of a young me in you. Some things I remember fondly, others I regret. My hope for you and your family is to find good where you are. You may not think any is there, but keep looking; you'll find it. Goodbye, Jack."

Brandon and Richard hugged Avery's leg tightly as the older boys wrapped their arms around him. Never had they entertained even one bad thought about their neighbor, but only now did they realize how much they loved this gentle soul. While he had their attention, Avery shared some parting words with the children.

"Boys, I watched you all grow up, and you know that I'm not much for talking, let alone telling people how to get along. I do want you to remember this, though: do right by your parents, and God will do right by you."

As he spoke, he extended his open palms slightly to either side, directing the attention to Jack and Patricia. The boys thought he looked like a tall, thin Moses. If anyone had credibility with the boys when it came to talking about how to treat people, it was Mr. Mangold, and they took seriously what he said. Though for the older boys, how the whole "God thing" tied into anything was a more blurry matter. Even Avery's endorsement of the "All Mighty" could not erase God's apparent scarcity of late, but Avery's word still carried weight with the boys. Finally, Jack and Patricia pried a tearful Richard and Brandon from Avery's legs, and the longtime neighbors said their final goodbyes.

Loaded up and settled into the car, the family sat still while Jack hesitated before backing out of the driveway for the final time.

"You left it in even better shape than when we moved in, Jack," Patricia said. "Whatever the apartment complex does with it, you can be proud of the condition that you left it in." Jack appreciated her words of affirmation. He liked to think that for all of the ups and downs, in the end he had left the house in good shape. For now, the house was to be a rental; Jack didn't want to think about what kind of shape it might be kept in, since the new occupants would not show the care of an owner. He liked even less the understanding that their former home was slated to be torn down altogether at some future point.

After taking a deep breath and backing out, Jack pulled to the edge of the Mangold property and put the car in park. He turned to explain to Patricia, but she stopped him with a hand on his arm and nodded. She had expected this to happen at some point before they departed.

Calmly and with a little hesitation, Jack exited the car and slowly walked back to Rommel's resting place. Tilting slightly to one side, the makeshift cross fashioned months ago was beginning to bear the scars of time. Jack removed Rommel's worn and faded leather collar form the cross. For that instant, Jack was not the hardened man who fought for survival each day. He was a boy, mourning the loss of his faithful companion. He rested his fingers on the soil above Rommel's remains, grazed the thin blades of grass with his fingertips, and bowed his head before returning to the car. The boys respected Jack's pained silence enough to remain quiet themselves.

"When you are ready, we can look around," Patricia said, gently breaking the silence. "I'm sure there is another one out there waiting for you."

"Maybe once we get settled in," Jack answered. "I'll think about it." Jack felt he was not ready yet but could see another dog in the Christopher home in the future. Though as far as he was concerned, getting another *Rommel* was an impossibility. He would never find another Rommel.

The family stopped to visit Charles, and though the stop was enjoyable, it was also, mercifully for all parties involved, fairly brief. Jack and Patricia's heads were reeling from everything that had to be done today, and though Charles loved his grandkids, there were times that a houseful of boys was more than he was used to, or quite frankly, wanted. Jack's father had a usual agenda for his days: eat breakfast; work on a crossword puzzle; sit out front for a while; work on a crossword puzzle. The arrival of a station wagon full of boys threatened to completely throw off that schedule. Happily, father and son were mutually contented by slightly under an hour of chat and the agreement that Charles would come to dinner in Pennsauken once the Christophers had gotten settled in.

As the Christophers started down the pike once again toward Pennsauken, they were treated to one final pass by Stratford Avenue. Jack did not even look over or slow down as they passed their old street. He felt there was little to gain by doing so now. While most the others strained to keep the old homestead in view, Jack's gaze stayed straight ahead.

Robert preferred to look at the Bat House one last time. He would wonder on many Saturdays to come if his exclusive band of dear friends were congregating, and what culinary novelties each had brought. No Bat House would be possible in Pennsauken. For Robert, trying to replicate that would be only be a great injustice to the original. Patricia had repeatedly encouraged the boys to "be yourselves" in the new house and make lots of friends, but Robert wondered if parents said things like that for more their own conscience than any encouragement for the children. He and Shawn HAD a strong circle of friends, but their part in that circle was now summarily disbanded.

As the Bat House slid from view though, Robert considered the possibility that his mother might be right after all. The past few years had taken their toll, not just on him but on the entire family. A new start, in a new area, and the ability to reinvent himself did hold a certain appeal, the more Robert thought about it.

Weaving through the main highways and secondary roads that would deliver them to their new life, each son stretched his neck to see the new territory. The Christopher boys peered out the windows, sometimes switching from side to side as their mother pointed out places of interest. The ride was not unlike a school trip. Many of the places that seemed like oddities to the Christopher boys were landmarks to the locals. Names and places that needed no explanation among locals in casual conversation would be an enigma to the unschooled new arrivals for a while. Tippins Pond, the Pit, Fabrizio's, "train hopping," the trestle, Pennsauken pool, Wharton's, Collins Tract, Pennsauken Mart, Ivy Lanes; these were all terms that comprised a currently elusive local language. Stares of clueless bewilderment were sure to appear on all of the Christopher's faces as the arduous learning curve played itself out in the months to come.

As they drove, the Christophers began to notice that scarcely a vehicle could be found traveling along the 45-minute drive to their new home. Neon signs that normally called to passing motorists 24 hours a day were now turned off. Parking lots of the "mom and pop" businesses stacked one alongside the other all along the pike were completely empty. These signs provided a source of amusement for the kids, made into a game as the brothers tried to discern what each little shop was selling. Interrupted only by an occasional gas station or cemetery, the store fronts and homes converted to businesses stretched endlessly. The Christophers began to feel as if they had their own private autobahn.

As they drove, Patricia and Jack surmised that the reason for the emptiness was the lunar mission. Since the Apollo 11 launch on July 16th, much of the nation had been in rapt awe, seldom allowing themselves to leave their televisions. In fact, bedding down using makeshift accommodations on the floor of the Stratford living room the previous evening, the Christophers watched the lunar landing with pride. Jack had not wanted to pack the TV up and be the only family in America that missed it. The entire family whooped with joy as the module touched down. At 4:18 the Eagle came to rest on the moon's surface, much to the relief of an entire nation. No other subject but that one moment was discussed for the rest of the night. Mattresses became lunar modules and sheets became space suits for many hours, until Jack told the junior astronauts that they had to get some sleep.

Pulling up to their new home, the Christophers immediately realized that not everyone was in front of the TV with the moon mission. A dozen or more youngsters were amassed on the sidewalk across the street from their house. Seemingly convinced that some form of invisible barrier precluded the new arrivals from seeing gawking neighbors, the local kids offered commentary to each other on the assorted items being unloaded from the moving van and guessed back and forth who the new neighbors would be.

After Jack pulled the car into the short driveway and the Christopher boys began piling out of the wagon, quiet conversations ensued across the street, or at least conversations the neighborhood kids thought were quiet. Seeing the five boys exiting the car caused the boys across the street to assess how this new dynamic might change the hierarchical formula of the neighborhood. The girls seemed to feel differently. Seeing Russell, Angela Lorena fell in love with his thick black hair, and all of the young ladies blushed and giggled when they thought that he may have thrown them a smile. Russell had in fact made an intentional gesture, and made sure that the girls noticed it. The smile was warm enough to let them know that he saw them and slight enough to convey that he really didn't care.

The collage of pint-sized humanity now nudged each other and gestured toward the Christophers' new home. The Christopher boys felt somewhat like a featured new attraction at a zoo. *The only thing missing are peanuts being thrown into the den*, Robert thought wryly. He wondered for a moment what his family looked like to the outside world, and wondered which of the gangly group across the street—some eyeing the new arrivals with trepidation and some with fascination—would be friendlies.

Practically the entire block of Remington Avenue that ensconced the new house was represented. Nelson and Darrel Nielson, for example, lived directly across the street. Nelson, aged 9, was destined to own and operate a major IT company. His younger brother Darrel was known in the neighborhood for his gift of almost total recall, a startling ability in a 6-year-old. Both brothers had a pasty complexion, with faint dark circles under their eyes, which gave the impression that they seldom ventured outdoors. They were also thin, with no discernable musculature. What they and their sister may have lacked in physical stature, they more than made up for in intellect.

Further up the street lived Sal and John Tempola. Both were stocky in build and had olive brown skin, and they both strode, rather than walked, as though their importance on the block was well established. Sal had the annoying habit of constantly clearing his throat in a dramatic fashion. His brother fancied himself as well informed on any subject and talked accordingly. He was known to drone on and on until one of the bolder boys would suggest that John "lay off it."

Making no motion to give way as the Tempolas walked up were Paul and Michael Nardella. Paul was a year older than Robert, and Michael would soon become fast friends with Russell, sharing both disposition and age. The Nardella's oldest brother, Dean, was fighting in

Vietnam, and the younger brothers showed their pride in his service by being as tough as they imagined Dean to be.

The Christopher boys were sure to meet all their neighbors soon enough. Some meetings promised to be contentious, while others were more cordial. For today, the street provided a degree of separation that would allow the current residents and the newcomers a little space.

The Christopher house was situated in a long block of homes that started with a 2-story red brick house on 36th street. Next to it sat a 2-story home of white aluminum siding, and this alternating pattern of brick and aluminum continued all the way to the other end of the block, 15 houses away. Correspondingly, each owner looked out their window to see the same style house across the street.

Looking both ways up and down the block, the Christopher brothers decided being in the center of the block was good. The walk would be equal distance either direction. They also liked being on what looked like the main road through this side of Pennsauken.

Standing beside the car as they awaited permission from Jack to venture inside, the boys watched the burly moving men in their blue button-down coveralls with the monogrammed nametags, and Robert was the first to observe that the yard was small compared to the Stratford house. With their car pulled up to within inches of the house, there was only 15 feet of driveway before it met the sidewalk. With just 60 feet of frontage, there was scarcely 10 feet of space on either side of the house before you were in the neighbor's yard.

The boys liked that the house looked considerably newer than their previous residence, hoping that it meant fewer jobs for them. Gone were the carved wooden gables and detailed trimwork. Telltale signs of individual craftsmanship were now supplanted by white aluminum gutters, white siding, and standard brick molding in a pale blue color around the windows.

A short, two-tier concrete walkway led from the right side of the driveway to the front door. On the front of the house to the right of the front door was a large picture window looking into the living room, and above the driveway on the second floor, the boys could see the windows of bedrooms upstairs. The boys were already fighting over the pecking order as it pertained to sleeping assignments.

Directly in front of the car on the lower left side of the house stood what used to be a garage. At some point it had been walled off and converted into a finished basement. The boys liked the notion of having big room to themselves instead of having a car sit there doing nothing profitable.

"Can we go inside now, Dad?" Russell asked with anticipation. As Patricia slowly led the group, Jack stepped off to the side at the front door and ushered them in. Falling in behind the last child, Jack closed the door behind him, which the workmen took as an unavoidable work stoppage and opportunity to light cigarettes and grab snacks from the moving van.

Just inside the front door, a narrow 15-foot-long entryway separated the front door from the kitchen. An archway to the right, 10 feet wide, opened into the living room. Except for the kitchen (and basement, though they didn't know it yet), all the painted walls in the house blended together in a neutral eggshell color. Single-sheet linoleum covered both the entry hallway and the kitchen floors. Solid white, with light blue tones and a slightly textured surface, the flooring was clean, but aesthetically uninspiring.

Just in front of the kitchen, an angled ceiling and staircase on the left led to the second floor, and inside the kitchen entryway, another staircase and angled ceiling led down to the basement. "Don't go down there yet," Jack warned the kids. On the back wall of the kitchen was the sink and window. On the left, a chocolate-colored stove and fridge were an earth-toned match to the light brown countertops.

"Everything looks in good shape," Brandon commented as if he had a clue as to what he was looking at. All of the boys liked the house, but were still trying to adopt this new dwelling as their own; none being quite sure what he was supposed to say. The lingering issue of room assignments overhung any other thoughts they had of the house.

Walking through a second archway, the new arrivals continued along the back of the kitchen, and into the dining room. Patricia took in the wonderful smell of her brand new carpet. Running the full length of both living and dining rooms, the thick powder blue rug covered a large open area from the back to the front of the house. Several of the boys began to roll around as they felt themselves sinking into the carpet's thick pile.

"I'm never leaving this room!" Brandon exclaimed excitedly. Jack was pleased to hear the boys offering unsolicited approval of the new home, as he knew that such things were important to Patricia. For her part, Patricia loved the narrow elongated windows that allowed sunlight into the living and dining rooms through their common perimeter side wall.

"I gotta go to the bathroom," Richard announced, seeking guidance from his mother as to where he should go.

"Don't pee on our new carpet, Richard," Shawn quipped and he looked quickly at his brothers for the signs that his joke had registered. He was happy that it had.

Patricia led the family up the steps to the second floor and pointed Richard to the right at the top of the stairs to find the bathroom. The boys looked eagerly around as they waited for Jack's revelation on room assignments. Two rooms were in the front of the house and one in the back. The boys chattered about possible outcomes as they waited for Richard to come back.

"All right guys, shut up and sit down," Jack quieted the restless boys playfully. All of the kids plopped down on the light blue hallway carpet.

"This room is ours," Jack said, pointing to the bedroom at the back of the house. "That means that you do not go in there. No popping locks with the coat hanger or any of that, understood?" Jack waited for each one to respond for clarification.

"Robert, you are the oldest, so you get your own room." Jack pointed to the first room on the left from the top of the stairs.

Having fully expected to share his room, Robert could not have been happier at this announcement. "Oh my gosh; oh, my gosh; you're kidding! Thank you," he yelled and quickly hugged Jack and Patricia before flinging open the door to his private domain. Patricia gave her son a cautionary warning as he entered.

"This is your room; that means that you clean it if you want it to stay that way. We can go over all of the guidelines later." Robert walked in circles around his room with his head tilted back, and arms fully extended out on either side. "Free at last! Can I hang a 'stay out' sign on the door?"

"Slow down there, sportscar," Jack said, wanting Robert to maintain perspective. "We can talk about that later."

While feigning excitement for Robert, Shawn was not keen on his own prospects. Two rooms were accounted for, with one left. Horrid visions of two sets of bunk beds in one room gripped Shawn's pained heart, and he began to sweat as Jack called his name.

"Shawn, you're next. Your room will be in the basement. We will set up your bed and furniture there. For now, the room will be open, but once we get settled in, I'll wall off your half of the downstairs. It's not as private as Robert's, but you have lots of room."

Shawn was speechless. He didn't care that he had not even seen the basement yet. He had heard three words that he cherished but never would have expected: "your own room." Whatever it looked like, he was sure that his accommodations were far preferable to that of his younger brothers.

"Can I go down?" he begged. Jack dismissed Shawn and addressed the last three boys.

Opening the last remaining bedroom door, Jack announced the obvious. "You three are in here. We will get a twin bed for Russell and bunk beds for Brandon and Richard." Jack looked at their faces and addressed the disappointment he saw there. "Don't worry, guys, everyone moves up sooner or later."

Russell appreciated his father's comments, but could not contain his disappointment when they entered the room and he saw that that privacy would be nonexistent.

"Oh crap," he muttered. "Problem, Russell?" Jack asked with a warning look. Judging by the tone of Jack's inquiry, Russell surmised

248

that "no" would be the most prudent answer, so that's the one he gave. Russell's disappointment was not shared by his brothers. Brandon and Richard were more inclined to imagine the fun that awaited the three of them rooming together.

As they headed back toward the steps, Brandon looked over through the open door into the upstairs bathroom.

"Yellow again? You've got to be kidding me!" The rest of the boys were just as surprised to see yellow tiles and walls not much different than their old bathroom. Worse, the one stark contrast was that the floor was covered with bright orange tiles. Jack intended to change the floor as soon as possible but decided not to tell the boys just yet.

"Well, it will certainly wake you up in the morning; that's for sure," Patricia quipped as she led the family, moving slowly and heavily, down both sets of stairs to show support for Shawn's new independent space. When she reached the bottom of the second staircase, Patricia sought the comfort of the last step for her aching back and legs. It seemed like her kicking baby was just as excited as the rest of the family today.

The first thought anyone had when seeing the basement floor of being a chess piece as black and red tiles checkered the full expanse of the 20' by 25' floor. Several squares had popped loose, but neither this nor the color scheme hampered Shawn's opinion of his room in the slightest. A column was perched below a steel I-beam running across the full length of the ceiling that marked the old dividing wall between the garage and its adjacent room, and outlines of the base of the old wall were notched into the floor. Even the boys could see the unlimited potential before them. Cinder block walls made up the outside perimeter. Brown walnut paneling covered the two interior walls. Shawn did not care a bit about any of these peripheral concerns. He was shocked and elated that he had finally rated enough to get his own room.

"We're going to divide this room in half and put the wall back up here," Jack said as he pointed to the outline of the old wall. Jack's intent was twofold. He wanted to let his son know that, in time, he would have an actual room with a door, but he also wanted to make Shawn aware that the half of the basement closest to the steps was a common area.

Once the room was divided, Jack did not want Shawn complaining that the other were in "his room." Patricia gave Shawn the same cautionary warning about upkeep that she had given to Robert.

"All right, let's go, everybody," Jack announced. "I'm not paying these moving guys to stand around doing nothing. Let's get out of here so that they can get back to work." As Jack led the family out the back door to the patio, to the right they noted a small, useable bathroom, and to the left, the washer, dryer, and laundry sink . A panel wall divided the laundry room from what was soon to be Shawn's room. Stepping out onto a large, flat concrete slab, the boys could see that the yard was just wide enough to have a catch with the football.

Beginning to move towards the front of the house, Jack announced, "Mom and I have a lot to do today, so we need you all out of our hair. Grandmom and Grandpop are coming over to watch Brandon and Richard; the rest of you go find something to do." Jack's dismissal from any work party came as a surprising relief to the older boys, who had pictured moving boxes all day.

Ginny and Bud had offered to come over and help them all move in. It was not as if they didn't have enough of their own projects to tend to. Bud and Ginny had recently moved from Pennsauken to the pricier neighborhood of Cherry Hill after Bud was promoted to oversee a much larger retirement fund. Ginny had always been fond of the spacious neighborhoods and quaint shopping district of East Cherry Hill, but not everyone was excited at their move. Their beautiful former house was just around the corner from the Christopher's new place. Bud and Ginny had tried, with only minimal success, to remove their grandchildren's perception that the move to Cherry Hill had anything to do with the Christophers' move to Pennsauken.

Ginny was pained that some of the boys believed she would move just to be further away from them. She planned to purge this notion as soon as possible the best way she knew how: by frequent weekend excursions and impromptu gifts, which when combined, promised to leave Bud's wallet progressively lighter.

Before the boys got their hopes too high, Jack tempered any thoughts that they may have had about completely avoiding work.

"Have fun, but there will be plenty for all of you to do soon enough. Go check out the neighborhood. Your new school is right on the other side of the block. There is also a ball field, and a big blacktop next to it. Don't go wandering off too far, though; you might get lost."

Robert couldn't resist ribbing his brother, "Yeah, we wouldn't want wittle Russell to get lost; would we, precious?" Patting his brother on the head added to the Russell's indignation.

"Robert, kiss my…" Russell started to fire back at his brother, but caught himself and looked up at Jack, who looked down expectantly to hear the rest of his son's outburst. Russell swallowed the last word and smiled, managing to save himself from punishment for cursing.

Jack turned to the youngest. "Brandon and Richard, you guys play out back. I'll dig you out some of your toys," he said, indicating that they were to stay within the confines of the black metal three-rail fence covered with steel wire mesh that enclosed the back yard on three sides.

"You three, it's 2 o'clock, and I want you all back by 5. I do not want you going toward 36th street," he said, pointing eastward toward Camden. "Do you understand me?" The boys nodded though they did not really understand Jack's concern. They were as yet clueless to the reason for Jack's implied cautionary tone.

Chapter 37
Jack and New Hostilities

July 20, 1969

Off to check out their new stomping grounds, the three boys disappeared around the corner toward the front of the house. No sooner had they left and Jack bent down to tie Richard's sneaker, when a shriek sounded from the front yard. Further raising the alarm was the fear expressed in the three familiar voices: "Leave us alone!" "We didn't do anything to you!" "Don't touch my brother!"

Jack bolted around the corner following the sound of his sons' cries. As he ran up the side of the house, Jack could see the frightened boys huddled behind one side of an oak tree that marked the property line near the sidewalk. A large man, obviously irate, fumbled to grab any of the boys from around the tree. The man's t-shirt was filthy and the open flaps of his unbuttoned flannel shirt flapped up and down with each uncontrolled movement.

"Wan are you kidsh doin in my bik yart? C'mere you li'l bashterdz."

Jack got to the attacker, and before the man could register that he was there, grabbed the dirty flannel shirt in a steel grip. Pivoting without stopping, Jack propelled the man through the air until he landed hard on his back in the Christophers' driveway. Giving the assailant no time to get to his feet, Jack drove his fist into the stranger's jaw, knocking him out.

Pinning him with a knee pressed into the side of his head, Jack could smell the heavy stench of whiskey. The assailant was about the same height as Jack, but stocky, with a pronounced paunch. His hair was black, and wildly disheveled. Still-idling in the street, a green Galaxie

500, jutted out 45 degrees from the curb; further evidence of the drunkard's reckless state.

Hearing the commotion, Patricia ran out of the door in time to see Jack hit the stranger. Her mind raced back to Jack's assault on Billson, and she was visibly shaken by the time she reached them.

"No, no; I don't want to start out like this! Who is he?" Before anyone could answer, she turned to the boys. "Are you boys ok?" Although shaken and confused, they were otherwise unharmed. Looking from their mother, over to the man on the ground, her sons could offer no explanation. Jack thought it best to move the boys along as soon as possible.

"You three go ahead; we'll figure this out. Just make sure you're back by 5."

As the boys started down the street, Jack and Patricia turned toward the creak of a storm door opening from the house next to theirs. From the dwelling emerged a middle-aged woman in a faded floral housecoat that seemed too heavy for the warm summer months. She had lackluster red hair bound in large green curlers and was carrying a pitcher of water. Her tired, saggy face showed years of alcohol, hard life, or both.

Walking toward the still-unconscious man on the sidewalk, she moved unhurriedly, as though this was a routine occurrence and there was no reason for alarm. Patricia turned to her sympathetically. Patricia's desire to begin life here on the right foot was unwavering. Jack did not share Patricia's inclination to sympathy in the least.

"I'm sorry, Miss, we don't know what happened. This is not the way we wish to start out as your neighbors, I can assure you."

Jack had heard enough and quickly cut Patricia off.

"Are you done, Pat?! What the hell do you mean we're sorry? This son of a bitch is lucky that I didn't kill him! What was he doing chasing my kids? Who is he anyway?"

By now, the woman reached the unconscious man and held the pitcher of water over his head.

"This "son of a bitch" is my husband," she replied to Jack.

Her words came as neither a defense of her husband nor a lament of their relationship. As she calmly voiced their affiliation in a pale, even tone, she slowly poured the entire contents of the pitcher onto her husband's head. As the water splashed onto his face and spilled into his gaping mouth, her drunken spouse awoke, spit the water out, and shook his head. Once awake, he put his hand to his jaw as pain from Jack's blow registered.

"C'mon, Jason, get up. You're home." The woman reached under the now-sitting man's arm, pulling him up on a pair of unsteady legs.

"Alice, who the hell ish dish," he mumbled, waving a wobbly finger at Jack. Patricia reasoned with her husband as Jack prepared for another altercation.

"Jack, no. He's drunk. Please just let it go."

As his wife led him toward the house, Jason took advantage of having learned his new neighbor's name.

"This isn't over, *Jack*. Not by a long shot, *Jack*."

Meanwhile, Alice was neither apologetic nor combative as she led her husband into the house and shut the door behind her.

Since the car in the street was still running and blocking half of the street, Jack climbed into it, pulled it safely into the driveway, and turned it off, leaving the keys in the ignition. In the back seat of the car were several fast food wrappers, empty soda cups, a dump truck and other toys. Jack's gaze fell on a scattered stack of nursing home brochures and handouts sitting on the front seat. He felt a tinge of compassion for Jason and Alice as he wondered what challenges they faced. Whatever their challenges, though, Jack had no intention of tolerating his neighbor taking it out on *his* children.

As he crossed back onto his own front lawn, Jack saw Bud and Ginny driving up the long straight stretch of Remington Avenue. With the older boys gone and Bud and Ginny here to keep Brandon and Richard occupied, Jack was hoping to get back to the business of moving into their new home.

Chapter 38
The Christopher Boys and Conquering New Territory

Rattled from their encounter with the frenzied stranger, Robert, Shawn, and Russell were reassured as they looked back to see their father still perched on top of the motionless recipient of his crushing blow. They hoped to find out who the guy was, and why he had been so angry at them when they got back home. For now though, they were interested in exploring their new neighborhood. Walking down their new street with both the degree of caution used when anyone is out of their element, and yet a degree of self-assurance, the brothers ventured forth.

Each of the tidy houses passed were simple, but well maintained. Meticulously edged lawns suggested that no one wanted to be the only neighbor with an unsightly yard. Several yards were enclosed with knee-high picket fencing. Most homeowners had made minor attempts to set their house apart from the others with a lawn ornament here, or a small fountain there..

As they walked, the boys heard two mothers calling back and forth to one another,

"Jeanine, have you seen my Dennis?"

"I think he's over at the school with Paul and Michael, Linda," came the reply. "Would you like me to have Edward ride over and tell him to come home?"

"That would be great, Jeanine. I have a pie in the oven and can't leave to get him. Are you going to Annette's on Thursday?"

Her counterpart obviously knew both Annette and the upcoming event. "Yes, I'll see you around 7."

As quickly as it had started, the conversation ended with the doors of both houses closing almost simultaneously. Moments later, the bike-riding courier was dispatched and raced down the street to his objective.

The boys exchanged looks. Would their mother be grafted into this complex maternal network? Nothing of such breadth and scope had existed in Stratford. The Christophers wondered at the implications of living in this buzzing hive of homes. Out of parental sight would no longer necessarily be out of mind, or out of reach.

Turning left at the large corner property at the end of the block, the brothers could see Ginny and Bud's old house on the corner next to the school. Watching strangers in the yard and coming in and out of the house left an empty feeling in the pit of their stomachs. They were still not convinced as to the true motivation for their grandparents' departure from the neighborhood. Seeing the house but being barred from going inside was painful.

As they crossed at the corner, the stranger on the bike passed by once again, this time traveling the opposite direction. The second rider on the back of the banana seat was an indication that the dispatched courier had accomplished his mother's directive. As the courier pedaled, he gave the Christophers a look to suggest that he was perplexed that their paths had crossed again. Venturing onto the school grounds, the brothers wondered why, in all of the times that they had visited their grandparents, they were never permitted to go beyond the confines of Bud and Ginny's yard. The boys felt they should know this neighborhood like the back of their hand by now. Faces currently nameless might have been quite familiar if only the boys had been given the chance to meet the other kids on the block before now.

Walking down the gentle slope of the schoolyard, the Christophers came across a large open lot that acted as a buffer between the sidewalk and the school itself. The size of two football fields, the large open plot made a good playing area for pickup games of football. A long, wide concrete walkway wound from the sidewalk all the way down to the school's entrance doors, and a 40-foot flagpole stood at the entrance on the other side of the walkway.

The large single-story building was brick, with Plexiglas windows that hand-cranked open. Behind the school was a vast 15-acre plot, mostly barren and open but for blacktops next to the building that were used for recess. A rudimentary baseball field stood on the far corner of the lot. The boys were anxious to see what the classrooms looked like, but only Robert and Shawn were tall enough to peer in through the bottom of the windows. Russell was forced to pull himself up above the red brick windowsills. His vantage point for looking in lasted only as long as his arms would hold him up. They worked their way around the school, trying to figure out which classrooms would be theirs by the standard year-round décor that adorned each room.

As they surveyed the last of the classrooms, satisfied that their inquiries had been answered, the Christopher boys were surprised by a voice calling to them from behind. Startled, at first they feared being reprimand for gawking into the classrooms, but soon realized the voice belonged to someone close to their age.

"Hey, kid," the still unseen speaker called again. Turning to respond, the three Christophers assumed a defensive posture, like soldiers who had been discovered behind enemy lines.

"Yeah," Robert replied. "What do you want?" Robert hoped to put his counterpart on the defensive by posting his response as a question.

"You're the new kids moving in, right?" the boy asked.

"Yeah," Robert replied, still not sure where the conversation was going.

"I'm Paul Nardello," the boy said. His voice was not unfriendly, but he did not move closer. The boy jerked a hand behind him to indicate three other boys throwing a football around. "That's my brother, Michael, and Sal and John Tempola. We were going to play two on two with my friend as a steady quarterback, but he had to go home."

"You must mean the 'bike' kid," Shawn said, referring to the second boy on the banana seat.

"The what kid?" Paul had no idea what the Christophers were talking about and began to grow a little defensive until Robert explained how they came up with that name.

"Yeah, that's my friend, Dennis," Paul said when Robert finished. "Anyway, if I steady quarterback, we could play three on three with these guys." Paul again indicated Sal, John, and Michael.

The brothers exchanged a look and nodded. "Cool, let's play," Robert answered for the group.

As the Christophers walked over to other boys, they did not see Paul nod to the rest of his group, or their returning nod. The invitation to play football was sincere; they really did need more players. What the Christophers did not know was that Paul and his group had talked and decided that the game would also provide a means to test how tough "the new kids" were and see where they fit in the neighborhood hierarchy. Paul called them together.

"All right, here's the sides: I'll steady quarterback. Sal, you've got 'Stretch,'" he said, indicating Robert. Robert wondered why they didn't just ask their names, but since he did not find the nickname offensive, he didn't bother to ask.

"John, you're covering 'Bones' over here," Paul went on, pointing at Shawn. Robert could not help but let out a little laugh when he heard Shawn's nickname.

"Kiss my ass, Robert!" Shawn said. He didn't find the name nearly as amusing as his brother did. Shawn well knew that he was lanky. He liked to think of himself as strong and wiry, and he was much stronger than his thin frame suggested. Shawn had developed a moppy head of curly sandy brown hair that gave him a wild appearance. Jack was not thrilled with the haircut, but finally relented to Patricia's continued pleading.

"Michael, you're on 'Stumpy' here," Paul called, finishing the lineup.

"Stumpy, my ass!" Russell started over to get into Paul's face until Robert directed him away. Michael tried, with little success, to psych Russell out by clapping in approval of the matchup. The players were paired according to age and relative size and were fairly equitable. The teams took opposite ends of the field, with the locals kicking off to the newcomers. Robert caught the opening kickoff and ran back the return.

258

Robert moved with determination and intent, still assuming this was just a friendly pickup game. He had no intention of using stiff arms or shoulder butts. Thus, he was shocked when the locals came after him as if they smelled blood. Robert was laid flat as John drove his forehead into his chest and the heel of his right hand into Robert's lower ribs, knocking the wind out of him.

"Yeah, baby! That's what I'm talking about!" John congratulated himself while his teammates patted him on the back. Shawn held out his hand to help Robert up, but his brother pulled away, preferring to get up himself. He lined up again, having said nothing.

The calculated assault on the Christophers continued unanswered for the first quarter. The brothers wanted to remain diplomatic on their first day in town, unaware of the intentional nature of the physical pounding they were receiving. Paul remained pretty evenhanded at steady quarterback, capitalizing on any open player without regard to which team they represented.

At the end of the first half, the score was 28 to 7 in favor of the locals. More importantly, the Christophers felt much more battered and bruised than their counterparts.

"This is bullshit, Robert," Shawn said in the first huddle of the second half, when he was sure his celebrating opponents could not hear him. "I'm done screwing around, friends or no friends!"

"I'm with Shawn; I've had enough!" Russell said. He had a bright red mark on the side of his temple from repeatedly getting slapped.

Robert made the call. "Alright, let's play straight unless they keep giving cheap shots; in that case, give it back. I just don't want to get Dad pissed off if anything happens." The brothers nodded. Getting beat with the belt was not the way any of them wanted to end their first day in town.

As they returned to the line, the locals had no reason to believe that anything had changed. Russell could see Michael twitching his fingers as he readied to inflict another blow. Instead, as the ball was hiked, Russell brought his elbow squarely across Michael's jaw, bringing him to the ground as Russell ran his pass pattern.

"I'm open; I'm open!" Russell yelled to Paul. Paul threw a clean spiral right into Russell's chest. Overjoyed, the young Christopher ran unopposed into the end zone.

"He hit my freakin' jaw," Michael complained. If he expected support from his friends, he was disappointed.

"All part of the game, Mike," his brother cautioned.

Now that both sides knew the rules, or lack thereof, they pursued them with vigor and tenacity for the rest of the second half. Robert had a crushing tackle on Sal, and Michael and Russell traded blows at the line. More importantly, an unspoken mutual respect was being forged between the teams.

The game might have continued this way to the end, but John decided to take the dirty tactics to the next level. He and Shawn had banged each other up fairly evenly. This next play, John thought, would be his decisive move. This play would establish without dispute that John had bested Shawn. While in his stance on the line, John picked up some fine powdery dirt. As the ball was snapped, John threw the dirt into Shawn's eyes, and when Shawn hit the ground, John pushed his head into the dirt with his free hand.

As the play concluded, Shawn lay almost motionless for a minute, face down in the dirt. As the boys moved back into the huddle, Shawn slowly stirred. He raised himself to his knees, rubbing his eyes as chunks of dirt fell from his mouth. John tapped Shawn on the shoulders.

"I bet you didn't expect that, Bones, did you?" he taunted.

Shawn sprang to his feet, casting a steady wide-eyed glare at John. Robert recognized the same wide-eyed look their father got when he was pushed over the edge. Robert could not remember seeing that look on Shawn's face before.

"So you think that's funny?! You think it's funny?" In an instant, Shawn pushed John to the ground and straddled him with his knees pinning John's arms down. Shawn drove his thumb repeatedly into the other boy's throat as John struggled to free himself.

"How's that? Is *that* pretty funny?!" Shawn yelled. His brothers looked on in shock, but Shawn looked as if he was only semi-aware of his surroundings, as if something had been unleashed in him that until now had been safely contained. He grabbed a nearby rock and raised it over John's head.

"I'll put this rock through your head," he shouted, which galvanized the boys around him. Robert ran over and pulled Shawn off as John's brother Sal helped his frightened sibling to stand.

"You wanna mess with me?! I'll f-ing kill you!" Shawn yelled as Robert dragged him over to a spigot jutting out of the wall to wash his eyes out.

Robert and Russell exchanged a look over Shawn's head. Neither remembered ever seeing this volatile side of Shawn before. Shawn was not the one to make bellicose threats, but in that moment, Robert and Russell did not doubt that assuming Shawn's threats were empty would have been a horrible mistake. Whatever had snapped inside him, Shawn had demonstrated every intention of driving the large stone into John's head.

After flushing the sediment from his eyes and soaking for a moment under the running water, Shawn walked back to the others with Robert. He appeared much calmer and perhaps even slightly embarrassed at his behavior. John was leaning over with his hands on his knees, massaging his neck. He swallowed hard several times as Shawn and Robert approached, unsure whether hostilities were about to be reignited. Instead, Shawn extended his hand,

"John, I'm sorry I lost it when you threw the dirt. It was stupid, and I really don't want to piss anyone off my first day here."

Shawn could only hope that his outburst did not make enemies of John and his brother. He was glad to see John return his conciliatory gesture.

"We're cool, Bones;" John said as they shook hands, "the dirt thing was stupid."

Shawn smiled in response. He was starting to like the "Bones" moniker. Paul began laughing now that the tensions had subsided.

"Dude, you are a freakin' nut! You scared the crap out of all of us."

Shawn's brothers said nothing but were in complete agreement with Paul.

"Remind me not to tick you off, Bones," Paul finished.

Shawn liked the notion that he was thought of as a wild cannon. Robert checked his watch as the others finished dusting themselves off.

"We've got to start heading home. If we're not back by 5, our father will go ballistic."

"Don't feel bad," Sal interjected, "our old man is the same way."

As the Christophers turned to head down Remington Avenue, their new friends joining them, they realized that they'd laid the foundations of a new reputation for the Christophers, especially Shawn. By the next afternoon the whole block would hear about the new "psycho" kid, who should not be messed with. When the group reached the Nardella house, Paul and Michael extended an invitation that confirmed to the Christophers had they been accepted.

"We just got the new Beatles album if you guys wanna come over and hang out tomorrow," Paul offered.

"Sounds cool; let me check with our old man," Robert accepted on behalf of his brothers. Before going into the house, Paul called out a friendly barb to Shawn. "Hey Bones…leave the rocks home ok?" Shawn laughed, and flipped Paul a jovial middle finger.

As they got near their new home, the boys could see the moving men climbing into their truck after settling up with Jack. Battered and dirty, they reported in to their father on time, avoiding any risk of punishment, though their disheveled appearance piqued Jack's curiosity.

"What the hell were you three doing?" he asked at the sight of them." You look like five miles of bad road."

"We met a couple of kids who asked us to play football," Robert answered, clearing the air before Jack could get the wrong idea. "It was a pretty rough game, but they were pretty cool. We're going over tomorrow and hang out. They have the new Beatles album."

Jack was satisfied with the explanation for their motley appearance, but wasted no time changing their plans for the next day.

"Don't make any plans for tomorrow. I told you that we have a shitload of boxes to unpack, and your mother isn't feeling well. You can call your friends and set up another day after dinner; now go in and get cleaned up for supper. I'm picking up a couple of buckets of chicken for dinner if you want to go with me."

Riding with Jack involved strategic calculation. Although one had to be on his best behavior, whoever went with him would probably be allowed to add his own personal preference from the menu. One large bucket of fried chicken would be quietly consumed shortly after Jack's return home. Later in the evening, as the Christophers, like much of the nation, gathered in front of their televisions, the second bucket would function as a late night snack.

As darkness fell, the moonlight streaming in through the side windows blended with the black and white images dancing on the television. Patricia, exhausted from her pregnancy and the excitement of the day, fought to keep from nodding off as she nestled into the corner of the couch. The monumental moment about to be transmitted on television was significant enough for Jack to allow the family to eat in the living room and paper plates with chicken in varying stages of consumption laid scattered throughout the room. All drinks, however, by order of Jack, were to remain in the kitchen. Jack and Patricia had spread a soft oversized blanket on the living room floor for the boys to lay on, as well as to prevent greasy fingers from rubbing on the new carpet.

As the five brothers lay sprawled on the blanket, the two youngest succumbed to their body's demand for sleep. All other eyes were glued to the TV, with the older boys afraid to miss any of the history unfolding before them. Watching the grainy images of the lunar module Eagle, with cutaways to the men inside the capsule, the family was filled with awe. Belief that anything was possible, a concept that had been far removed from any of their hearts in light of the trials they'd faced over the past few years, again beckoned to them.

This first night as a family in their new home felt really comfortable, the best that hearts had felt in a long time. Perhaps, just perhaps, the family had found a pocket of breathing room. The utilitarian existence they had been living had worn on them, and it had taken a great toll on Jack and Patricia's marriage. Perhaps now healing between them, long overdue, could now begin.

Jack's new job was going well, a new addition would soon join the family, and the home on Remington Avenue promised a new start. Jack wondered what life would hold if he were able to finally shed the pains of his troubled life. For too long, Jack was resigned to carrying the weight of life in silence. Could he leave all of his demons behind him in Stratford? Having traveled for so long by himself, enclosed in a capsule of his own making, Jack had denied himself the right to consider the dangerous possibilities of a life that could be different, and perhaps even better.

At 10:39, the family looked on as the Eagle's door opened on an unpredictable and exciting new world. Wondering if the planning, pain, and risk had been worth all of the effort, the nation collectively held its breath. Slowly, Neil Armstrong emerged from the doorway and began his descent toward the untouched foreign lunar surface. At 10:56, the Christopher family burst into cheers as the first footprint was pressed onto the moon's surface. Brandon and Richard were jolted out of their oblivious slumber by the shouts that accompanied this historic moment. Perhaps this night, the Christophers, too, had been jolted out of their coma of hopelessness. Only time would tell, but for tonight, the Christophers rejoiced with millions of others at a single footprint made by one man willing to take a bold step.

Chapter 39

The Christophers and a New Hope and a New Enemy

September 30, 1969

"Mr. Christopher, you may come in with your wife for the delivery if you'd like; I just need to get you a gown." Several heads in the waiting room turned slightly as the nurse excitedly offered the recently approved opportunity to Patricia's husband. Several of the men were anxious to hear his answer.

"No, thank you just the same nurse; I was there for the most important part. I'll just wait here till the baby comes out." The need to wear a gown did not entice Jack to take the nurse up on her offer. Most of the men in the room could be heard fighting to suppress their amusement at Jack's reply. Not so amused was the nurse, who chaffed at the father-to-be's offhand dismissal of the chance to witness his son's birth. She found the attempted joke glib and distasteful. Normally diplomatic, the nurse made no effort to hide her indignation in this case.

"Very well then, Mr. Christopher, I just suppose that you can wait right here." A heavy emphasis on 'Mr.' and 'here', coupled with the distinct clomping of her rubber-soled shoes as she stormed away left no question as to the nurse's opinion. Although several of the expectant fathers were obviously elated, most sat staring at nothing. A few read the paper, more concerned about whether Atlanta would clinch the NL West title than anything going on in the recesses of the delivery rooms.

Ginny and Bud were again more than happy to spoil Richard for the day. By now the boy knew what to expect and looked forward to being indulged for the day as much as his grandparents enjoyed indulging him. The other Christopher boys were in school, passing on Jack's offer to come along or spend the day with their grandparents. None wanted to fall behind and risk getting into trouble only weeks after school had started. This was a whole new school and set of teachers to get used to.

All of the brothers were excited about having a new family member, and most hoped of course, for a boy. As much as they loved their mother, they felt that 2 girls in the house were sure to radically throw off the established patterns of the household. No burping, fart jokes, or gross forms of amusement would be permissible any longer. Only Brandon cared little which gender came home. His only thought was that a new baby's arrival was certain to move him up a notch in the slow-moving pecking order.

At 11:37 am, after a little over an hour of waiting with no word, a tall, attractive nurse strolled into the waiting room. Her entrance into the room did not go unnoticed by most of the men, as she was both beautiful and much friendlier and more bubbly than her predecessor. Jack was sitting half asleep with his arms folded and legs stretched straight and was one of the few who did not notice the woman come in. Since his butt rested on the edge of the hard plastic seats, Jack shifted consistently, trying to get reasonably comfortable.

"Mr. Christopher, Mr. Christopher!" As the nurse tapped him gently on the shoulder, Jack could smell the hint of perfume before opening his eyes.

"Mr. Christopher, if you'll follow me, I'll take you to see your wife and new son. Congratulations!" The other men in the room envied Jack, hoping that their wait would soon be over as well. Looking around as he followed the nurse, Jack was relieved to have graduated from the waiting room. As they walked down the hall, the pleasant nurse updated Jack as to his wife's condition.

"Your wife is doing fine but is understandably tired. Right now your son is down in 'Observation and Weighing'; they should be finished up any time now. He's a beautiful boy. I think that he weighed in at 8 pounds, 8 ounces." Stopping as they arrived at Patricia's room, the nurse directed Jack in and continued on her rounds.

"You may go in, Mr. Christopher. Congratulations once again." Maintaining her friendly disposition, Jack could see the nurse switch right over to her next charge.

Jack announced himself before entering to be certain that he had the correct room. "Pat? Is it ok to come in? The nurse said that you could have visitors." Patricia's voice when she answered was faint, and Jack could tell that his wife was exhausted. And yet, through all of her exhaustion and pain, Patricia was absolutely glowing as only a mother can in those beautiful, satisfying moments when she first beholds her newborn.

"He's beautiful Jack; wait until you see him. If he doesn't look like your father, no one does. I could see the resemblance as soon as they handed him to me." Jack could not have been happier. To hear that he had another son was exciting enough. To be able to show the child to Charles, and for his father to see the uncanny likeness for himself, was more than Jack could have hoped for.

"How are you feeling, hon? Did everything go OK?" Jack wanted to rescind the question as soon as he had asked. Patricia wasted no time making her husband pay the price for his open-ended question.

"Well, Jack, I feel as good as could be expected after pushing 8 pounds of baby out of me after 9 months. How about you?" Patricia laughed at her own zinger as Jack signaled with his finger that the point went to his wife.

Behind Jack, a nurse wheeled the baby's transport unit back into Patricia's room. Jack looked down happily. He was in fact, a beautiful baby boy with stout arms and legs. Jack thought that he looked like a little linebacker. Sporting a head of thick, black hair, the child made not a sound as the nurse handed him to Jack.

"He's a quiet one, isn't he, hon?" Jack asked. Patricia thought it best to keep their expectations realistic.

"He sure is, Jack, but let's not jinx him. He has only been here for an hour," she teased.

Holding his son for the first time, Jack saw him as a confirmation of a new beginning for the Christophers. Wide blue eyes looked back at

Jack as the proud father kissed his son's head, and took in the one of a kind smell of his son's hair. Jack leaned over and kissed Patricia's forehead.

"It will be nice for all of us to be home together in a few days. We'll keep the visitors down while you recover," Jack added. "You need the rest, and I'm a lousy back-up host." Patricia laughed in agreement.

"Don't make me laugh, Jack; it hurts."

Jack handed the baby back to Patricia as he suggested a name to his wife.

"I have a name for him Pat, and I want you to tell me what you think. 'Ryan Charles Christopher.' His friends will call him 'RC.'" Jack was pleased when Patricia reached over and took his hand.

"I like it Jack. I really do.

As the nurse entered the room to check on Patricia and Ryan, Jack thought that he should let his wife rest.

"You need some sleep, and the kids will be home in a little while, so I'd better get going. They are all doing fine, so don't worry." Patricia really missed her boys, but had every confidence of their well-being with Ginny there.

Jack kissed his wife as he brushed back her hair, and she nodded.

"Tell the kids I'll be home soon and to behave." She laughed to herself knowing that the boys dared not act up, especially without their mother there to intercede for them.

"I'll see you tomorrow, hon." Jack rubbed the top of Patricia's foot as he left the room.

A hint of unfamiliar optimism came over Jack as he walked to the Lady of Lourdes Hospital parking lot. Jack did not try to dismiss or argue himself of out the feeling this time. Today he had every reason to foster a brighter outlook. As he drove down Haddon Avenue, Jack gave into the impulse to pull into Henderson Florists. Walking out with a large arrangement highlighted by cotton candy cattily , lipstick phalaenopsis, and Vera jumbo amaryllis, the thought that Patricia would be shocked to see such a lovely display on the dining room table when she arrived home pleased him. The purchase was uncharacteristic enough these days,

268

but Patricia was certain to come to tears when seeing such an extravagant display.

As Jack positioned the vase of flowers safely in the passenger's seat, the intoxicating aroma of the floral combination filled the station wagon. Making his way around the vehicle to the driver door, Jack grabbed the roof rack as a sudden jolt of numbness gripped his feet. For a split second, it was as if they were of no use to him. Jack felt incapacitated as the sensation passed through both legs. Then, as quickly as it came, the feeling passed, and he moved his tingling feet again. Disconcerted initially, Jack remembered how the edge of the plastic molded seat in the waiting room dug into the backs of his upper thighs. His circulation must have been cut off by his protracted time in that chair. This explanation made so much sense to him that by the time he pulled away from the flower shop, he had almost forgotten the incident. He calculated that he would easily be back at the house before the kids returned home from school.

As he turned onto Cuthbert Boulevard, Jack decided he liked this more relaxed disposition. Perhaps it was time to retire the unflinching 24-hour guard that stood over his mind and heart. The struggles of the recent years, some admittedly self-inflicted, and the deep imprints of a painful upbringing, had scarred him. That he always expected the worst and was unwilling to be caught off guard seemed to him a natural outcome of necessary diligence.

"Let go and let God," his mother had always said, advice he had never been able to take. Nor was he yet ready to turn everything over to a seemingly absent God just yet. Perhaps at this juncture, he was ready to incline slightly toward hope. Whether the optimism would remain long enough to assure Patricia that she was witnessing a new beginning remained to be seen.

Jack made the left onto Cuthbert, which started a slow and gradual downhill ride past affluent colonial-style homes on either side. He played over the route to come in his mind. He would soon pass over Cooper River Park, a spacious and popular park frequented by residents from the surrounding townships. After the park, bearing right on a steep uphill grade would include a landscape change as he passed through an industrial park lined with building suppliers and heavy equipment rentals. This line of businesses was broken by a seemingly endless cemetery on the left. From a blind spot at the top of the hill, the road banked left past Camden Catholic High School on one side and a short distance later past the Courier Post newspaper building on the other. Jack anticipated the left turn at the far end of the massive Courier Post building. This 3-mile trek would leave him only a short trip through back streets to home.

Jack was enjoying the neatly manicured lawns of the colonial homes as he drove when he suddenly heard the engine of the Country Squire scream, and he was thrown back against the driver's seat. Jack struggled for control as the car inexplicably careened down the hill! He fought to slam on the brakes but found himself under attack by an adversary that could not be intimidated, reasoned with, or even seen. Numbness had overtaken both feet as the dead weight of his own foot, devoid of sensation, acted like a brick on the gas pedal! The same numbness moved into his hands. The indiscernible assailant struck fear into Jack's heart like no man had ever done before.

He gripped the steering wheel on either side with his elbows, and the wagon clipped a mailbox at the bottom of the hill as Jack leaned left as far as he could to navigate the curve. Swerving back and forth between lanes like a slalom skier, Jack feared taking an arm off of the wheel to move the dead weight of his leg off of the gas pedal. A cascade of sparks flew from underneath the vehicle as it bottomed out over the crest of the tiny Cooper river bridge. The shower of sparks and the swerving that preceded it also caught the attention of a police officer sitting in his cruiser at the mini-golf course at the foot of the crossing.

The car screamed past the building supplier, the uphill curve doing little to mitigate the runaway speed of the car. "Shit! Shit! Shit!" Jack yelled as he struggled to turn the steering wheel to the right with his lifeless arms. "I'm not going to make it!" Cresting the hill as the flashing lights and siren of the police cruiser followed right behind, Jack failed to regain control. Unable to navigate the curve, Jack felt the car jump the

270

median into oncoming traffic. This insufficient turn almost brought him head on into an oncoming motorcycle. The biker fishtailed into the right lane, the rear of the bike just missing the grill of the car as the rider flashed past Jack's view.

Popping as it impacted the median, Jack's front tire shredded as the Country Squire crossed back over onto the other side of the roadway. The wagon went airborne as it jumped onto the front lawn of the Courier Post. Sliding uncontrollably on the wet grass, the car impacted the steel pillar supporting the lighted sign. Mercifully, the deflated tire acted as an anchor as it dug a rut through the freshly watered grass. The back right quarter panel struck the support column, and the station wagon came to an abrupt halt.

The flashing lights of the police car reflected onto the dashboard as Jack looked up through the windshield. Although unhurt, he was still unable to move. Sprawled across the passenger seat, his legs hung lifeless by the gas and brake. Near Jack's head on the passenger floor, the flower vase lay shattered, its previously exquisite contents now lying in a tangled heap. Jack reached for the door handle, but his fingers could not register the steel of the release.

Pellets of glass rained down on Jack as the police officer shattered the passenger window with his nightstick. Jack heard him calling to him. "Are you OK? Hang on, I'm gonna get you out! We've got to get away from the vehicle!"

Jack called out in desperation from inside the car. "Ni ne elp. Ni gnat peel…my negs."

As the officer pulled him clear of the accident, Jack thought of Patricia and tried to explain to the officer. "Nel…my wife…plees."

The officer's primary concern at the moment was for Jack's safety. "We have an ambulance on the way, Sir; please just lie still."

The officer laid Jack on his back and took a blanket from the trunk of his squad car, placing it over Jack.

Leaning over Jack with his hands on both knees, the patrolman expressed his suspicions as to the root cause of the accident.

271

"Sir, how much have you had to drink today? You were swerving all the way back at Cooper River."

"Ni non't nrink.," Jack replied as clearly as he could.

Shortly thereafter as the ambulance and another squad car arrived, the officer turned to the EMTs and said, "Looks like a DWI. He was all over the road a few miles back. You guys can take him to Lourdes to get checked out. We'll ask for a blood sample, and then bring him down to the precinct for processing. He has no lacerations or other visible injuries but can't stand up. No shocker there."

The EMTs nodded, but did not speculate on Jack's condition. As they transported him to the hospital, the police drove to Jack's house to notify his family. Ginny explained that Jack's wife was in the hospital, having just given birth.

"She's at Lady of Lourdes Hospital, and Jack should be with her. Why? What happened? Is somebody hurt?" The policeman refrained from providing any details, primarily because he really knew very little himself.

"We'll have your daughter call you as soon as possible, ma'am. I assure you everything will be OK."

When the police told her about the accident, Patricia feared for Jack's condition, but did not concur for one minute that he had been drunk. The officer, however, was even more convinced that Jack had done a little too much celebrating when he heard about Ryan's birth.

"I can tell you that my husband has not been drunk a day in his life!" Patricia said, adamant about setting the record clear. "I don't know what the problem is, but I can tell you it's *not* drinking. "

The officer and his partner were not swayed to change their opinions, but they respected a wife's desire to defend her husband, and, in consideration of her condition and the stress that the situation had placed on her, they did not argue against her assertion.

"You've been a great help, Mrs. Christopher. Your husband is conscious and on his way here. We won't disturb you any longer. Oh, and congratulations on the birth of your new baby."

272

If Patricia recognized that they did not believe her, she did not have the time to worry about it. The new mother immediately began a flurry of calls to address immediate needs. She asked Ginny and Bud not to say anything to the boys when they arrived home. They all agreed that worrying the children made no sense when they did not have any details. Bewildered as to what might have happened, Patricia took some solace in the report that Jack was conscious.

Jack started to regain feeling in his hands and feet shortly after arriving at the hospital in the ambulance. By the time he had been checked in, he was functioning enough to articulate his ordeal to the emergency room personnel. Jack also had a few choice words that he wanted to share with the police officer. Given his relatively quick recovery as he recounted the accident, the doctors were inclined to believe that Jack had not been drunk.

"We don't doubt your story, Mr. Christopher, but the police will need to see your bloodwork to confirm your innocence. Either way, we would like to keep you overnight for testing. If your episode was not alcohol related, and we have no reason to think that it was, we need to find out what is going on. I will set up a battery of tests to start as soon as possible and send the results to your primary doctor. Who would that be?"

"Dr. Scherring in Somerdale," Jack replied. Dr. Scherring was a longtime friend of the Christopher family and the only physician that Jack trusted. In addition to being a top-rated practitioner, Dr. Scherring was affable and had a low-key disposition. He had gained jack's respect when Jack's mother was ill by often going out of his way for her. He had a way speaking gently but directly, and Jack knew Dr. Scherring could be counted on for frankness.

After the immediate flurry of activity in the emergency room, Jack insisted that he at least be permitted to call home and calm the fears of his children, unaware that the boys were currently in the dark. Bud and Ginny however, were relieved to hear Jack tell them himself that he had no major injuries, and they gave the phone to Robert when asked.

"I'll need you to take charge for a couple of days, Robert," Jack told his oldest. "Grandmom and Grandpop will make sure that the others know that I have put you in charge."

Robert appreciated the confidence in him in his father's voice, but the conversation took Robert back to when Jack was in jail. The responsibility again weighed heavy on him.

As Jack was being settled into a room for the night, the results of his blood work came back. Since his blood contained no alcohol, the township officer was satisfied that the accident was not a police matter. The arresting officer went so far as to call Jack's hospital room and apologized for presuming he was guilty of drunk driving. Also encouraging was news that the Country Squire was salvageable, though it had fared far worse than Jack in the accident. The vehicle had sustained considerable damage on both the front right and rear left quarter panels, but this was the least of the family's concerns.

Settled into his room for the night, Jack could not have been happier to see Patricia walk into the room. As late as it was, and both spent by the end of the long day, they still found renewed strength in seeing one another. After asking for several hours to leave the maternity floor long enough to see her husband, Patricia was finally given the go-ahead. She walked in and kissed Jack as he slept. Slowly awakening, Jack smiled at Patricia as evening rain danced against the window behind her.

"I'd bought you some flowers," he said with a rueful smile, "but they didn't make it. If I had known I would have bought the cheap vase," he joked.

"Just take it easy, hon," Patricia whispered softly. "I'll see if they will let me bring the baby down tomorrow. You may be running around all day, but I'll try."

Too short-lived had been the earlier excitement and exuberance of Ryan's entrance into the world. As the night finally gave into midnight, Jack had more questions than answers for the day to come. What malady had beset him? Was this just a strange fluke, or did the accident portend something bigger and more ominous? Cold steel bedrails replaced the warmth of hope that had been coursing through Jack's body. That hope had been circumvented by an emotion that had always been unfamiliar to him. He felt fear as never before in those frantic flashing minutes when he was stripped of all control of both body and circumstances. Not knowing; that's what was killing him.

Chapter 40
Jack and the New Siege

October 19, 1969

Laying flat on his back in the middle of the living room carpet, Jack raised his arm at the elbow, and let his forearm freefall back onto the floor with a slow, rhythmic "thump." Thump…thump…thump. Trying to drive the constant tingling feeling from his arms, Jack also hoped to block out Ryan's cries from upstairs. It had been about 3 weeks since the accident, and Jack had no more information than that first night in the hospital. Nothing had changed in his understanding of the new enemy.

What had changed were Ryan's quiet nights of cooing. Now his piercing screams could be heard throughout the house. Piercing as the sound was, the inconsolable wails were enough to fray anyone's nerves, but the effect was magnified many times over for Jack. Though Jack cared little as to the name the malady, he had begun recently suffering from hyperacusis. Noises that to most might seem nominal sent shards of pain through his head. He was convinced that the condition resulted from the accident, although Dr. Scherring assured him that the timing of the events was coincidental and unrelated.

Unaware of their father's condition and oblivious to the very real and detrimental impact noise had on their father, the boys thought that most of his complaints were just designed to impose arbitrary authority and control. When out of earshot, the boys had begun to mimic his complaints with a hint of sarcasm. "Stop crunching that apple! Don't slam the damn cabinet! Put down that friggin' bag of chips!" Hidden rebellion among his sons, however minimal, fertilized the seeds of resentment that had sprouted deep within their young hearts.

276

For her part, Patricia tried her best, but she was also worn down by the constant wailing. When Jack said once again, "Can't you shut him the hell up, Pat? That screaming is driving me nuts!" she answered more honestly than she'd intended.

"I'm sorry, Jack; there's nothing that I can do until Ryan gets over the colic. That may be tomorrow or it could be 2 months from now; I have no way of knowing." Patricia immediately second-guessed herself, and she thought that the last bit of information just slipped out and probably did little to make Jack feel better. Patricia had almost suggested that her husband take a walk down on 36th street to pick up cigarettes, but stopped short, recognizing that this would only have reminded Jack of two recent events that did not sit well with him.

First, his driver's license had been put on medical suspension for the next 6 months, leaving him unable to drive. For now, he needed Patricia to chauffer him anywhere he needed to go. As Jack put it, he felt like "some damned invalid."

Compounding the frustration was Dr. Scherring's recommendation that Jack not walk for extended distances until they knew more. Another flare up may be possible, and the doctor did not want such things to occur as Jack was crossing the street.

Jack thought of their earlier meeting with the doctor and grimaced.

"So now you're telling me that I can't walk and I can't' drive. That doesn't leave me a whole hell of a lot of options, Doc," Jack had said. Now he found that lying around with a baby screaming was almost more than he could stand. The increasing frequency of strange symptoms with no answers left Jack prone to bouts of depression. These episodes made life that much more difficult for everyone, as the melancholy seemed to spread like a virus throughout the family. At least he would get some information when he and Patricia met with Dr. Scherring on Monday. Dr. Scherring would have the results of Jack's spinal tap and associated tests, and hopefully a diagnosis. At the very least, this would give the Christophers a starting point from which to address the problem.

As he and Pat talked, the sound of his arm thumping on the floor harder and harder punctuated the conversation.

"Hopefully we'll have some kind of answer from Dr. Scherring when we see him, Jack. I know this is frustrating." Jack rested the back of his head down on the carpet with his eyes closed, saying nothing, as both arms continued to fall alternately to the floor.

Patricia returned upstairs, cringing as she opened the bedroom door. Dragging her tired, sleepless body into Ryan's room, she hoped to bring her baby some measure of comfort.

Chapter 41
The Boys and an Afternoon's Reconnoiter

Later That Day

Robert had been tasked with taking the rest of the boys outside, anywhere, for the next few hours to lessen the tensions at home. Although not thrilled with having been saddled as the babysitter once again, given the current mood within the home, Robert had no intention of remaining indoors anyway.

Lately, home was often the last place Robert wanted to be. Even school felt more comfortable. Robert had successfully made the big move from elementary school to Junior High. Being the "new kid" made little difference, since a hundred other former 6th graders had to run the same gauntlet he did. It had not been as easy for all the other brothers.

Brandon had been thrilled to start kindergarten, which allowed him to traverse the same hallway as Russell and Shawn. Despite being warned beforehand, Brandon had developed the irritating habit of calling out to his brothers every time that he passed by them in the hall. This could repeat itself perhaps four or five times a day. "Hey, that's my brother Russell! That's my brother Shawn over there. Hey Shawn!...Hey, Shawn!...Shawn!" After a while the older brothers resorted to turning their heads away while cringing, all the while marked for playful taunts by their classmates. Such recurrences had made the first few weeks of school painfully long for Shawn and Russell.

Now, walking down 36th Street, the clan made their way to the peak of the 36th Street Bridge. As the older boys stopped periodically to allow Richard to catch up, Brandon reveled in not being the junior man in the group. Brandon was intent on capitalizing on this raised status while he had the attention of the others.

"Hurry up, Richard. My gosh, you are so slow!"

"You still wet the bed, Brandon, so don't make fun of me!" Richard shot back. He was doing his best to keep up and in no mood to be made a scapegoat. Richard's comment sent the older brothers into a fit of laughter and knocked Brandon's ego down a few pegs.

"He burned you, Brandon," Russell laughed.

When they arrived at the top of the bridge, the older brothers lifted the two youngest up to peer over the concrete wall to the steel tracks 70 feet below. A string of boxcars stretched as far as the eye could see. The train tracks cut through a vast expanse of otherwise untouched sandy dunes covered in tall wild grass and weeds. Russell thought the dry wispy tops of light, waving grasses almost invited a lit match. *What a beautiful, waving, poetic picture that would be*, Shawn thought.

The boys realized that the trains were not alone down on the tracks as they passed under the bridge. The brothers watched as several figures in the distance jumped out of the adjacent underbrush and onto the side of a passing boxcar. The figures disappeared inside the car momentarily, and boxes flew out of the car through the air, crashing onto the stony tracks below.

"Check it out; they're robbing the train!" Robert said. "See if you can tell what those guys are stealing."

From their vantage point, the boys could see uniformed cops converging on the violated car, running across the top of adjacent boxcars and climbing down their steel ladders. Soon after, the boys watched as frightened train robbers jumped from the moving car, landing on the stony ground below before running off. Covered by the thick underbrush, the thieves eluded capture but were unable to grab any of the loot now lying alongside the tracks. Slowing as it pulled into the cannery behind the brothers, the cargo train had presumably reached its destination. Leaving the damaged boxes beside the train tracks, the railway officers moved on with the rest of the convoy's cargo.

"Let's go find out what they threw off of the boxcars!" Robert's suggestion was met by the others with enthusiastic approval. Only Shawn was quiet, appearing preoccupied with looking down over the railing to the rocky ground below.

"Come on Shawn, move it," the others called as they began to make their way down the steep slopes to the train tracks below.

"Robert," Shawn called to his brother in an eerily calm voice. "If someone were to jump from here, do you think that they would die right away; I mean as soon as they hit the tracks?'

Robert thought the question awkward, and the fact that Shawn had not moved, apparently waiting for an answer, disconcerting.

"I don't know, Shawn, and I'm really not interested in finding out. Let's go see what was thrown off the train." Robert was happy that Shawn seemed satisfied and moved to join his brothers they as slid down the soft gray sandy embankment to the tracks below. Stopping to ensure that the train cops were not still in the area, the brothers hunched over as they moved down the tracks. Coming upon the discarded contraband, the Christophers were thrilled to see assorted candies spilling from the broken boxes onto the track bed.

"Yeah, baby!" Robert whooped. "Load up with as much as you can; we have to get out of here! We don't know if the cops will come back." Robert was not interested in spending any more time than necessary on the exposed open railroad tracks. Quickly stuffing their pockets, the Christophers disappeared into the tall grasses. Winding their way through the brush, the brothers passed several abandoned campfires and finally emerged at the fence along the rear property of the school. The Christophers cut across the open grasses toward where the Nardella brothers and several others were playing football.

The pants and jackets of the Christophers were brimming with pilfered confections, and bars of candy repeatedly fell out of overloaded pockets as the boys walked. Aware that bringing all the sweets home without being challenged by their parents was impossible, Robert planned to capitalize on the acquisition that had befallen them. He convinced his siblings to give the excess candy to their friends. The bleak picture Robert painted of Jack's reaction to his sons coming into the house with stolen candy was motivation enough for the others to share the bounty of their endeavors with the neighbors.

"Where did you get all of this stuff?" Mike Nardella asked.

Not inclined to share the details their adventure on the train tracks, Robert responded, "We found it," in a voice that made clear that no further details would be forthcoming. Mike and the others cared little how the Christophers got the candy. Robert's strategic move paid off: not only had he and his brothers found favor with the neighborhood top dogs, but the Christopher brothers were solidifying their reputation as town badasses.

The boys consumed or discarded the last vestiges of the day's bounty before arriving home, Robert and Shawn checking the younger ones for any obvious oversights.

The house was surprisingly quiet as they attempted to sneak in the front door. The boys saw that Jack was fast asleep on the living room floor but before they could go to their respective rooms, Patricia came down the steps from Ryan's bedroom. "Shhh!" their mother signaled with a finger to her lips. "Not a word. Ryan just went to sleep," Patricia informed them while abruptly ushering them all down to the basement.

"We had a great time!" Richard piped up. "Mom, we got candy from the box next to the train, and shared it with all of our friends!"

Shawn, Robert, and Russell were incensed that it had only taken Richard 30 seconds to bring all of their careful planning to naught. Brandon was just content that *he* was not the one who betrayed the unspoken trust. Patricia's suspicious and angry gaze shot over to Robert, who was bracing for the imminent interrogation. Much to his surprise and relief, his mother just raised her hand in exasperation and went back up the steps. What the boys did not realize is that hour upon hour of Ryan's screaming and her husband's foul mood had left Patricia with little energy for another battle. Their near escape from Patricia's anger did nothing to mitigate resentment toward the spoiler of their plan.

"Richard, you little shit, why did you have to run your mouth?" Robert gritted through his teeth.

"You couldn't keep quiet for one minute. You are never going with us again!" Shawn added.

Notifying the youngest that he would be ostracized from the group in the future brought him to tears; his crying voice growing ever louder. Shawn finally convinced Richard that the threat was all in jest, just to keep their mother at bay. The boys remained in the basement until Jack woke for supper and their mother called them up. They decided separation from Patricia was the best available course of action. Besides, none of the brothers were too hungry the rest of the afternoon.

Chapter 42
Jack and the Enemy Named

Saturday, November 15, 1969

Lingering odors of pine cleaner and rubbing alcohol surrounded Patricia and Jack as they waited nervously in the reception area of Dr. Scherring's office. Over the 6 weeks following the accident, Jack had undergone a battery of invasive tests while trying to keep life as normal as possible, hoping to find the cause of his bouts of numbness. Recurring symptoms had grown considerably worse in recent weeks, though Jack had made every attempt to hide his debilitations from both Patricia and Dr. Scherring. Most distressing for Jack were uncontrolled fits of shaking in both legs, suppressed only by pressing down on his bent knees with both hands. More recently, he'd started having intermittent blurred vision that he tried his best to attribute to some unrelated cause.

Exacerbating simmering tensions in the Christopher household, Ryan continued to have colic. Sleep deprivation and piercing migraines led Jack to put his hand through several walls in frustration. His frayed nerves rode on a razor's edge, and his aggravation fed the increasing discord that occupied the Christopher home daily. Even he and Patricia found themselves with little to say to each other as of late. Both found the silence of the waiting room refreshing, and neither wanted to ruin the solitude by speaking. They sat next to , but slightly turned away from each other; each lost in troubled thoughts while they waited for the consultation.

Behind closed doors, the doctor conducted a final review of Jack's test results. As the receptionist finally escorted Jack and Patricia into his office, he saw Jack's eyes immediately fix on the thin stack of reports in

284

his hand. Jack was disconcerted that such a thin collection of papers could so profoundly impact the rest of his life. Dr. Scherring seated himself at a small modest desk and collected his own thoughts before speaking. Leaning forward with both elbows on his desktop, Dr. Scherring spoke slowly, seeming to choose his words carefully.

"Jack, I've had my suspicions as to what your condition might be, but we needed the tests you've been through to be sure." Jack shifted nervously in his chair as Dr. Scherring closed in on the heart of what he was waiting to hear. "Unfortunately, the results of your lumbar puncture confirmed my initial concerns. What you have, Jack, is a disease called Multiple Sclerosis...or MS."

Patricia's eyes filled with tears, and she instinctively reached over and took Jack's hand in hers. Hearing the condition given a name suddenly made all of their fighting seem petty.

"What the hell does this mean for me, Doc?" Jack asked. Hearing a name for the disease left him no more informed. Dr. Scherring continued to explain in his steady baritone voice.

"When we analyzed your spinal fluid, we found a large number of antibodies. Patterns within those antibodies indicate an abnormal autoimmune response within your brain and spinal cord. What I am saying, Jack, is that your body is attacking itself. The myelin, or coating on your nerve endings, is being stripped off, leaving scar tissue. This scar tissue essentially blocks the signals to and from the brain. It means that your muscle groups begin to stop talking to various sections of the brain."

Patricia needed to break the flow of information to process it, and she held up her hand to get Dr. Scherring's attention.

"Doctor, please tell us...is this temporary or permanent? Is there a cure? What do we do now?" Patricia's voice cracked slightly as she struggled to control her emotions. Jack's expression changed little while he struggled to take in what Dr. Scherring was telling him, and what the implications were for his life.

"The truth is," Dr. Scherring continued, "that we really have no way of telling how far Jack's condition will digress. We have a scale that we use to identify levels of disability. Measurement on the scale ranges from one to ten, one being the least disabled."

Jack looked at Patricia and back to Dr. Scherring. "And what is a 'ten'?" he asked hesitantly.

Dr. Scherring paused for what to Jack and Patricia seemed like forever. His delay was deliberate, but not to increase anxiety. Instead, he hoped to slow the couple's runaway thoughts and give them time to deal with what he was saying. He now spoke slowly, not condescendingly, but carefully and gently, as a father to his son.

"Multiple sclerosis, or MS, is a very unpredictable disease. Jack, I'm not going to pull any punches. Right now, based on your symptoms, I would say that you are at a level three. You currently have mild disability in both arms and legs. There is a chance that you may stay at level three and never get any worse. Going down to a two is unlikely but still possible. We do, however, need to be prepared for possibilities at the other end of the scale." Patricia winced as Dr. Scherring delved into those more frightening prospects.

"It is just as likely that you may experience a slow, steady digression of your motor skills, vision, and cognitive ability. MS attacks every part of the body; however, I do not want to spend a lot of time concentrating on symptoms that you do not have yet. We would do best to take it as each day comes. There is not cure, but we can try to manage your symptoms as best we can. First, you want to keep your muscles moving; don't give up and stop exercising. Take walks, do light exercises, anything to keep those muscles active. I will prescribe some medications for the spasms, as well as the pain, and involuntary shaking. There is shaking, isn't there, Jack?"

This question was the doctor's way of gently letting Jack know that he was well aware of his patient's probable symptoms, even without Jack voicing them. In short, Jack had not succeeded in hiding anything from Dr. Scherring. Jack did not volunteer any information about his blurred vision, but did admit to more muscle spasms and involuntary shaking than previously shared.

"There is a little shaking, Doc, and the spasms and cramps keep me up at night." Dr. Scherring understood Jack's discomfort but was never quick to administer sleeping pills.

"Well, let's try to alleviate the spasms first and see if that allows you to sleep."

The remaining minutes of the visit were spent by the doctor suggesting support groups and resources that the couple could pursue. With great tact and sensitivity, Dr. Scherring did his best to prepare, not only Patricia and Jack, but the rest of the family through them for the potentially drastic changes they may experience. As they left the doctor's office, both Jack and Patricia were emotionally drained, but at least their relations had thawed enough for them to address the immediate concerns at hand.

Patricia could tell that Jack had some numbness in his feet, because he had been dragging his foot slightly as they walked to the car, though he said nothing. Patricia dared not point it out after such a draining meeting with Dr. Scherring. She knew that Jack found it emasculating enough to be in the passenger's seat as they pulled out from Dr. Scherring's parking lot onto the road.

To Jack, this was no different than a schoolboy being taxied to and from afterschool band practice. He lamented that the State had stripped him of control of his driving privileges. Each day, with few exceptions, Patricia had to take Jack to and from the shop.

His condition had not gone unnoticed at work either. While his new employer was much more sympathetic and accommodating than Kutter Metals had ever been, certain realities still existed, and Jack knew it. He was having trouble feeling the metal plates when trying to pick them up and he sometimes had difficulty guiding the heavy sheets through the cutter. Finding himself on disability at some point loomed over Jack, and he detested even thinking the word.

Jack felt like, one by one, all the vestiges of self-determination, control, and predictability were being systematically stripped away from him. Perhaps the most stinging affront was that his own body was failing him. Attacking itself cell by cell, appendage by appendage, Jack's body

287

offered no hint as to when, where, or to what degree it would be stricken next. A disability incurred as the result of another accident, a contagious disease, on any foreign intrusion on his health would have been bad enough. Being told by Dr. Scherring that his own body was attacking itself brought unimaginable grief and frustration. An unwilling host, Jack still could not stop his own internal assault.

Patricia, as much as she wanted to, could not even offer her husband a comforting "you'll be OK," with any degree of confidence that her words were true.

When they pulled into the driveway at home, exhausted and filled with unanswered questions, Patricia and Jack could see Jason Dorgan sitting on his front steps. Leaning over, half slumped with his head resting against the black iron hand rails, Jason raised an oversized drinking glass to his lips, but not much deductive reasoning was needed to understand that the glass was filled with liquor. Raising his head slightly as he heard their car doors slam, Jason leered with hatred at Jack, but said nothing. Dorgan wanted Jack to know that he had not forgotten the previous confrontation and was in no mood to extend forgiveness. Dorgan was drunk but retained enough self-control to refrain from challenging Jack.

Meeting Patricia and Jack at the front door, Ginny held Ryan, who was giggling as he pulled at the graying strands of his grandmother's hair. Ginny could see that her daughter and son-in-law were too tired to recap the results of their doctor's visit, and she did not press them for an update. Striving to keep the conversation to a minimum, Ginny spoke only enough to fill them in before leaving.

"Ryan's been perfect," Ginny said, much to Patricia's delight. Ryan pulled himself close to Patricia's neck as his grandmother handed him over. "Robert, Shawn, and Russell are running around with their friends somewhere. I told them all to be home by 4 o'clock. Richard is glued to the television, and Brandon has been moping around all day. He wouldn't tell me what was bugging him. Listen, honey, I'll leave you both be. I can see that you are tired."

Ginny kissed her daughter on the head as she left, then turned to Jack. She leaned over and kissed him on the cheek just as his own mother once did. Her hand remained rested gently on the side of Jack's cheek.

"Take care, Jack; we'll be thinking of you."

"Thanks, Mom, I appreciate your concern."

Both Ginny and Jack meant their sentiments. For those brief few minutes, Jack felt like a son. Both Jack and Patricia were thankful for Ginny's sensitivity.

Once in the house, Jack headed straight for the couch, worn out by the troublesome prognosis Dr. Scherrer had given them and a now growing migraine. Almost as soon as his body was prone on the couch, Richard climbed up on his father's stomach, saying nothing. Nestling his body between Jack and the back of the couch, Richard continued watching television in silence. Jack welcomed his son's unspoken show of affection and rested his left hand across his son's chest as Jack faded off to sleep.

As she went upstairs, Patricia could hear a faint sobbing. She stopped mid-stairs and tuned her head to determine its origin. The low, tired crying was coming from behind the door to Russell, Brandon, and Richard's room. Turning the doorknob, she was surprised to find the door locked and the room's occupant unresponsive to muted requests to open the door. Patricia had no intention of waking Jack, who she knew would be in no mood to learn of such a household infraction.

Patricia went into her bedroom closet and retrieved a metal coat hanger she could use to pop the lock. Quietly gaining access, she found the boy's room had all of the curtains lowered and the room lit only by the few rays of light that managed to sneak past the drapery's edges. Brandon was kneeling on the floor with his upper torso laid out across the bed. His face was buried in his old Davey Crockett cap; his muffled sobs became more distinct as his face turned to see Patricia's approach.

Brandon's eyes, tear filled, red, and tired, made it evident that the crying had been going on for some time. Kneeling next to her son,

Patricia placed one hand upon his quivering back, rubbing gently as she tried to comfort him.

"Honey, what's the matter? Why are you crying up here all alone?"

Brandon's reply gripped Patricia's heart.

"Why don't you and Dad like each other anymore? You yell at each other all the time. Even when I go to bed I can hear you both yelling. The other kids in class talk about Thanksgiving coming, and family stuff. We're never like that now. All that we do is yell."

Patricia ruefully remembered that she and Jack had gone through several heated arguments lately as Richard's colic had worn thin any patience they may have had. Everything bothered Jack: every noise, misplaced item, or slightest interruption. Patricia had no more tolerance for being corrected, admonished, belittled, or demeaned, and their confrontations had grown much more vocal recently.

"If you think that someone else can do better, feel free to look, Jack! I'm damn tired of you nit-picking everything that I do! What do you want from me?" she had shouted the previous evening as she slammed the cabinet door closed.

"There you go, playing the friggin' martyr again, Pat! For all I give a shit, you can take the whole bunch and move to your mother's! Don't think that you'll get a penny out of me either."

"You're not even sure that you can make it around the house, Jack. How would you live here alone?" Patricia said. She had meant this as an observation, but Jack did not take it as such. He hurled his coffee mug through the kitchen window, watching as it disappeared into the darkened back yard and the broken window was one more thing they'd needed to have replaced.

Patricia continued rubbing Brandon's back as she thought of what to say. Trying to explain all of the conditions that had strained the couple's relationship would have been pointless. Before she could speak, Brandon continued.

"Sometimes I lay at the top of the stairs in the dark and listen to you and dad fighting. Why do we have to move away again? I finally have friends here; kids that like me and don't make fun of me." At this last

290

revelation, Brandon started hyperventilating. His mother held him close and began to cry with him as she rocked Brandon back and forth.

"We're not going to move, honey, I promise. Sometimes parents say things that they don't mean when they get mad. Daddy and I love each other even when it may not sound like it. Look at me…you will not have to leave your friends."

At Patricia's assurance, Brandon composed himself enough to stop crying. Patricia opened the drapes, letting in the afternoon sun.

"Dad is asleep on the couch. Why don't I bring you up some lunch and a soda? You can calm down a little and then maybe find some of your friends."

Brandon nodded but stopped her as she turned to go downstairs.

"Can we not tell the others, Mom? Can this just be between us?" Patricia assured her son that she was sensitive to the need for confidentiality.

As she fixed lunch for Brandon, Patricia wished that she was as confident of family cohesiveness as he portrayed to her son. It was certainly true that she and Jack made foolish, unintended remarks in the heat of confrontations. There was no way of measuring with any degree of accuracy how wide the gap between Patricia and Jack really was. As with Dr. Scherring's unavoidably ambiguous prognosis, Patricia could not presume to know what awaited their marriage in the dark days to come.

When she took Brandon's lunch upstairs, Patricia found him asleep on his bed; his tiny resources depleted by the multitude of tears shed. Leaving his lunch tray on the end table, Patricia paused at the foot of the steps to watch Richard fast asleep next to Jack. Jack, still napping, found a temporary escape from the uncertain prospects that awaited him.

Chapter 43
The Christophers and a Christmas Battle

December 1969

On the last day before Christmas break, each classroom at Baldwin Elementary school celebrated with a long anticipated party, and the classes were adorned with students' holiday crafts. Paper snowflakes hung from the ceiling of the common hallway. Lining the back of each room were tables with colorful holiday deserts and juice provided by the students' mothers. Candy canes made of painted macaroni adorned the glass panels of each classroom door. Highlighting the event would be the Christmas play put on by the sixth graders, followed by Santa's arrival in the gymnasium.

Looking forward to the Christmas break, Shawn and Russell were just glad Brandon seemed to have stopped pointing them out all the time. They had found his enthusiasm amusing the first few times, but after 3 months, it was just humiliating. The habit had not done Brandon any favors socially. Though it did not, in and of itself, cause his classmates to ostracize him, it was certainly part of the framework that contributed to his social isolation from all but a few of the students. Unlike his older brothers, Brandon never had acquired good social skills. Even Richard appeared to have more poise and self-confidence than his older brother.

Brandon's lanky gait, swinging arms and his pale, thin body still made him the object of occasional ridicule. Moreover, try as he might to be accepted, any contributions Brandon made to a conversation either in class or out often came across as disjointed and clumsy. His overzealous interjections often had nothing to do with the topic being discussed, and the forced contributions tended to make the other children shy away from him. Brandon was often left alone at his desk during any free time, or standing on the playground while others broke into groups. One or two other students were also socially stranded at recess, and at times the three of them gravitated toward each other in mutual support. These were Brandon's closest "friends".

Brandon had not lied when he told Patricia he didn't want to lose his "friends." He truly believed this to be. In reality, Brandon had no real friends. He usually walked to school by himself as he watched other groups laughing and chatting. No one happily anticipated his arrival at school. Brandon's glaring social awkwardness masked an intelligent and creative young boy. He just could never seem to learn the language that everyone else was speaking.

Home was where Brandon most often felt the acceptance and security that was always just out of arm's reach at school. Here, he could be himself. As frictions between Jack and Patricia increased, home life was also constantly unsettled. Jack always seemed to be annoyed with him, and Brandon tried his best to avoid Jack whenever possible. Consequently, each day promised more stress than a 7-year-old should feel. School fed his fears of going home, and at home he worried what the next day of school would bring.

Brandon's older brothers also felt the strain but coped with the increased strife at home by putting distance between themselves and their house whenever possible. Russell and Shawn hung out with an ever-growing group of kids that occupied the corner across from Ginny's old house. Everyone respected Russell's strong, quiet personality and still remembered Shawn's "psycho" reputation, which made him something of a curiosity.

Robert had recently begun to break off from the corner gang and spend time with his own circle of friends from Junior High. Robert's tall, lean frame had begun to fill in considerably. His arms, once thin and lanky, were now thickened with defined muscle and pronounced veins that helped him gain the respect of others in his new school. He never said too much to his brothers about any aspects of life in junior high school. His grades were exemplary, and Patricia often commended her son for his academics. The others found it odd that Robert would periodically remove his shirt when he got home, and hand wash it instead of throwing it into the laundry. Shawn and Russell had their own suspicions, but Robert would neither confirm nor deny anything.

Even as they struggled to cope with the stress at home, the boys knew about Jack's illness in only the simplest of terms. Patricia and Jack had told them that Jack's condition may worsen, but they'd spelled out no details of what "worsen" might entail. Jack and Patricia decided that no good would come of painting a picture of what *might* happen, because even the two of them did not know what *would* happen.

By mid-December, Jack retained no hope that his condition would improve as time passed. Lately, the pattern of symptoms allowed for several good days, with minimal numbness and shaking, followed by as many horrible days that felt like they would never end. Jack was especially grieved that his sons were witnessing the difficult end of the impervious man they had always known and that both he and they were fully aware of his deterioration, even if nothing was said.

While he possessed, at least on his good days, traces of his former stature, Jack decided to celebrate Christmas in a unique way. Perhaps his actions were the overt display of a boyish notion, an attempt to feel strong and in control again, or maybe a cruel, deliberate dig at Patricia. Ultimately, his motivation did not matter; the end result was the same either way.

On Christmas day, while Patricia was out delivering tins of homemade cookies to some neighbors, Jack summoned the boys into the living room. Earlier in the morning, Shawn, Russell, and Brandon had each received a Spy Probe Assault Rifle for Christmas. These black, realistic looking rifles fired a white plastic bullet hard enough to leave a stinging red spot on bare skin from 50 feet away.

Originally afraid they were about to be punished for an as-yet unrecognized transgression, the boys were relieved when Jack said, "Guys, grab your guns and help me turn over the couch. It's time for some holiday destruction!" Their defensive posture disappeared as they helped Jack flip the couch on its side. For the first time in memory they felt like Jack was just another big kid playing with them. They huddled behind the cushioned fortress with Jack as he motioned toward the Christmas tree on the opposite end of the living room. Bathed in twinkling multicolored lights with unwrapped presents at the base, the tree's beauty was almost pristine. The thought of holiday destruction involving the scenic setting at the other end of the room piqued the boys' excitement.

Jack laid out the shooting gallery's ground rules.

"OK, two teams: me, Russell, and Brandon on one team; Robert, Shawn, and Richard on the other. Each person gets three shots. You have to pick out what ornament or ball that you are aiming at. You get one point if you hit it, and zero points for uncalled kills. I'll keep score, and Robert will go first. The most points after five rounds wins. Go ahead, Robert."

Robert settled in, sighted his target through the magnified crosshairs of the plastic scope, and called out an ornament.

"Look at the clear glass angel with the village inside of it. It's hanging directly above Brandon's skateboard." Robert waited until everyone verified his target before clearing himself to shoot.

"We see it, Robert; take the shot." Jack's authorization rang in Robert's ears as he lined up the shot one more time, taking a breath and holding it just as he had seen the snipers in the war movies do. Robert squeezed off the round and watched as the glass angel exploded. The village inside the ornament fell to the carpet below, along with silver glitter that had been encased for over twenty years. His brothers erupted in congratulatory cheers, even the opposing team.

"Nice shot Robert!" Jack yelled.

"Beat that, scrubs!" Robert shouted in challenge to his competitors.

And so it went on, back and forth, for the next hour. Larger Christmas balls made a loud distinct "pop," while the smaller, heirloom ornaments required a greater level of marksmanship. For the boys, this one rare hour of pure fun was worth the cost of every decoration on the tree. Beneath the dimmed living room lights, on this most special of nights, Jack Christopher was truly just another big kid.

The boys may have wished that the seed of the night's camaraderie could have been harvested and spread beyond the borders of this one precious night, but they all understood that relations and family dynamics were sure to return to their previous state in short order. Thus, the joking, laughter, and teasing shared as they rolled around and systematically dissected the Christmas tree made it all the more precious.

When all of the shots had been fired, only a few of Patricia's keepsake ornaments, hidden on the back side of the tree, survived the onslaught. More than 30 years of purchased, gifted, handed down, and meticulously cared for ornaments lay in a multi-colored, shimmering, crystal glass heap beneath the tinseled branches.

"All right, let's clean up this mess, guys," Jack directed, as if sweeping up the aftermath would prevent Patricia from noticing.

When she arrived home, Patricia looked at the emptied, disheveled tree and burst into deep, heavy sobbing. Her grief was so heavy that she did not yell at Jack or the boys, but ran upstairs into her bedroom and locked the door. Jack made his way up the stairs with some difficulty, leaned against the bedroom door, and apologized for his thoughtless actions. He promised to let her shop carte blanche next year for tree trimmings. The very inception of the game was unwise, he admitted, but never malicious in its intent. Jack just thought that it seemed like a cool thing to do with the kids.

Patricia ignored Jack's pleading, which did little to remove the hurt, but Patricia conceded to herself that this action was not inconsistent with his impulsive past history. Jack rarely analyzed and pondered. Most often, he just did, and worried later about any repercussions.

For the rest of day, Patricia and Jack did not exchange a single word. Patricia remained in the solitude of their bedroom, emerging only briefly to go to and from the bathroom. For their part, the boys felt bad to have hurt their mother so much, but not enough to completely regret having participated in Jack's afternoon mayhem.

Chapter 44
Jack and the Enemy's Advances

January 1970

For several weeks following the decimation of her tree trimmings, Patricia performed her duties as wife and mother at a bare minimum. There would be no niceties, no baked treats, no last-minute rides for the kids, no special touches around the house, and most assuredly, no sex. Patricia sent an unmistakably clear message to Jack and the boys: "don't piss me off." Eventually, Patricia got past the initial fire of indignation, but a smoldering ember continued to lie just beneath the seemingly inert ashes; just enough to remember.

When Dr. Scherring communicated his initial diagnosis to Jack and Patricia, he had tried to exercise great caution not to foster any misplaced hopes without triggering emotional hopelessness. The hope that Jack's MS was less severe was reasonable. Relapsing-remitting MS or RRMS tended to plateau at a lesser level of disability and stay there or even decrease. That was the best outcome that could be logically hoped for, but based on Jack's test results and early experiences, Dr. Scherring feared that Jack would not have the best outcome.

With each passing month, Jack's body had shown that Dr. Scherring's fears were warranted. Given the extent of scarring in Jack's head and spine, the doctor was tragically confident that his patient's condition was likely to digress into secondary progressive MS. Perhaps the cruelest trait of Jack's probable condition was that the patient would experience brief periods of remittance from painful and debilitating symptoms. On these days, Jack and Patricia vainly latched onto a fragile sliver of hope that perhaps Jack's body was healing itself. They wondered if staying any further digression was possible. Soon thereafter the malady returned with a vengeance, often more severe than it had been previously, destroying any expectations for recovery.

Within the month after 1970 had been ushered in with an illuminated ball on Times Square, Jack knew that his employer would soon have little choice but to place him on disability. Paresthesia in both of Jack's hands had become more and more frequent. Even walking to his machine had grown ever more difficult, and standing for hours on end, once something he didn't even think about, was now visibly arduous and physically painful.

By February, his blurred and sometimes double vision made it impossible to run his press without risking another injury. With every "thunk" of the cutter blade slicing steel in two, jack's hyperacusis tormented him to the point at which he became nauseous from the pain. Sporadic bouts of involuntary shaking and footdrop became daily occurrences.

Dragging his foot behind him was embarrassing enough for Jack, but this also marked the point at which Dr. Scherring felt that he needed the additional support of a cane. No matter how much worse conditions would get in the days to come, no matter the extent to which his body may someday give in to itself, the sheer anguish he felt on the requirement of this first means of supplementary support was unparalleled. Any misplaced delusions of total recovery or escape from this terrible disease were brutally shattered forever. Everything else from this point addressed not the potential for recovery, but management of any digression. The only positive effect of the wooden cane was the merciful delay of leaving work on disability.

Any delay in going out on disability was tauntingly short-lived. In March Jack was placed on disability. He hated the sound of the word "disability," but the burning and tingling had made it impossible to carry out the simplest of tasks, and Jack knew that the company had no other choice. He went out of his way to assure Wes Morgan that he understood their difficult position, and that there were no hard feelings. Once again, this time through no fault of his own, Jack was out of a job.

Adding to Jack's sense of humiliation, his driver's license was permanently revoked for medical reasons in late March. Now restricted to the house and however far he may try to venture walking, Jack watched circumstances over which he had no control dictate the course of his life.

Patricia made subtle changes around the house as discreetly as possible. She bought larger coffee mugs in the hope that the oversized handles would be easier for Jack to manipulate. She tried to preserve his independence. Going to the bathroom was now a half hour event as Jack had more trouble going up the stairs. At first, he would let only Patricia help him. She stood behind him with her hand in the small of his back as he struggled to ascend the steps. Bracing her back foot, Patricia was often the only reason that Jack did not fall back onto the hallway floor below. He also needed help in the bathroom manipulating his zipper and positioning his penis. His once-pronounced forearms now denied Jack the coordination to make us of the bathroom tissue.

Even worse, his disability checks, though steady, were little more than half of his normal pay. This time, restrictions imposed by his own body would not allow Jack to make up the difference. He had not been employed long enough to be vested, and so his union "package" of benefits would not go with him.

By the time the thoughts of many turned to vacation and the last sweltering days of school gave way to summer, Patricia was working part time. As a result, the older boys now had to help Jack walk up the steps and make use of the bathroom. With both parties on edge, but unable to avoid such awkward moments, father and sons found the trauma almost unbearable. Jack's frustration at his circumstances spilled over and he often berated the boys for their efforts.

"Push my back so that I don't fall down the damn steps! Are you that stupid?" At times, despite the boys' best efforts, Jack would urinate on the floor and toilet seat. "Look, you made me piss all over! Help me downstairs and then clean this up."

His sons felt compassion for their father's struggles but wished he were more understanding. "I'm sorry, Dad; I'm trying," would be the typical emphatic reply.

By midsummer, Jack's muscle tone had diminished considerably, and he now experienced frequent fecal incontinence, which added to the stress of the family. Over the summer, the older boys' friends often hung out in the Christophers' basement. Some days, they only convened there before walking together the 2 miles to the Pennsauken pool. Other times the group camped out in the basement all day; 10 to 15 teenagers bullshitting, flirting, or playing games. The smell of fecal matter would sometimes waft into the basement as Jack called for one of his sons. As might be expected from boys their age, Jack's sons did not demonstrate much sensitivity to how their father must have felt, and the brothers almost always argued about whose turn it was to go upstairs.

By August, Dr. Scherring told Jack that he had deteriorated from a level three to a five on the Kurtzee Expanded Disability Status Scale. He also said that though there was always the possibility for improvement, counting on such a change too much would be unwise.

What his sons could not see and could not appreciate was the torment Jack felt every day. Alone in his own house, usually in the living room, Jack spent long hours bitterly questioning why he had this terminal sentence placed on him. While Patricia worked to help pay the mounting bills, Jack spent the long days alone, devoid of even a friendly adult voice. Thankfully, once a week one of his brothers always stopped by to visit and help Jack shave. Joe or Charlie would walk through the door purposefully lighthearted and positive. It was only during these visits that Jack could tell someone he could trust, and who would understand, that he was truly afraid for the first time in his life.

Jack's body continued to deteriorate. By the end of summer, his body was a remnant of its once-powerful frame. Jack's face now had a hollow, jaundiced appearance as he lost more and more weight. As measured by his children, good and bad days were gauged by how much their father was involuntarily shaking. Jack was determined to function on his own as much as he could, so his pained family watched as hot

300

cups of coffee trembled and spilled over, even using the large mugs, while he fought to control them. Where once his voice compelled others to jump in response, now Jack was left waiting until others decided to come to him.

Though the boys retained a healthy fear of Jack because of his strong personality, as young men often do, the older sons also carefully pondered how to use the present situation. Jack was no longer able to dole out the punishment that had always kept his sons in check. The boys, at times, took greater risk that they would be caught in a transgression than they might have had Jack still been able to wield his belt.

One such occasion involved one of the days that Jack had needed help after a bout of fecal incontinence. Brandon's brothers convinced him that if he went up to help his father, they would include him in their plans the next day. This was an offer that Brandon could not pass up,

Fulfilling their promise to spend the following day with Brandon, Robert and Shawn offered to play "cattlemen" with him. Even as he began the game with his brothers, Brandon remained oblivious to the activity's origins or rules of play.

"Lay on your stomach, Brandon," Shawn invited in a tone that promised his brother fun and adventure. Brandon happily complied without hesitation, taking the prone position on the cool basement tiles.

"Now we're going to pretend that you are the cattle and me and Shawn are the cattlemen," Robert further explained. "You start out tied up in the barn and have to escape and hide; when you do, we come and find you again." Brandon painted pictures of a colorful game in his head as Robert talked.

"Now give us your hands and feet, buddy," Shawn directed. Brandon offered his feet, bending both legs at the knee, and put both hands behind his back. His brothers secured both hands and feet individually, and then tied the two together with a small connecting rope. To this they attached a longer rope with a slipknot draped around Brandon's neck.

301

"You are now our captured cattle, Brandon!" Shawn and Robert continued playfully. "If you don't escape by the time we get back, that means that you go to the slaughter house!"

Brandon excitedly played along. "I'm going to escape, you wait and see! Mooo, Moooo" he jested.

"All right, we'll be back," Robert jokingly warned as he and Shawn each picked up a small bundled towel and headed out the back door. With that, they left Brandon tied up on the floor, and headed to Pennsauken pool.

Brandon laid there motionless for 10 minutes planning his escape. Finding it more difficult to free himself than expected, he grew increasingly nervous. Finally, impatience caused Brandon to begin kicking his feet and jerking his arms in frustration, which caused the noose to tighten around his neck. Panic set in as his air supply became more and more restricted with each kick of his feet. He fell over onto his side and his face began to turn blue just as Patricia came down the steps with an armful of laundry.

Patricia screamed as she saw her son choking on the floor. She ran into the kitchen and grabbed her sharpest blade. As she cut the noose from around Brandon's neck, she could hear his heavy frantic gasps for air, and as she comforted him and listened gratefully to his breathing return to normal, she contemplated retribution for Robert and Shawn.

His older brothers had not intended to hurt Brandon. The fact that he could have been hurt or even killed never crossed their minds when they invented the prank. This assurance, however, did little to soften their mother's heart. Patricia scolded her sons that they never would have attempted such a stunt if their father was well, but if they thought that she was soft on punishment, the boys were sadly mistaken. Both boys were grounded for 2 weeks with no TV, no visitors, and no phone calls. By the end of their sentence, Robert and Shawn thought they might have preferred their father's swift justice instead.

One of the difficult lessons that Jack learned in his first year of battling MS was that time could no longer be measured in terms of days, weeks, or months. These common benchmarks were soon irrelevant. The

302

confines of his home, the absence of normal patterns that accompany a job, and the distorting effects of some medications had blurred these lines. Time was now measured by doctor appointments, the length of remissions or relapses, and how long it had been since Jack's initial diagnosis. Nor did the future provide anything good to anticipate. Looking too far ahead was unhealthy for both Jack and Patricia, as the present view of the future offered little hope.

Jack's greatest pleasure in that first year, and an escape from concerns of the future, was playing with Ryan on the living room floor. Many of Jack's motor skills were only slightly better than his son's, and their jerky, disjointed movements were very similar. Jack saw a beautiful innocence and joy in Ryan that eased his struggling heart as his son wrestled with Jack's face and hair. By the time the leaves of autumn released their grip on the trees, Ryan's increasing mobility made keeping the toddler in Jack's reach more and more difficult. The plethora of medications throughout the house also became more of a concern as Ryan was able to open drawers and rummage through the lower cabinets.

Magnifying the misery of the disease itself, many of Jack's medications had troubling side effects. Over time, they slowly rotted his teeth, causing some to fall away completely. Jack's rugged jaw line shifted out of alignment, causing severe pain at the joints. Dr. Scherring had prescribed Valium to help offset his patient's anxiety, but the Valium itself caused sleeplessness and loss of balance.

Butabarbital was prescribed to help Jack sleep, and Inderal to mitigate the tremors and uncontrolled shaking. These, too, were not without negative side effects. Inderal sometimes exacerbated jack's depression and left him with a sore throat and cold hands and feet.

Elavil seemed to work to ease the depression, but sometimes caused dry mouth, nausea, and numbness. Fiorinal took away the dry mouth, assisted by the cubes of ice Jack constantly chewed, but produced a constant ringing in his ears, which further interfered with his sleep. Darvon worked fairly well to relieve pain racing through Jack's spasming muscles and joints, but caused him to hallucinate, rendered him jaundiced, and left him wondering if he might be better off ending the whole damn mess.

Considering Ryan's mobility and Jack bouts of depression, Patricia took the precaution of collecting the multiple bottles of drugs, many double ordered and stuffed in various drawers throughout the house and stored them in a locked steel box in her closet. She had meant to keep them primarily from Ryan and to ensure that Jack did not take them incorrectly, either accidentally or purposefully, but she was not unhappy that they were also more difficult for other family members to reach.

She did not know that Robert had actually been tempted to take some medications. On one of the limited occasions that Robert mentioned Jack to his friends at school, he happened to bring up the list of drugs that his father required.

"Rob, do you know how much money you could make off of all that stuff?" one of his friends asked immediately. "Man, you are sitting on a gold mine! You could sell out a whole bottle by the time lunch was over and go home with a pocket full of cash. We can help you get rid of it if you were to give us a cut of the profit."

Robert was tempted by the offer. He reasoned that the money would solve a whole lot of problems for Patricia, and he could keep a percentage. Something in him, however, told him that such a venture was fundamentally wrong. Besides, what would Bud think if he learned that the grandson he had invested so much time in was nothing but a drug dealer? Robert was not willing to risk such shame, much to his friends' disappointment.

Chapter 45

Jack and Brandon, and a Winter Détente

December 1970

Only 3 weeks before Christmas, the first snow of the season fell softly as most of the Christophers slept. Night had mercifully ended a particularly contentious day. Jack's uncontrolled shaking and acute ear pain left him especially irritable. Unfortunately, Robert and Shawn were so engrossed in heated disagreements of their own that they ignored Jack's simplest requests.

While trying to land a heavy glass mug against Robert's head, Shawn missed and shattered the cup against the upstairs hallway wall. Later, while running from Robert, Russell managed to track heavy mud footprints across the living room carpet. Adding to Jack's frustration, he was unable to do more than yell at the fighting brothers.

Using the upstairs bathroom was now untenable for Jack, as Brandon was too small to safely help him up the precarious staircase. Instead, positioning himself on the couch, Jack had Brandon bring him the urinal that he used in these circumstances. Brandon moved the receptacle where his father needed it and turned away to give his father some measure of privacy. He could feel the unit filling up and felt uneasy and anxious to dispose of its contents as soon as possible. In his haste to get to the bathroom when Jack was finished, the boy caught his leg on the corner of the glass and chrome coffee table and fell forward headlong. Losing his grip on the urinal, Brandon watched it fly across the room, hurtling against the far wall. With a hollow "thud," the urinal hit the floor, contents spilling all over the living room carpet.

"You stupid son of a bitch!" Jack called in frustration. "You ruined the damn carpet! Useless. You're friggin' useless! Go get some towels and clean as much of that up as you can, till your mother gets home."

A little more than 2 hours later, Patricia arrived home after her 12-hour shift at the Harvest House Cafeteria inside the Woolco department store. She was painfully aware that each day every problem and confrontation that Jack and the boys had would be waiting for her the moment that she walked through the front door. The 20-minute ride home from work was the closest thing to a break that Patricia could reasonably expect. Her own body was beginning to rebel from the months of physical and mental strain.

Now, as everyone else slept, only Jack and Brandon remained awake. Trying not to be heard, Brandon cried softly as he sat midway down the second floor staircase. He gazed down at his father watching the Johnny Carson Show in the living room, the television providing the room's lone illumination.

As Brandon sat on the steps, the shouting, fighting, and his own mistakes of the day replayed in his mind. The smell of wet carpet lingered in the hallway from Patricia's attempt to clean up the mess. Jack looked up to see Brandon sobbing quietly as his son was perched on the steps.

"What are you doing up Brandon? Go the hell to bed."

"I just…ah, wanted to say…ah…that…ah…I'm sorry, Dad. Can…ah…I come down?" Brandon's reply was delivered with nervous puffs of air every few words.

Jack could tell that his son was upset, and would never go to sleep until he got out whatever it was that he needed to say.

"OK, Brandon, just for a few minutes, and then you have to go back to bed."

Composing himself as he entered the living room, Brandon dried his eyes on the edges of his shirt and sat quietly on the floor. He sat Indian style next to the couch near Jack's head and looked at the TV. Neither father nor son spoke for several minutes as they watched Don Rickles perform his standup routine as they sat in surprisingly comfortable silence. Finally Brandon found common ground for beginning a conversation.

"He's one of your favorites isn't he, Dad? I like when he's on this show."

Jack could tell that Brandon was really trying to connect, and he responded in kind.

"I've watched this every night for as long as I can remember. It always relaxes me before bed." Returning to the comfortable quiet, they watched Johnny Carson banter with Ed McMahon, and Brandon reached up and rested his small hand on Jack's. He was surprised at how cold Jack's hand was, but pleased that his risky gesture had not been rebuked.

Finally, Brandon posed the question that had drawn him to his contemplative position on the steps. "Dad…" Brandon's tone had changed almost to that of a man talking to another man. "…why do we fight so much, Dad?" Direct and concisely delivered, his inquiry begged a response though his voice trailed off and cracked on the last few words. Jack reached down and rested his arm over his son's shoulder.

"Brandon, do you remember during the summer, when you shut the car door on Russell's finger? He yelled 'oh shit!' even though I was standing right there. He didn't think about cursing; the words just came out because of what had just happened. So much has happened this year, Son. For me, many days feel like my finger is being slammed over and over again." Jack paused as if he were marinating in his own words as they sank in. "Do you ever feel like that, Son?"

Brandon turned his head to look straight into his father's eyes. Jack could see the tears welling up in Brandon's eyes and fought to suppress his own.

"I feel like that all the time. Dad. Why did God make you so sick?" His last question started Brandon sobbing as he rested his head next to Jack's chest. Jack's answer was as much for himself as it was for his son.

"I don't know the answer to that, son. I ask myself the same question every day. Sometimes my medicine makes me cranky too. I have always hated taking any pills; now that's all that I do anymore."

"Are you going to get better, Dad?"

307

Jack was all too aware of the true answer, but he knew that his son was not ready to hear it.

"It's always good to think that it's possible, right, son?" Brandon smiled at the freedom Jack had given him to believe that recovery might be possible.

"I love you, Dad." Brandon poured out his heart, desperate to hear Jack's response.

"I love you too, Brandon." Jack's reply was intentionally emphatic to assure Brandon that the feeling was genuine. "Even when we both have bad days and it doesn't seem like it, I want you to remember that, OK? Chances are we are both gonna have some bad days, and we will probably argue again."

Brandon knew that his father was right; there would be more arguments, and the stinging words would hurt every bit as much as they had before. Hearing his father finally verbalize his love provided Brandon with a future soft spot on which to land when his heart was in freefall.

After a few more minutes of the Tonight Show, Jack nudged Brandon off to bed. "You've got school in 6 hours, son; you better go to bed."

"Not if it keeps snowing," Brandon hoped aloud.

"Well, just in case, you had better get going."

Brandon hugged his father's neck as he stood to leave. "I'll always remember this, Dad." His words sounded almost like a prophecy.

"I'm glad you came down, Brandon."

As his son trudged wearily off to bed, Jack realized that he had needed to hear love affirmed as much as Brandon did. Too many hours alone to ponder his present condition had a way of compressing even the smallest negative thoughts together into a dense wall that obstructed any hope-filled view of the future.

This opaque mental barrier to optimism was not restricted solely to Jack. Disputes between brothers that would one day be remembered as innocuous were now fanned into flame by the internal strife and daily frustrations heaped on each family member by their present

308

circumstances. Remaining indefinitely mired in difficulties, with no foreseeable end in sight, each one of the Christophers' nerves stood raw and sensitive to the slightest affront or perceived indignation.

Each Christopher responded to this oppression of spirit in different forms. By this time, Robert could think of nothing better than to somehow remove himself from the entire matter. Now 14, Robert carried painful memories etched by his younger days. With constant uncertainty and almost-constant anger at home and no clear answer as to what, if any benefit would come of all their tribulations. Robert counted the days until his 17th birthday. He could then extricate himself from his troubles by joining the military, going to college, or doing anything that allowed him to relocate.

Shawn was well aware of Robert's intentions and resented him for it. Robert's prospects for leaving left Shawn feeling abandoned and holding the bag. Shawn's reputation in the neighborhood mirrored his growing bitterness and feelings of inferiority that manifested with his lashing out at his brothers as much as with others. In his mind, the next insult or disparaging remark was always just around the corner. Shawn was not even sure who to blame for Jack's illness. Was it the failure of the doctors, indifference of God, or both? Not knowing who to rightfully hold in contempt left him angry at everyone.

Russell had no such doubts as to where the blame should be laid. If God were all powerful and all knowing, as Russell had repeatedly been assured every Sunday morning, then why was his father still so sick? Either the church was lying or God was not the deity that He had been purported to be. If God were not to blame for inflicting Jack with multiple sclerosis, then He was at the very least indifferent to the infirmity. Aunts and uncles with the best of intentions continually offered Russell what he considered empty platitudes: "God is in control. It's all for good in the long run. You have to have faith." Russell's disdain for these admonitions was palpable after a year of watching his father struggle to hold a cup or walk across the room. The glaring dichotomy between God's perceived goodness and the family's circumstances was not easily reconciled in Russell's sharp but troubled mind.

Brandon's recent encounter with Jack calmed the boy's heart to some extent. For Brandon there existed no seething anger or resentment toward either God or his father. Instead, he became convinced that taking the guilt for Jack's condition upon himself was the best and most logical action. If Jack must suffer, then the least that Brandon could do was deny himself the carefree life of an eight-year old. Brandon decided to impose upon himself the mantle of martyr. Volunteering for every unpleasant task that had to be done, he emptied urinals and changed dirty linens: anything to which the natural inclination should have been avoidance.

He was motivated more to do penance for some intangible sin than from any altruistic intent. Brandon wondered if the stress he had brought into Jack's life contributed to his father's present condition. Did losing Rommel trigger some sort of rebellion in Jack's body? Brandon had begun to feel that the only way to live with himself was to deny himself the happiness that eluded Jack. Sadly, this mindset had a detrimental impact on anyone around him. This added to his difficulty making friends. His always unhappy disposition cost him friends, which in turn fueled his negative, guilt-laden self-image. Brandon himself did not make the connection between his own morose outlook and his lack of playmates.

Richard and Ryan were the only family members spared, for now, the pain of chronic distress. Only particularly loud and heated arguments registered any discomfort for them. Richard's boundless confidence and independence kept him preoccupied with his own affairs. Barely more than 14 months old, Ryan was blissfully ignorant to the daily contentions within the Christopher household.

Chapter 46
Jack and the Start of the Final Battle

April 1971

A strange and unfamiliar quiet settled over the house the day after Easter as the morning light shone through the multicolored Easter grass strewn across the living room floor. Only 24 hours earlier the faux grass had been meticulously arranged in six baskets, along with candy and small gifts. Robert had contended before Easter that he was too old for a basket, but he was secretly relieved to find that his mother had let him enjoy the morning surprise one more time.

There were few pleasant surprises in the Christopher household in the weeks and days leading up to Easter. In March, a motorized bed had been installed in the dining room. Jack welcomed this, as it spared him the difficulty and humiliation of trying to make it up the steps. Less exciting was the confirmation that he would now spend 24 hours a day on the same floor.

Worse, just before Easter, Dr. Scherring had informed Jack and Patricia that Jack's condition no longer allowed him to rely on a walker to get around. His condition had now digressed from a level five to a level seven on the EDSS scale, and hypotonia had left Jack hunched over as he tried to maneuver the walker. Neither Christopher contested the doctor's decision. They knew he was right, but this concession did not ease the devastation the blow had on Jack's morale.

Jack did not need a doctor to tell him his condition had deteriorated considerably. He now had respiratory difficulty as his lungs fought his body's attempts to shut down. A frighteningly chronic shortness of

311

breath left him constantly uneasy, and vertigo and vestibular ataxia meant he had little or no muscle coordination or sense of balance.

Dr. Scherring had always encouraged Jack to keep his muscles moving, even if someone else had to put the muscles through their range of motion. As Dr. Scherring explained, inactive muscles atrophied. Though Jack was usually very respectful of his doctor, he thought that this idea was ridiculous: *What the hell good is it to watch someone else move my damn arm for me?* He wondered. The symptom that sealed Dr. Scherring's decision, though, was the neuropathic pain that sent shocks through Jack's body. Considering these symptoms in their totality, the doctor had little choice but to move Jack to a wheelchair.

Therefore, Jack's brothers Joe, Charlie, and Richard, who came up from Texas, stopped by on Easter to convince Jack to stay with them at Charlie's house for a few days. Of course, whether Jack knew it or not, he really had no choice, but was being essentially kidnapped. Patricia could think of no better way to lift Jack's broken spirits than to hang out and laugh with his brothers. She knew as well as anyone that this was not just a social visit. Jack's brothers would spend the next few days building a ramp for his wheelchair.

Richard had not seen his brother since the diagnosis, and was crushed to see how frail Jack had become. He thought back to a hot summer day when they were young men and they'd sat in Richard's car waiting for a street light to change. Both men had their windows down while they made casual conversation. Jack rested his arm on the door, his fingers tapping to a Johnny Cash song on the radio. As Richard began to pull away, Jack exchanged words with a large irritated man walking by. Richard never understood which man, or perhaps the sweltering summer heat, sparked the altercation, but he saw a sudden flash of sunlight reflect off a butterfly knife as the pedestrian opened a long, deep gash on Jack's forearm.

The knife made a 'ting' sound as it hit the side of the car then fell to the street. Before he or Jack could react, the assailant ran around the corner of a nearby pharmacy. Jack said not a word but he sprung out of the car while it was still rolling forward. Richard called out, but Jack was already around the corner, so he pulled over and waited…and waited…and waited. Thirty minutes later Jack emerged from around the corner of the pharmacy; his shirt, forearms, and hand were bloody. As he walked toward the car, he took off his white short-sleeved button-down shirt, so he was just in a t-shirt. He wrapped the shirt around his arm. When he got back in the passenger seat, Jack held his bloody appendage out the window to avoid messing up the car's interior.

"So," Richard had prompted, hoping his brother would pick up the conversation from there.

"So what?" Jack replied, seeming genuinely unsure what Richard was asking.

"So, where the hell did you go, Jack? What happened?" Richard had asked, irritated at having to inquire a second time.

"Oh," Jack replied as a slight smile came to his lips. "I gave him his knife back." That was all he said then and all he'd ever said about the matter.

Richard looked at the frail man in the wheelchair and tried to reconcile him with the brother who would chase down a larger man and come out ahead in the altercation. Excusing himself to the bathroom, Richard worked to regain his composure and hide his grief.

Richard was every bit as strong-headed and direct as Jack was. His time in the state seemed to make him the quintessential Texan. He pulled no punches, and hated it most when he felt like anyone was jerking him around. Richard had become a Christian in Texas, though he was never inclined to beat his brothers over the head with it. Every once in a while he would say something about Christ and salvation, though exactly what he was trying to say was often lost on the rest of them.

Jim also planned on coming in from Texas in a few days. The brothers would all be together for the first time in several years. Jack's sister Annie promised to come over and feed her hungry brothers. "Little Annie" as Jack called her, and their other sister Janet, had inherited their mother's culinary skills, and the team could masterfully replicate many of the best-loved family dishes. The aroma coming from the kitchen at previous gatherings brought back fond recollections of their beloved mother as the two girls worked like a well-oiled machine. Jack had a tender spot in his heart for his sisters. He had always been their protector, the one they could count on when a less than polite suitor called on them. Understanding that he could not be their protector anymore broke Jack's heart.

When Patricia had preemptively informed the younger generation of Christopher boys their uncles and aunts would be arriving in several days, she had to dispel several myths about Texas. Their uncles would not be riding a horse, although Richard and Jim were more than proficient with an 18-foot bull whip. Several years back, the older Christopher boys watched Richard's son Bobby snap a cigarette out of Jack's mouth at the filter from 15 feet away. No one was quite sure who was craziest: Bobby for attempting the feat or Jack for letting him do it. Patricia also explained that the men would not be wearing six shooters. This clarification left young Richard Christopher particularly disappointed. The final and perhaps most important clarification was that the wheelchair ramp their uncles were building was not a skateboard ramp and was not to be used as such.

With Jack staying with his brothers, Patricia decided she could enjoy a rare quiet breakfast in the kitchen the day after Easter while the boys were in the living room watching TV and raiding their Easter baskets, Brandon chopped at a solid chocolate bunny with a knife. He rested the bunny on his leg as he thrust the long narrow blade into the bunny, chopping off bite-sized chocolate chunks. Although his siblings derided their brother's lack of common sense, none bothered to inform Patricia of the looming danger. They did not have to wait long for the inevitable; taking his eyes off of the rabbit for a second to look at the cartoons on TV, Brandon drove the knife several inches into the top of his right thigh.

He felt, simultaneously, a deep surge of pain and the desperate desire not to utter a word. Afraid to remove the knife from his leg, he stood straight up and looked around the hallway corner into the kitchen hoping to sneak up the steps undetected.

314

Brandon made it into the bathroom and locked the door behind him while still supporting the dangling knife as it hung from his leg. "Oh my God, oh my God, oh my God," he repeated in rapid succession while trying to think of what to do next. Unable to think of anything else, he pulled the knife out and watched in horror as a steady stream of blood flowed out of his upper thigh.

Perhaps fortunately for Brandon, he had not made it into the bathroom unseen. Russell saw Brandon turn the corner into the bathroom and was curious as to why his brother had appeared so frightened. He pressed his ear to the bathroom door in time to hear the knife hit the floor and Brandon's panicked conversation with himself. A great satisfaction filled Russell as he ratted Brandon out to his mother.

"Mooom, I think Brandon stabbed himself; you better come up here!"

Patricia cut short her cherished quiet breakfast, ran up the steps, and finding the door locked, began banging on it.

"Brandon, open up! Do you hear me? Open up this door!"

Brandon made a futile attempt to cover while he tried to think of a way out. "I'm going…to the bathroom!"

Patricia was incensed. "You are not going to the bathroom dammit. Now. Open. This. Door!"

Brandon, unable to think of another way out and increasingly worried by the blood he couldn't seem to stop, opened the door. Patricia immediately fixed on the blood-soaked towel on her son's thigh.

"I'm getting a little dizzy, Mom," Brandon admitted as he sat down on the edge of the tub.

Patricia moved the towel just long enough to see the size of the cut and called out to Russell. "Run over and get Mrs. Nielson! The rest of you go down stairs," Patricia ordered the rest of the mini crowd that had gathered outside the bathroom door.

"I told you he was dumb enough to do it," Shawn said to Robert as they turned back downstairs.

Patricia held the towel to her son's leg and murmured reassurances as they waited the several minutes it took for Mrs. Nielson to arrive with her medical kit. Arlene Nielson was the neighborhood's only registered nurse and was always the first one called in an emergency. Arlene was gracious and never seemed to mind the imposition, no matter what time the call came in. She quickly determined that Brandon had not hit a vital artery and that the puncture was a narrow, clean, deep wound. She took over applying direct pressure and after a few minutes the bleeding had slowed to a trickle.

"It's too narrow for stitches, Pat," she said once she was sure the bleeding wouldn't restart. "Just keep it clean and watch for infection. He's going to be sore and limping for a few days but should otherwise be fine."

Patricia thanked her neighbor profusely, but knew Arlene would be insulted if she offered payment. Patricia found the entire incident completely embarrassing. There was no logical way to explain how her son managed to thrust a knife deep into his own leg. Patricia was thankful that Jack did not have to be here for all the commotion.

"Hey, Brandon, got any chocolate? Hey, I think I'll cut this chocolate rabbit up by laying it on my neck!" Brandon's brothers wasted no time teasing him about the incident. Happily for him, over the weeks that followed, and as his limp became less pronounced, the taunts from his brothers died down considerably.

Jack returned home several days after Easter. The time with his brothers had restored some of the spark in his eyes. His brothers had treated him as in old days, with equal ribbing and sarcasm. Despite his pain and lack of mobility, Jack felt like one of the boys again. Jack's brothers and sisters had all come back to the house, the men to begin construction of the wheelchair ramp, and the women to first make lunch.

They also had plenty of time for socializing. Charles had taken it on himself to draw up the official plans for the ramp, and he had ordered the materials and had them delivered to the house while the brothers were at Charlie's. Charles, ever the perfectionist, had troubling visions of the six brothers each having their own plans, going in six different directions. Having the materials and his plan already on site would hopefully ensure a consensus, especially with him having covered the cost of the materials.

Though they'd treated him the same verbally, Jack's family gained an appreciation for the level of assistance that he needed in the days he'd stayed with them. They saw the many medications that needed to be administered at precise times. Helping their brother with the simplest of needs enabled them to understand that caring for Jack was a 24-hour-a-day task. Jack's brothers and sisters were thankful for Patricia's tireless attention to the growing daily needs of their brother.

After an abbreviated lunch, the young Christopher boys, except Ryan, were dispersed into the neighborhood so that they would not be in the way of ongoing construction. While Jack's brothers and sisters enjoyed incidental conversation and friendly banter over lunch, Patricia rolled Jack toward the front door for his afternoon appointment with Dr. Scherring.

"We'll see you in a couple of hours," Patricia called out as she maneuvered Jack's wheelchair to the door. "Janet, Annie, lunch was delicious. It is wonderful to have you all here." Patricia was not just being polite. She truly enjoyed hearing the lively laughter and love that flowed back and forth wherever Jack's family got together.

Jim rose from his chair as one would expect a Texan in matters of courtesy. At 6'5", Jim was by far the biggest of Jack's brothers, and muscles bulged from his white T-shirt.

"Pat, let me take Jack to the car for you."

Patricia was reluctant to interrupt the rare gathering but knew she would need some help. "Thanks, Jim. Let me get Jack down to the car, and I'll stop back in. I could use some help lifting him into the seat."

"OK darlin', just come and get me whenever you need help," Jim offered as he slowly sat back down.

Patricia rolled Jack past the threshold onto the front step and closed the door behind her. Jack let out a grunt with each step as a jolt of pain accompanied Patricia's lowering him down.

"I'm sorry, Hon; I'm trying to get it down as gently as possible."

Clearing the last step, Patricia pushed the wheelchair down the short, angled walkway and navigated the two steps down into the driveway. She turned to take Jim up on his offer for help but had only gone a few steps when she was recalled to the car by a sarcastic male voice.

"Oh look, it's the cripple and his wife." Jason Dorgen had come out of his house and now rounded the car toward Jack, leaning his right hand on the hood of the car for support as he did. He seemed in the early stages of his daily inebriation.

"Jason, go home! Just leave us alone." Patricia ran back to put herself between Dorgen and Jack.

"Get out, hyou son-of-a-bish!," Jack yelled to Dorgen in his increasingly slurred speech.

"You're not so tough now, are you, Jack." Dorgan pushed Patricia aside and slapped Jack violently across the back of the head, sending him reeling against the side of the chair.

"Nlet me get my handsh on you, you bashtard!" Jack wanted so much to be able to rise from his chair as he watched Patricia fall to the ground.

"Still want to hit me, Jack?" Jason danced from side to side tauntingly smacking Jack's head. "Oh, I forgot; you're a cripple now!"

"Stop, stop!" Patricia screamed shrilly. "Jim…Richard…please help me!" She called as Dorgen pulled Jack by the collar, and threw him onto the ground.

"How does it feel, JACK?" Dorgen called. He was so intent on his long-awaited retribution that he failed to notice the front door opening and Jack's brothers running out onto the lawn. First out the door was Jim, who ran with his enraged siblings toward Jason. As Dorgen leaned over Jack, Jim grabbed the drunk man by the back of the shirt and spun him around. Before Dorgan had a chance to look Jim in the face, the Texan's fist came crashing into his eye socket. Dorgan's head struck the side window of the car, sending a crack the full length of the glass.

Richard's anger at seeing Jack on the ground would not let Jim strike the only blow. Richard grabbed Dorgen by the arm and snapped it

318

at the elbow as he had been taught before his deployment to Korea. Jason screamed in pain as the bone snapped.

"Don't kill him!" Patricia's cry was not only for Jason's sake but also out of legal concern for Jack's brothers. Jim held Dorgen up, half conscious by his throat against the car. He looked straight into Dorgen's face as he squeezed his throat.

"Son, if you set foot in this yard one more time, I swear that I'll come back here and kill you." Jim and Richard grabbed Jason under the armpits and threw him face first on his own front lawn. Dorgen dragged himself into his house.

While he did, Jim and Richard settled Jack back into his chair. Upset by his sheer helplessness and embarrassed by his inability to protect Patricia, Jack shook with anger and frustration.

"Come on back in, Jack," Richard said. "That doctor can wait."

"I'll call and reschedule, Hon," Patricia quickly agreed. She knew Richard was right. Jack was in no condition to go through any routine appointment.

As Richard pushed Jack in front of them, Jim took Patricia's arm and held her back for a moment.

"I'm sorry about the window, Pat; we'll be sure and fix it."

Patricia nodded absently. She was glad that the boys had not been there to witness Dorgen's assault on their father.

Back inside, Jim and Richard lifted Jack into his bed and adjusted the motorized positioning of the back and foot until Jack was comfortable. Over the next hour the family did their best to forget the traumatic events of the late morning. They would wait to start the carpentry work on the ramp until tomorrow, though they did start grading the ground as the afternoon reached its latter stages.

As Jack closed his eyes and settled in, he could picture his mother cooking for him as a young boy. Fondly familiar aromas floated into the dining room from the kitchen as Annie and Janet worked on dinner, darting out into the living room between tasks to contribute to the stories and recollections that flew back and forth across the room. Tales of earlier days were recalled with enthusiasm and excitement.

319

To the Christopher boys now seated on the living room floor, the stories offered a glimpse into their father's boyhood. Robert and Shawn found many of the stories amusing but a bit redundant, since they'd heard them several times over the years. The younger boys found the tales fresh and riveting.

The next few days were productive, with no repeat of the difficulties of the day after Easter. The older generation Christophers finished the long, sleek ramp and painted it a deep courthouse red. As he'd promised, Jim replaced the car window. Dorgen made no other appearances outside his house. With time to spare after the ramp's completion, Jack's brothers also made several much-needed repairs around the house that Jack could no longer tend to. Sagging gutters, a water-damaged kitchen floor, and a roach infestation that accompanied the rotting floor were all rectified. Floor tiles that had been popping off in the upstairs bathroom were all reseated and sealed.

When the time came to leave, each of Jack's siblings gave him an extended hug and quiet verbal assurances of their love for him. Richard and Jim were heading back to Texas, and the others needed to return to their own family responsibilities. Annie and Janet promised to return in a few weeks and make Jack some of his mother's delectable fried chicken.

"We could have the chicken and watch some of the home movies that we have in the attic," Jack suggested. He looked forward to the return visit by his sisters as much as the fried chicken.

Before he left, Richard pulled the kids off to the side in the kitchen for some parting counsel.

"I want all of you boys to listen to your father and help him when he needs it, OK? I love you all, but I will come back and beat your asses if I hear any different." The Christopher boys believed their uncle on both counts.

Sitting on the front porch in his wheelchair with Patricia, Jack watched his beloved family load into their cars and drive down Remington Avenue. Jim playfully waved his Stetson out the window as if on a cattle drive. Jack wondered to himself if he would be there for any future family gatherings. Far worse than missing the events completely

320

was the possibility that his body would be present and little more. What if he was unable to participate in any activities or add anything to the family banter? He would be reduced to an object of pity and the subject of one-sided conversations describing what Jack "used to be like."

He and Patricia returned inside to the children's promises to be cooperative and curtail any in-house fighting. Uncle Richard had put the Texas Fear of God in them. Jack was thankful for that, though he wondered how long it would last. He was even more thankful for the new ramp. Not having to endure the repeated jarring of the steps would be an enormous relief.

Chapter 47

Jack and Rebellion and a Tactical Retreat

December 1971

Jack was right to wonder how long the boys' commitment to Richard's warning would last. By winter, the Christopher boys could not restrain themselves from finding a more entertaining function for the ramp. When Jack and Patricia were out, the brothers turned the ramp into a sledding slope. The excited boys ran through the kitchen and hallway onto the front steps, using the front porch as a launch platform. With the smooth pitched incline frozen over with recently laden snow, both sled and rider were propelled across the front lawn, down the curb, and into the street. One of the brothers, acting as a spotter, registered the rider's stopping point with an empty soup can. The boys had leaned a piece of plywood against the curb on the opposite side of the street just in case there was enough momentum to land the junior luger in the neighbor's lawn. Accomplishing this notable benchmark promised increased stature and great cheers.

The brothers initially enjoyed the ramp by themselves, but it did not take long for a crowd to line up along the ramp, ready to take their run from the kitchen. Unfortunately, the boys misjudged how long it takes to clean up hundreds of slushy footprints from the kitchen and hallway, and they were shocked to see Patricia and Jack arrive home before cleanup was complete. It had also not occurred to them that the sled marks and gouges in the yard would be a dead giveaway, irrespective of any cleaning efforts.

They also could not have foreseen the effect of what they thought was harmless fun would have on Jack. Jack had no doubt that the boys would never have attempted such a stunt if he were still able to dole out corporal punishment. In his mind, his disability was being flaunted by his sons. Even the ramp, for all of its practical benefit, now represented something more insidious to Jack. Chronic pain, constant medication, and the inexorable progression of the disease itself had taken a toll on his mental state.

Dr. Scherring was adamant about Jack's need to get out of bed and move around the house for a while each day. Increasingly combative with everyone else, Jack was still respectful of his doctor, but as he watched his condition decline, Jack viewed these mundane exercises as more and more futile. Trying to maintain this daily "therapy" was physically painful for him and heart-wrenching for everyone else. Patricia and the boys strained to encourage Jack to continue for his own good. Unfortunately, they could hold up nothing tangible to offset his resistance. Sessions were often filled with cursing, hurtful remarks, and frustration for all involved.

For Jack to get out of bed, Robert and Shawn pivoted his body 90 degrees by swinging his cold lifeless legs over the edge of the bed and readied themselves to lift their father's dead weight into the wheelchair. Meanwhile, one of the younger brothers propped himself against Jack's back to prevent him from falling back onto the bed. Shawn and Robert would then lift their father awkwardly off the bed and onto his wheelchair or commode. This grueling process was necessarily repeated several times each day, each time bringing the same pains for Jack.

"Ow, you're crushing my side! My foot is all twisted up! Untwist my leg, dammit!" Jack would call.

He could feel the straining biceps of his two sons pressing against his side; a chiseled feature that he had long since lost. After the sledding episode, the crushing helplessness that he felt, and the conviction that the therapy ordeal gave him little benefit reached its apex. Jack announced, with no tolerance for debate, that he no longer intended to use the wheelchair. He would remain in bed, except for extreme emergencies.

"Dad, please!" Brandon cried. "We won't complain about whose turn it is to clean the commode anymore! You can't just stay in bed all

323

the time." Patricia had no doubt that there was no changing her husband's mind. This was one of the few aspects of his life that Jack could still control.

Chapter 48

Jack and the Christmas Insurrection

December 1971

Christmas 1971 felt like a 3-week torment in which the heart is daily torn open that it may relive the previous day's pain and discontent. Idyllic songs of festive tidings and warm fireside gatherings only amplified the despondent days and nights leading up to Christmas Day. Unable to even afford a tree, the family saw the surrounding decorations as a macabre taunt at their misfortune. School parties and community events celebrating the holiday season were viewed with dread. For the Christophers, the real blessing would be when it was all over and the manufactured joviality could cease. People could then go back to their normal, unpretentious lives for another year.

Patricia solicited no Christmas list ideas from the children. Encouraging wishful thinking seemed fruitless and cruel, as she had no money. When she thought no one was around, Patricia cried deep mournful petitions to God. "God, I don't even know what to say to you anymore. What do you want me to do? What is it that you are trying to pull out of me? Do you even see my kids? Have you any idea how much it hurts to see their pain every day? I am trying to picture what you get out of tearing Jack down a little more each day, and why you insist on doing it in front of the boys. Forget the damn presents! I can't even feed my kids. You let them walk out the door each day having eaten nothing but salad croutons! Salad croutons!"

Patricia's long simmering anger burst forth more and more as she voiced her frustrations. "I have really, really tried to keep the kids pointed toward you, to not get angry, not get discouraged. You're

325

destroying the one thing that I have, the only thing that I ever asked you for, and for what? Can you at least tell me that?" Her inflection turned from one of anger to an exhausted daughter pleading for an answer from the Father.

Unable to bear their mother's sadness another day, Robert recruited Shawn and Russell to rectify one source of the family's misery. "We're getting a damn tree one way or the other. Tonight, we are going to find a tree somewhere." Under cover of night, scarcely 3 days before Christmas, the brothers ventured out into the darkness. Several hours later, they were dragging an 8-foot tree up the wheelchair ramp as pine needles left a trail behind them.

Expecting a flood of joy and appreciation from Patricia, her sons were surprised when, instead of accolades, they got anger and grief.

"Where did you get this tree? Did you really think that a stolen Christmas tree would make me happy? Do you know how humiliating this is? We are taking this back right now!"

The boys tried to convince their mother that since the tree was cut down now anyway, she might as well make use of it, but they had no luck changing Patricia's mind. Instead, Patricia dragged them back to the offended neighbor's yard, forcing them to confess. As upset as the property owners were, they had compassion for Patricia's situation and the awkward position her sons had put her in. When Patricia promised full restitution as soon as possible, they took her at her word. For the boys, Patricia found every dirty job she could think of as punishment.

On Christmas morning, no children came rushing down the stairs. Most cared little if they came downstairs at all. They knew that no carloads of gifts and trimmings came at midnight to create a great surprise on Christmas morning. Bud and Ginny were struggling like many in the economy and had no means of repeating the gesture. Patricia had thought of decorating with what she had but decided it would add insult to injury.

In the morning, the family members straggled downstairs over the course of a few hours. Each tried as much as possible to pretend that this day was no different than any other. The boys knew that they were in denial, but none wanted to talk about all they were missing out on. Most painful for them was knowing how terrible Patricia felt, but being totally unable to change her sadness. When Patricia came downstairs shortly after 10 am, her eyes were red and it was obvious that she had slept little the previous night.

Robert and the boys expected Jack to warn them, as he did most mornings, to keep the noise down and stop roughhousing. When he didn't, they felt a bit guilty for judging him so quickly and tried to compensate by offering to help him or get him some refreshments.

"Dad, do you need any ice to chew on, or something to drink?" Robert called. "Let me know if I can get you anything."

Hearing no response from the dining room, the boys went to the kitchen to forage through the cabinets for anything that could suffice as breakfast. Patricia came into the living room and kissed Jack on the forehead as he slept.

"Good morning, hon, can I get you anything?" Jack looked uncomfortable. His upper body was twisted; his left arm hanging over the right rail of the bed. She carefully rolled Jack's shoulder, allowing him to lay flat on his back. She noticed that his arms and legs felt particularly limp, offering no tension or resistance at all.

"Jack…Jack…you'll have to wake up for a few minutes." Adjusting the fitted sheets, Patricia went out of her way to jostle her husband out of his slumber. When she reached across Jack, she felt the spilled contents of a medicine bottle spread across the bed beneath Jack's blanket. She looked at her husband's pale skin and the dark shadows beneath his eyes and her heart sank. She fought panic as she called his name louder and louder, and tapped his cheeks. At his lack of response, Patricia grew ever more frightened, and she started slapping Jack's face repeatedly.

"Jack! Jack! Please wake up! What did you do?"

A month's supply of butabarbital had been left on Jack's dinner tray after his last dosage. Months of strain, distraction, and exhaustion had allowed the once tight controls over Jack's medications to grow lax. Patricia figured that he managed to fill his hand with enough pills to try

327

to end his own life. Jack must have decided that this was another area of his life that he could still control.

In the bright late morning sun, Jack's skin had taken on an ashen gray look. Jack's breathing was shallow and abbreviated. Slapping her husband's cold skin until her hand ached, Patricia pulled his hair as well in a frantic attempt to revive Jack. She screamed for Robert, and he came running in from the kitchen.

"Oh God! Oh God! Robert, get a pot of ice water now!"

Robert brought in a large stock basin of cold water from the kitchen and poured it over Jack's head. The shock elicited a scant, barely intelligible grunt.

Hearing Patricia and Robert's frantic cries, the rest of the Christopher boys ran up from the basement and raced to Jack's bedside. Seeing their father drenched with water in his own bed frightened and confused them, and they deluged Patricia with frantic questions.

"What's the matter, Mom?" "Why isn't dad moving?" Patricia had no time to provide any details.

"Dad needs a doctor now! Call the emergency number on the fridge, Robert. You have to help me keep dad awake."

She did not want this image seared into any of the boys' minds.

"Robert, stay here and help me. Shawn, take everyone else upstairs and do not let them come down," she ordered through tears. "Go in my room, check on Ryan, and stay there!"

Shawn grasped the gravity of his mother's words and physically pushed his siblings up the stairs. Patricia heard confused cries and repeated questions from her room as Russell, Brandon and Richard grilled Shawn.

"I called, Mom; they're on the way. What do I do now? What do I do?" Feeling helpless, Robert prayed that his mother had a directive for him. For all their fights and contention over the years, Robert loved his father and did not want to fail him now.

"Just keep yelling at him, Robert. Do anything that you have to until the paramedics get here."

Robert yelled anything that he could think of, and with Patricia's permission, continued slapping his father across the face. "Shit! Wake up you son-of-a-bitch! Yell at me…anything!"

Several minutes later, the EMTs were racing through the front door; they quickly had Jack on a gurney and were sliding him back down the snow-covered wheelchair ramp. Jumping into the ambulance with Jack, Patricia left Robert to try and calm the others. After a draining few hours for all the Christophers, Patricia was able to call home and confirm to the boys that Jack would be OK after having his stomach pumped.

He could be expected home in a few days, once he'd recovered and suitable arrangements could be made for psychiatric evaluation and counseling. Patricia chastised herself for leaving the bottle on the dinner tray. She had tried so hard to remain diligent about locking Jack's pills back up. Before approving Jack's return home, the hospital required all medications to be securely locked under tight control, with only Patricia having access to the prescriptions. Jack often sent the boys to have prescriptions refilled, sometimes weeks before the medication had run out.

Jack's return home was quiet, with no fanfare and no mention made of the event. Jack was exhausted from all of the procedures and testing while in the hospital, and he had gotten pissed off more than once while there, especially when nurses woke him out of a sound sleep to make sure that he was resting. Now, all Jack wanted to do was sleep. First he wanted the boys to know he appreciated their efforts to accommodate his needs and make him feel welcome.

"Thanks for the picture, Richard. It looked just like me." Richard had drawn a picture of his father with bulging muscles, standing next to a much smaller house. Jack was pleased that Richard had chosen a vibrant depiction of him. He could have just as easily portrayed Jack sick and in bed. He turned to the rest of the boys.

"Thanks, kids, for everything. I'll be OK. I'm sure," Jack tried to put any fears to rest, but his tired, raspy voice did not do much to help his assertion.

329

He could not reassure them that he regretted the suicide attempt. Indeed, he would have preferred that he had been successful. He understood why Patricia and the boys had worked so hard to keep him alive, but his position on the wisdom of his decision had not changed.

His principle motivation had not been to end his own suffering, though that certainly would have been accomplished. His primary goal was to expedite what he viewed as the inevitable. As Jack saw it, his death would mitigate the financial burden on the family. Patricia and the kids would be able to move on with their lives, and he would no longer hang like a millstone around their necks.

Of course, none of Jack's calculated and deliberate reasoning factored in the emotional devastation his suicide would have caused his wife and children. The great unanswered "why" promised to haunt the survivors even beyond the short-term grief. Even a note would do more to ease his own guilt than to lessen the pain of a grieving family.

Patricia and Jack had not discussed the matter in any detail. The fatigue brought on by his suicide attempt and everything that followed left Jack without the emotional reserves or physical strength to indulge in recapping the incident beyond his own thoughts. He was well aware that the new controls implemented over his medication now made a second attempt nearly impossible. Falling into a long awaited sleep in his own bed, Jack was begrudgingly resigned that yet another aspect of control over his life had been denied him.

Chapter 49

The Christopher Boys and Dissention in the Ranks

Summer 1972

Jack's declining physical condition and its detrimental impact on the family's emotions, finances, and social dynamics were the broad brush strokes that composed the backdrop of the Christophers' lives, but day-to-day life still went on in a never-ending series of smaller vignettes. Ever-shifting rivalries, collaborations, betrayals, and dramas played out against a constant gnawing anxiety. One brother pitted against another, or this pair against that pair; these small dramas were every bit as important to the boys as anything their parents faced..

By the summer of 1972, the stress was taking an increasing toll on the boys. Brandon's symptoms may have been the most overt. He began to feel the need to wash his hands every 2 minutes. Aside from taking up the bathroom all the time, this irritating compulsion inconvenienced everyone while they waited for Brandon. They had to wait in the mall while Brandon washed his hands. They had to pull over on the way to Ginny's at a diner so Brandon could wash his hands. Overwhelmed, Patricia sought advice from Ginny and hoped this was a phase he would grow out of.

Slightly more disconcerting was Brandon's tendency to grab his brothers' forks from the table before they had finished eating so that he could wash them. Standing behind his brothers like a hawk, he swept in unannounced, liberating them of any cutlery they did not have their hands on. Brandon had also become fearful of robbers and had begun to set booby traps on the doors using rope and cinder blocks. Patricia quickly brought this to an end after Robert was struck in the abdomen by a swinging block.

Brandon was not the only brother who reacted to the stress with bizarre behavior, and incidents such as these were daily occurrences for the boys by now. As they got older, the boys became quite inventive in their mayhem.

In the early morning hours of Independence Day, a succession of explosions rang out as eight M80's decimated a string of mailboxes on the Christopher's street. Although Robert and Shawn denied any involvement, little time had passed before one of the neighborhood boys cracked under pressure and confessed, bringing the rest of the vandals down with him. Of course, the Christopher's mailbox standing as the lone survivor left a fairly obvious clue who some of the culprits were.

Regularly returning home to find that someone had been burned, whacked with a hockey stick, stopped by the police, or threatened, Patricia by now took it all in stride. The wilting rose of Stratford was long gone. After hearing the latest conflict recapped as she walked in the door, Patricia casually opened the latest foreclosure notice from the bank.

Much more concerning to her than the mailed financial threats were the rolling papers and small pipes that fell out of pants pockets as she did the laundry. Since several of the boys shared clothing, Patricia did not know who had worn the pants last, but concluded that the items could not belong to Robert. He was still anxious to go into the Navy as soon as he was old enough. Taking drugs would jeopardize all his plans. His grades in school were good, as he knew they would have to be to qualify for a good school after boot camp. Shawn and Russell, on the other hand, had little or no interest in their education. They also had been spending more and more time hanging out together. By the end of summer, the two seemed uninterested in much of anything but hanging out with friends and sneaking alcohol and pot past their mother.

These evolving dynamics often left Brandon home to help care for Jack. Ironically, spending day in and day out together lead to a more acidic relationship between Brandon and his father. As Jack's physical and mental condition degraded, Brandon was often in the line of fire. Compounding matters for Brandon was his acute social awkwardness. He had few friends at school to speak of and few that let him tag along in the neighborhood. He often found himself feeling isolated and utterly alone.

One afternoon in September, Brandon watched from the kitchen table as an outsider as Shawn and Russell laughed with friends downstairs. Five beautiful teenage girls and seven guys convened many weeknights in the Christophers' basement. One girl in particular caught Brandon's attention, Lorraine. Tiny, with short black hair and olive skin, Lorraine had a fun, fiery personality. She was always playfully extolling the beauty of her near-perfect behind. The rambunctious little Italian cutie had a crush on Russell and would sit on his lap and play with his thick black mane. Brandon wondered what genetic benefit he had missed out on, and Russell had so abundantly received. All of the girls loved Russell's confident, quiet personality.

Brainstorming as he sat in the kitchen, Brandon desperately searched for some way to "one up" Russell for Lorraine's attention. Then it dawned on him. *Sheer genius*, he thought. Reaching into the utensil drawer, Brandon withdrew a butter knife, taking the end of the blade between his thumb and index finger. How quirky and amusing Lorraine would think him to be if he were to embed the knife into the dark walnut paneling beside Russell's head. Lorraine's amused smile would be well worth any brief discontent on Russell's part.

Descending down the first few basement steps unnoticed, Brandon was partially obscured by the angled ceiling above the staircase. Slowly he leaned over and peeked to his left past the wooden trim of the overhead. There was Lorraine, bubbly and flirtatious, mussing Russell's hair and leaning in so that he could smell her perfume. Taking it all in stride, Russell was cool, calm, and semi-detached, which might have been why the girls fought so hard for his attention. Anticipating the adulation and kudos that he would receive from the others for scaring Russell, Brandon was already patting himself on the back for his ingenuity.

Lining up his trajectory, Brandon threw the knife sidearm off of his hip. A shimmering silver blur reflected the lights from the ceiling fixture as the blade continued on its inevitable path. Instead of hearing the crack of his knife impaling the wood paneling, Brandon heard Russell scream in pain as the knife struck him on the side of the head.

"Owww, my head! What the hell was that?"

Russell jumped up, sending Lorraine crashing to the floor. Blood flowed from his scalp, his anger growing as he saw the blade that had pierced his scalp laying on the tiles at his feet.

"I saw Brandon throw something and run," one of the girls chimed in.

Shawn and Russell bounded up the staircase, their feet hitting only one step as they raced after Brandon. Russell had fire in his eyes as he felt the warm blood still flowing down the side of his face. He stopped in the kitchen, and holding a dish towel to his head, Russell and Shawn searched the house for Brandon. With Patricia at work, their brother had no advocate to call for intercession.

"Where are you Brandon?" Russell screamed. "I am going to friggin' kill you! Do you hear me?!"

"What the hell is going on out there?" Jack called. He could hear all of the commotion from his bed, and his voice revealed a mix of frustration and anger that he was out of the loop and unable to intervene.

Shawn and Russell stopped at the foot of the foyer steps to listen for signs of their antagonist, while Shawn answered Jack's inquiry.

"Brandon stuck Russell in the head with a butter knife!"

"Tell him I said get the hell down here…now!" Jack responded with the expectation of compliance, but his slurred speech and stuttered words diluted the impact of his message.

The boys stopped at the front door, which was closed, so Brandon had not left the house. Suddenly the two heard a "pop" as Brandon pushed the button on the doorknob, locking himself into the bathroom. Brandon shuddered inside the bathroom as two pairs of heavy footsteps drew closer to the door, prompting him to brace his full weight against it.

The doorknob jiggled as Shawn tried to turn it. Denied access, Shawn and Russell appealed to Brandon's need to obey his father.

"Dad said come downstairs now!"

Brandon weighed his options. He was convinced that if he left the bathroom he would never make it downstairs to report to Jack. His brothers had every intention of beating him to a pulp as soon as they could get their hands on him.

When they got no response, his brothers moved on to plain threats. "You can't hide in there all day, you bastard! Open up or I swear I will rip this door off!"

Brandon knew that Russell, though normally low key and easy going, exercised no restraint if provoked to anger. Brandon felt secure enough in his position that he went the added step of taunting his brother. "Why don't you get your girlfriend Lorraine to fix your head!"

Suddenly, Brandon's head bounced off the door as Russell and Shawn threw themselves against the other side. They continued to yell back and forth through the door for a few moments, and then Brandon heard only silence from the other side. He had just assured himself that perhaps the two had given up when a violent shove against the door sent him reeling to the bathroom floor. He wondered how Russell had moved the door so far, not realizing Russell had landed squarely against the other side after a running start.

Brandon started to panic again as the white hollow core door began to split with the sound of splintering wood at each forceful kick. With each blow, the entire door seemed to bubble out, and then contract back into position. Brandon's options were limited, but he could start to see light showing through the cracked door.

"You got nowhere to go, Brandon! I'm gonna kick your ass!"

Frantic, Brandon looked to an improbable means of escape. Opening the bathroom window, he gauged the drop required to land on the concrete patio below. A round metal freestanding ice bin sat directly below the window.

Brandon looked between the drop and splintering door. Under the incessant kicking the two halves of the door were being pushed in

335

opposing directions. One or two more good kicks would give his rabid siblings the access that they so desired. Fear of Russell's retribution cured Brandon of any apprehension about the precarious drop to the ice bin. Brandon climbed out the window and hung for a moment from the windowsill. He released his grip just as Shawn's foot broke through the door. He landed squarely in the ice bin; the momentum of the fall was absorbed by the bending of the receptacle's aluminum legs.

Brandon rolled onto the grass, his face grinding across the green blades. A mound of dirt accumulated in his mouth as he slid across the lawn. He was on his feet and running as soon as his momentum stopped. Russell stuck his head out the bathroom window just in time to watch his brother frantically jumping over the back fence.

"When you come home, you're dead, Brandon. Dead!" He yelled out just as Brandon disappeared between the two neighbor's houses behind them.

Brandon knew that returning home was impossible until Patricia came home from work. Until then, he sat perched underneath the underpass of the 36th Street bridge. Hunkered down in the white sandy soil, he remained there for hours until around 4 pm, eventually chased out by the increasing number of rats running along the bridge's rafters.

Returning home to the relative safety of Patricia's presence, Brandon was summarily grounded for a week. For the next month, his head pivoted constantly as he scanned his surroundings for impending danger. Russell never forgave or forgot an offense, and Brandon knew Russell would patiently wait to exact his revenge. In the meantime, Russell found a degree of gratification in watching Brandon's obvious state of chronic fear.

Chapter 50
Patricia and the Wish for a Separate Peace

November 1972

Clusters of cockroaches convening in the middle of the kitchen floor scampered to safety beneath the fridge and oven as Patricia turned on the kitchen light, breaking the early morning darkness. Troubling as the presence of the insects was, their ranking on the ever-growing list of problems that demanded her constant attention was so far down that Patricia barely noticed the bugs on entering the room. Dripping water lines under the sink were again seeping under the floorboards and attracting the unwanted guests. Patricia had tried fixing the leak herself, only to make it worse. Cooking pots now sat underneath the multiple leaks within the base cabinets. Towels were placed in the bottom of the pots to at least minimize the irritation to Jack from the constant drip…drip…drip…from within the cabinet. The catch pans allowed only 24 hours before spilling over on to the bottom of the cabinets.

Wearily plopping herself down in the booth style seats at the kitchen table, Patricia waited for her tea water to boil in the open saucepan. She forwent coffee, fearing that the percolator might wake Jack. She looked at the pile of dirty dishes in the sink. The boys had promised fervently that they would do the job while she was at work the day before, but greasy water slicked near the uppermost rim of the sink, forming a slimy ring completely around the basin, told Patricia that the boys had gotten only as far as filling up the sink before becoming distracted by some other unrelated venture.

Arising an hour early was the price that Patricia was willing to pay for a few precious minutes to herself before a full day of demands both at home and at work. Soon she would wake Ryan and get him ready to be dropped off at his Aunt Rosemary's. Thirty minutes' drive in the opposite direction from her work, the daily trip had been well worth the additional miles over the preceding year. Rosemary was raising three rambunctious kids of her own, two of whom were only slightly older than Ryan. Another boy in the house kept her children occupied, and was no more trouble to care for than her own. Rosemary had experienced her own setbacks over the years and had never forgotten that Patricia had always been a strong advocate for her.

Patricia forced herself to refrain from dwelling on how nice it would be to let Ryan sleep in and awake at his own leisure. Spending the whole day together as Ryan shadowed Patricia from room to room filled his mother's deepest hopes and aspirations. She would be reminded of those early years with the older boys back in Stratford. Such fanciful thoughts, however, did not reflect her present reality, did nothing profitable, and to the contrary, invited melancholy with them.

Rubbing her face to clear an uncomfortable night's sleep from her eyes, she paused to look at her hands as they were outstretched in front of tired pupils. Turning her hands from palms to backs, Patricia wondered where the soft gracefulness had gone. The once nimble fingers were now rough and coarse, a condition cultivated by scrubbing floors at the Woolco cafeteria.

At the risk of submitting to self-pity, Patricia harkened back to the pot roast dinners she made for the family in Stratford. How happy she had been with the freedom to create in her own kitchen. She was thankful that she had not wasted those days bemoaning things she did not have! Those years were some of the most precious in her memory. Why was her present attitude so different? She spent too much time and emotional resources remembering what she used to have or worrying about the future. Feeling herself sliding down a self-imposed spiral of self-pity, Patricia ceased her jaunt back to bygone days, all too aware that overindulging in memory would make the coming day more difficult.

She would need every ounce of available energy in the coming week. The Woolco was sure to be packed with shoppers buying Thanksgiving decorations and supplies before the holiday arrived next week. Many of those overbearing shoppers would eat at the in-store cafeteria. Satisfying the demanding and often rude patrons would exact every bit of emotional and physical strength from Patricia for 12 hours. Many of the diners conducted themselves as though they were seated in a five-star restaurant, treating Patricia and the other workers as the lowly hired help. Though she was tempted more than once to scream, "This is a cafeteria, you idiot; get over it," her own dignity and the need for the job prevented her from doing what was most certainly an invitation to get fired.

The demands of the past 3 years had done more than weathered her hands. Care had carved lines around her eyes, and Patricia's face was etched with the weight of her responsibilities. Years of lifting Jack in and out of his chair and bed had transformed Patricia's delicate arms with muscle and sinew.

The water in the saucepan across the room boiled as Patricia stood. She took pliers from the top of the stove and absently used them to turn off the burner, which did not have a control knob. Since half of the burner control knobs had gone missing over the past several years, the pliers held a permanent place next to the range. No rational explanation for their removal had ever been offered, and Patricia never received one confession from any of her sons. The control knobs just somehow "disappeared".

Pat fixed her tea, taking care not to clink the spoon against the sides of the cup. She sat again and had just raised the drink to her lips when she heard her husband's low call from the dining room.

"Pat, is that you in the kitchen? I need to use the commode."

Placing the steaming mug on the table, Patricia walked into the dining room. As the tea cooled, Patricia positioned her husband onto the receptacle, got him back into bed, and woke Ryan for the trip to Rosemary's. Eventually the refreshing cup of tea grew cold, left on the table as a reminder to Patricia on her arrival home of the loss of those few quiet morning moments.

Chapter 51
The Christophers and Finding Grace

November 1972

Dressed in uncomfortable, ill-fitting suits that had long since seen their finer days, the boys walked the 10 blocks home from St. Joe's church with Patricia on Thanksgiving. The Country Squire had driven its last mile a few days before, and though Jack's brother Charlie had agreed to loan the family his brand new white '72 Dodge Dart for as long as they needed it, he was not able to bring it over until the following week.

Shawn thought the family looked like a traveling billboard for poverty, though he did not say this aloud. Robert and Shawn had warned the younger boys not to ruin this day for Patricia. Attending church together still meant the world to their mother, though few if any of her sons shared her enthusiasm.

Still, they had managed to behave during the mass, and Patricia was able to enjoy the service without interruption. The older boys bided their time scanning the rows and quietly pointing out any good-looking girls, using their fingers to silently rate attractiveness from 1 to 10. After running out of cute girls, the brothers started back at row one and looked for people with freakish features or habits. Ryan provided a degree of levity to their pew when he thrust his hand into the collection basket. The entire row was amused, laughing aloud in the middle of the worship hymn.

Patricia looked at her sons walking slightly ahead of her on the way home and mused about the sermon they'd just heard. As the priest talked about learning to be thankful in all circumstances, Patricia listened intently. The art of gratitude in the midst of adversity currently eluded

341

the weary mother, but if such a condition of the heart were possible, she wanted to attain it.

Just down the street, an enormous banner was hanging from the facia boards of the Nardella house. Bold blue letters on a king-sized bed sheet read, "Welcome Home Corporal Dean." Mrs. Nardella's son had finally come home from his last tour in Vietnam. Many soldiers' mothers were not so fortunate as to fly such a banner. Patricia wondered what it must have been like for Dean Nardella's mother, wondering day after agonizing day for months if her son was alive. Patricia felt deeply grateful that she never had to endure this mother's nightmare with any of her children. She was indeed learning gratefulness in adversity.

She thought of other blessings. The country was in the middle of a deep economic recession, evidenced by gas rationing, 17% inflation, rampant unemployment, and soaring costs for the most basic of food staples. Many families had no idea where their next meal was coming from. Patricia took this into perspective as she and her children were walking home anticipating a full Thanksgiving dinner.

The difficulties of the Christophers' challenges and setbacks could not be discounted. However, Patricia agreed with the admonition of the priest's message. Enduring the daily barrage of troubles and disappointments was only possible if the family maintained some degree of thankfulness for what they did have.

As they walked ahead of her, her sons brought Patricia an increasingly thankful heart as they tormented and joked with each other. All of her sons were healthy, something that she could no longer flippantly take for granted. Repeated support from her mother and siblings as well as Jack's family meant so much over the years. This too, Patricia felt profound gratitude for. Many struggling families were not surrounded by loving relatives.

She committed herself to complaining less and thanking more even as she dealt with trying days. Instilling gratitude in the boys would be impossible if Patricia did not feel the benefits herself. If God were there, and if he were inclined at all to bestow any benefit or blessings to her family, Patricia believed that she was the linchpin. If she gave up hope,

342

the Christopher boys were certain to lose any connection to God and to be set adrift in a sea of troubles and tribulation. Patricia had no intention of letting that happen.

If Patricia could hear her son's thoughts, her musings would have been confirmed. Catching only a few words of the priest's message here and there, the boys were somewhat less ethereal in their viewpoint. How easy it was for the priest to drone on about a thankful heart while he passes a plate around and people give him money, Robert thought. *I'd be freakin' thankful 7 days a week if people threw their money to me.*

As they got within a block of the house, Patricia gave the boys permission to run ahead and get out of their church clothes. "Don't wake your father if he is asleep," she cautioned them. Their departure gave Patricia an entire block to walk by herself, with a groggy Ryan sleeping intermittently in her tired arms. Slow casual steps permitted her to make the most of this brief time alone. Spending a few quiet moments with Ryan was a rare treat.

Patricia spent the rest of the morning cleaning and completing a myriad of assigned tasks that the boys had left unfinished during the week. Patricia found great satisfaction in being able to return to work on Monday knowing that all of the clutter and disorganization had been rectified. Initially inclined to have the boys help her, truth was that she spent more time and energy getting them started than just completing the task herself.

Later that afternoon, Jack agreed to his wife's request to sit at the head of the makeshift dinner table in his wheelchair. His adherence to his vow to stay in bed caused bedsores, which made sitting in his chair for any period of time painful. Unlike his wife, Jack saw no benefit to further use of his chair. He understood that Patricia's request to sit at the table head was a kind, but symbolic gesture to reaffirm him as the leader of the household.

Patricia intentionally outdid herself preparing the holiday meal. Jack's heart grew a little lighter as the smells from the kitchen took him back to those early days in Stratford. It was nice to have his wife home, popping her head in and out to talk while she cooked. The interaction was a welcome change from his usual long, lonely days at home.

The festive dinner table was beautifully set and displayed. Robert and Shawn helped Jack into his wheelchair and made him as comfortable as possible then politely took their places with their younger brothers. Ryan and Richard were too young to remember the extravagant meals in their former residence, but the comparison was not lost on the older boys.

Patricia, still thinking about the things she had been pondering earlier, suggested something different for the meal.

"Before Dad prays, I want you to each tell of one thing that you are thankful for."

Russell volunteered to begin: "I'm thankful that I'm not as dorky as Brandon!" His attempt at humor struck a comedic chord with his brothers but was quickly rebuked by both parents.

"That's enough, Russell" Jack snapped. He could tell that this was important to Patricia.

"I want you to be serious for one minute." Patricia continued. "I am sure that there must be something that you boys are thankful for."

Whether to express true thankfulness, please their mother, or just get through the exercise in order to eat, each son gave a reasonable account of appreciation for life's blessings. Patricia was genuinely pleased with their answers and asked Jack to bless the meal. As they all joined hands, Shawn could not help but notice how lifelessly Jack's arm lay across the table. He took his father's cold hand in his own and gently squeezed, the extent of Jack's infirmity hitting home in his heart. The strong hands that had once comforted him and commanded his respect could now barely signal that they even existed.

Bowing their heads, the family listened as Jack said a prayer of thanks in a trembling voice.

"God, thank you for this meal, and all of Mom's love and hard work that went into making it. Thank you for all that are here, and we remember those who have left us. Forgive us for hardened hearts, and taking what we have for granted, for not loving each other the way we should."

The boys looked up dumbfounded but stayed silent as Jack's prayer strayed from a simple meal blessing into something very different. They had never heard Jack talk like this before. It was as if he had entered into a private conversation with God and the rest of the family was listening in on the exchange. As he continued, Patricia could feel Jack's attempt to squeeze her hand, as if referring to aspects of their relationship too. The man who had once boasted that his god was in his back pocket, the man who resented even going to church, was at this moment reclaiming his faith.

Though his family had no way of knowing this, Jack's unplanned prayer was the result of countless hours alone without anyone to talk to. Isolated within the confines of his bed, Jack Christopher began talking to the only one who was there to listen. God Himself. Conversations transpired that even Patricia had not been privy to, for Jack had said nothing to her about them. These were not the flowery conversations heard in church or public prayer. Jack's prayers had none of the pretentiousness of carefully chosen words or grammatically perfect sentences. Instead, in those dark early morning hours, Jack cursed God for his trouble-filled life.

"What the hell are you doing to me? Are you that egotistical that you demand to be called 'good' and then allow this kind of shit to happen?" Jack held nothing back, itemizing event after wretched event in his life when he felt that God had abandoned him. After a few days, Jack began to feel God's reply as if the Lord was speaking to him.

"Jack, these are the times when *you* had disappointed *me*. Didn't you know that I too, can be hurt? I love you, but the pain in my heart is no less than what you say I have done to you. Your trust in me was unabated as long as I did exactly as you say. Such positions make me not your Lord, but your slave. I have written you a letter telling you exactly how I feel and think and act, but you have read none of it. You then hate me for not explaining why I do the things that I do. We have our differences, Jack. Let's work this out, just between the two of us. Often I

345

had wanted so much to talk to you, but you just turned me away. Remember, many days at St. Anne's with your mother when you were young, I called to you. Your mind was always somewhere else. Now we have the house all to ourselves, Jack," and so the conversation began.

Many discussions were heated, some were tender, others left unfinished. Jesus reminded Jack that his own life on earth had been anything but enjoyable. He had been lied to, mocked, beaten, and killed; hardly a sheltered life.

"Jack, had I not done all of that, I could never have talked to you, and you would have been forbidden from talking to me. Whether the pain was worth it is up to you. I love you, and I will show you a place that will make all of your pain worth it. I would not lie to you, but until you see me for who I really am, and believe, we are separated. I cannot make you into all that you can be in this life and the next.

Only a few weeks before Thanksgiving, after many conversations and exhausting exchanges, Jack Christopher found his piece of heaven in the quiet solitude of his darkened room, but he told no one of the change in his heart. Even now as he finished the holiday prayer, Jack would reveal nothing of his conversations with God. His newfound faith was no assurance that he would never curse or argue again, or that he did not still loathe his physical circumstances. What was certain in Jack's heart was that something better awaited him.

Jack finished praying, careful not to overindulge in front of his hungry family.

"Father, thank you for each one here, and bless this food, and our time together, in Jesus' name, amen." The closing line of Jack's invocation struck the family as unfamiliar, but refreshing.

Remaining in the wheelchair for another half hour, Jack engaged in small talk with the boys. Though awkward at first, the boys were soon cutting each other off to share an anecdote with their father. Eventually, the pain from the bedsores and being seated in the same position for over an hour forced Jack to return to the relative comfort of his bed. Exhausted, he barely had the energy to take the meds Patricia brought him before he dozed off to sleep. After dinner, the boys helped clear the table so that Jack did not have to hear dishes clanking together all night as Patricia cleaned up from the holiday meal by herself. Russell found a tactful way to avoid the messy work by strategically offering to watch Ryan downstairs until the cleanup was completed.

As the boys went to bed, Patricia filled a single wineglass with a deep Merlot, and sat quietly on the living room couch. This day had ended peacefully, without any sudden demand for intervention. Looking over at Jack, she was happy to see her husband sleeping comfortably. She leaned back on the couch and watched as the full moon shone through the living room window, the light dancing across the carpet. If only more days could end on such a pleasant note. Recounting the blessings of this day, Patricia placed her half-filled wineglass on the table before fading off to sleep.

Chapter 52
Robert and Forward Movement

May 1975

Patricia finished giving Jack breakfast and cheerfully reminded him that their families would be coming over later in the day. Two and a half years had passed since Jack's last Thanksgiving seated at the table. By now his condition could barely be classified as "living" by any normal standards. He weighed scarcely more than 170 lbs, and bony joints could be seen jutting beneath the skin of his thin, frail frame. Racked with pain and denied any use of his arms or legs, Jack's only noticeable movement was to turn his head as Patricia fed him. Hollow cheeks accented each painful wince of his face as he felt the torment of his collective maladies. He was able to communicate, between the disease and the medications, and his reasoning was often fleeting. He was often delusional and seemed to become more combative as each day passed. By early Spring most days were filled with shouting and arguments. Jack often told all of the boys that he wished their children would be just as screwed up as his were.

He frequently reminded Brandon especially that he would amount to nothing. Although Brandon understood that the meds were responsible for his father's comments, they still cut long-lasting wounds into his heart. On one occasion, Brandon raised the motorized foot of the bed as high as it would go in a fit of anger, and left the house, leaving Jack stuck in the painful position for 15 minutes before returning to lower the bed back down.

Even attempts at humor among the boys often had a cruelty. One afternoon, Russell carried Ryan into the house, blood running down his

348

face. "Ryan was hit by a car, Mom!" Russell yelled to Patricia as she rushed to her blood-covered son. Crying frantically, she took Ryan over to the sink hoping to wash off enough blood to assess his injuries. As they got to the sink, Ryan jumped back, threw his arms in the air, and yelled, "Surprise! It's fake blood!" Patricia fell to the kitchen floor as the strain on her nerves and jolted emotions overwhelmed her.

Now Patricia was facing another overwhelming event. Soon Robert would be leaving for Navy boot camp in Chicago. His impending departure was more than his mother could bring herself to think about. Reassurance that the country was no longer at war held little consolation. There would be no communication at all with her son for the next 13 weeks.

Large tufts of deep red hair fell to the floor in the bathroom as Shawn guided the electric razor back and forth across Robert's head. Robert's hair was now cropped more closely than Jack had ever required, but he decided that having his hair already in specs on arrival at boot camp would not be a bad idea. As Shawn worked, Robert stared at the bathroom wall, and for the hundredth time over the course of life in Pennsauken, counted the missing tiles; following the moldy grout lines. One thing was certain, he would not miss this bathroom.

After Shawn finished, Robert brushed hair off of his lean, muscular 6'3" frame. He had yearned to get away on his own for as long as he could remember and was anxious to begin naval training. As Jack's condition had declined in recent years, his brothers all viewed Robert as the functioning head of the household. Deprived of the normal pursuits of a high school teen, Robert had no time for dates, sports, or proms. He worked after school to supplement the family income and then came home to arbitrate sibling disputes.

Patricia appreciated the sacrifices her oldest son was making, which made her doubly vehement in her support for him to go out and start his own life. College was not even a remote possibility for now, but she hoped prudent handling of his money while in the military might make a secondary education possible She had no doubt that Robert's departure would leave an emotional as well as a practical void, not only for her, but among his brothers as well.

Robert came down the steps and leaned over in front of his mother, inviting her to rub his fuzzy scalp. Though amused that his head now looked like a ripe Georgia peach, seeing her son devoid of his red locks drove home the certainty of his impending departure. For his sake, she tried to hide the hurt as much as possible, and focused instead on preparations for Robert's going away party.

Both Jack and Patricia's families would soon begin arriving. Normally, the house's state of disrepair left Patricia embarrassed at the idea of people coming over, but Jack's condition now demanded that someone be in the house at all times, making hosting a party somewhere else too difficult. Besides, unease over the house paled in comparison to the sadness brought on by the thought of Robert's upcoming flight to Chicago. Patricia was relieved when all of the guests began arriving. Noise generated by the music and multiple conversations distracted Patricia from her sad musings.

Relatively speaking, Jack was having a good day and was glad to see most of his brothers, Annie, and Janet. His siblings took turns, one at a time, sitting with him.. Far different was this visit from the loud raucous joking they had shared a little more than 4 years earlier. Tonight, Jack's answers were short, and strained attention was needed to hear his voice at all. His head often swayed slowly to and fro, and with his eyes wide open, he often seemed to be looking off into some unknown, remote world. His blue eyes sometimes rolled back in mid-sentence, and Jack would close them as he struggled to regain his thoughts. Though he lit up each time one of his siblings sat down beside the bed, his condition brought tears to their eyes as they walked away.

Patricia had positioned the stereo in the basement, hoping to minimize discomfort to Jack's ears. Most of the younger guests had gravitated there, leaving their parents upstairs. Robert was now welcomed into the circle of veterans among his uncles. Soon to be a military man himself, Robert was, for the first time, told firsthand accounts of combat during their enlistments. Not all the conversations

350

were serious. Jack's brothers, in particular, were loud, funny, and animated, and began giving Robert pointers on how to handle girls in his many ports-of-call overseas.

Overhearing, Patricia laughingly set her brothers-in-law straight.

"My son doesn't need any pointers, because my son will never leave the ship in any of those places!"

Jack's brothers burst into laughter as Robert shrunk in his seat, not quite sure if or how to answer his mother. He was proud to have the honor extended of sitting with men that he so admired.

"Have a beer, Robert," a voice called as a bottle was passed to him. "Your first one. If you're old enough to get shot at, you're old enough to have a beer." Robert politely declined, not that it would have mattered. Patricia was right on top of the exchange.

"He's not one of the boys yet, not at home."

"Oh, come on Pat," the men teased. "The next thing you know, you'll be telling him to stay away from women!" Patricia answered in kind.

"Not all women…just *those* women."

Robert had expected no gifts and was pleased when family members began handing him envelopes and cards containing money. Robert proudly told Patricia that he would be happy to give half of his gifts to her to help her catch up on bills, but Patricia flatly refused.

"That is your money, Robert. Now is the time to start your life, but thank you."

As the evening progressed, the conversations became quieter and the groups more subdued. After a while, the older folks convened to reminisce, and several of the younger boys started a game of Monopoly. With the guests otherwise occupied, Robert called Shawn to the back of the house, speaking quietly to avoid anyone else hearing.

"Let's go up onto the roof." Robert signaled Shawn to back door. The patio light was turned off, and the only light at the rear of the house was what came from the kitchen window. Carefully leaning a 12-foot wooden ladder against the lower pitch, Robert led the way. They climbed onto the steep upper pitch and reclined where the front and rear pitches met. The cool evening breeze was more pronounced on the roof than it was at ground level. Sitting 20 feet above the yard, the brothers looked out over a cloudless evening sky.

"Here," Robert said as he pulled two beers from his thin jacket. "Don't tell Mom, or I'll have to kick your ass," he joked.

Shawn popped the cap and took his first swig, before retorting, "You better wait until they teach you that kung fu shit before you make your move. Remember, I'm the psycho!" Robert saluted Shawn's comeback by gently tapping his beer bottle to his brother's.

An uneasy silence lingered for several minutes as each waited for the other to say what they were both thinking. Robert could hear the slight tremble in Shawn's voice as he broke the silence. "I'm gonna miss you, Rob; not that I don't care about the others, but…" Robert saved him the discomfort of explaining.

"Same here, bro," he interjected, staring straight out into the night sky. "We've seen a lot more than the rest of them have. I just don't know why I could never seem to measure up.," he mused. "Maybe when I come home in uniform, Dad will be proud."

"Maybe it's like any other family, Rob," Shawn ventured. "The first one is the experiment, and that just happens to be you." He paused as if searching for words. "I don't know what's gonna happen after you go," he said finally. "For you, someone will be on your ass 24/7; you won't have to decide what to do. I'm not so sure about us back here. Mom always felt safer when you were around."

Robert reminded Shawn of his repeated wish over the years that he were the oldest child.

"You're top dog now, Bones. It's like when we were in the Double Digit Club; you just moved up the social ladder." Both brothers laughed at the reminder of their secret society and the memorable days at the Bat House.

"I'm surprised you never asked Denise out, Rob; you know she only joined to hang out with you."

Robert was not sure how true Shawn's observation was, but he liked to think that it was right. Still, he was not about to let his brother off so easy.

"Tell ya what, I'll ask Denise out as soon as you ask lighthouse girl. What was her name?"

It did not take Shawn long to recall that fond day, and the girl's sweet Irish accent.

"Kati...I wonder whatever happened to her," he said wistfully.

After a few moments, each with his own memories, Robert came to the reason he had called his brother onto the roof.

"Listen, bro, I don't want you to feel like I'm abandoning you. I just wanted to make sure we were cool. We've been through a lot together, and I want you to know that you can count on me. Maybe Mom can bring you to my boot camp graduation."

Robert's last suggestion reminded them both that he would be leaving in a few short days. Shawn turned his head to wipe his eyes as Robert's coming absence sank in. Robert decided to lighten the moment.

"Besides, Bones, you're too crazy not to come out on top."

Shawn started laughing, and accidently released his grip on his-now empty beer bottle. As it slid down the steep pitch, he lunged instinctively for the bottle, lost his place on the roof, and began to slide down the front pitch after it. Before he reached the roof edge and fell onto the driveway, Robert grabbed him with one arm while holding onto the ridgeline with his other hand.

"I can't keep saving your ass like this," Robert quipped as he pulled Shawn back up. They moved carefully down the roof toward the ladder as the sound of shattered glass signaled the bottle's fall.

In the kitchen, Patricia heard the quick scampering on the roof and stuck her head out the rear dining room window just as the young men were climbing down the ladder.

"What are you two doing up there?" she called out.

"Ummm...looking for something." Unlike Shawn, who could lie without flinching, Robert was not so adept at deception. Even he did not know what his stuttering explanation was supposed to mean. Seeing them both reach the ground safely, Patricia did not stop to pursue a further answer. She would easily put it all together in the morning when she cleaned up the broken glass in the driveway.

When the last of the guests had gone and his brothers were scattered throughout the house, sleeping in one corner or another, Robert approached his father's bedside. He had not spoken to Jack much over the course of the evening.

Even while seeing his father's exhausted state, part of him saw no reason to let go of the anger and resentment that his early years had fostered. Jack had been unswervingly harsh to his firstborn son. Robert could never justify getting his head slammed for giving a wrong answer. He sometimes wondered if Jack feared that getting too close to his son would hinder the boy from standing up for himself. Watching Jack as he doted over Ryan in recent years made Robert want to cry out to his father, asking him why they could not have enjoyed that same kind of relationship.

Robert looked at his father dozing in his bed. He felt increasingly distant and removed in his relationship with Jack. Did that make him as insensitive as his father had been to him? Feelings of hurt and rejection aside, Jack had helped bring Robert into this world. He had stood by the family while he could. No doubt, Robert had wounds that would take years to heal, if they ever did, and Jack inflicted some of those wounds. Was Robert inclined to take that same knife and inflict vengeful blows on his father now that he could not fight back? Jack slowly came out of his slumber as his son approached.

Stopping at Jack's bed, Robert found him tired but in good spirits after having so many visitors. He leaned over and brushed his father's slightly greasy hair back from his forehead. As sick as Jack was, he still retained his jet-black hair. Robert kissed Jack on the forehead and felt some of his anger and resentment leave him. This was his father.

"Thanks for the party, Dad. I still have two days before I have to leave." As Robert began to stand back up, Jack thrust his wobbly forearm forward as best he could. The dead weight glanced off of

Robert's shoulder, but Jack's son realized what his father was trying to do. Robert took Jack's hand and placed it around the back of his neck.

Suddenly, a beautiful clarity came over Jack's face. His eyes did not wander but looked straight into Robert's. Jack's change in countenance was not lost on Robert. He watched as the fire returned to his father's eyes. As Jack began to speak, the words did not dribble out as in recent years. Instead, his speech was surprisingly crisp and forceful.

"Robert, I am damned proud of you. Your uncles are proud of you." After speaking, Jack fell back and leaned against his pillow, still looking at his son. The fire in Jack's eyes and voice had died back, but had not been wasted.

Robert could tell that the glowing comments from his uncles had pleased his ailing father, but he had not expected Jack to come right out and say the words to him. He felt like bursting into tears and hugging his father, but he refrained, fearing that doing so might substantiate any lingering fears of weakness.

"Thanks, Dad; it really means a lot to me hearing you say that before I go to boot camp." Robert managed to keep his composure as he again kissed his father's brow with tears in his eyes. "I'll see you tomorrow, Dad. Thanks again for a great night."

"Good night…," Jack responded through a fading, tired voice as Robert turned off the living room light. "…Son" Jack's words struck Robert's heart.

As Robert walked up the darkened stairs toward his room, he saw his mother at the top of the steps sobbing quietly.

"Mom, are you OK?" he whispered with concern in his voice.

"I didn't want you or your father to hear me. I ran up here from the kitchen when I heard your dad tell you how proud that he was of you. I know how much that means to you, Robbie."

Patricia had not called him by that name in years. She wrapped her arms around her son, resting her head against his chest for a moment.

"You're always going to be Robbie to me. You know that, don't you?" Robert held his mom to let her know that her name for him would always be fine. Finally, Patricia pulled away and dried her eyes.

"You'd better get to bed, son," she said, smiling at him. "You have a lot of ground to cover before you leave."

Robert wasn't quite ready to say goodnight. He was glad to be getting on with his life, but he did not look forward to that final heart-wrenching goodbye. "Thanks Mom, for everything." Robert hugged her again, like he did not want to let go. It was an expression of gratitude, not just for the party, but for a lifetime of sacrifice and unconditional love for her children.

Chapter 53
Shawn and a Tactical Miscalculation

Late October 1975

Patricia had not heard from Robert since attending his graduation from boot camp in August, she was excited to get his letter despite its less than thrilling contents. He thanked her again for coming to his graduation and bringing Shawn along. They'd had a wonderful weekend together in Great Lakes, swimming and tracking down every food that Robert had craved during his 13 weeks of training.

After boot camp, Robert had transferred to Pensacola, Florida, for some type of electronics training, and the letter briefly mentioned saying something about radar. He noted that he was doing very well in his studies, but more importantly to Patricia, he sounded happy. Along with general updates, her son had written to let the family know he would not be able to make the trip home in 2 weeks for Thanksgiving. His training schedule had been extended, and going on leave was out of the question. Even this news was relayed matter-of-factly, without distress or anger, and hearing Robert's positive disposition through the letter was a great measure of comfort for Patricia.

Though the boys missed their older brother, his departure had given Shawn and Russell a boost in mood, in the form of improved living conditions. Shawn moved into Robert's old room. Russell was equally pleased, as now he had his own room in the basement. Hopes of having equal halves of their room evaporated for Richard and Brandon since they had to share their room with Ryan.

Petty complaints aside, the sleeping arrangements had improved for all of the boys to some degree.

Robert also asked how Jack was. He knew from her letters to him that Jack was now out of the hospital after a bout of respiratory distress. His lungs had accumulated considerable fluid buildup, and when his breathing became very labored and difficult, Patricia felt he needed more help than she could provide. Jack had been placed on assisted breathing for several days until his respiratory distress was relieved.

Patricia did not plan to burden Robert with unnecessary details before he came home on leave in December, so she would not include Dr. Scherring's gently made suggestion that they consider placement for Jack in a continued care facility. For now, it was enough for him to know that his father was feeling better.

She sighed when she thought of the conversation with Dr. Scherring. She'd appreciated his delicate handling of such a sensitive subject, and he seemed to understand that he did not need to push the issue. Patricia admitted that Jack's care requirements were rapidly surpassing what she could deliver. For Jack's sake, Patricia acknowledged that delaying for much longer was counterproductive to providing him with the best care. Dr. Scherring promised that he could circumvent a 2-year waiting list to one of the best nursing homes in nearby Cherry Hill.

Though she could wait to tell Robert and the other boys, she knew she could not delay in making the decision. Later in the afternoon that she received Robert's letter, she prepared to meet with Dr. Scherring and discuss all that would be involved with any decision regarding Jack's care

She called Shawn down for last-minute instructions.

"Shawn, I have to go out for a while, and you are in charge." Shawn thought that his mother's declaration had a nice ring to it. "Russell is over at the Nardella's and I'm taking Brandon to get sneakers. Check on Dad, keep track of your brothers, and put the meatloaf in at 3 o'clock. Oh, and no fighting. I'm serious. I have enough to worry about without having to play referee. I'll see you later." Shawn nodded, but moved quickly toward the living room. At 17 years old, he thought himself way past kissing his mother goodbye.

As Patricia walked out the front door, she noticed Ryan standing in the flowerbed just to the left of the steps. Leaning over with his hands on his knees, he was staring intently just in front of him at the base of a small ewe in the center of the bed. Patricia stood for a moment, staring at the same place without seeing anything that might have so fascinated her son, before she turned to her youngest in puzzlement.

"Ryan honey, what the heck are you doing?" she asked. Ryan responded without lifting his head, or diverting his eyes from the ground.

"I think we have mice, Mom. I saw a big mouse run into this hole." Patricia stepped onto the dirt to get a better look. Behind the bush was what appeared to be a deep symmetrical hole nearly 3 inches across. Patricia was startled at the size of the opening.

"Are you sure something went in there, Ryan?" she asked.

"Yep, he was big and dark brown." Ryan had no doubts as to what he had seen. "When I came out the door he ran into the hole."

Since Patricia had no time to address the situation, she delegated the investigation to the current man of the house.

"Tell Shawn to see if he can find out what it is but don't do anything until I get back."

Ryan assured his mother that he would convey the message, and watched Patricia and Brandon get into the car and drive away; then he ran into the house to deliver the message.

Standing outside of Shawn's room, Ryan banged on the door and shouted: "Shaaaawn! Mom said that you have to find out what went down the mouse hole outside."

"What the heck are you talking about, you dork?" Ryan had just turned away when the door flung open and an irritated and bewildered Shawn demanded clarification. Ryan repeated his mother's instructions. Shawn followed his younger brother hesitantly, put off by the task. When he saw the tunnel, his interest was considerably piqued. He and Ryan were the only boys home; that meant any course of action he took would not be immediately questioned.

"That's not a mouse hole, Ryan, that's a rat hole! A river rat hole! River rats are nasty, and they can grow bigger than a cat." Shawn had

359

seen similar tunnels in the sandy soil surrounding the railroad tracks down by the Delaware River.

"We're gonna kill those nasty bastards."

"Yeah, let's kill the bastards," Ryan mirrored his brother's enthusiasm, though he had no idea what they were actually going to do. He followed Shawn as he headed straight for the basement and the thin sheet metal door that led into the crawl space under the living room and dining room.

Entering through the noisy metal panel, Shawn crawled through the cold, dry sand with a foot of headroom to spare above him.. His suspicions were confirmed as he shined the flashlight through the dark dusty room. Spaced throughout the crawl space were eight more tunnels identical to the one outside. Exiting the crawl space, Shawn made his way to the kitchen under Ryan's inquisitive and watchful eye. Careful not to speak loudly enough for Jack to hear in the other room, Shawn called John Tempola. Ryan listened to Shawn's side of the conversation as if it were new TV program.

"John, listen, does your dad still have any more of those gopher bombs we threw in the holes down at the pit? We have a bunch of rats under our house. Cool…can you bring some to my house? Thanks…see ya."

Minutes later, John appeared at the door with a smile and a fistful of "gopher sticks." Each rectangular rodent bomb was 5 inches long and half an inch square. The tiny units were packed with a hard granular composite, and a dark green fuse protruded from the end of each stick. There was a dangerous appeal to their appearance that fueled the boys' excitement. Patricia would be relieved to learn that the rodents had been eradicated when she arrived home. Shawn wanted to show that he was ready to live up to the responsibility place on him with Robert's departure.

Shawn laid out the game plan to John and, much to Ryan's surprise, included him in the conversation: "John, you and Ryan drop one in the hole outside. I'll do the holes under the house and meet you in the kitchen." Ryan wasn't sure what was going to happen, but it had to be cool if it involved using a lighter. As Shawn returned to the crawlspace, John and Ryan readied themselves atop the single tunnel outside.

"Are you ready to do this, Ryan? I'll let you light it while I hold the smoke bomb."

Hearing John's offer, Ryan was beside himself with anticipation. Not only did he get to watch but also had the thrill of lighting the fuse! Holding the lighter with both hands, Ryan awaited John's signal.

"Fire it up!" John yelled. Ryan lit the green stem, and a small steady flash descended toward the tube. Suddenly an immense cloud of yellow smoke spewed from the smoke bomb as John dropped it into the hole. Before they could step away, John and Ryan caught a small whiff of the noxious sulphur vapors. It was as if a hot iron had been pressed against their lungs. Both boys doubled over in a violent but momentary coughing fit. Finally wiping their watery eyes, they recovered.

"Oh man, that stuff is nasty!" exclaimed John as he wiped his runny nose. A steady chimney of yellow smoke arose from the tunnel, convincing John and Ryan that nothing could have survived their fumigating efforts.

They quietly made their way to the basement, taking care not to awaken Jack. They found Shawn on the basement floor, gagging even worse than they had. A cinder block held the sheet metal door closed as a small amount of the now familiar smoke seeped out the access. John ran over to the laundry basin and filled a watering can before bringing it back to Shawn.

"Hold out your hands." John directed as he poured water into Shawn's hands. Shawn splashed the water into his eyes, flushing the burning sensation out after a few minutes.

"There was a ton of smoke," Shawn described as he cleared his burning lungs. "As I dropped the last one, and I couldn't find the door. I almost passed out."

It took Shawn a bit longer to recover from the troubling symptoms, but once he had, the boys assured themselves that they had all survived and the rats had not. The trio high-fived each other in congratulations and moments later, they stood in front of the fridge, searching for a celebratory snack. The sound of coughing in the other room interrupted their foraging. This was not a normal cough but one that signaled immediate distress. Before they could go out and check on Jack, they smelled the now-familiar noxious smell and began coughing again themselves, their eyes burning from the vapors. As Shawn watched in horror, smoke from the crawl space rose into the dining room.

"Open the windows! Open the windows!" Shawn screamed. John turned on the kitchen fan and the boys scrambled to open all the first floor windows. The smoke in the room seemed to multiply exponentially.

The boys heard a moaned, "Oh God," as Jack fought to breathe.

"Ryan, get outside!" Shawn yelled and turned to his friend. "John, help me get my dad out the door!" As the haze thickened, the boys each grabbed Jack under the arm after turning his body so that his head hung over the side of the bed. By then all three were gagging, with snot running out of their noses. Jack moaned again as pain shot through his body when his legs fell to the floor. The boys dragged him across the room, down the hall, and out onto the front porch.

Jack gasped for air as his eyes watered. The boys had positioned him sprawled across the front steps, and pain radiated down his back from the sensitive bedsores that had been dragged across the carpet and now pressed against the hard concrete. Blood spotted the back of Jack's white T-shirt as his bedsores bled.

Ryan noticed the blood first.

"Dad! Dad! Somebody help him!" he cried in terror.

"Son of a bitch! Get me off of these steps!" Jack moaned.

Soon after attempting to render aid, they heard the screaming siren of a police cruiser racing toward them and saw Mrs. Nielson coming as fast as she could to help Jack. She had seen smoke pouring from the Christopher's windows. The siren from the firehouse now joined in, tearing into Jack's ears. The police car skidded to a stop in front of the house, and the officer jumped from his car and ran toward the front door.

"Everybody's out, but my dad needs help!" Shawn cried as he pointed toward Jack.

A flurry of police and fire activity ensued on the front lawn for the next hour as the ambulance took Jack to the hospital. Once they'd cleared the house of any existing or potential fires, the firemen ventilated the house using a large portable blower. The officers took statements from the boys and determined it was an accident. They assured Shawn that they wouldn't file criminal charges, but he and John would still have to answer to their parents.

Shawn was worried about his mother's reaction, but he was more concerned to see Family Services on the scene to investigate. Finding Jack gagging and bleeding on the steps left police no alternative but to call the agency.. Now they would need to determine whether the environment was even safe for Jack to return. .

As Patricia headed home after her meeting with Dr. Scherring, she had no idea of the maelstrom she was about to face. The meeting had been cordial and productive. She and Dr. Scherring did not make a definite decision, but they had reviewed the financial, legal, medical, and emotional implications of Jack moving to and living in a nursing home. Patricia had committed to developing a permanent resolution by the end of the year, completely unaware that people she didn't know had already begun making the decision for her.

Brandon first registered concern when they turned the corner of Remington Avenue and saw the flashing lights.

"They look pretty close to our house, Mom."

Patricia had no doubt that the convergence of flashing red and blue lights was not near her house but *at* her house. The meeting with Dr. Scherring was forgotten as the possible reasons for so many emergency vehicles swam through her mind. As she slammed the car door and she and Brandon ran towards the house, her first thought was for Jack.

"Where is my husband? Is Jack OK?" she asked the first policeman she saw. "Somebody, *please* tell me what happened!" Putting her trembling hands to her cheeks, Patricia looked back and forth for someone to give her answers. A brawny police officer in sergeant stripes walked briskly to her. He had just finished talking to Shawn, John, and Ryan when she pulled up.

"Mrs. Christopher, I'm Sergeant Tyler. Your husband will be fine. There was an accident in the house, and we needed to take him to Cooper Hospital for treatment and observation."

Patricia interjected, "What's wrong with him? How long will he be in the hospital?" Her words faded as she realized that the officer had no way of answering.

Seeing her distress, Sergeant Tyler said the next words as gently as he could. "Mrs. Christopher, Family Services will need to evaluate when and if it is advisable for Mr. Christopher to return home. There were multiple fumigating bombs ignited inside the house, which caused your husband to go into respiratory distress. Apparently your sons and their friend were trying to exterminate some rodents. The boys are all OK, but shaken up. It was clearly a mistake and not done maliciously, so we won't file any charges, but I will need you to sign my report."

Patricia barely noticed the firemen behind them stowing the last of the gear onto the trucks, or, despite the officer's care, his last comments. Her mind was now focused on the statement that Jack may not come home at all.

"What…what do you mean 'if' Jack should come home? Why shouldn't he come back home?"

The sergeant was patient but firm. "Mrs. Christopher, that is a determination that someone from Family Services will need to discuss with you. I can certainly give you their number, but I am not qualified to provide details. Now, if there is nothing else that I can do for you, I'll try to get everyone out of here."

After the sergeant politely excused himself, Patricia walked to the boys. Assured that they were fine, Patricia skipped cordial greetings and directed her attention to Shawn. She leaned over and put her face within inches of his nose. Speaking through gritted teeth, she tried to control her anger.

"What the hell did you do? All that I asked was that you watch Ryan and check on Dad from time to time. How hard was that? Instead I come home to people all over my front lawn, and they tell me that Dad might not come home. Are you trying to drive me over the edge? Let me tell you, Shawn, that I am pretty damn close!"

A younger Shawn would have fallen apart with doubt and self-loathing. By 17, though the self-doubt was ever present, anger had replaced sulking or crying. Shawn took to his feet.

"Let me guess, Mom, Shawn screwed up again, right? I was trying to get rid of the damn rats that we live with! But it's no different than the last 17 years of always being such a damned disappointment to you. Well here's another one for you, Mom; Me and Russell are quitting school! It's all bullshit and a waste of time. We're signing ourselves out next week. It's not like we haven't been cutting classes for most of last year anyway! Now at least if will be official!"

John had watched the beginning of this exchange cautiously, waiting to see if he could interject on his friend's behalf, but when Shawn mentioned leaving school, he decided nothing he said would be helpful. With a half-hearted wave of farewell that neither Shawn nor Patricia noticed, he turned and walked toward his own house.

As Shawn's friend made his way home, spittle formed on Patricia's lips as her shock and anger boiled over. Shawn could only think of how pissed Russell would be that he had blabbed of their plans.

"They tell me that your father may not be coming home, and you wonder why I'm angry? Well let me tell you something Shawn, and you can tell your brother. You want to quit school? Go right ahead! Understand this though—by God, you are going to get a job and pay rent, both of you! It's one or the other, so, since you and Russell are so good at planning, you two do your little planning and decide! You have just one week from the day you both drop out to find a job, and not one day more. If not, you'll find all of your clothes piled on the front lawn.

If you think I'm bluffing, try me. If you try to live here without school or a job, I'll call the police. I have enough to deal with every day without you and your brother throwing more on me. I have had enough!"

Shawn snapped back, "I'm practically an adult! You can't tell me what to do anymore!"

Patricia answered her son in a calm steady voice. "You're right, Shawn, and I'm not telling you what to do, but I damn sure am telling you what you are not going to do. You and your brother are not living in this house unless you are either in school or have jobs.

Patricia stormed into the house around a quiet Brandon, who'd sat on the front steps through the exchange, looking at the small dots of blood left by Jack's injuries. He watched her go past, but made no move to follow.

Patricia managed to get into the front door before she began sobbing. She moved through the house, slamming closed each of the open windows. The movement helped dissipate her anger, though not by much. She was still so furious that it took her a while to realize that Ryan was now following her, apologizing fervently.

She turned and reassured him that she didn't hold him responsible.

"Your brother was in charge. He should not have let you get involved at all. BUT, the next time anything like this comes up again, I want you to remember the mess that you got yourselves into today, and say "no". Ryan nodded eagerly, relieved that his mother's anger was not directed toward him.

Patricia continued to look through the house, taking stock of the damage. The meatloaf had never been put in the oven, and the noxious fumes had ruined a good portion of the exposed food in the house. As she started cleaning up and throwing away the ruined food, Patricia reconsidered her immediate response to Shawn's actions but then stopped. Granted, he was trying to help by killing the rats, but by just charging ahead and not thinking through what could happen, he might have killed Jack, and he risked not only his own life but Ryan's and John's. It was inexcusable, she decided. Now she faced a nightmare with the authorities to try and get Jack home for what little time they might still have together before he would have to move into the nursing home.

Once the kitchen was cleaned up, Patricia walked across the street to thank Arlene Nielson for rushing over to help. Though Arlene had unassumingly returned home when the police and ambulance arrived,

Ryan mentioned her in his many apologies. Arlene looked surprised but pleased to see Patricia.

"No thanks needed," she said to Patricia's embarrassed appreciation. "What are neighbors for?" She saw that Patricia still looked a little shaky and put a steadying hand on her shoulder. "Listen, why don't you come in for some coffee and to get off your feet?"

"I'll have to take a rain check, Arlene," Patricia said with a grateful smile, "but I would love to stop over tomorrow. I got the worst of the residue cleaned up in the kitchen, but the rest of the house is still a mess after all this excitement."

"Wonderful then," Arlene answered. "I'll have desserts and coffee ready around 2 o'clock." As they parted, both women wondered why they had not gotten together before. The closest they had come was when Arlene ran over to the Christopher house in an emergency.

As she was walking back into the house, Patricia felt a prickle of unease as she saw Jack's empty bed in the dining room. The house was quiet, but it was not a serene quiet. Jack had sometimes had to stay at the hospital for varying durations, but now, with no idea when or if he was coming home, the room exuded an unfamiliar hollowness. For all their discord over the years and the understanding that Jack would eventually need to move to a facility with professional care, Patricia found that she dearly missed her husband's presence. She was not ready to lose him.

Ryan's request for fish sticks snapped Patricia out of her musings. She smiled gratefully at her youngest son. What she needed at that moment was simplicity: a plate of fish sticks and French fries, sitting with Ryan and Brandon watching TV; that was as much as Patricia could handle after a day like today. In the morning, she would go to see Jack and figure out what to do about Shawn and Russell. For tonight, fish sticks were as complicated as she wanted to get.

Chapter 54

Shawn, Russell, and Patricia, and a New Cold War

Late October 1975

An uneasy quiet fell over the house after Patricia's ultimatum to Shawn and Russell. The younger boys kept asking when Jack was coming home, and Patricia had done everything she could think of to convince Family Services that Jack would be safe there.

Unfortunately, although visitors from the agency were cordial, they insisted that Jack be transferred to St. Jude's nursing home in Cherry Hill. The agency was not satisfied that returning home was in Jack's best interest, nor could they promise that it ever would be.

When she visited Jack, Patricia found the nursing home to be a top-rate facility. Apparently Dr. Scherring had seen to it that his patient reside in one of the best nursing homes. That did nothing to alleviate the guilt that gripped Patricia. Part of her wanted so much for Jack to be home with her and the kids, but she also wondered if pursuing his return was self-serving. Jack received compassionate 24-hour care at St. Jude's. Deep down, Patricia understood that the time had come for Jack to have professional care and relief from his symptoms that she could not provide. Patricia would give consent for Jack to live at St. Jude's though it would mean that all of his social security and disability payments would go toward payment. By now, her consent was merely a formality.

What really crushed her was how he had left. She could not help but seethe with anger that Jack had been given such a disrespectful exit from their home. She had spoken barely a word to Shawn or Russell since the incident, and they had not spoken to her. When circumstances forced them to occupy the same room, they maintained a cold politeness.

Brandon, Richard, and Ryan found the whole exercise to be unfair and draining. The three youngest boys did their best to avoid any conflicts. Although Brandon had noticed that his older brothers developed the particular habit of removing a pillowcase of personal items every few days, he did not inform Patricia.

Despite the current tensions between them, Patricia did her best to maintain the usual rules. For example, she had always prided herself in letting her sons enjoy some privacy. She wanted the boys to feel as though their bedrooms were a haven of sorts from the surrounding turmoil. Therefore, she kept any incursions into them to a minimum.

By the end of October however, handling Jack's affairs, the growing discord, and Shawn and Russell's frequent absences had created something of a laundry crisis. Dirty clothes, usually deposited in the hallway hamper, were instead piling up in bedrooms. When Patricia noticed a pungent odor in front of the bedroom doors on a day she knew the boys were going to a Halloween party and would not arrive home until late or the next day, she felt she had no recourse. She popped the lock on Shawn's room and began collecting the clothes piled up on the floor. Besides solving the problem of the lingering stench, Patricia hoped that the gesture of doing their laundry might be a starting point for renewed cordial relations.

Patricia worked her way across Shawn's room, picking up article after article of clothing. She finally worked her way over to a pile of clothes on the floor of the doorless, closet. Working through a pile of what appeared to be mostly Shawn's clothes, Patricia heard the sound of tinkling glass.

"The least they could do is take their cups downstairs," she complained to herself as she moved jackets to reveal the items underneath.

Looking down in dismay, Patricia was painfully conscious that this was not an innocuous pile of drinking glasses. She pulled an emerald green translucent cylinder from the mound. It had a rounded bowl at the bottom, with a long thin glass tube jutting up 45 degrees from the base. Inside the bowl, Patricia could see a small amount of residual water with a smell similar to oregano. Beneath this first bong was another and another, intermixed with smaller pipes and scattered rolling papers. Patricia was livid at the thought that Shawn and Russell were smoking pot in her house, only feet away from Richard and Ryan.

Patricia decided that only a serious retribution would be proportionate to the offense. She wondered if she was being vindictive as she called Richard and Brandon up the steps to help her, but then decided a little vindictiveness was appropriate, and felt good..

Richard and Brandon chorused, "What Mom?" with less than ardent enthusiasm at her call.

"How would you guys like to smash some glass?" Patricia answered and was rewarded by rapid footsteps on the stairs. Brandon and Richard were not sure of their mother's intent but both loved the invitation to smash things. Patricia moved the boys to the front window and handed the paraphernalia to them one at a time, instructing that the items be dropped out on the driveway below. Richard and Brandon enjoyed the destructive pastime, and both feared that the other would get the last item. They liked watching the glass fall and smash into colorful shards. Viewed from the second floor, the shattered glass formed an interesting tapestry of red, green, blue, and yellow.

In the early morning hours following the Halloween party, Patricia could hear Shawn and Russell fumbling as they came in the house. Patricia listened to their laughter as they told each other to be quiet at a decibel level that clearly meant they were drunk. They must have missed seeing the broken glass in the driveway and remained blissfully oblivious to her incursion until the next morning. Patricia did not look forward to the inevitable confrontation, but she didn't fear it either. As Patricia turned out the nightstand light, she promised herself a good night's sleep.

Chapter 55
Shawn and Russell, and Retreat

Early November 1975

Shawn and Russell went about their morning routine inside the house, still unaware of the shock that awaited them just outside the window. Patricia had cautioned Brandon and Richard not to tell their older brothers anything before Shawn and Russell saw the shimmering glass in the driveway for themselves. Brandon and Richard laughed to themselves at breakfast over their secret. At first, Russell and Shawn, hung over, nursing headaches, and bleary-eyed, had no interest in why their younger brothers were laughing. Patricia sat at the kitchen table with a fresh cup of coffee, reading the paper.

By the time the older boys put on their coats to depart, checking that they had ample smokes and matches, Brandon and Russell could hardly contain themselves, waiting to see the coming reaction. Finally, the older boys muttered "Bye" to no one in particular and walked out. As soon as front the door closed, the three youngest pressed their faces against the front picture window. They watched in rapt attention Shawn and Russell's steps slow as they noticed the morning sunlight reflecting beams of light off of the scattered glass like tiny prisms. Shawn first noticed that the pile of glass was under his window. He could not immediately put his finger on why, but he noted to Russell that the color and shade of the glass pieces seemed strangely familiar. Finally, he noticed remains from a stem tube with the mouthpiece still attached.

"Are you shittin' me? Fifteen bongs and pipes, and she throws them out the window?" Shawn yelled, kicking the pile of debris and scattering

371

it even further. Russell simply stared in shock. Shawn raced back into the house at full speed, ripping the front door open as hard as he could.

"Lady, what the hell were you thinking?" he screamed at Patricia. "You go into our room and smash our stuff. We weren't bothering you with it! Did the power kick make you feel better?" Patricia did not move from the table, but calmly looked up at Shawn.

"*Your* room, *my* house, *my* rules! If you want to bring drug crap into my house and leave it around your brothers, I'm going to throw it out." Shawn grew increasingly red through this speech as Russell rejoining him, exploded.

"Half those pipes weren't even ours! How the hell am I going to replace them?"

"You should have thought about that before you brought them into the house!" Patricia's calm voice and face made her lack of sympathy perfectly clear. Both Shawn and Russell were livid.

"You know what, Mom? If breaking stuff is so much fun, let me try it." Quickly looking around, Shawn grabbed a deep blue decorative wine goblet that Brandon had bought Patricia the previous Christmas after doing odd jobs. "How 'bout this, Pat?" Shawn took off running out the door with Patricia running behind him.

"You give me that back right now!" she screamed.

"Now you know how it feels!" Shawn sneered as he thrust the goblet onto the cement in front of him.

"You bastard!" Brandon cried as Patricia held him back from running at his brother.

"Fine. Well, I've got news for both of you," she said, pointing a trembling finger. "You'd both better find a place to live because you are not coming back into this house. I don't care where you go, but all of your clothes will be on the front lawn in the morning, whether it's raining or not! I'm done! I don't want to talk to either one of you!"

Russell jumped in. "Good! See how long this piece of shit house holds together without anyone to help!"

Patricia looked sadly from one to the other. "When have either of you ever lifted a finger to help me?" she asked, turning back into the house.

"You won't have to worry about us any more, Mom," Shawn yelled as he lit a cigarette and began walking away with Russell. "We are moving in with Tom in Cinnaminson; anything to get out of this hellhole!" Patricia did not even know who Tom was.

After she ushered the three youngest boys back into the house, Patricia grabbed a broom and began to move all of the glass into one pile. Her arms strained against the weight of it, but as her chaotic thoughts finally overwhelmed her, she fell to her knees and began to cry in deep, heavy sobs. She barely flinched as small shards of glass cut into her knees

None of this would have happened if Jack were well, she thought. Her sons would never have attempted this behavior if Jack were well. What more could God do to her? Was disabling Jack a shot at the entire family?

Patricia lifted her head when she felt a reassuring hand on her shoulder and saw Arlene Nielson. Arlene smiled gently at Patricia and spoke with a nurse's practiced calm.

"Why don't we go over to my house and have that coffee. I think the mess can wait, don't you?"

Patricia stood up, and small trickles of blood trickled down her legs from both knees. "We'll get you patched up, as well," Arlene said. Patricia was embarrassed by the spectacle that had played out on her front lawn and wondered how much of it Arlene had seen and heard, though she did not ask.

Early Sunday morning while Patricia was at church with the three youngest, Shawn and Russell pulled to the front of the house in Tom's white Grand Torino. As promised, their clothes were piled in the center of the front lawn despite the light rain. Hurrying in case their mother should return, the young men threw their soggy belongings into the trunk. Shawn used his house key to run into the house and grab a roast out of the refrigerator. The meat would be a gesture of good intent to

Tom. Since they had no jobs at the moment and couldn't offer rent, the roast prevented them from walking into their new home empty handed.

Over beers and a few bowls of reefer, Tom, 10 years Shawn's senior, went over the ground rules for their stay; what rules there were. Shawn and Russell were convinced that this new arrangement far surpassed anything at home, but they did feel some remorse for some of the things they'd said to Patricia. They decided the only thing to do was wait it out, and see what happens.

Chapter 56

The Christopher Family and the Hardest Détente

1976

Despite the anger and resentment on both sides, perhaps it was not surprising that Patricia's relationship with Shawn and Russell had thawed somewhat by the New Year. Patricia tried to look on the bright side. While she was not thrilled with their living arrangement, or the drug use that the environment fostered, her sons *were* on speaking terms with her. Further, both sons now had jobs and were trying to take on some responsibility. Shawn was a prep cook at a nearby country club and Russell worked as a mechanic's helper.

Neither side discussed the possibility of the boys returning home, but they stopped to visit once or twice a week. Patricia usually prepared a bag of food and toiletries for them to take as they left. Shawn and Russell insisted that her efforts were appreciated but not necessary, but this was something Patricia insisted on. And though they would not have admitted it, even to each other, both Shawn and Russell liked knowing that Patricia insisted on giving them these things as much for her peace of mind as for their physical benefit.

For Patricia, the weekly get-togethers had the added benefit of reinforcing an image of family continuity for Brandon, Richard, and Ryan. She felt that financial and medical strains were enough for them to deal with; they didn't need the added fear that the family was falling apart.

Brandon, in particular, worried Patricia. The responsibility he imposed on himself in recent months left no room for frivolity, and when Patricia expressed concern over his growing paranoia, Brandon flatly rejected her promise that things would get better. Citing the events of the preceding years in Pennsauken, not to mention the difficulties in Stratford, he asked how his concerns could be considered paranoid. If paranoia was an irrational fear, how could recalling actual events and worrying about their repeat be irrational? Despite his increasing melancholy, Brandon was smart, and he spent the free time he allowed himself reading political history, and books on the securities market.

Richard, now 12, was as purpose driven as ever. He never told anyone what his objective in life was, but his determination was clear. He was not about to let circumstances or people get in the way of his happiness or aspirations. If Richard could not go around adversity, then dammit, he would go through it. Would he have liked to have Jack home and healthy? "Yeah, but that's not real life, and the dude isn't here," he reminded himself. "What am I supposed to do but move on?" he asked Brandon. Patricia sometimes wished that a little of Richard would rub off on Brandon, and Richard sometimes wished it, too. Brandon's "whining" and downtrodden attitude was a source of frustration for his younger brother.

Ryan was looking for a safe, secure paradigm of life and family, and as of yet, he had not found it. Career day was difficult at school as other kids brought their fathers in to talk about life on the job. No one could reasonably explain to him why God did not allow him the same experience. Still, of the boys, Ryan sometimes seemed the happiest. Jack had lavished great affection on Ryan from the day he was born, and thankfully, Ryan could still recall wonderful times with his father. His body had been the last to feel secure in Jack's strong arms. Moreover, unlike Brandon, Ryan possessed an exuberance and outgoing personality that encouraged his mother to believe that he would overcome the family's difficulties.

Constant, unwelcome change results in a sense of unease. When the expected daily rhythm is perpetually interrupted, the heart feels as if it never knows what's coming. Always be on alert, and in the presence of this constant crisis state, nerves can be left frayed. Overcoming this deviation from the norm was Jack Christopher's goal throughout most of his life. For him, a successful, contented life was one that minimized if not eradicated change. Unfortunately, his endless search for stability in his life led to change and unpredictability within Jack Christopher himself, until his reactions contorted against every perceived imposition on what he considered the normal cycle of life.

Patricia had joined Jack in his quest, trying during much of their life together to provide him the stability at home that he craved. In the long months that followed her reconciliation with Shawn and Russell, Patricia learned about the pain of the paradigm that stood opposite constant change. As 1976 progressed into 1977 and then 1978, she found herself wondering how to cope with the pressures of life when nothing seems to change at all. She woke each morning to the same challenges and difficulties that bid her goodnight the previous evening. Worse, she could not look ahead to the point when circumstances would improve, or when her hopes for herself and her family would be any closer to fruition.

Between breathing and death is suffocation. Although breathing is better, in her darkest days, Patricia began to understand the argument that even death is preferable to a constant state of feeling suffocated. In the 730 days that life went on but did not seem to change, Patricia's fondest wish was to find a breath of fresh air that never seemed to come.

Jack's condition showed no signs of improvement, but little, and very gradual deterioration. When Brandon asked one day if they had done Jack a disservice by saving him after his suicide attempt, Patricia was shocked, but did not know how to answer. Certainly, saving his life was the right thing to do when they came upon Jack in such distress, but she understood Brandon's point. Jack still had bedsores, and he battled constant dehydration, piercing ear pain, and almost complete immobility. He seemed just alive enough to endure suffering. His bowel control was nonexistent, and his lungs were slowly succumbing to the MS and filled with fluid more and more frequently.

Along with the physical pain was Jack's emotional despondency. He was alert enough to know where he was and that he could do nothing about his circumstances. At 46 years old, he was surrounded by patients nearly twice his age. His mental facilities were sufficient to let him endure the humiliations of daily procedures, but his disease denied him the ability to express his displeasure.

Even rest was elusive and fleeting. Several times a day a food cart with a squeaky wheel would make its way down the light green tiled hallway. For patients who never received visitors, the noise was reassuring; for several moments another human being would be coming in to talk to them. Since Patricia often came to visit with the kids, Jack did not find the food cart comforting. Jack was also bothered by the constant smells of lingering fecal and urine odors mixed with the pungent aromas of pine cleaner and disinfectants; such was an expected, natural cycle.

Hardest for Patricia was when Jack signaled her to lean close and whispered, "Why can't I just die, Pat?"

When Jack was first sick, Patricia prayed for a miracle in her husband's life. As the years passed, that too became more and more difficult. She could not bring herself to pray that God would take him, yet she held out no hope for improvement.

Adding to the feeling of suffocation were the near-constant collection calls. With no compassion or mercy, the calls persisted day after day, month after month, angry voices demanding payment of one sort or another. Patricia felt the guilt of watching her three youngest boys often head to school wearing tattered clothing handed down from their brothers and knowing they were teased and tormented at school for it.

As the seasons passed without the prospect of a brighter tomorrow, Patricia did everything she could to tamp down the seeds of bitterness in her heart and in her sons'. In the summer of 1978, Patricia feared that the cumulative years of fending off adversity had brought the level of stress and physical exhaustion to a point of critical mass for all of them. Against her own better judgment, she skipped a mortgage payment and the electric bill, loaded up the car, and took Brandon, Richard, and Ryan on a 5-day trip to Maine. She hoped to avert her own nervous breakdown and provide an escape for the kids. The trip was on a shoe-string budget, but her sons did not seem to know or care. For 5 days, they could all be a normal laughing family. Experiencing a clambake in Boothbay Harbor while staying at an old roadside motel planted a seed of hope in their hearts.

Patricia desperately wanted her boys to see that life did not always have to be about crisis management. So much could be found in the simple joys of everyday living if they looked. All the phone calls from collection agencies would be well worth the aggravation if Brandon, Richard, and Ryan could learn this one lesson. Driving to and from Maine, and the many stops along the way, enabled the boys to see a world outside of their difficulties at home. Patricia hoped her sons could find a world of loving people, most of whom did not judge them as inferior. Watching her sons in the rear view mirror as she drove, Patricia smiled to see them breathing in the fresh air of life, even if just for a moment.

Chapter 57
Brandon and Friendly Company

November 1978

As Brandon looked out the window during history class at the cascading colors across the autumn trees, he thought back to the beautiful mountains of Maine. The countryside was surprisingly beautiful, and Brandon began to wonder how many other majestic places were out there to be explored. His mother had accomplished the purpose of the trip in his heart.

Before his thoughts wandered too far, the warning bell rang and snapped Brandon out of his daydream. History had always been his favorite class in school, and this year was no exception. In fact, this year's history class was possibly the single greatest class since the beginning of Brandon's formal education, for Brandon had acquired a piece of prime real estate. Mr. Johnson had decided not to use alphabetical order to determine seating assignments, but instead opted for a first-come—first-choice format. Normally banished to the maze of nondescript seats in the middle of the room, Brandon was for the first time enjoying the perks of sitting in the back row.

Over the previous year, Brandon had outgrown the remnants of the gangly appearance he'd had as a young boy, and he no longer sported disproportionate appendages or a puppet-like walk. With his thoughtful, quiet disposition, the solitary pursuit of weightlifting appealed to him, and since he spent almost all of his free time alone anyway, Brandon had been lifting weights over the last few years. His arms and chest were compact and well defined, and his back now formed the sought after

"V." Though Brandon was still too naïve and self-doubting to recognize their interest for what it was, girls in school had begun to notice him.

Even if he had recognized their interest, for all of his burgeoning physical strength, Brandon was still clueless when it came to actually talking to a girl. He immediately froze and began stuttering when spoken to by anyone of the opposite sex younger than his mother. Most of the girls who spoke to Brandon found this endearing, as it assured them that their babbling classmate entertained no untoward thoughts and was, in fact, harmless.

Brandon's discomfort in talking to girls did not diminish what he felt was one of his rear-row seat's major advantages: its proximity to two of the most attractive girls in the school. To Brandon's right in the back of the room was Susan Wells. Tall and thin with perfect cream-colored skin, Susan had angelic features framed by short satin smooth blonde hair that curved up in short gentle waves at the bottom. Her full mouth, wide blue eyes, and delicately turned up nose reminded Brandon of the close up photos in magazines selling high-end jewelry, and she was always dressed in the most tasteful outfits; every aspect of her appearance always in place.

To Brandon, Susan seemed to come from another time, or another world. He wondered whether she'd had formal etiquette training. How else could she move like that, he wondered, as if even the simplest motion was a graceful dance. Even though she never seemed forced or pretentious, or even dramatic, he found just watching her fluid movements pleasant, almost reassuring. Brandon often wondered what type of home life cultivated such refinement; certainly not the mayhem and dysfunction that he lived with.

What Brandon most appreciated in Susan was that for all of her refinement and attractively delicate mannerisms, she was not pretentious or aloof. When she talked to Brandon, on the few occasions they exchanged words, she actually listened to what he was saying and responded to it. Brandon was all too aware that Susan was out of his league. She was in Student Government, French Club, and various school choirs. It was enough to know that someone like her would talk to him, even for a few minutes.

Contrasting with Susan on his right, another high-school beauty, Donna Marie Siperavage sat on his left. Donna seemed to be on a mission to squeeze every ounce of joy and excitement out of each day. In addition to a captivating face, Donna had a toned, athletic body and curly blonde hair that bounced playfully on her shoulders as she walked. She carried her lithe frame equally well no matter what she wore. She might wear jeans and a blouse on Monday and a knockout dress on Tuesday. Brandon liked to guess what fashion choice she had made before Donna entered the classroom.

Laughing and optimistic every day, Donna was smart as well as athletic. She often encouraged people to "live outside their comfort zone," which struck Brandon as amusing. He had been doing that most of his life, just not on purpose. Perhaps he did have something in common with this beautiful blond. Her piercing blue eyes and infectious smile made Brandon feel like something good must be out there; even for him.

In this one class, seated between two friendly, vivacious beauties, Brandon could almost relax. In their happy company, he briefly escaped the strains of his life. To Brandon, any escape was welcomed, yet temporary infusion of joy.

Chapter 58
Jack and the End of Hostilities

May 1979

Jack's roommate had been temporarily transferred to another room to provide the Christophers a measure of privacy as they gathered around his bed. A chilly dark rain blanketed the early spring sky, and raindrops tapped against the windows as the family sat in silence, each member seemingly lost in their own thoughts.

Robert was thankful he'd been able to get emergency leave from his ship, currently moored off the coast of Japan. He'd taken a taxi to the nursing home immediately after getting off the plane in Philadelphia.. Patricia held Robert's hand tightly. She hadn't seen him in over a year, and though she wished his reunion with the family had been under happier conditions, she was greatly comforted having her oldest son home.

Holding Jack's foot, Russell listened to the squeaky wheel of the dinner cart as it came down the hall, just as it had so many times before. This time, though, the cart went past the door to Jack's room without stopping. Russell cried quietly as he thought back to the times in Stratford that they'd walked home from Grandpop's house, Jack looking over his boys with a watchful eye. Brandon interlaced his fingers with his father's, squeezing gently and feeling Jack's valiant attempt to squeeze back one last time. Jack fought to keep his eyes open as Shawn dabbed his father's brow with a cool damp cloth.

Richard and Ryan watched the heart monitor intently. The sound was turned off, but glowing lines made sharp spikes with each heartbeat. They knew that the spikes were bound to cease very soon and felt unable to look away. Patricia watched Jack struggle to draw each breath and thought again how his illness had changed his face. His cheeks were sunken, and his cheekbones protruded outward, and his teeth seemed to no longer fit in his mouth.

Robert rose and leaned over his father's bed. He kissed Jack's forehead and pressed his cheek to his father's. In this moment, he thought how foolishly trivial so much of his anger and resentment had been. How many beautiful memories had been lost to pride or indifference, certainly from Jack but also from his children? As he watched his father's life ebb slowly away, Robert lamented to himself the times that winning an argument seemed more important than his relationship with his father.

"I'm so sorry, Dad; I want you to know how much I love you," he said. Jack tried to turn his head toward Robert, and Robert thought he was speaking, but he could not discern the words. When he saw tears forming in his father's eyes, he broke down and left the room.

When he came back in after a moment, Patricia pulled a chair up to the bedside. She lowered the rail and held her husband's hand tenderly while caressing his cheek. Tears streamed as she spoke softly.

"We're all here, Jack, and we love you so very much. You have always been the strong one." Patricia laughed through her tears as she remembered how unpredictable Jack was and how that attracted her to him when they met. "You always wanted strong boys, Jack, and you have them. You raised six fine sons who know how to overcome and survive."

Patricia could see her husband smile slightly at her words. As she spoke, all six boys rested their hands on their father.

"We know you're tired, Jack. It's been a long road, and you never let yourself rest." Patricia could hardly get the words out as she continued. "It's your turn to rest, Jack. You've finished the race." At these words the boys abandoned reservations and began to weep uncontrollably.

Patricia kissed Jack's cheek tenderly and pressed her face to his. "I love you, Jack. The boys love you. Know that we will always love you. It's your turn to rest."

Patricia rose and stepped back, allowing her sons to come to the head of the bed, one by one. As Ryan stepped back, he began to weep in heavy, mournful sobs and ran out of the room. He ran blindly out of the main entrance and stood in the downpour, drawing hiccupping breaths as rain and tears intermixed. Robert followed him out. He let him sob alone for a few moments, and then put his hand on Ryan's heaving shoulder. Minutes later they both returned to the room, Ryan soaked and Robert's uniform heavy with rain.

As the family gathered around Ryan to console him, Jack's back arched and a loud groan issued from his body. Richard turned to the heart monitor, but no spike appeared. As the family stood staring at the bed in silence and in the absence of Jack's labored breathing, Brandon felt as though the entire world had stopped. Then, just as quickly, it started again, and ceased as a nurse hurried into the room. She turned to face the family hesitantly, and steeled herself to make the difficult announcement.

She did not need to say anything. Her eyes met Patricia's, and she saw that Patricia already knew. Jack Christopher was gone. Brandon ran to his father, throwing both arms around Jack's waist.

"Dad! Dad, it's me; wake up! God, *please* wake him up!"

Patricia gently pulled Brandon away from the bed and to her side. For all their sakes, she ushered her sons out of the room as the nurse started to pull the sheet over Jack's still form.

As Patricia led the family into the house on returning home, she was surprised to realize that her overriding feeling was numbness. They had focused so much and for so long on dealing with Jack's illness, she had no notion as to where her family should go from here. She knew that life would not give her much time before she needed to decide on a course of action for the family, but she felt completely incapable. At present, at least, comforting the kids and saying goodbye to her husband were paramount. She would focus on that.

The family remained in the living room for several hours, laughing as they remembered Jack's fearlessness and stubborn determination. Through tired tears, the older boys shared stories that the younger ones had not heard. Richard and Ryan took in every detail until they slowly faded to sleep. Though by early morning, nearly all the boys were asleep, they all stayed downstairs, not wanting to leave the security of the group.

Several days passed before the magnitude of events began to sink in. Patricia often found herself staring at Jack's wheelchair in the corner or the cane propped up in the hall closet.

"How could they put someone else in dad's room so soon?" Russell asked as he walked past his father's old room on the way to the nursing home activity room. It seemed disrespectful to find another patient in there the day of Jack's funeral. St. Jude's permitted Patricia to hold Jack's memorial on site to save on expenses, an idea championed by the nurses who'd cared for Jack over the years.

Preparations were simple, as expected. Dark blue curtains on metal framed stands ran the length of one long wall of the activity room, hiding the large round folding tables from the view of those coming to pay their respects. Flowers at the far end of the room provided a floral backdrop to the casket, which rested on a black, felt draped, gurney. Nursing home staff had arranged 10 rows of light brown metal folding chairs, 10 across, in the 60' X 30' foot room, with a set of seven chairs off to the side for Patricia and her sons.

As more mourners arrived, the staff put out additional chairs to accommodate the additional guests. The Christopher boys looked out at the faces, many unfamiliar, and wondered how many of them had their own memories of Jack that no one else may ever hear.

Afterward, they all agreed that the memorial service was beautiful. The nursing home chaplain shared a fitting message of how God promised to restore Jack to full health as Jack trusted in Him. Shawn appreciated the idea but wondered why God had to wait for death to give life and full health. One by one relatives and friends stepped forward to share sometimes funny, sometimes touching recollections of life with Jack.

Throughout the service and greetings from those who came up to pay their respect, the Christophers were touched by the words of comfort, but they shed no tears themselves. In fact, Patricia, Shawn, and Brandon found themselves often rendering comfort to others as some were overcome with grief before the open casket.

As the last of the mourners passed by, Brandon's aunt gently pulled him off to the side.

"Brandon, honey, I'm a little worried that you're trying too hard to be strong," she said in a soothing voice, "It's OK to cry." Brandon respectfully considered his aunt's and then replied in the same soothing tone.

"But is it OK *not* to cry?" he asked. His question was genuine one. This was what he felt and he thought some other members of his family felt too after crying so many tears for so long. Jack was no longer suffering, and his family was free from helplessly watching him decline.

As the parting guests went out the entrance doors, a fresh spring wind blew up the hallway and into the memorial room. As she felt it, Patricia looked around and watched her boys take a deep breath of the fresh, clean infusion of air.

Chapter 59
Jack and the Final Homecoming

Jack dimly heard his family around him and understood their sadness but did not share it. As his eyes drifted shut for the last time, he waited for the much talked about light to beckon him as a peaceful warmth flooded his body, but it did not come. He heard no angelic songs to usher him into eternal bliss. Regaining his vision, Jack found himself dwarfed on either side by pristine rolling green hills. The deep blue sky around him was interrupted by neither cloud nor celestial body but was seamless. He saw a walkway of translucent gold just ahead, and when he turned to look behind, he saw untouched grassy hills. To his right in the small enclosed circular patch of grass he stood in was an ivory bench with intricate carvings of pomegranates and clusters of grapes. The bench was exquisite in the simple beauty of its carving but nonetheless seemed out of place.

For the first time in his life, Jack felt unpressured to do anything or be anywhere. Jack looked down at himself and saw the toned, chiseled muscles that he had known in his 30s. He felt better and healthier than he ever remembered feeling on earth. Jack looked at the bench, but felt no inclination to sit right away. He was thrilled to be standing again. He thought about walking over the hills but decided to stay on the path.

Just as he started, to walk, he looked up and saw a man in a seamless white garment approaching. Jack fell on his knees in worship, crying tears of joy.

"Lord it's you! It's you! I'm finally…"

"Home," Jesus finished as he bent to cup his hands on either side of Jack's face, guiding him to his feet. "Welcome home, my son. Many here have been looking forward to your arrival. Everything that I have promised you is now before you. Your struggles and trials are over. Your sincere faith on that day that you called out to me has opened my kingdom to you."

Unspeakable joy filled Jack's heart as he embraced Jesus and yet…

"You have a question, Jack," Jesus interjected. He directed Jack's attention to the bench. "This bench was prepared for you. You may ask me anything, and you and I can talk as long as you wish. I have many things to tell you. Some words will be honey to your ears; others will be very difficult."

Jack took a seat on the bench, but he hesitated to ask the burning question in his heart. Jesus did not sit but stooped in front of Jack, as a father would before his child. Jack noted that Jesus had offered him the freedom to ask anything and decided to speak freely.

"Lord, why was there so much pain? Why did Gary Mayer have to die like he did? If you saw all of these things coming, why didn't you stop it?"

Jack looked at the Lord's face but saw no irritation. "Jack, look out there and tell me what you see." The Lord pointed directly across from where Jack was sitting. Jack looked out at an expense of open grasses that rose high above him, and rolled slightly from left to right.

"Just a big hill, I guess," Jack answered.

"And what do you see behind the hill, my son?"

Jack looked into the distance but was somewhat confused by the question. "I can't see anything," he said, "the hills are too high. I'm not sure what you want me to say."

"You cannot see past this mountain." Jesus said in a serious tone. "I look beyond it to the next one, and the next, and a thousand hills beyond. I see them before they are there, and I see them long after they had been laid flat against the earth. How then do you become a judge over me, and the purposes and motivations of my heart?

"Later you will once again see the one you called Gary Mayer. He can tell you whether or not I am faithful to my words. How I work, and what I speak into another life is not for you to know, as what I speak into your life is not for others. If you cannot see past this hill, how then will you see my plans, or see how the lives of those I love affect each other.

"One who knows that he has been bitten by the viper does not rail against the prick of the physician's needle, for he knows that death is racing through his veins. All who walk the earth have been bitten by the viper, but not all understand that they are dying even as they live. The man that refuses the needle grows angrier as his condition worsens and curses the physician until his dying breath. The man that knows he is dying suffers the prick of the needle and is thankful that the physician saved him. Your life, Jack, was the pinprick needed to save you from death. My motivations and purposes are as different and numerous as there are people on earth; but in your life, that is how I worked."

Jesus and Jack continued talking. Jack had no way of telling whether he had been seated for an hour, a year, or a hundred years.

Finally, Jack stood to embrace the Lord, whose arms were extended to him, and the bench with the brass feet disappeared. Jack understood that his struggles on earth would no longer haunt him. Side by side, Jesus and Jack stepped onto the golden walkway. From the moment his foot hit the shimmering pathway, Jack Christopher was filled with perfect understanding. This perfect understanding was accompanied by perfect peace. Jack could not worry if he tried to.

As they began walking, the two resumed their conversation. Jesus no longer addressed him as Jack but used a name that only they two knew. Jack had never heard the name before, but it was familiar, like it had been created just for him. A short way down the winding path, Jesus directed his son's attention to the top of a nearby hill. At its crest, a towering willow stood with its boughs 50 feet above the roof of a large cabin directly underneath. White smoke rose lazily from the chimney and disappeared into the willow's full branches. Round ivory pavers formed a quaint winding path from the golden walkway to the cabin.

Outside the cabin, Jack could see a number of people seated at a large, long table, though he could not tell who they were from his vantage point. When they arrived where the golden path and ivory walkway met, Jesus hugged his son and kissed his cheek.

"We have no end of days together, my child, and no tears, no trials, and no evil to torment the soul. Breathe in the fresh breath of eternal life. Those atop the hill find great cause for rejoicing today. Go to them, and be blessed."

Jesus turned and continued walking down the golden path as Jack walked up the gentle slope toward the cabin. When he was near the top of the hill, one of the figures seated at the table rose and started down the path toward him. As the figure approached, Jack recognized the youthful, radiant beauty as his mother. Joy beyond measure filled his heart as his arms embraced his beloved mother as her embrace was returned in kind..

As they walked to the table, Jack recognized faces that he had not seen since his youth: Grandpop, Grandmom, so many others. He realized that some faces were not there, but Jack left that to the Lord's sovereign oversight of His own kingdom. A single empty place setting and chair occupied the lavishly prepared table.

"This seat at the banquet is yours, Jack," his mother whispered joyfully. "Welcome home, son. Welcome home."

Chapter 60
The Christopher Family and Room to Breathe

October 1983

In the little more than 4 years since Jack died, the family had begun to carve out a long anticipated new normal. Winter of 1982 had been particularly stressful, so Ginny had funded a ski trip for Patricia, Richard, and Ryan to Attitash, New Hampshire. The family group stopped over in Littleton for several nights on the way home, which was all the time Patricia needed to fall in love with this quaint New England town. The tight-knit community reminded her of Stratford's daily continuity during her early days with Jack. She was convinced that he would have loved Littleton. More importantly, Patricia had no doubt that Littleton would be a great environment for the two boys still living with her.

Visiting Littleton was one thing, but living there year round often proved to be something quite different. Common wisdom from the locals for potential new residents was "Live here for one winter, and you'll know if Littleton is your new home or not." True enough, Patricia and the boys found the change to be challenging, but not without its inherent advantages. Though the boys seemed to love the rugged outdoor life that Littleton offered, adjusting to life since moving the previous spring had sometimes been a little tough.

As the billowing morning fog wafted across the valley, Patricia surveyed her new home with satisfaction, and a muted degree of personal pride. Granted, calling the appendage that jutted out from the back of the modest two-story cabin a "deck" would be something of an exaggeration. However, the 6' x 4' timber decking, enclosed on three

392

sides by a rustic, two-tier post railing, invited Patricia outside to enjoy her morning coffee. Sturdy, and freshly sealed, the open porch proved to be the perfect grandstand from which to view this glorious New Hampshire morning. A wide swath of pristine grass stretched 200 yards from the porch, sloping gently downhill to the tree line below. Even as the cool mid-October air gently rustled yellow and auburn leaves on the trees, the lawn retained its deep green color.

"Jack would have loved such a lush, green property," Patricia thought to herself. With only two cabins on either side, her virtually unobstructed view extended for over a quarter mile to her right and left. The peaceful band of grass seemed to go on forever. Beyond the grass, the forest presented a soothing blend of color. From her place on the porch, Patricia could see the far bank of the Moore Reservoir just over the treetops.

While savoring her coffee, Patricia watched as thick billows of low-lying clouds moved up the river, obscuring the far bank from view. She was enthralled with the slow moving leviathan of vapor, and she stood and watched for twenty minutes as the soft mass worked its way across the horizon to meet the base of the mountain.

At the sound of cracking wood, Patricia turned with excitement to see branches six feet above the forest floor give way as a bull moose emerged from the woods. He stopped cautiously, sampling the tender late-season grass. Patricia's heart raced as she strained with every fiber of her being to remain quiet. She had never been so close to such an imposing, majestic animal. The sheer size of the beast left Patricia in awe.

Suddenly the porch door flew open, sending the creature back into the brush for cover.

"Mom, breakfast is ready, and me and Rich need a ride to the Crags," Ryan barked. The "Crags" was the boys' shorthand for Killburn Crags, a popular hiking trail of modest difficulty. The hike was a nice, free way to enjoy the day.

"A bunch of us are hiking to the top," Ryan finished.

"Ryan, you just…" Patricia began to explain the opportunity that Ryan had just chased away, but thought better of it before she did, resigned that the moment was now gone. She decided to just be thankful for those precious 20 minutes of solitude.

Though driving her boys over to Killburn Crags might have been inconvenient, Patricia really didn't mind; she was encouraged by any signs that Richard and Ryan were assimilating.

"Mom, when you drop us off, please don't go on and on about being safe," Ryan continued. "We won't get eaten by a bear or killed by a moose, I promise. We're going to hang out up top, and Brett's mom said she will bring us home."

"That's fine," Patricia answered. "I will only tell you once: stay on the trail and NO fires!" This last admonition was directed toward Richard, who sometimes seemed overly preoccupied with campfires and all things flammable.

The boys hurriedly finished breakfast, and Patricia could hear their footsteps thundering off of the walls as the two barreled up the narrow wooden staircase single file. Splitting off to their respective rooms, the brothers began stuffing their backpacks for the day's hike while Patricia finished the dishes.

As Richard and Ryan dashed downstairs and tried to get out the front door before Patricia could think of any more concerns about hiking, Richard attempted to belatedly relay a message without breaking stride.

"Oh yeah, Mom, the school called. Friday off is fine. Mrs. Gerst needs you to help in her class on Monday. Aaaand…something about next week."

Patricia brought the duo to a halt.

"Whoa, whoa! If you expect a ride to the Crags, I want the whole message."

Richard threw his head back and let out an exaggerated sigh of frustration and Ryan immediately followed suit.

OK, Mom," Russell said with the air of one who had already done his duty and was being asked for more. "The school called. You can

394

have Friday off. Mrs. Gerst needs a room assistant on Monday. They will also probably need you for 3 days next week. NOW can we go?"

Patricia smiled and grabbed her keys. She was thankful that the new school year had brought her steady work as a room assistant. The pay was not great, but the school was very flexible with scheduling.

Patricia had also begun making dolls again, and the craft had proven lucrative over the spring and summer, providing a reasonable monetary cushion. Her seamstress talents had also provided an introduction of sorts with the women in her new community, who respected her skill and ability.

Pulling up to Killburn Crags, Patricia was relieved to see a group waiting for Richard and Ryan. The past 6 months in Littleton suggested a lot of promise for the boys. As the boys raced out of the car, Patricia called out one final warning.

"Have a good time, but be home no later than 5, both of you. I've worked too hard getting ready for tonight to spend it running around looking for the two of you."

Surprisingly, Patricia got no sarcastic remarks in response to her warning. Instead, both called back their assurances.

Patricia hoped so. As she drove home, she went over the many tasks still to complete. So much still needed to be done. The marinade had been soaking into the beef tenderloin she planned to serve, but she still needed to dig pictures out of storage and put them out.

Shawn and Russell were coming tonight! This would be the first time since their abrupt eviction years before that her sons would not only visit but stay for several days. Based on Patricia's recent conversation with Shawn, her sons were as eager for the visit as she was. Shades of Pennsauken would be relived as the brothers would double bunk in each room for the next 3 nights. Patricia offered to sleep on the couch, but her prospective guests would not hear of it.

Patricia smiled to think of how her relationship with Shawn and Russell had evolved; not immediately of course. Even after the boys started coming for weekly family dinners, tension stayed high for a long time. As their futures improved though, Russell and Shawn came to the conclusion that getting kicked out was one of the best things that could have happened to them. Though it had taken a while, they had grown into responsible men. Shawn found his niche as a chef, and Russell ran a shift repairing industrial factory equipment.

Patricia's only regret was that Robert and Brandon would not also be there. Robert found traveling with the Navy addicting, had re-enlisted, and fully intended to make it his career. Several of his Division Officers had recommended him for Officer Candidate School and he had not been able to get leave to make the trip.

Brandon was in California trying to break into stand-up comedy, with an ever-changing degree of success. He joked to Patricia that if he was going to get laughed at, he might as well get paid for it. She knew that behind the one-liners, he still grappled with much of the pain and bitterness he'd felt in his early life.

As the sun set, Patricia peered out the kitchen window and down the long, straight stretch of road that led to the house. Few visitors came up this way, so any headlights would surely signal her boys approach. Richard and Ryan had come home and just finished quick showers when they heard an excited shriek from the kitchen.

"It's them; I know it! That's got to be them!" Patricia trembled as the headlights came closer, slowing at each house and then turned into her driveway. As the car went dark and silent, Patricia burst out the front door, uninterested in even pretending composure. Running to the passenger door, she threw her arms around Russell as he got out of the car.

"Oh Russell, I'm so glad to see you! We are going to have a great time together!" Russell warmly returned the hug.

'It's good to see you, Mom," Shawn said more cautiously as he came around the front of the car. Patricia pulled him close, hugged him tightly, and whispered, "You don't know how much this means to me." Shawn pressed both hands behind Patricia's shoulders as he hugged her, relieved that his fears on the drive up were unfounded.

As Richard and Ryan came out to greet their brothers, Patricia pointed to the car.

"I don't recognize this. Did you get a fancy new car, Mr. Chef?" she teased. Russell and Shawn exchanged a look.

"We had to borrow it, Mom," Shawn answered. "We had some extra packages to bring up and needed the space. C'mere; take a look."

Patricia did not see anything unusual about the car, so Shawn linked his arm in hers, walked her around to the rear hatch, and opened it up as Russell continued to smirk. She saw numerous boxes stacked inside but still didn't understand why her sons were so excited to show them to her.

"Open one up," Russell directed while pointing to a square green carton. Anxiously opening the lid, Patricia saw several beautiful Christmas tree ornaments neatly wrapped in tissue paper, and she burst into tears.

"How did... Where did you?" Patricia was overcome with joy.

"Some we bought; most we were given. We told our friends the story and asked for donations," Russell said, still grinning. "Many of the mothers wanted to give us even more of their decorations. We thought you would be happy."

Patricia assured her sons that she could not have been happier, not so much because of the ornaments, as much as she liked them, but because her sons were finally here.

"It's good to be home, Mom; it's good to be home," Shawn echoed.

As they began carrying in the boxes, the first few scattered snowflakes graced the October skies.

Chapter 61
Brandon and the Peaceful Accord

Early March 1989

Brandon had difficulty finding the headstone. Ten years had passed since he and his family had said goodbye to Jack, and they were not an easy 10 years for Brandon. Anger at God, Jack, and himself had festered unresolved for a number of them, leaving him often unable to find joy in his own life. Though he'd found love, and his wife's presence in his life was a great comfort, he still rose each day with no confidence that any peace awaited him. As an adult, Brandon understood that the pleasures of a normal childhood had been lost to him and could not be reclaimed. Worse, as he and Dianne considered starting a family, Brandon feared the father that he might become to his own children.

He'd planned this trip for some time, and he prayed that he would finally be able to release the pain and resentment that lingered in his heart. Finding Jack's headstone, he brushed away stray leaves and knelt just in front of the white marble. He pulled an envelope from his pocket, opened it, and withdrew several pages. Brandon leaned forward and kissed the stone before he began to read.

Dad,

As I write this letter, I am looking at the only two pictures that I have of you. Aunt Annie sent them to me last week. You were only 13 at the time, and you looked so happy and full of life. I can't help but wonder what you must have dreamed about back then, the things that you wanted to do in life. What happened,

Dad? What stole your dreams? I know that you had a difficult childhood; that much we have in common. I am sorry that you had it so rough.

Mom had dreams too. All that she ever wanted was a husband and kids that loved her. I think we can both say that there were too many times that we denied her that. I know it was hard when you got sick, but we could have dealt with it much better if we had been a closer family.

I think of all the times your words cut into me. Only recently did I think about the disrespect and sharp words that I used toward you.

There were times when we both caught a glimpse of what we hoped for. When you took me down to Atlantic City, we watched "Big Jake" on the boardwalk. I am surprised that I remember that trip so well. I wish I could have seen more of that side of you

"Hate" is a strong word. We both said it, and we both heard it far too often. No one should hear it as often as we both used it. Dad, I often did not agree with you and many of the things you did, and my own selfish attitude did not help matters much. I watched in tears as the years of illness drained the life out of you. Oh, how it hurt to hear you cry out "Just let me die!" Next to seeing Jesus, my greatest hope is to see you in heaven, and maybe, just maybe, learn the reason for it all. On that day, we will embrace each other in perfect love.

Thank you for bringing me into this world. You always wanted us to be tough enough to make it, and if wanting that was an expression of love in some of the things you said and did, I thank you. I am sorry that in the past, when I spoke of you, foolish anger brought up more negatives than good recollections. I do have more positive memories than I usually speak of, but you have my word that this habit will change. Too many years have passed to continue being angry.

You are my father, and I love you dearly. I am weary of resenting, regretting, and complaining. God, by his grace has given you peace in death. How, I wish to begin enjoying that same peace in life with my family. It is the peace that surpasses all understanding and can only come from forgiving one another, as Christ forgave us. Dad, I forgive you, and ask that you extend your forgiveness to me. I will always remember that day in the darkened living room, when you told me "I love you." That night has seen me through countless lonely hours. Until we embrace again in perfect love, I look forward to having your strong arms around me once again. Goodnight, Dad.

I love you,
Brandon

Brandon refolded the letter neatly and returned it to the envelope, placing it carefully in the center of Jack's headstone. He reached into his pocket and pulled out two faded plastic figures. One was a green army soldier firing a rifle from the prone position; the other was a knight on horseback thrusting forward a lance. Looking at these remnants from his youth, Brandon thought back to a carefree day so many years ago.

Placing the figures facing each other on either end of the headstone, Brandon again kissed his father's name etched on the marker and stood slowly back up.

"It's your turn to play for a while, Dad. I can come back for those later."

As Brandon made his way through the fresh, falling snow back to his car, he felt as if a great burden had been lifted from his shoulders. He looked around at the peaceful scene and smelled the crisp sweet air and began to sing, "Da-vey, Davey Crockett..."

END

Acknowledgments

To God: For a loving mother who is so selfless, and for restoring my relationship with a father long ago passed on. Thank you for the grace that saw us through so many difficult years.

To my wife Dianne: For loving me while working through the fallout from my early years. You are my voice of reason that has loved me enough to confront me, and helped me laugh again.

To Gena: For typing my handwritten (chicken-scratch) manuscript into something workable.

To Kim: For your passion for this book, beautiful editing, and tireless effort on *Breathing Room*.

To Jessica: For your remarkable cover design, patience over several years of questions about all things computer-related, and your gift and talent for illustration that you so readily shared.

To Danielle: For allowing your son to be on the cover, and for capturing on camera his perfect expression.

To Rich and Anna: For your generosity and friendship; when Superstorm Sandy wiped us out, you restored our hope and kept the dream alive.

To Daniel and Albright Rugby: For your continued encouragement and support.

To Charity: You are Breathing Room's 1st die-hard fan!

To Pennsauken Township and All Around Pennsauken Newspaper: For being the first to give *Breathing Room* a voice. Thank you for your early and continued support!

Laura Gonzalez

I cannot overstate my gratitude for the time, resources, and talent that you have invested in me over the past two years. *Your* 20 years of business experience as a media consultant, and *your* business mentoring skills have changed my life. Your heart for others, and desire to see *their* dreams come true, is inspiring. I am thankful for your friendship and have often said that if not for you, *Breathing Room* would still be sitting in my top dresser drawer.

Livewithlaura.com/authormentor

About the Author

Raised in poverty through most of his formative years, Steven Lange is no stranger to struggle and turmoil. Early medical hardships, financial strife, and family conflicts gave Steven a raw, unpretentious edge that translates into his writing. His work aims to challenge social norms, value systems, and the veracity of people's thoughts and actions. He lives with his wife and two children on Long Beach Island, New Jersey.

You can visit Steven online at

stevenlangebooks.com

For more exclusive information from Author Steven Lange connect on social

media.

stevenlangebooks.com/connect/

Also available as a three-part ebook series.

CPSIA information can be obtained at www.ICGtesting.com
Printed in the USA
BVOW02s1820050915

416693BV00005B/50/P